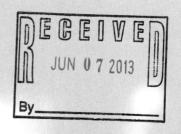
new moon

THE GRAPHIC NOVEL   VOLUME 1

STEPHENIE MEYER

ART AND ADAPTATION BY YOUNG KIM

Yen
Press

New Moon: The Graphic Novel
Volume 1

Art and Adaptation: Young Kim
Inking Assistant: Ashley Marie Witter
Background Assistant: Haya C.

Yen Press
Hachette Book Group
237 Park Avenue, New York, NY 10017

www.HachetteBookGroup.com
www.YenPress.com

Yen Press is an imprint of Hachette Book Group, Inc.
The Yen Press name and logo are trademarks of Hachette Book Group, Inc.

First Edition: April 2013

ISBN: 978-0-316-21718-7

10 9 8 7 6 5 4 3 2 1

RRD-C

Printed in the United States of America

new moon

THE GRAPHIC NOVEL   VOLUME 1

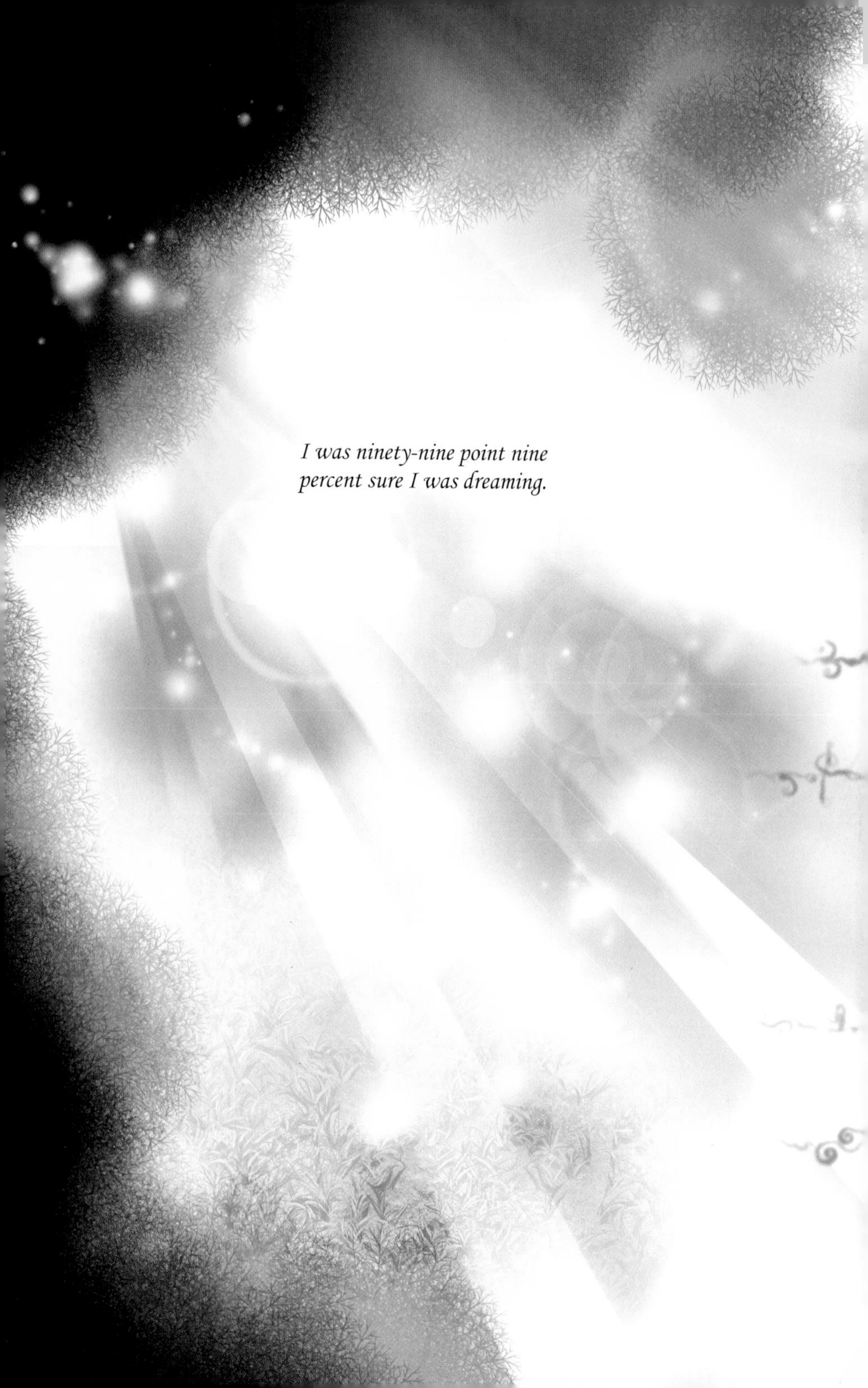
I was ninety-nine point nine percent sure I was dreaming.

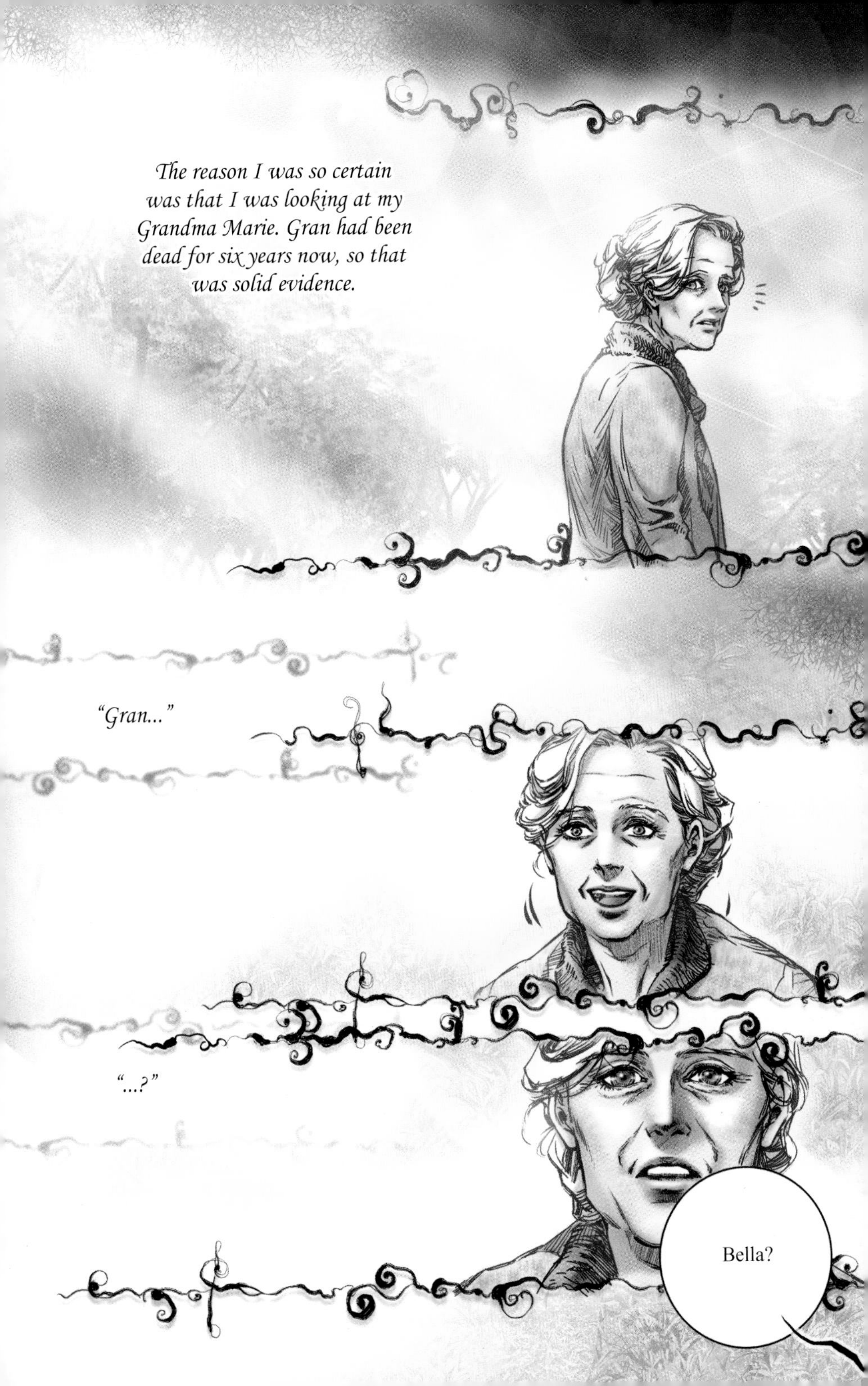
The reason I was so certain was that I was looking at my Grandma Marie. Gran had been dead for six years now, so that was solid evidence.
"Gran..."
"...?"
Bella?

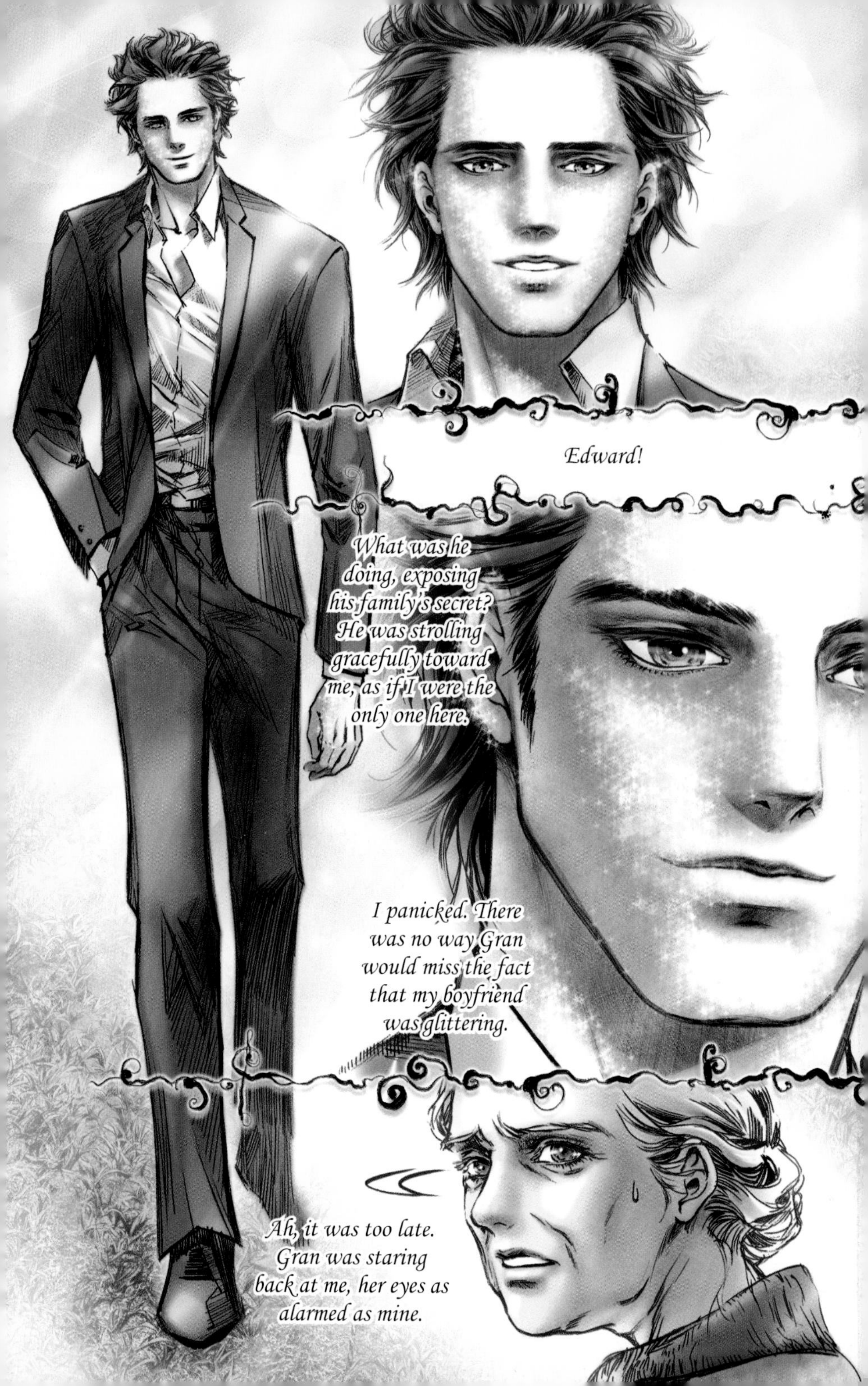
Edward!
What was he doing, exposing his family's secret? He was strolling gracefully toward me, as if I were the only one here.
I panicked. There was no way Gran would miss the fact that my boyfriend was glittering.
Ah, it was too late. Gran was staring back at me, her eyes as alarmed as mine.

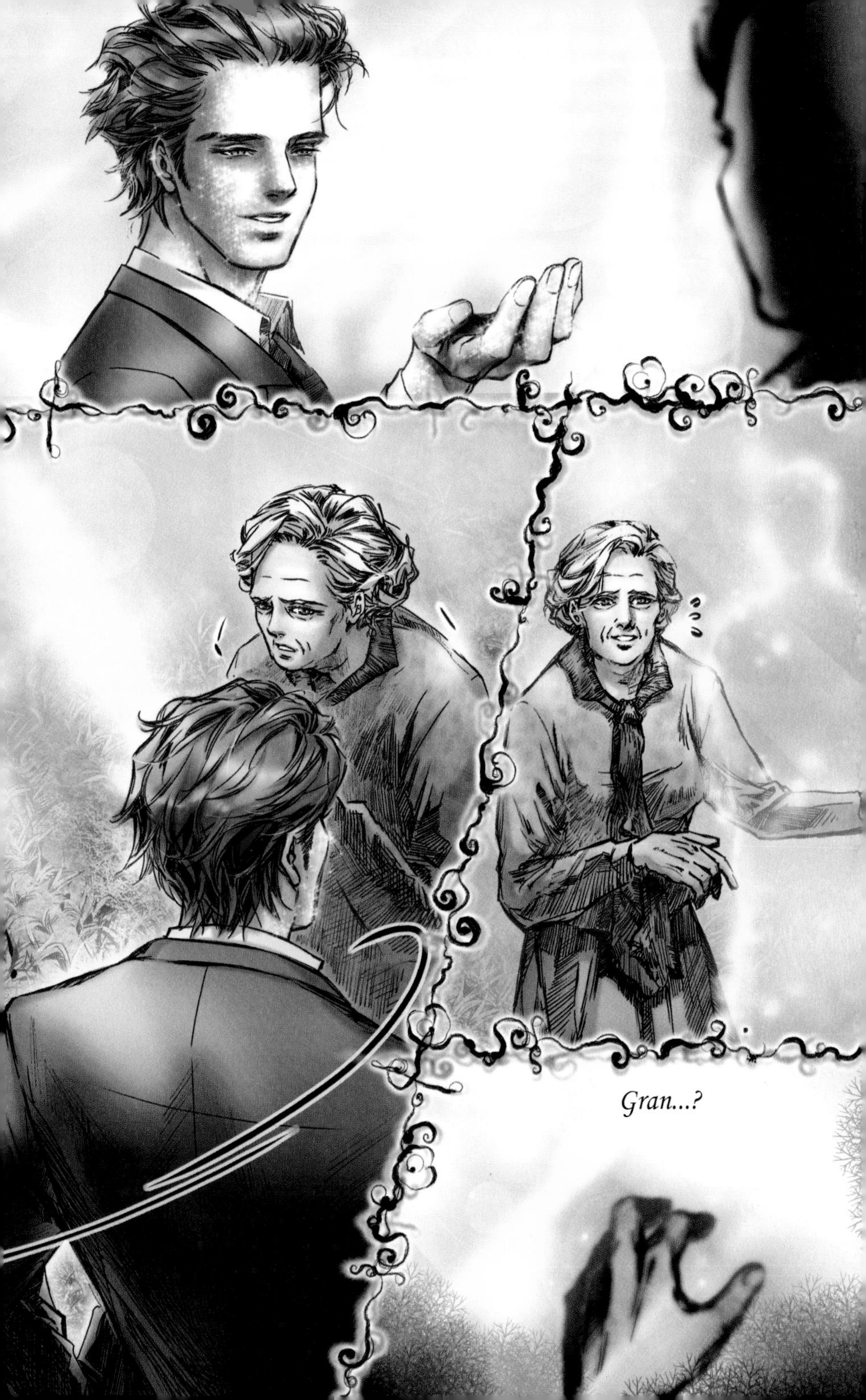
Gran...?

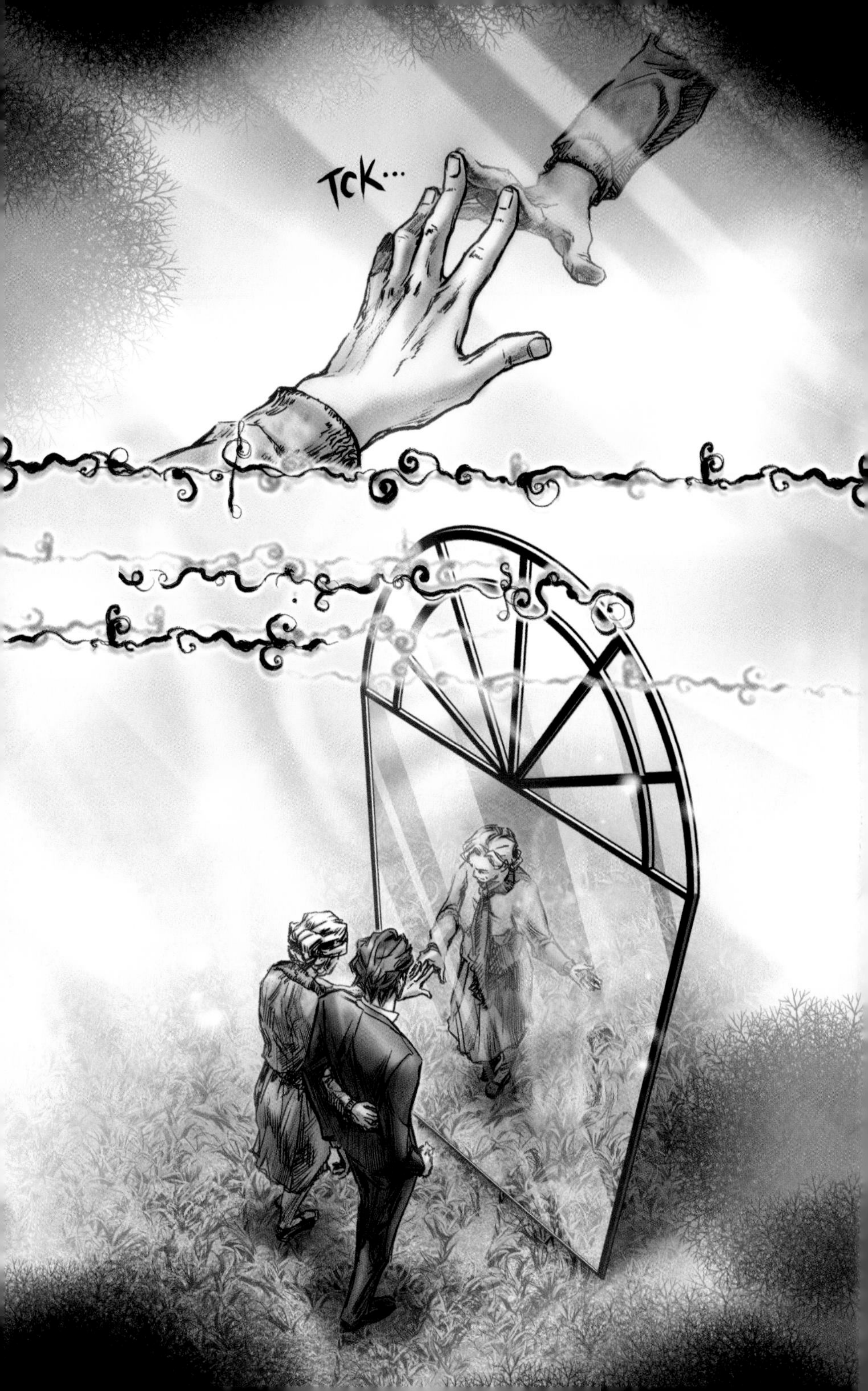
TCK...

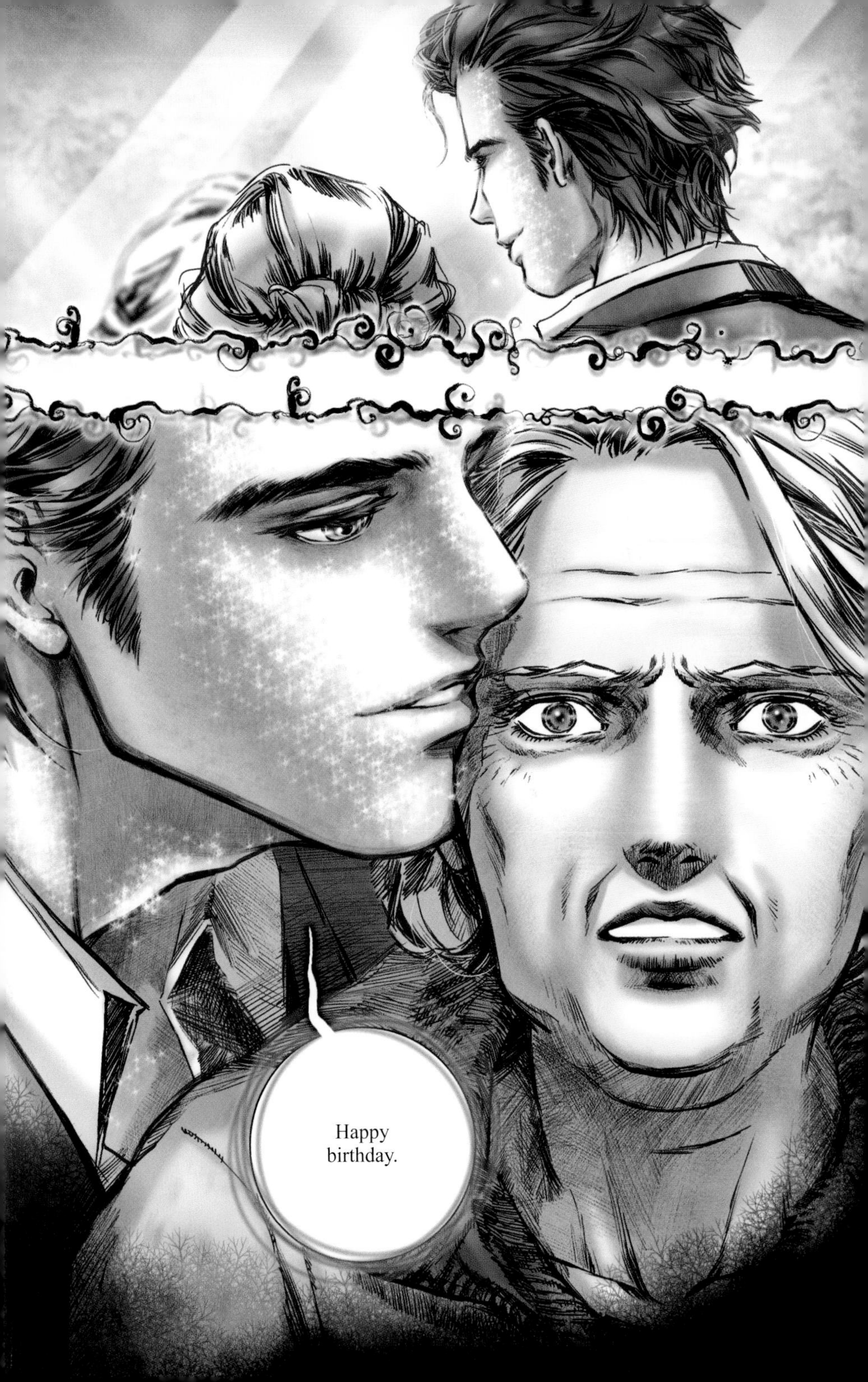
Happy birthday.

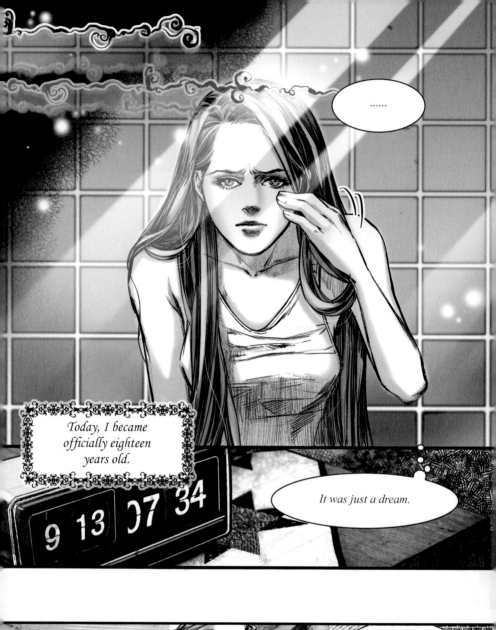

......

Today, I became officially eighteen years old.

It was just a dream.

9 13 07 34

Bella~!

FORKS HIG

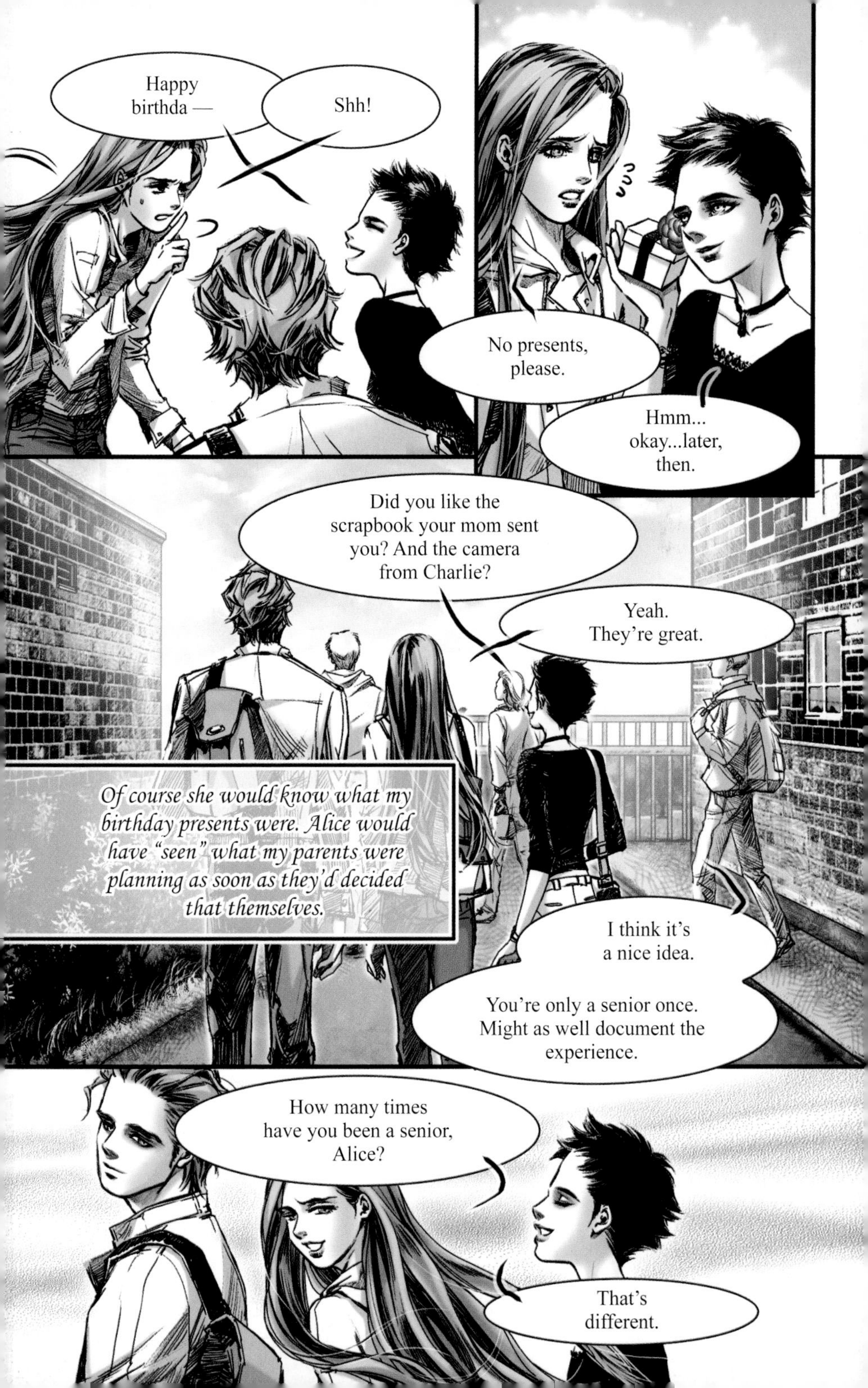
Happy birthda —
Shh!
No presents, please.
Hmm... okay...later, then.
Did you like the scrapbook your mom sent you? And the camera from Charlie?
Yeah. They're great.
Of course she would know what my birthday presents were. Alice would have "seen" what my parents were planning as soon as they'd decided that themselves.
I think it's a nice idea.
You're only a senior once. Might as well document the experience.
How many times have you been a senior, Alice?
That's different.

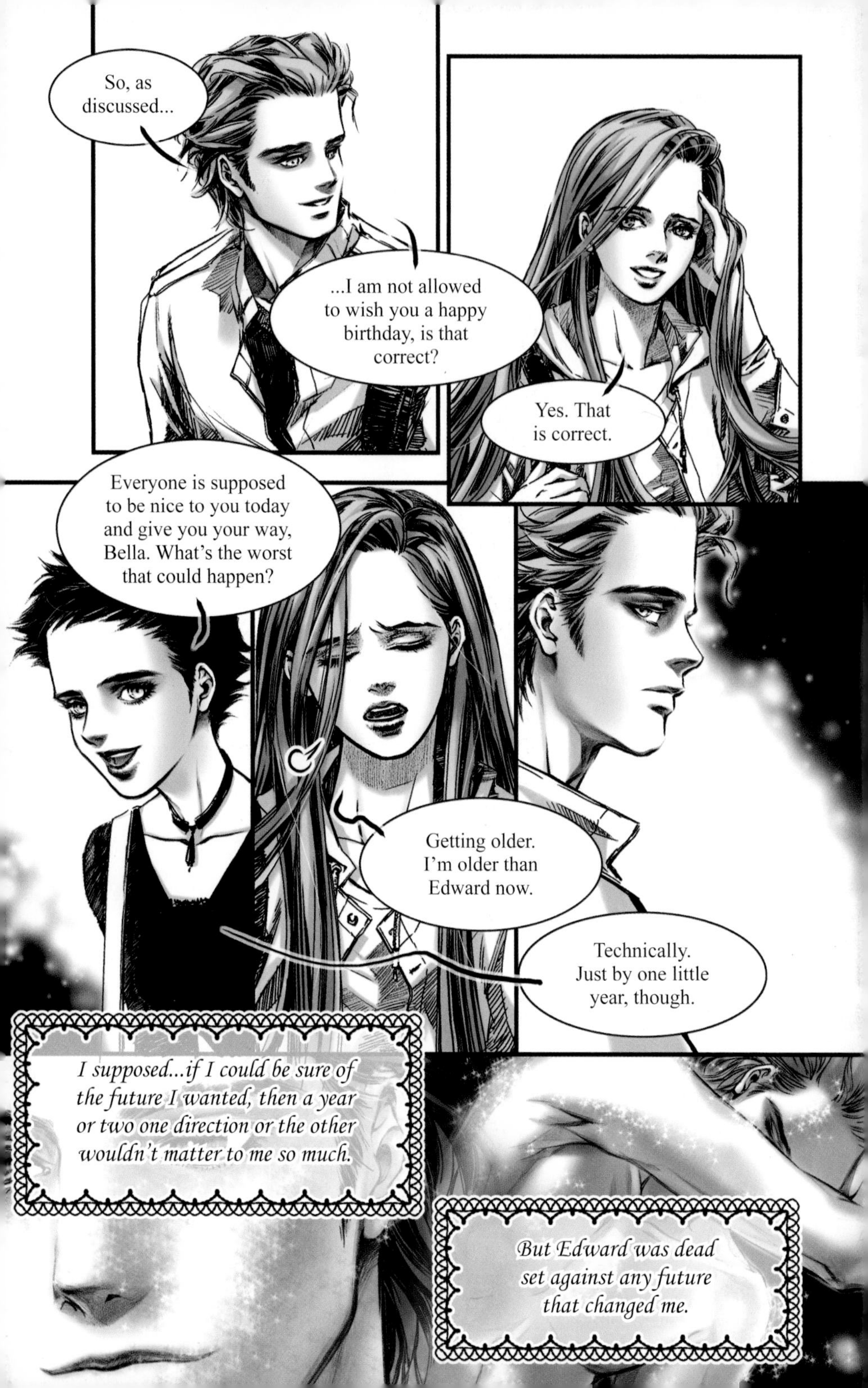

So, as discussed...
...I am not allowed to wish you a happy birthday, is that correct?
Yes. That is correct.
Everyone is supposed to be nice to you today and give you your way, Bella. What's the worst that could happen?
Getting older. I'm older than Edward now.
Technically. Just by one little year, though.
I supposed...if I could be sure of the future I wanted, then a year or two one direction or the other wouldn't matter to me so much.
But Edward was dead set against any future that changed me.

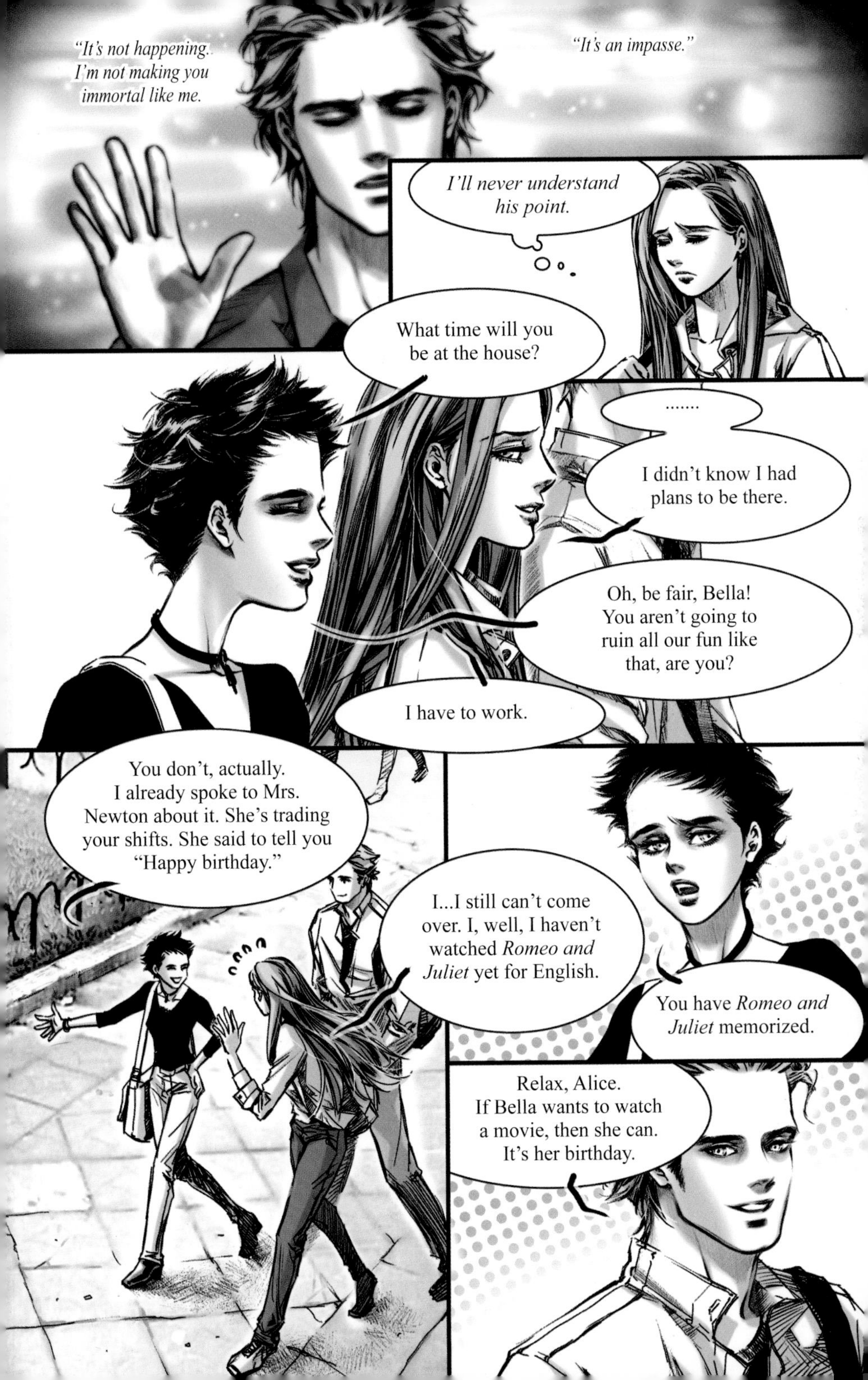
"It's not happening. I'm not making you immortal like me.
"It's an impasse."
I'll never understand his point.
What time will you be at the house?
....
I didn't know I had plans to be there.
Oh, be fair, Bella! You aren't going to ruin all our fun like that, are you?
I have to work.
You don't, actually. I already spoke to Mrs. Newton about it. She's trading your shifts. She said to tell you "Happy birthday."
I...I still can't come over. I, well, I haven't watched *Romeo and Juliet* yet for English.
You have *Romeo and Juliet* memorized.
Relax, Alice. If Bella wants to watch a movie, then she can. It's her birthday.

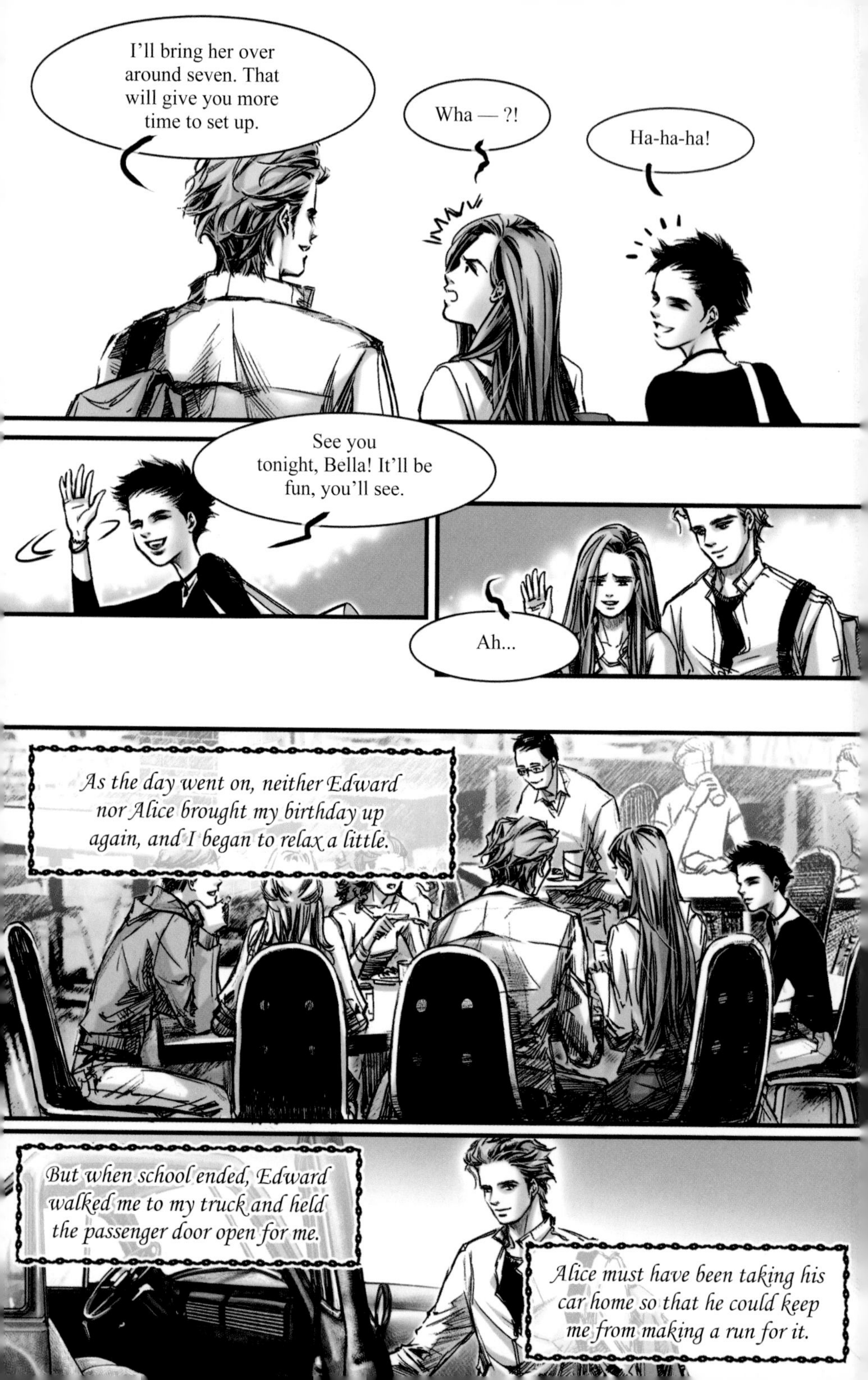
I'll bring her over around seven. That will give you more time to set up.
Wha — ?!
Ha-ha-ha!
See you tonight, Bella! It'll be fun, you'll see.
Ah...
As the day went on, neither Edward nor Alice brought my birthday up again, and I began to relax a little.
But when school ended, Edward walked me to my truck and held the passenger door open for me.
Alice must have been taking his car home so that he could keep me from making a run for it.

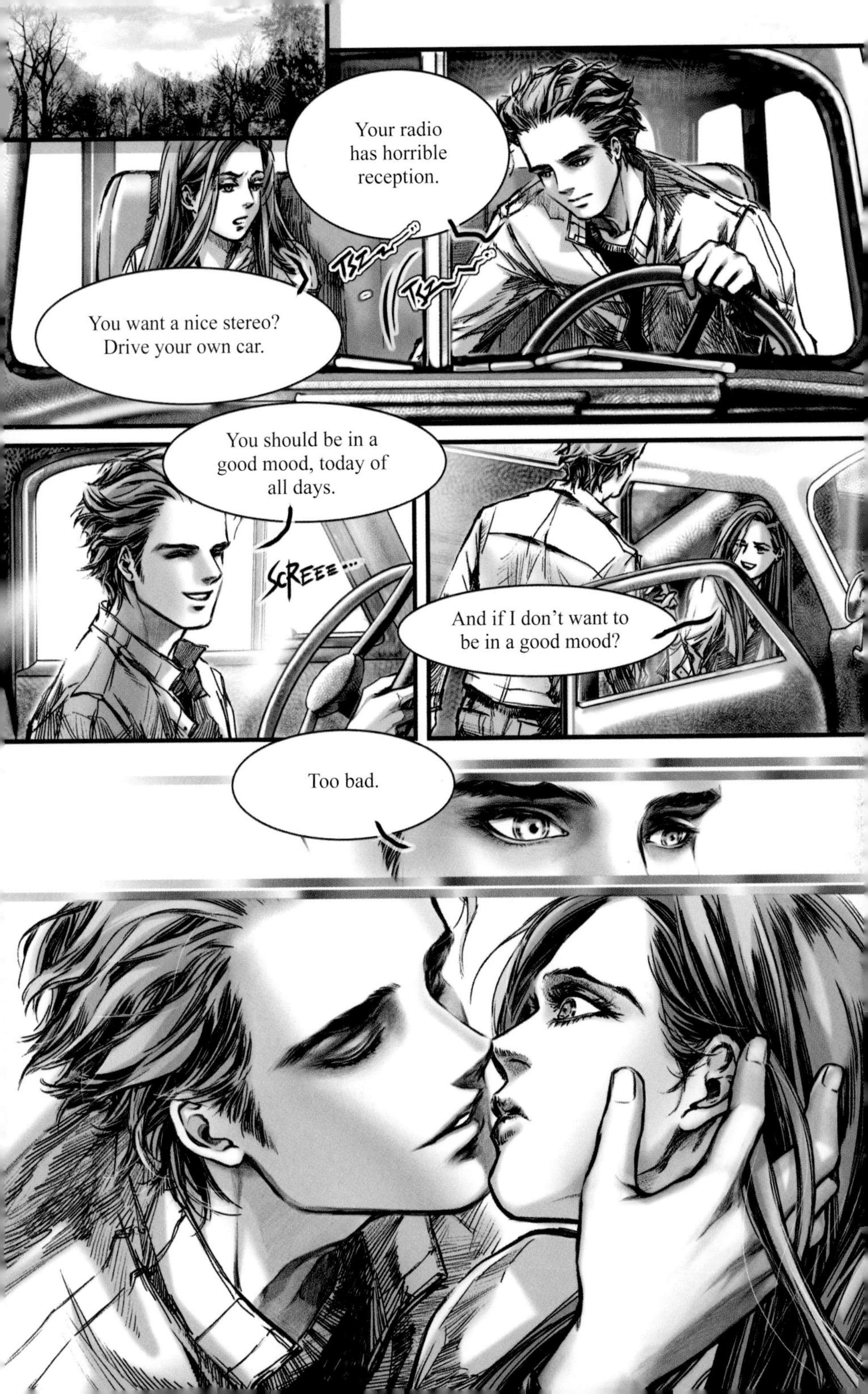
Your radio has horrible reception.
TSZZ...
TSZ...
You want a nice stereo? Drive your own car.
You should be in a good mood, today of all days.
SCREEE...
And if I don't want to be in a good mood?
Too bad.

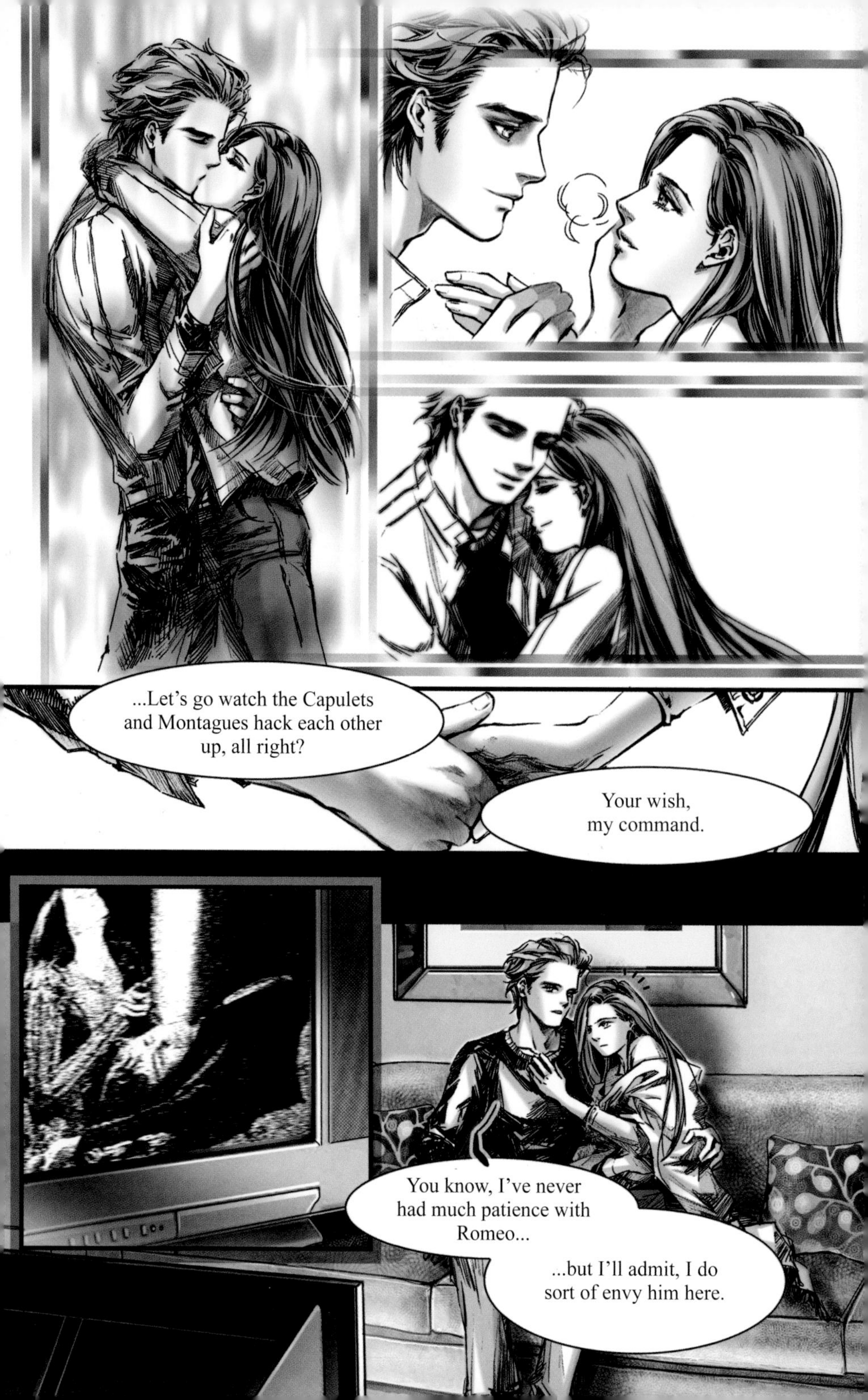
...Let's go watch the Capulets and Montagues hack each other up, all right?
Your wish, my command.
You know, I've never had much patience with Romeo...
...but I'll admit, I do sort of envy him here.

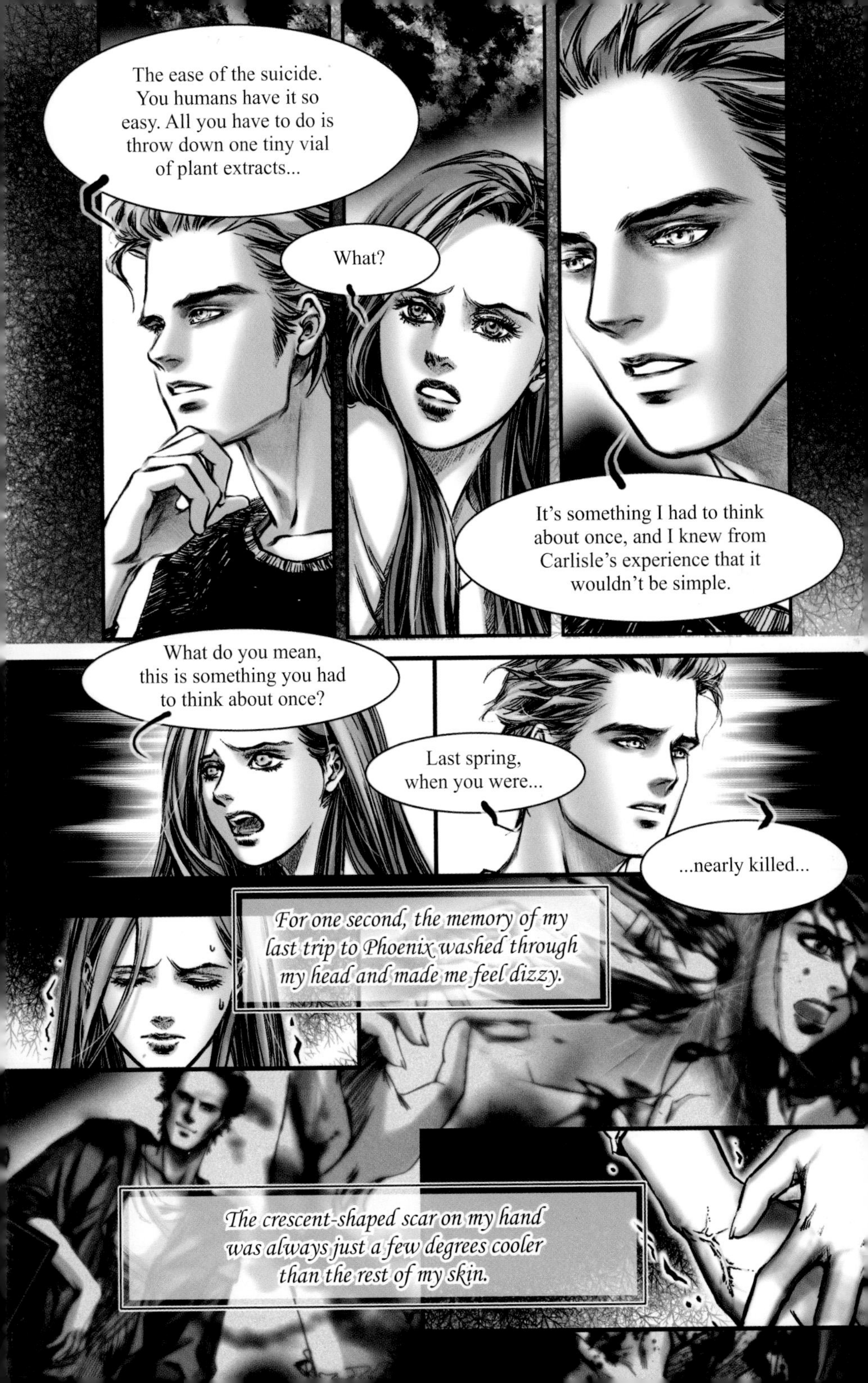
The ease of the suicide. You humans have it so easy. All you have to do is throw down one tiny vial of plant extracts...
What?
It's something I had to think about once, and I knew from Carlisle's experience that it wouldn't be simple.
What do you mean, this is something you had to think about once?
Last spring, when you were...
...nearly killed...
For one second, the memory of my last trip to Phoenix washed through my head and made me feel dizzy.
The crescent-shaped scar on my hand was always just a few degrees cooler than the rest of my skin.

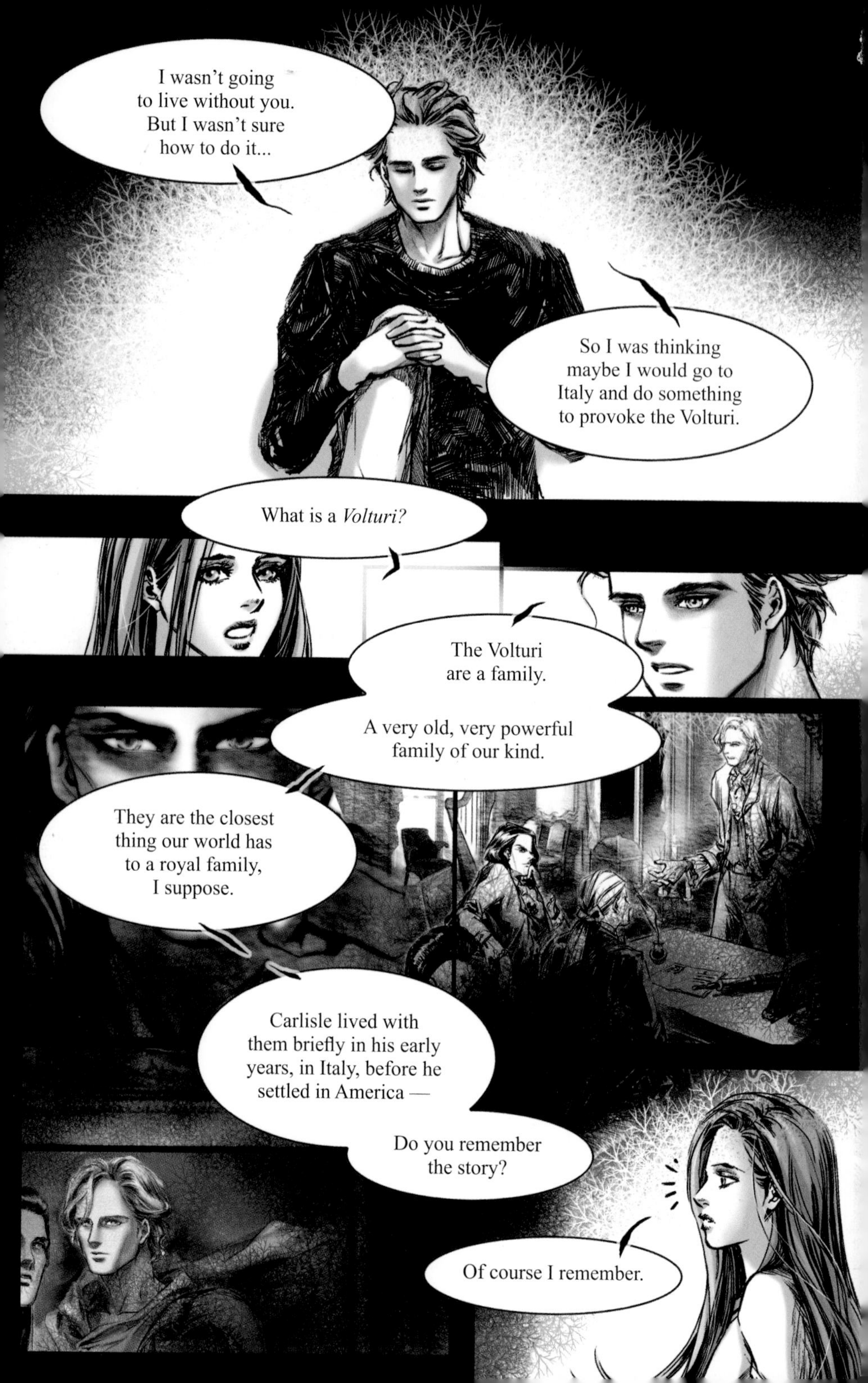
I wasn't going to live without you. But I wasn't sure how to do it...
So I was thinking maybe I would go to Italy and do something to provoke the Volturi.
What is a *Volturi?*
The Volturi are a family.
A very old, very powerful family of our kind.
They are the closest thing our world has to a royal family, I suppose.
Carlisle lived with them briefly in his early years, in Italy, before he settled in America —
Do you remember the story?
Of course I remember.

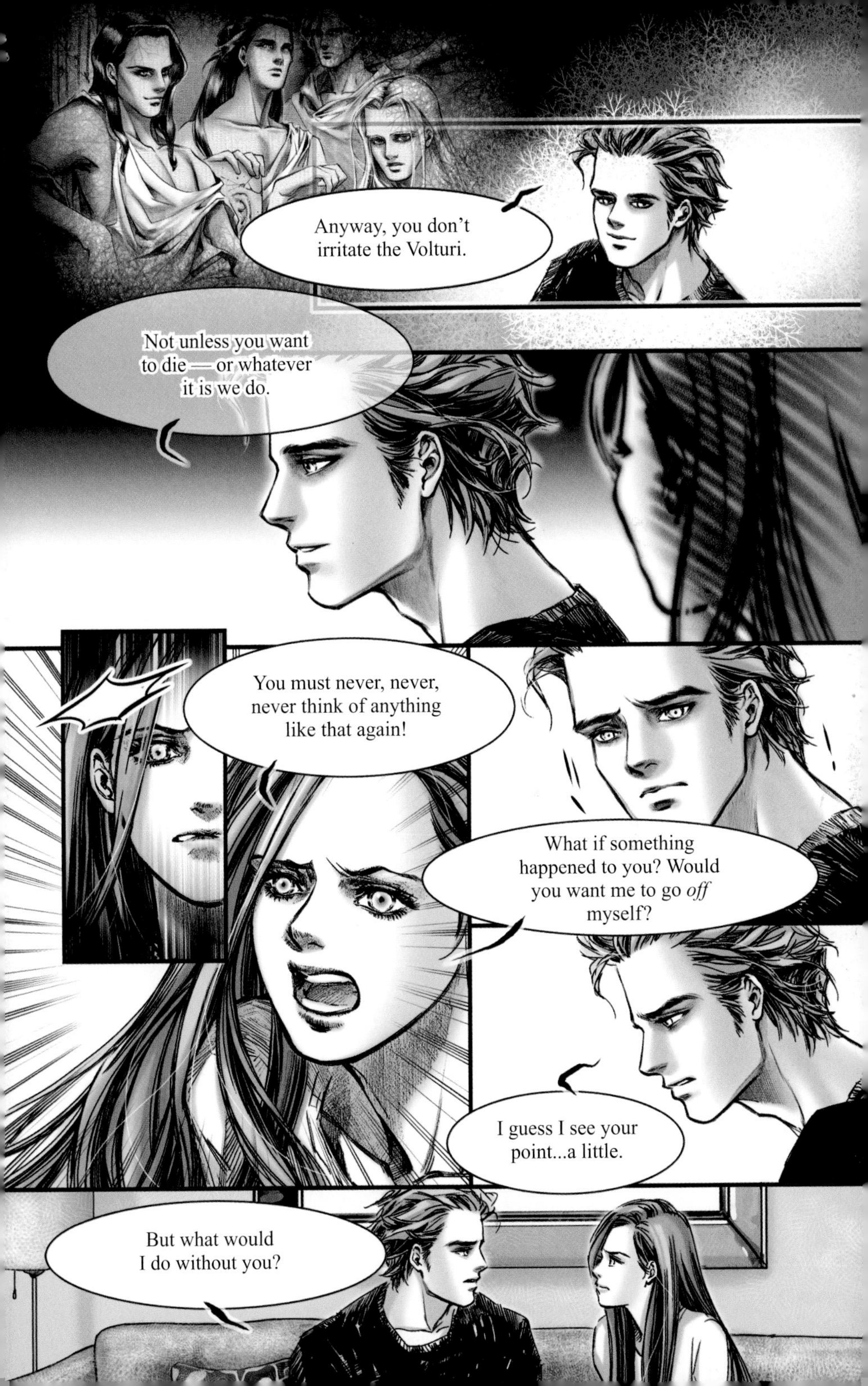
Anyway, you don't irritate the Volturi.
Not unless you want to die — or whatever it is we do.
You must never, never, never think of anything like that again!
What if something happened to you? Would you want me to go *off* myself?
I guess I see your point...a little.
But what would I do without you?

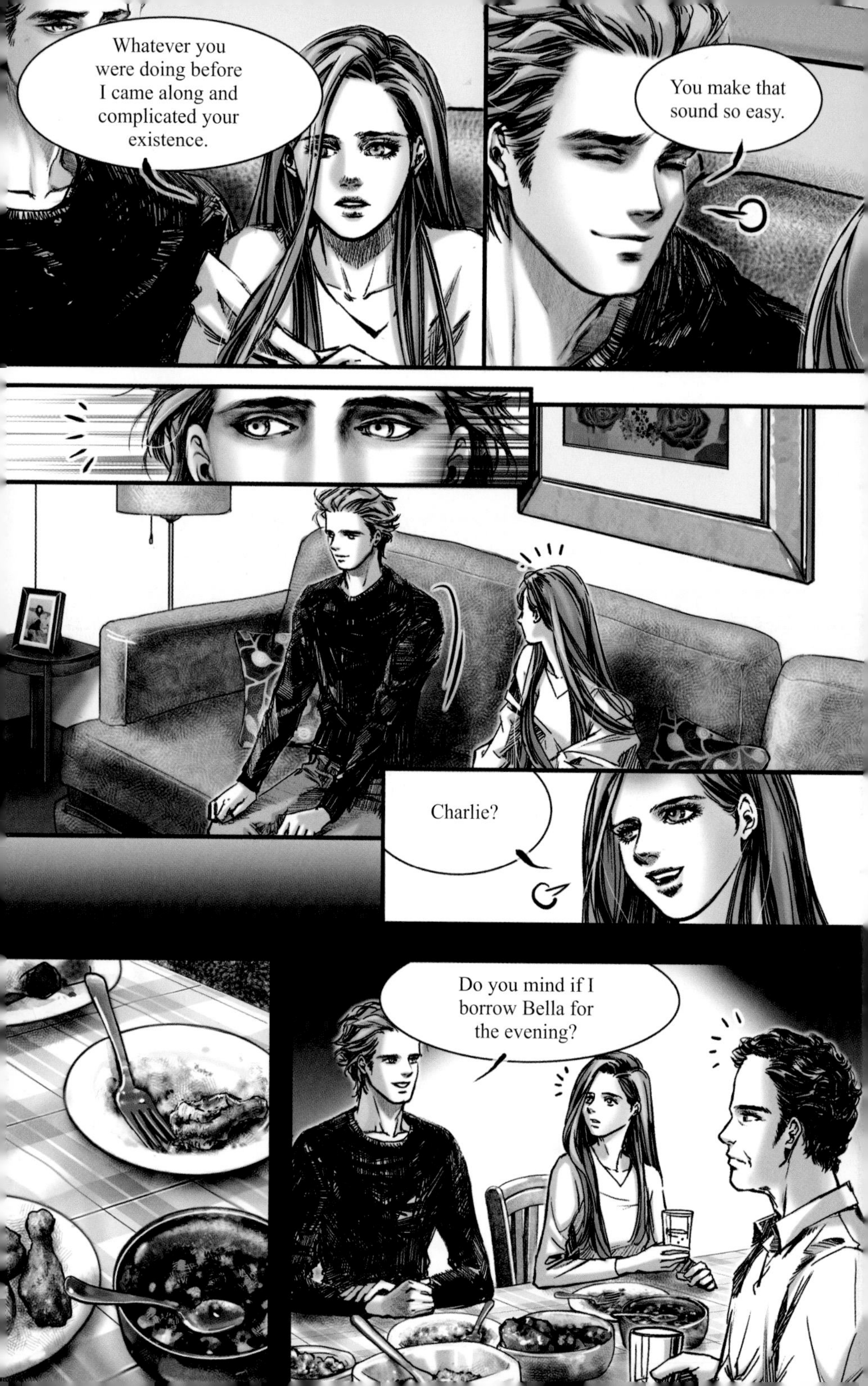
Whatever you were doing before I came along and complicated your existence.
You make that sound so easy.
Charlie?
Do you mind if I borrow Bella for the evening?

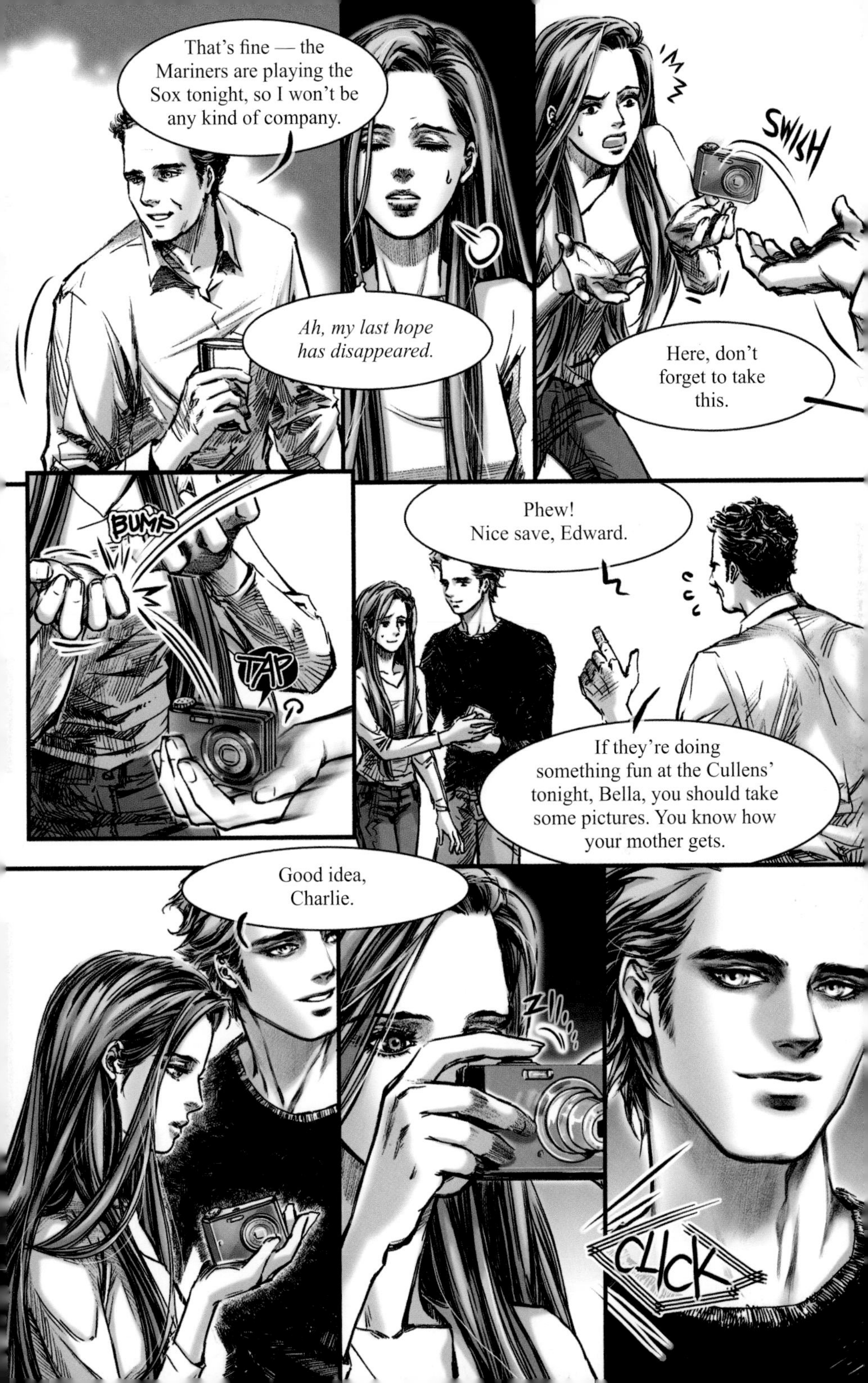
That's fine — the Mariners are playing the Sox tonight, so I won't be any kind of company.
Ah, my last hope has disappeared.
'MM
SWISH
Here, don't forget to take this.
BUMP
TAP
Phew! Nice save, Edward.
If they're doing something fun at the Cullens' tonight, Bella, you should take some pictures. You know how your mother gets.
Good idea, Charlie.
CLICK

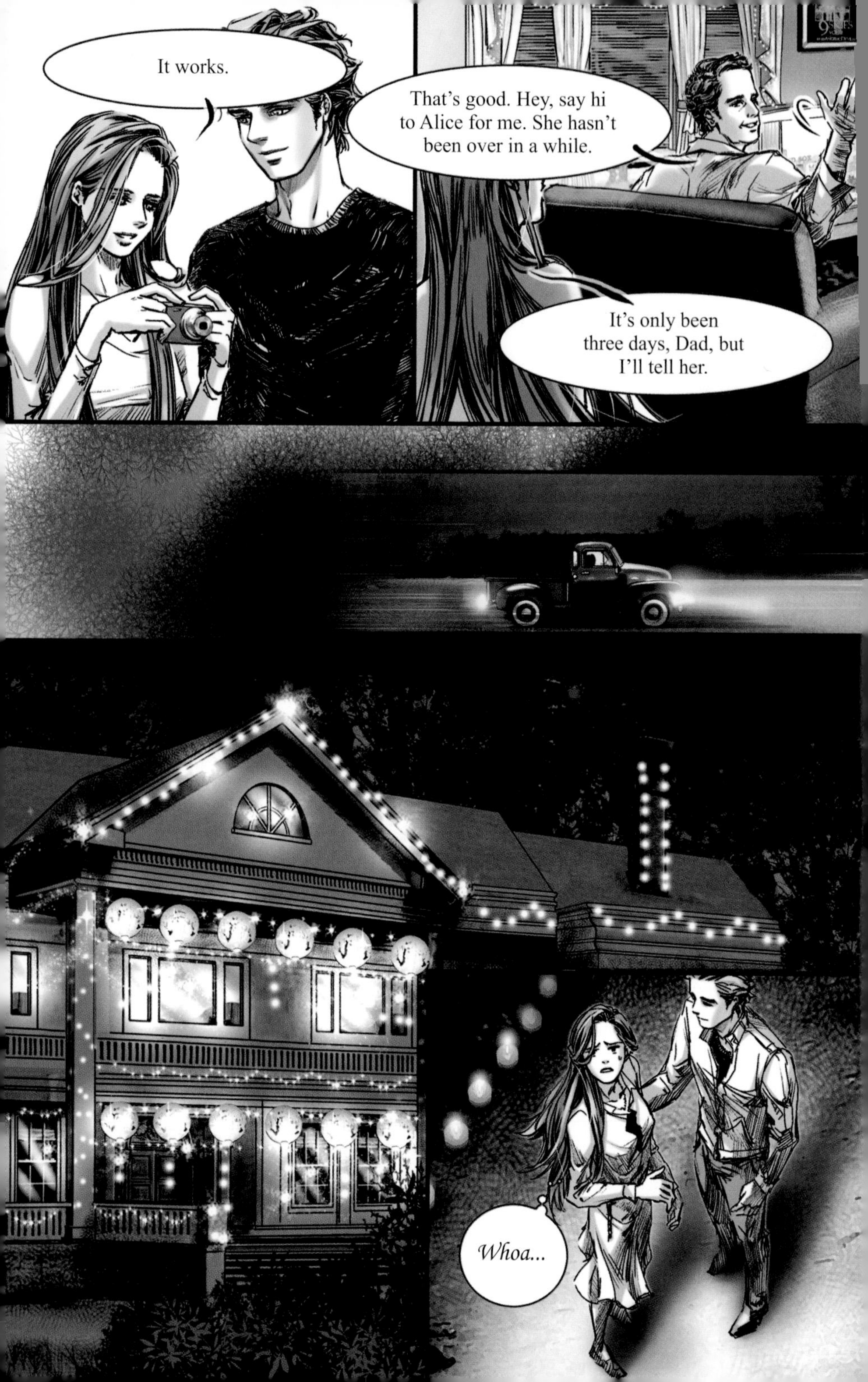
It works.
That's good. Hey, say hi to Alice for me. She hasn't been over in a while.
It's only been three days, Dad, but I'll tell her.
Whoa...

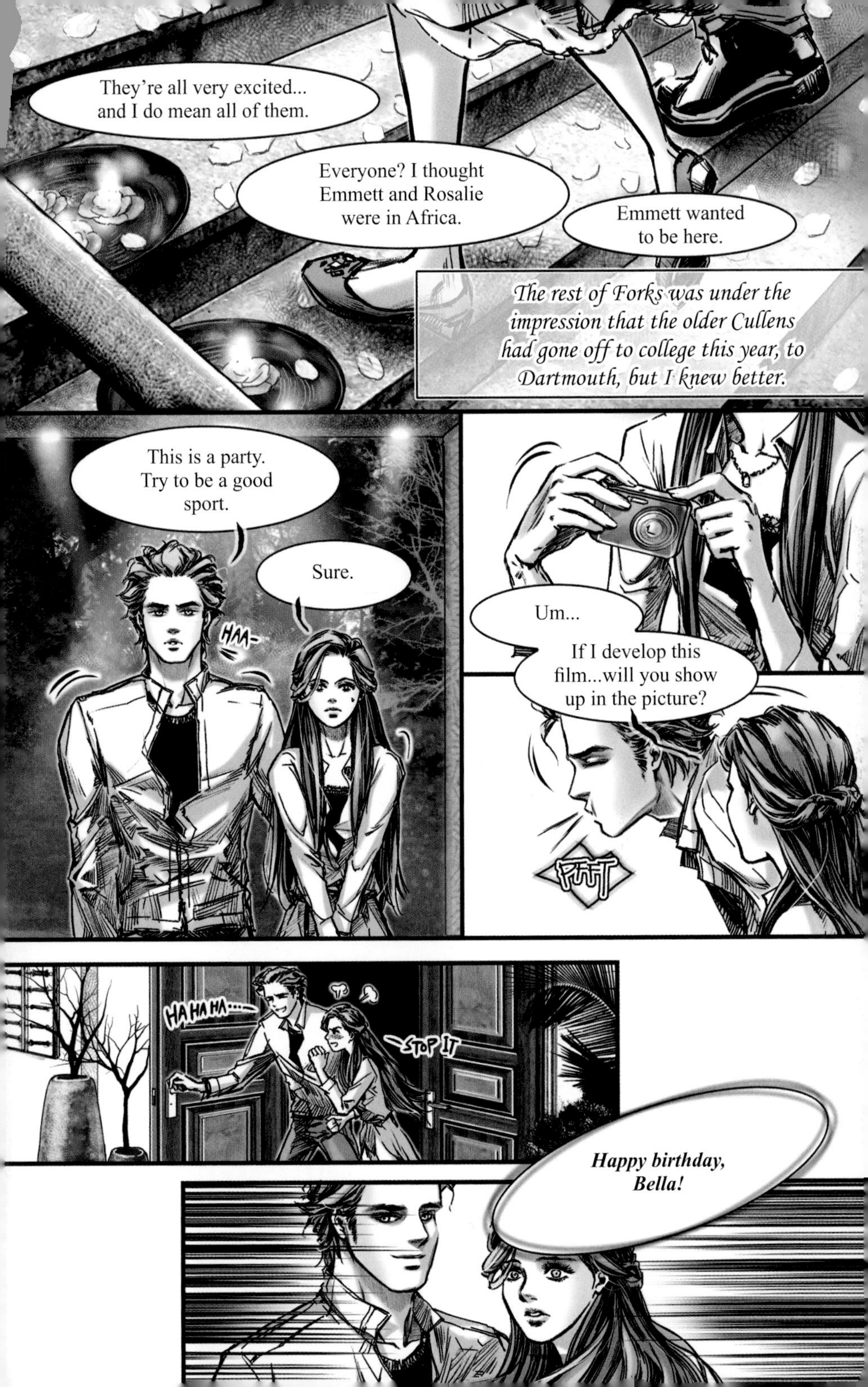
They're all very excited...
and I do mean all of them.
Everyone? I thought
Emmett and Rosalie
were in Africa.
Emmett wanted
to be here.
The rest of Forks was under the impression that the older Cullens had gone off to college this year, to Dartmouth, but I knew better.
This is a party.
Try to be a good
sport.
Sure.
HAA-
Um...
If I develop this
film...will you show
up in the picture?
PFFT
HA HA HA...
STOP IT
Happy birthday,
Bella!

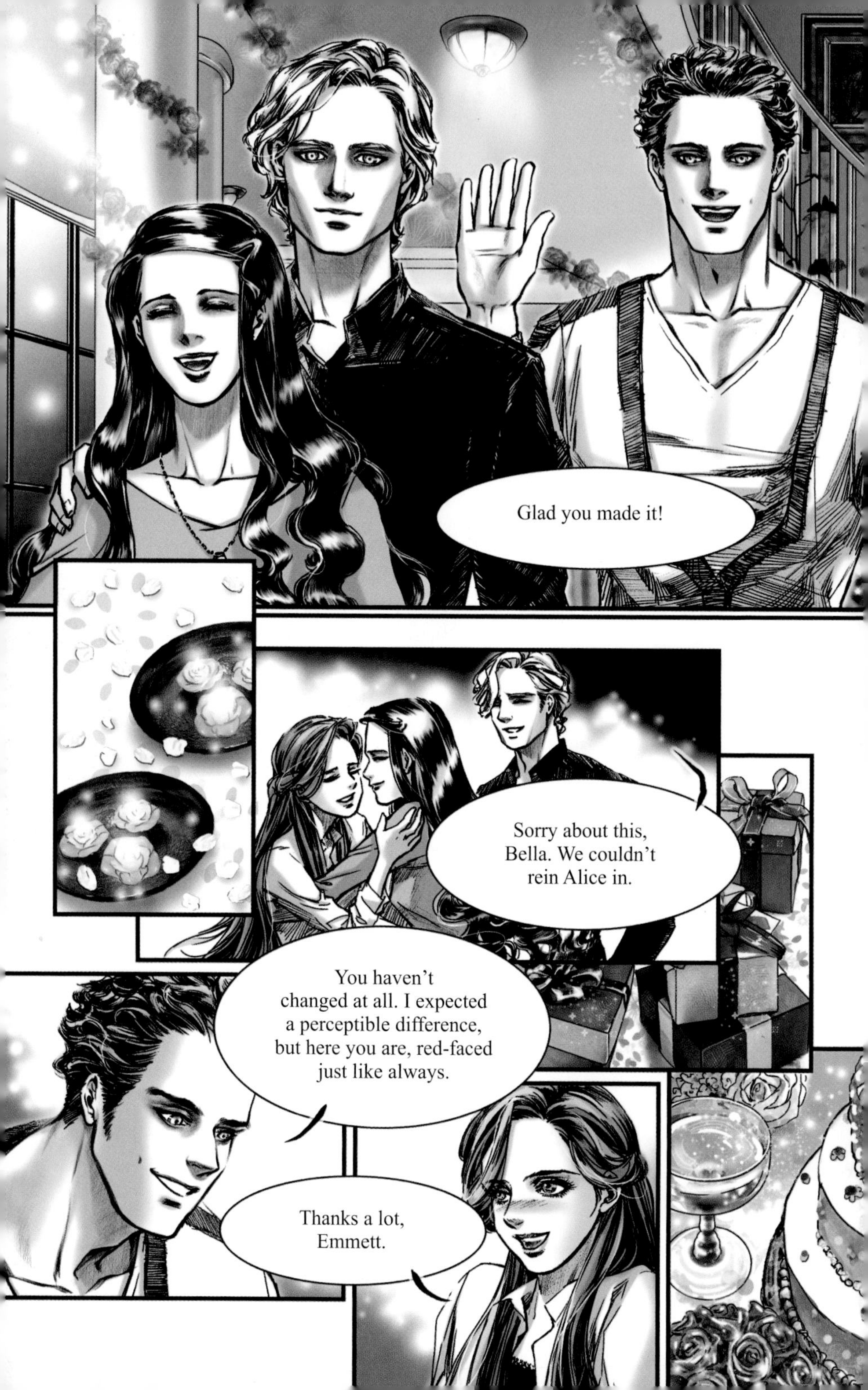
Glad you made it!
Sorry about this, Bella. We couldn't rein Alice in.
You haven't changed at all. I expected a perceptible difference, but here you are, red-faced just like always.
Thanks a lot, Emmett.

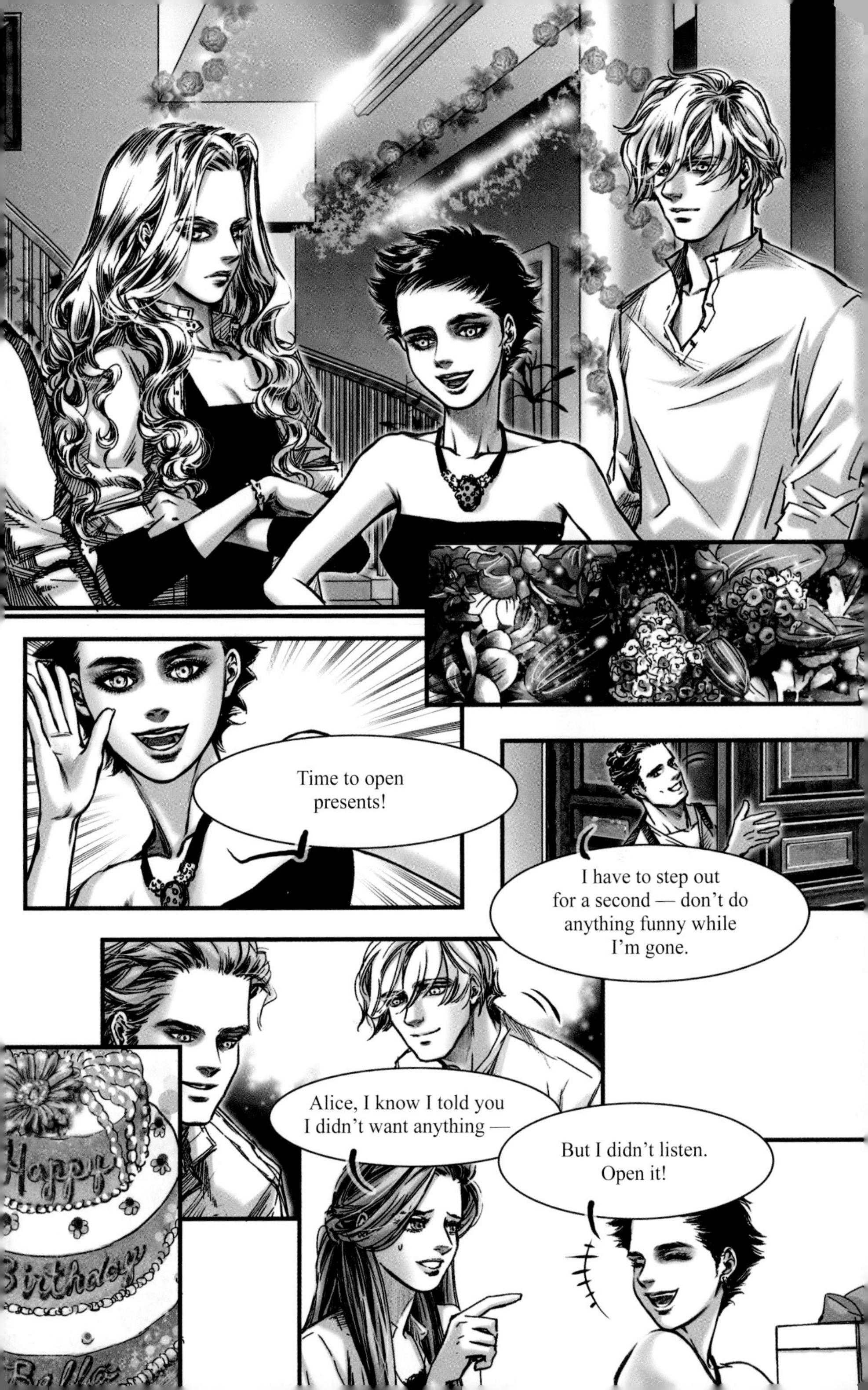

Time to open presents!
I have to step out for a second — don't do anything funny while I'm gone.
Alice, I know I told you I didn't want anything —
But I didn't listen. Open it!
Happy
Birthday

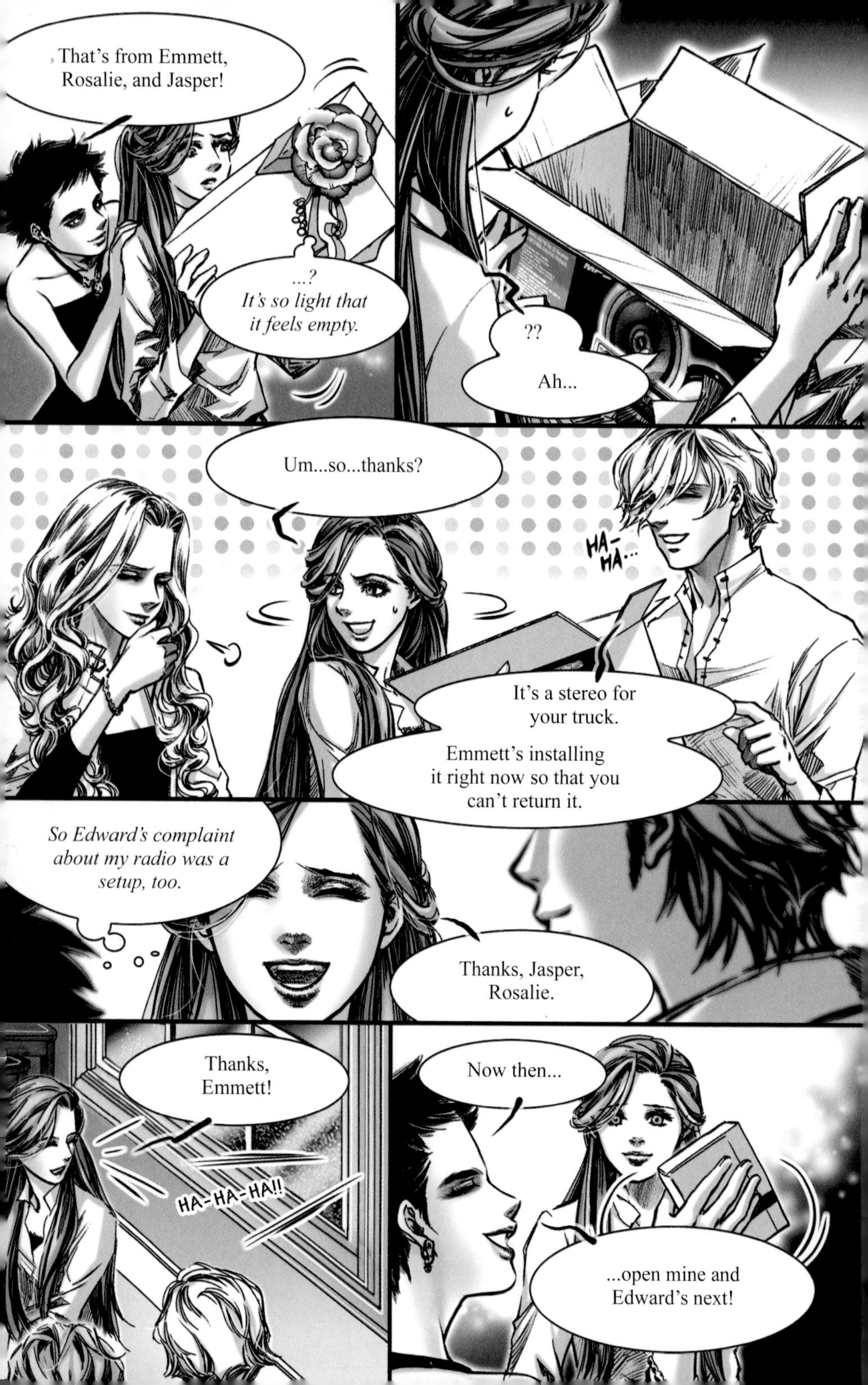
That's from Emmett, Rosalie, and Jasper!
...? It's so light that it feels empty.
??
Ah...
Um...so...thanks?
HA-HA...
It's a stereo for your truck.
Emmett's installing it right now so that you can't return it.
So Edward's complaint about my radio was a setup, too.
Thanks, Jasper, Rosalie.
Thanks, Emmett!
HA-HA-HA!!
Now then...
...open mine and Edward's next!

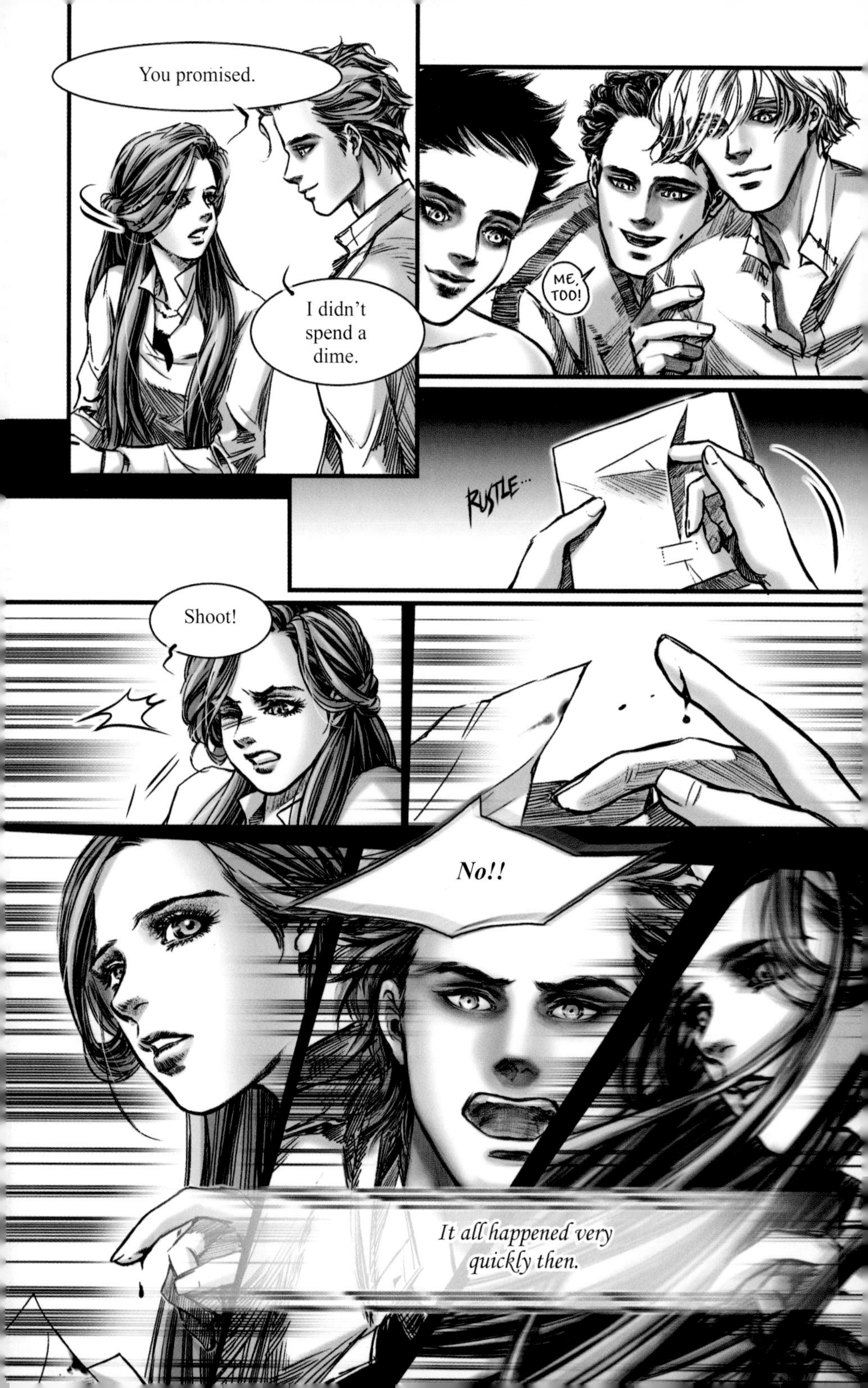
You promised.
I didn't spend a dime.
ME, TOO!
RUSTLE...
Shoot!
No!!
It all happened very quickly then.

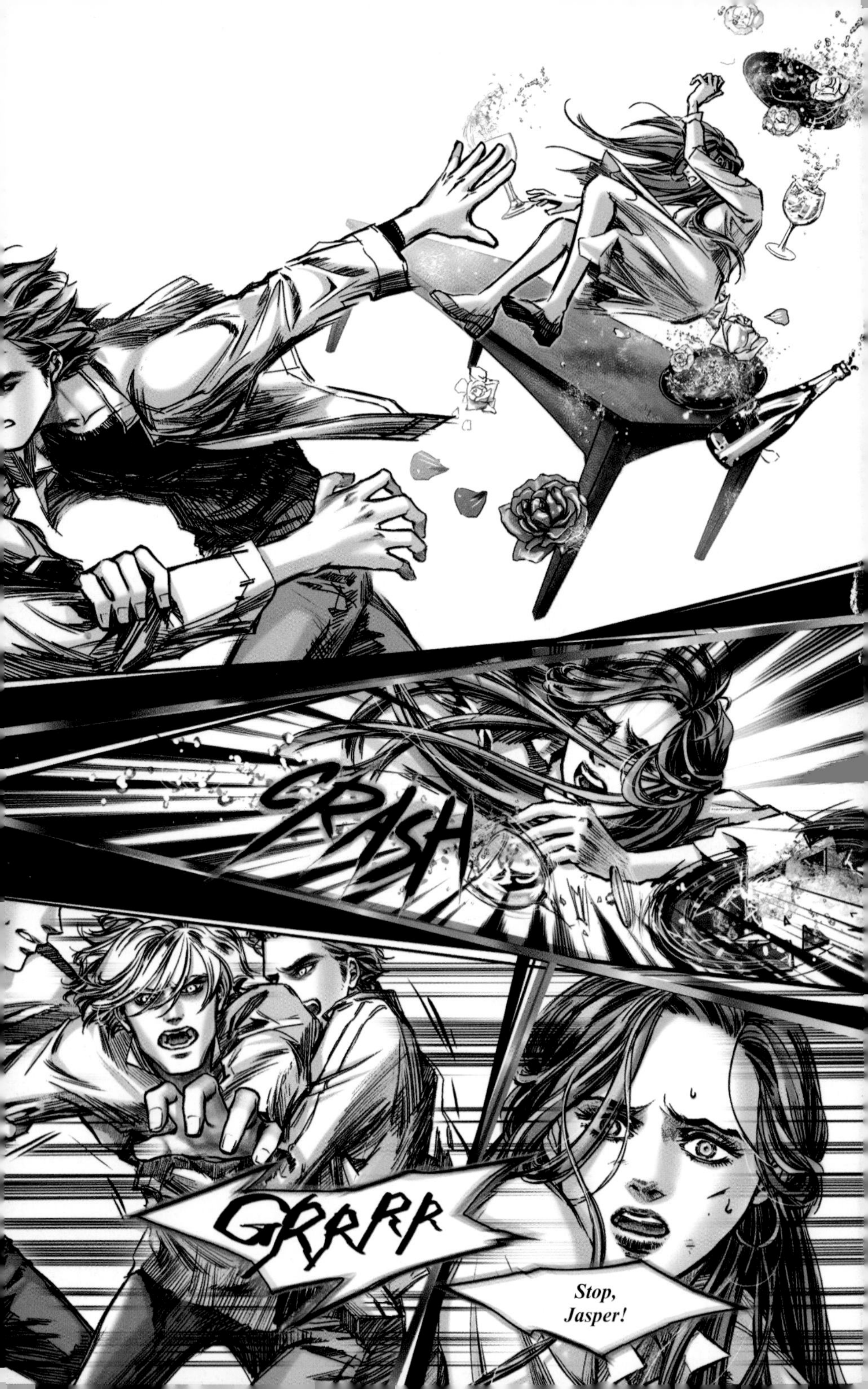
CRASH
GRRRR
Stop, Jasper!

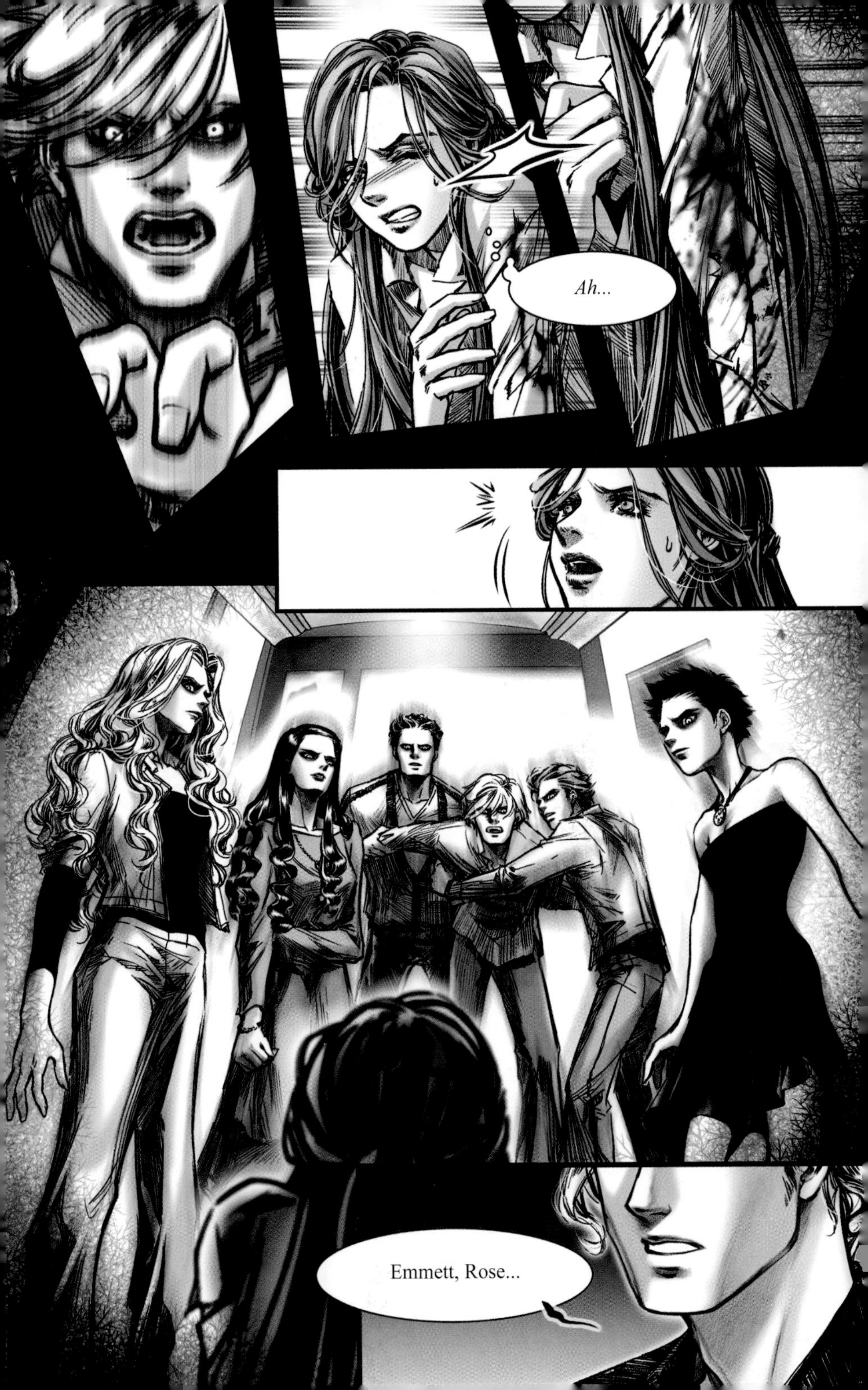
Ah...
Emmett, Rose...

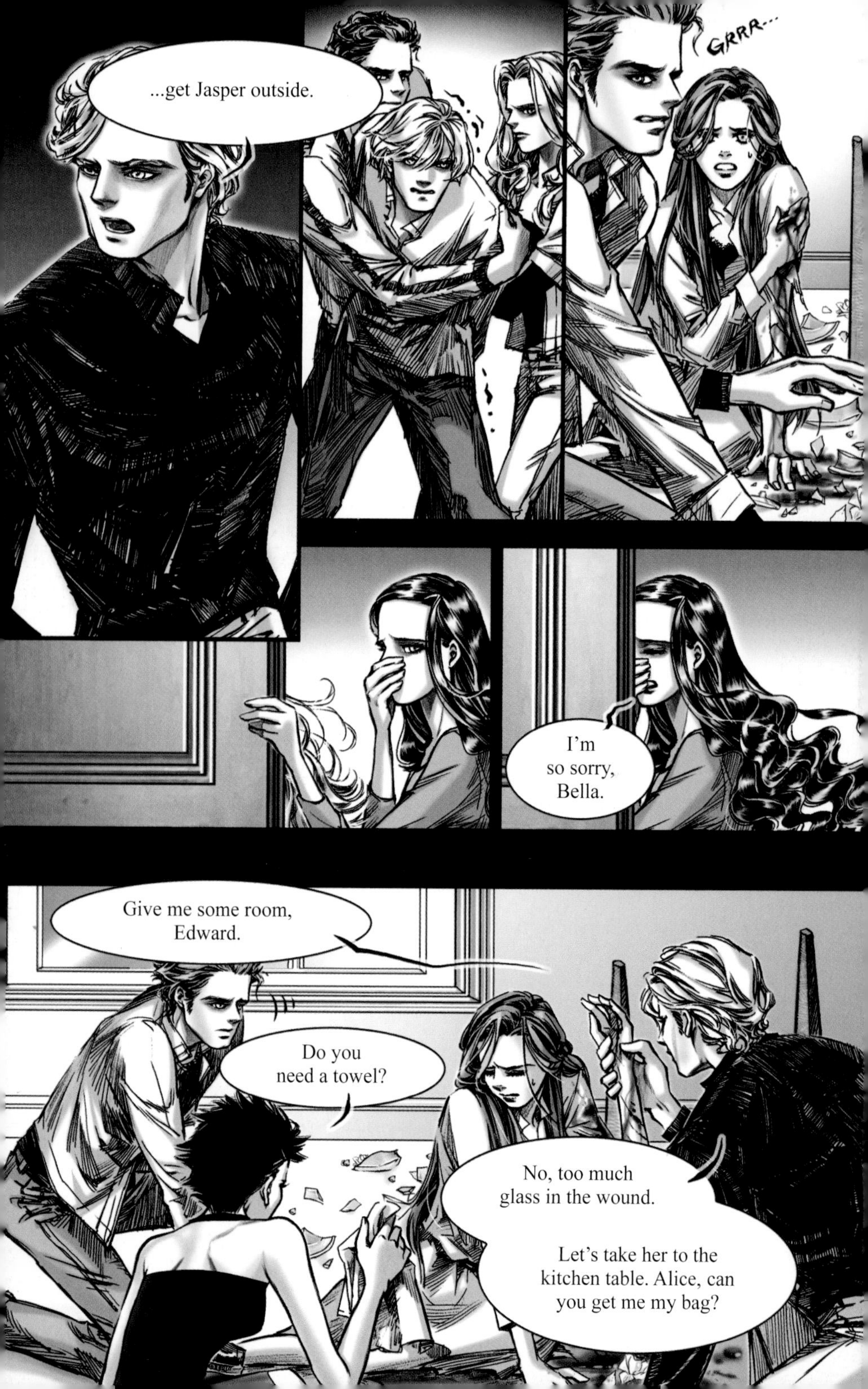

...get Jasper outside.
GRRR...
I'm so sorry, Bella.
Give me some room, Edward.
Do you need a towel?
No, too much glass in the wound.
Let's take her to the kitchen table. Alice, can you get me my bag?

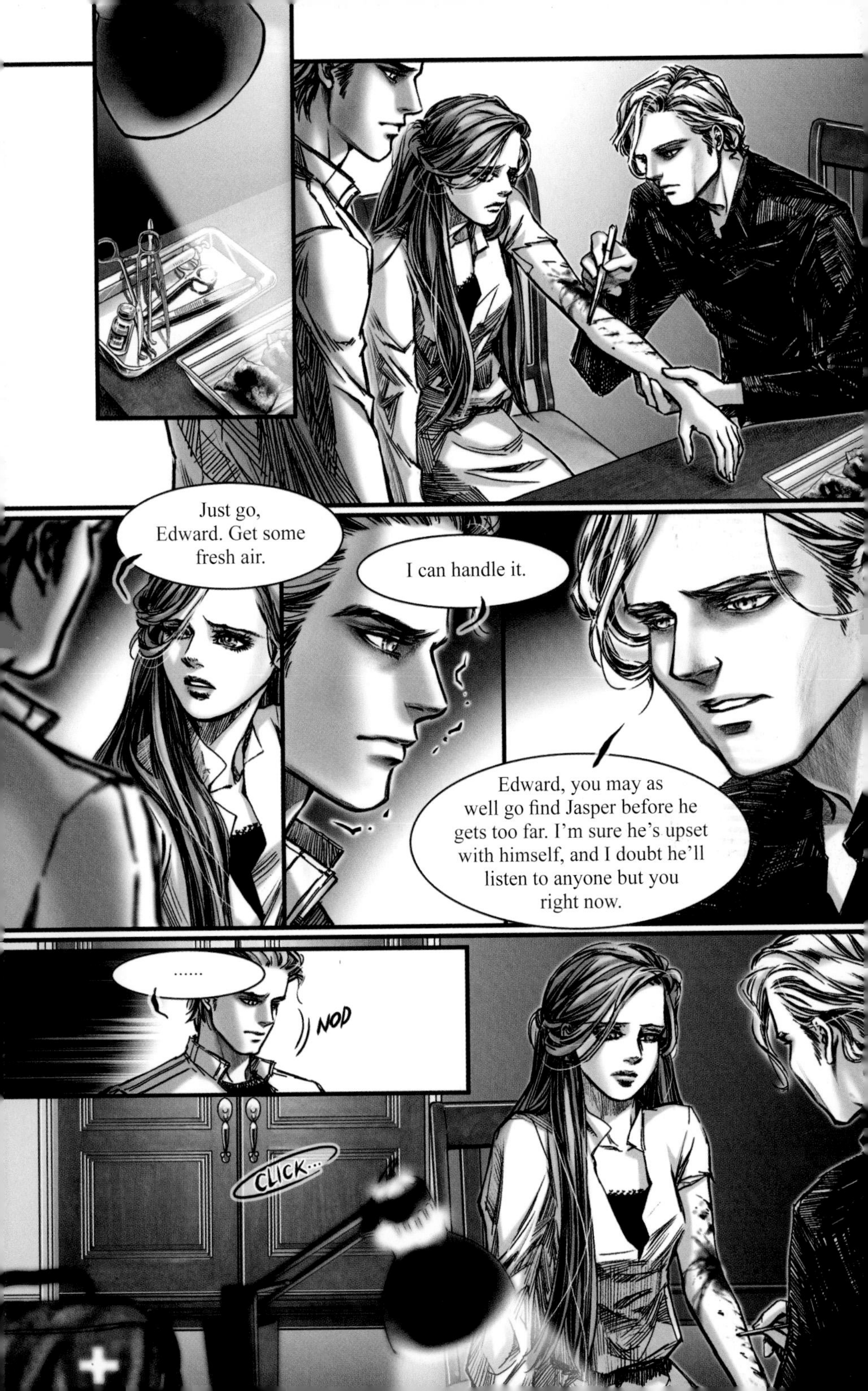
Just go, Edward. Get some fresh air.
I can handle it.
Edward, you may as well go find Jasper before he gets too far. I'm sure he's upset with himself, and I doubt he'll listen to anyone but you right now.
......
NOD
CLICK...

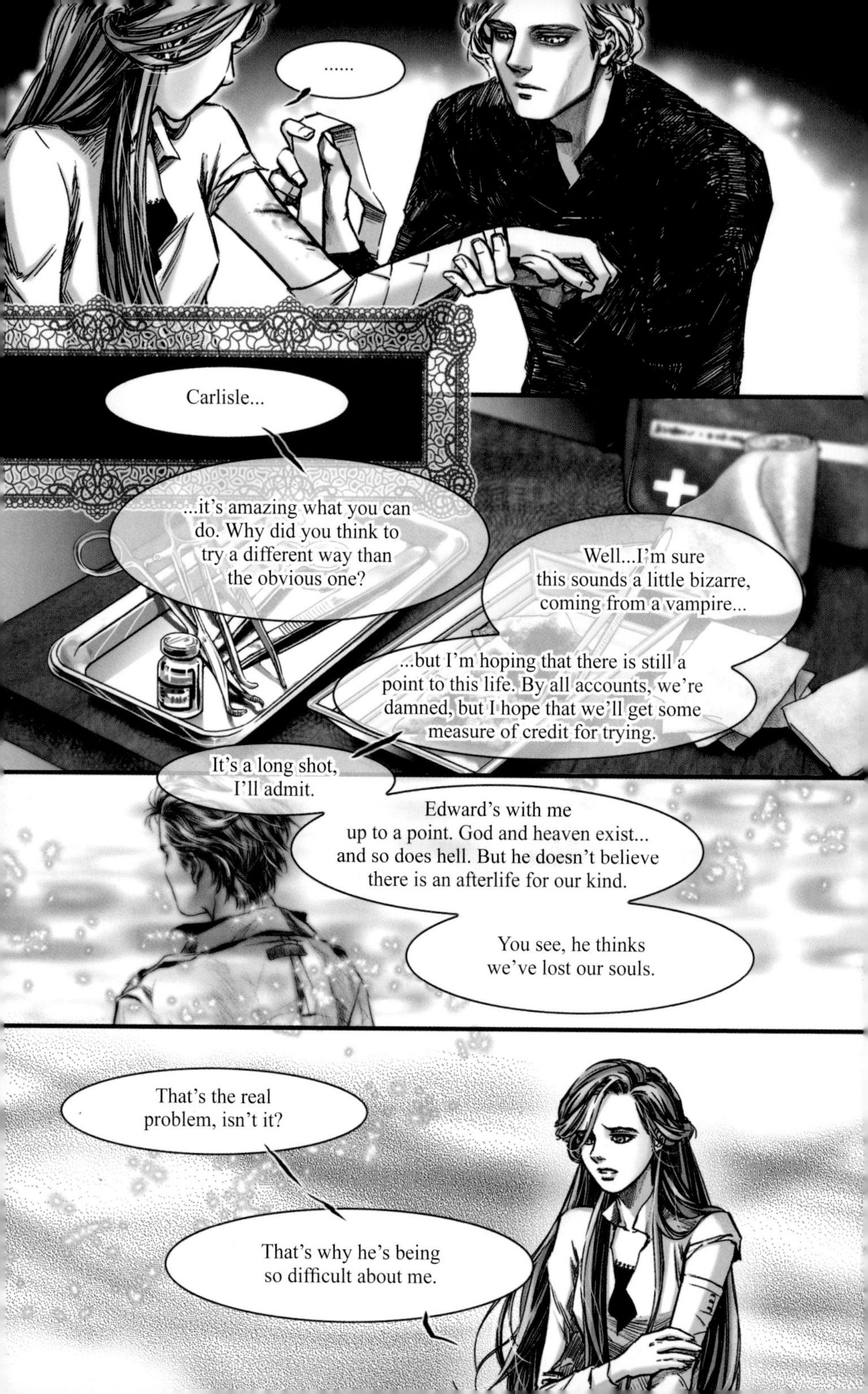
......
Carlisle...
...it's amazing what you can do. Why did you think to try a different way than the obvious one?
Well...I'm sure this sounds a little bizarre, coming from a vampire...
...but I'm hoping that there is still a point to this life. By all accounts, we're damned, but I hope that we'll get some measure of credit for trying.
It's a long shot, I'll admit.
Edward's with me up to a point. God and heaven exist... and so does hell. But he doesn't believe there is an afterlife for our kind.
You see, he thinks we've lost our souls.
That's the real problem, isn't it?
That's why he's being so difficult about me.

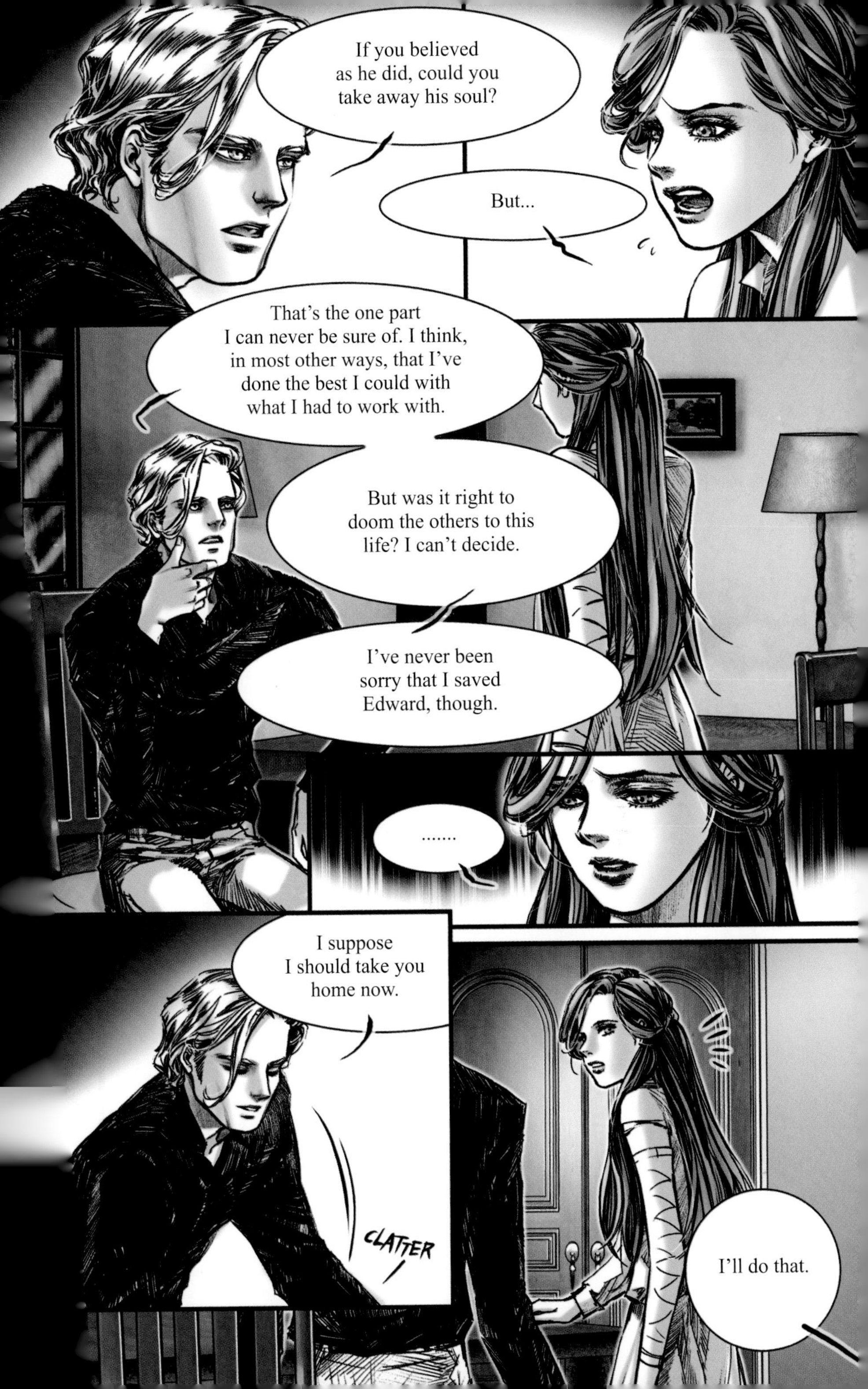
If you believed as he did, could you take away his soul?
But...
That's the one part I can never be sure of. I think, in most other ways, that I've done the best I could with what I had to work with.
But was it right to doom the others to this life? I can't decide.
I've never been sorry that I saved Edward, though.
....
I suppose I should take you home now.
CLATTER
I'll do that.

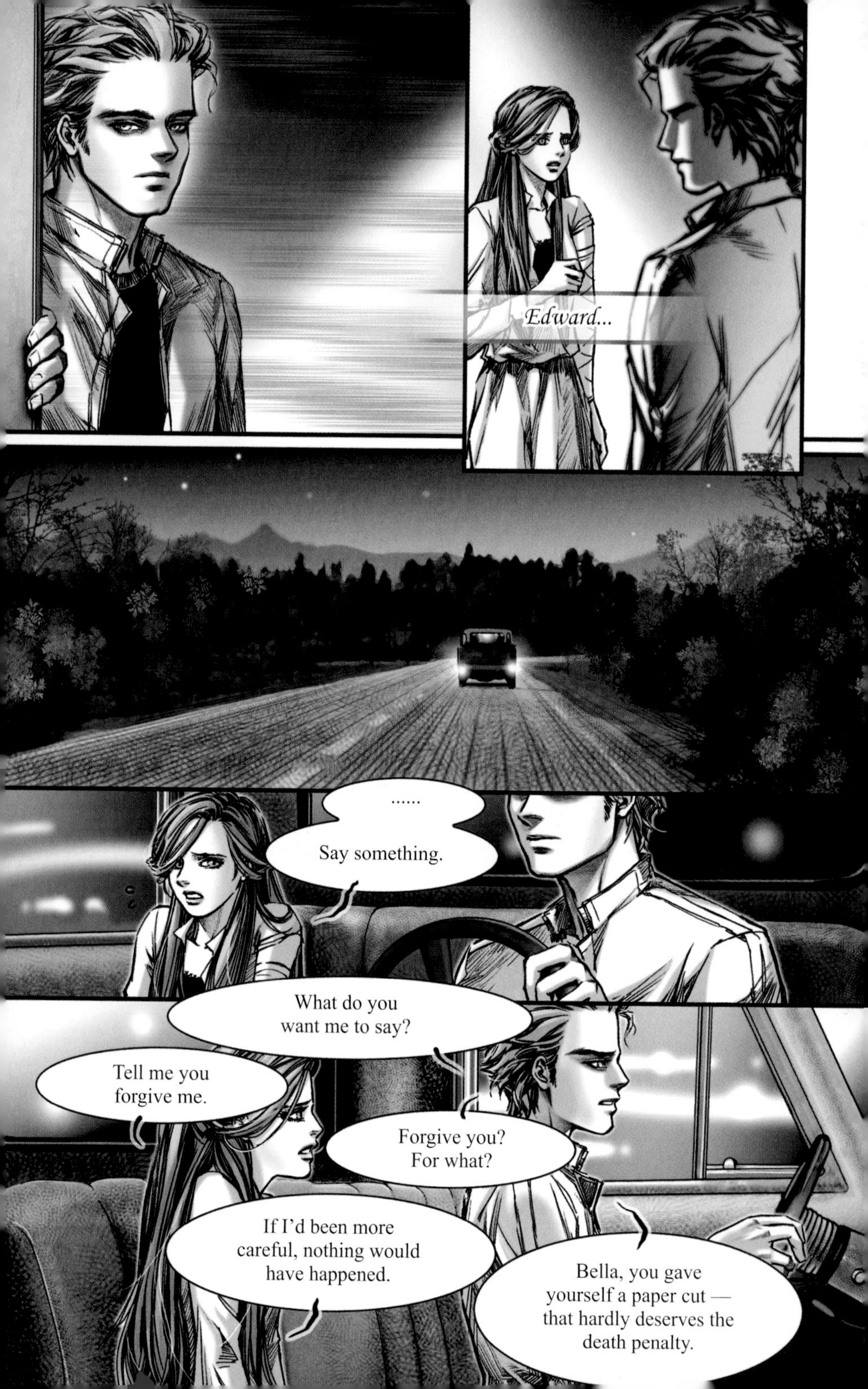
Edward...
......
Say something.
What do you want me to say?
Tell me you forgive me.
Forgive you? For what?
If I'd been more careful, nothing would have happened.
Bella, you gave yourself a paper cut — that hardly deserves the death penalty.

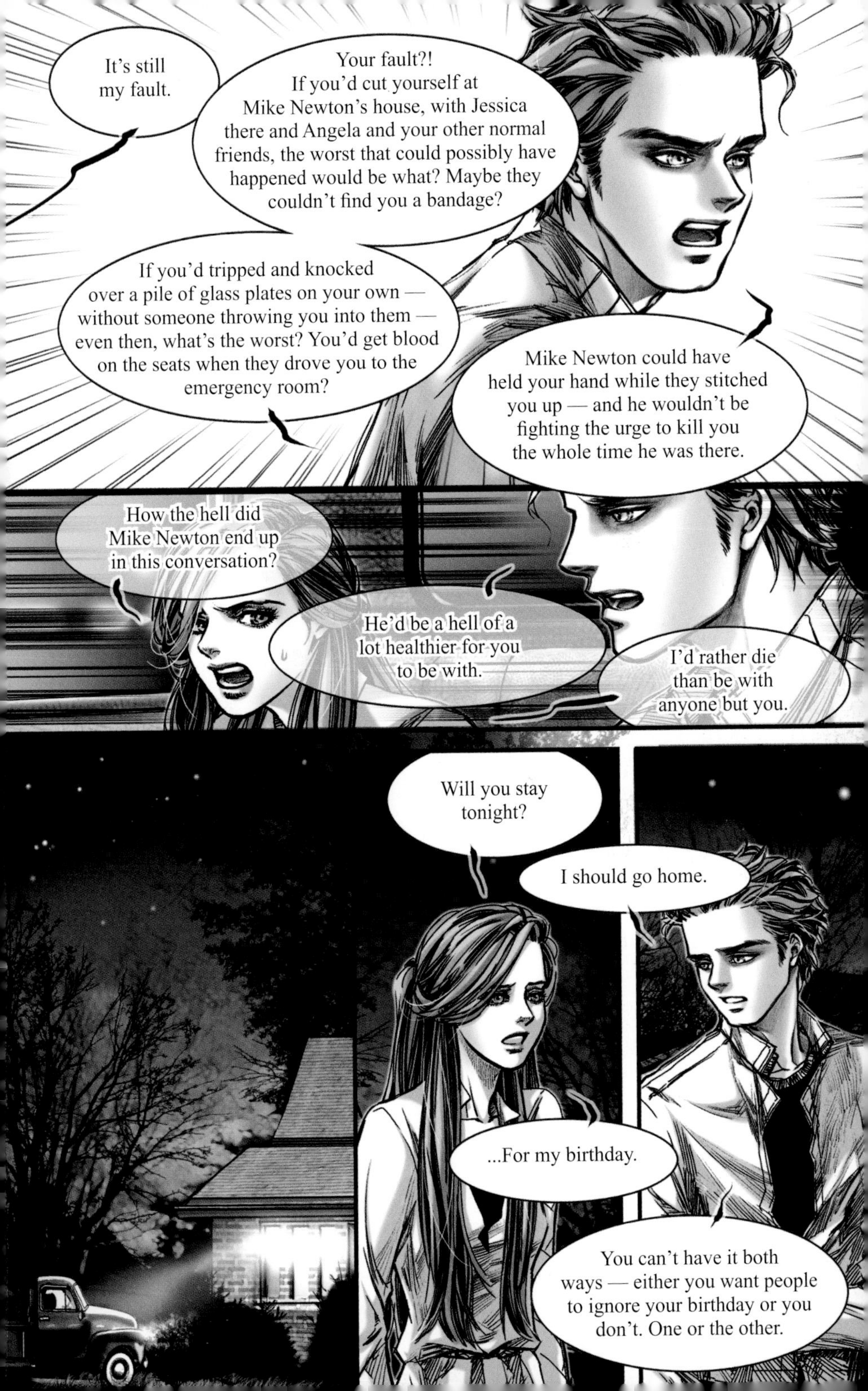
It's still my fault.
Your fault?! If you'd cut yourself at Mike Newton's house, with Jessica there and Angela and your other normal friends, the worst that could possibly have happened would be what? Maybe they couldn't find you a bandage?
If you'd tripped and knocked over a pile of glass plates on your own — without someone throwing you into them — even then, what's the worst? You'd get blood on the seats when they drove you to the emergency room?
Mike Newton could have held your hand while they stitched you up — and he wouldn't be fighting the urge to kill you the whole time he was there.
How the hell did Mike Newton end up in this conversation?
He'd be a hell of a lot healthier for you to be with.
I'd rather die than be with anyone but you.
Will you stay tonight?
I should go home.
...For my birthday.
You can't have it both ways — either you want people to ignore your birthday or you don't. One or the other.

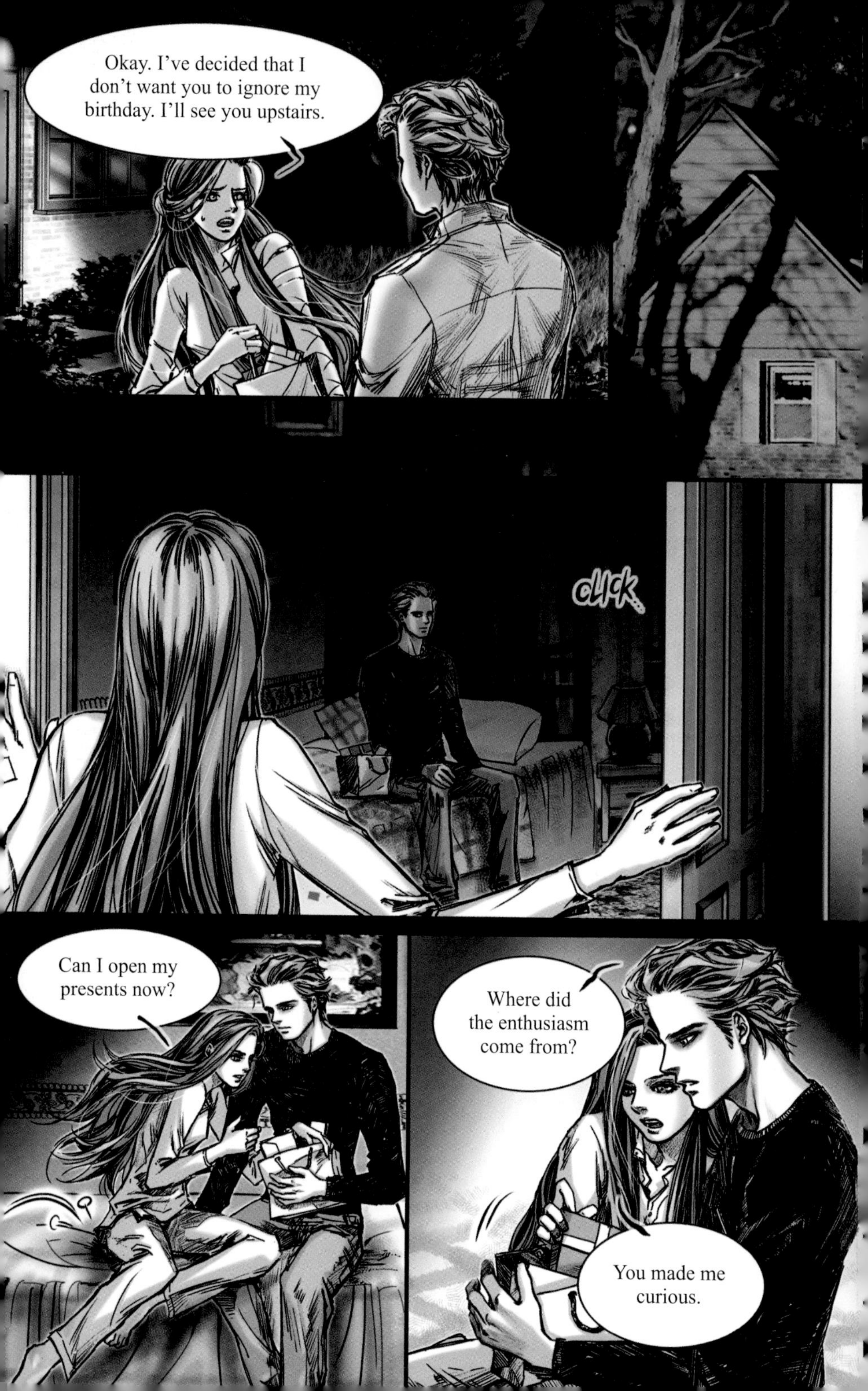
Okay. I've decided that I don't want you to ignore my birthday. I'll see you upstairs.
CLICK
Can I open my presents now?
Where did the enthusiasm come from?
You made me curious.

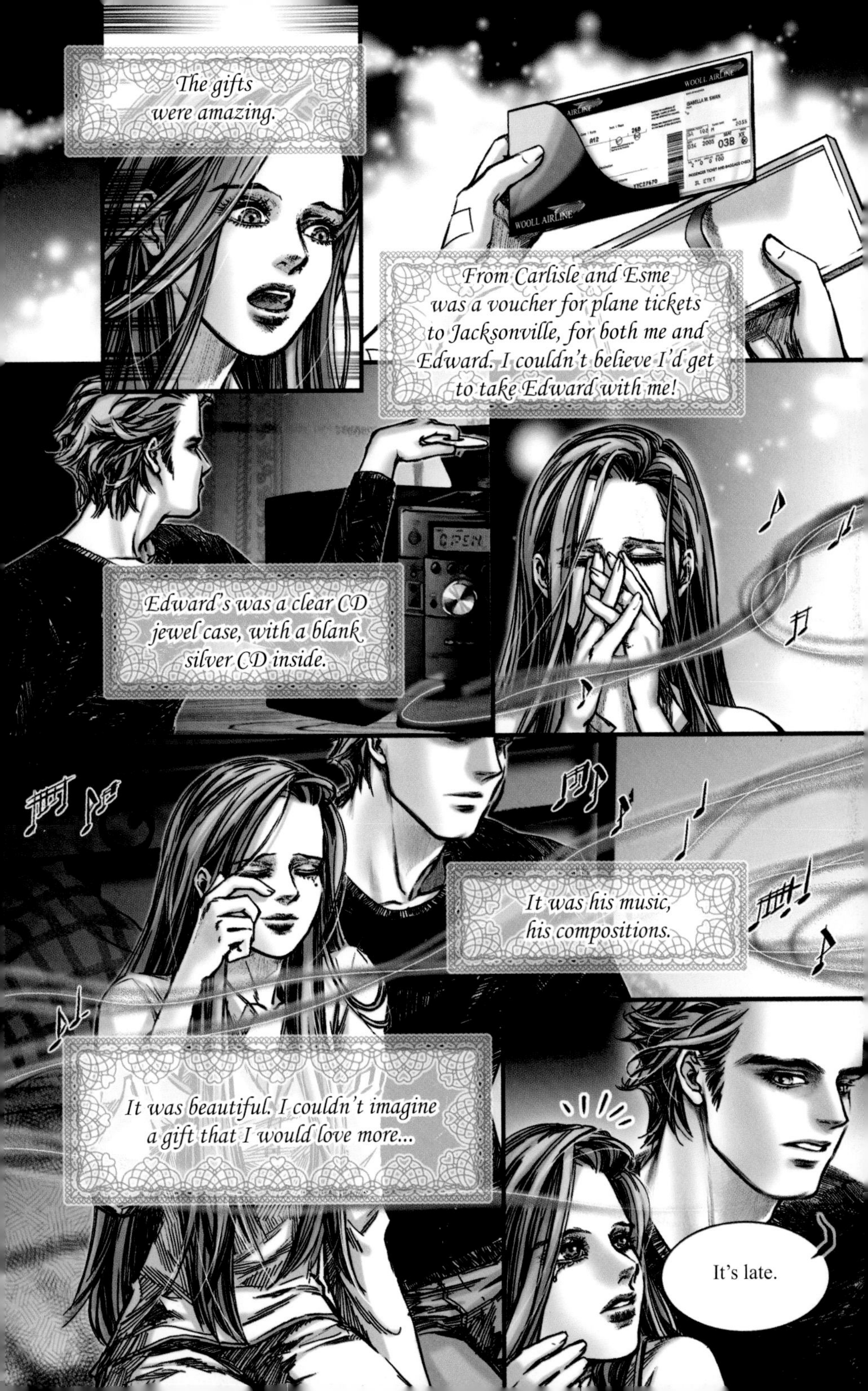
The gifts were amazing.
WOOLL AIRLINE
From Carlisle and Esme was a voucher for plane tickets to Jacksonville, for both me and Edward. I couldn't believe I'd get to take Edward with me!
OPEN
Edward's was a clear CD jewel case, with a blank silver CD inside.
It was his music, his compositions.
It was beautiful. I couldn't imagine a gift that I would love more...
It's late.

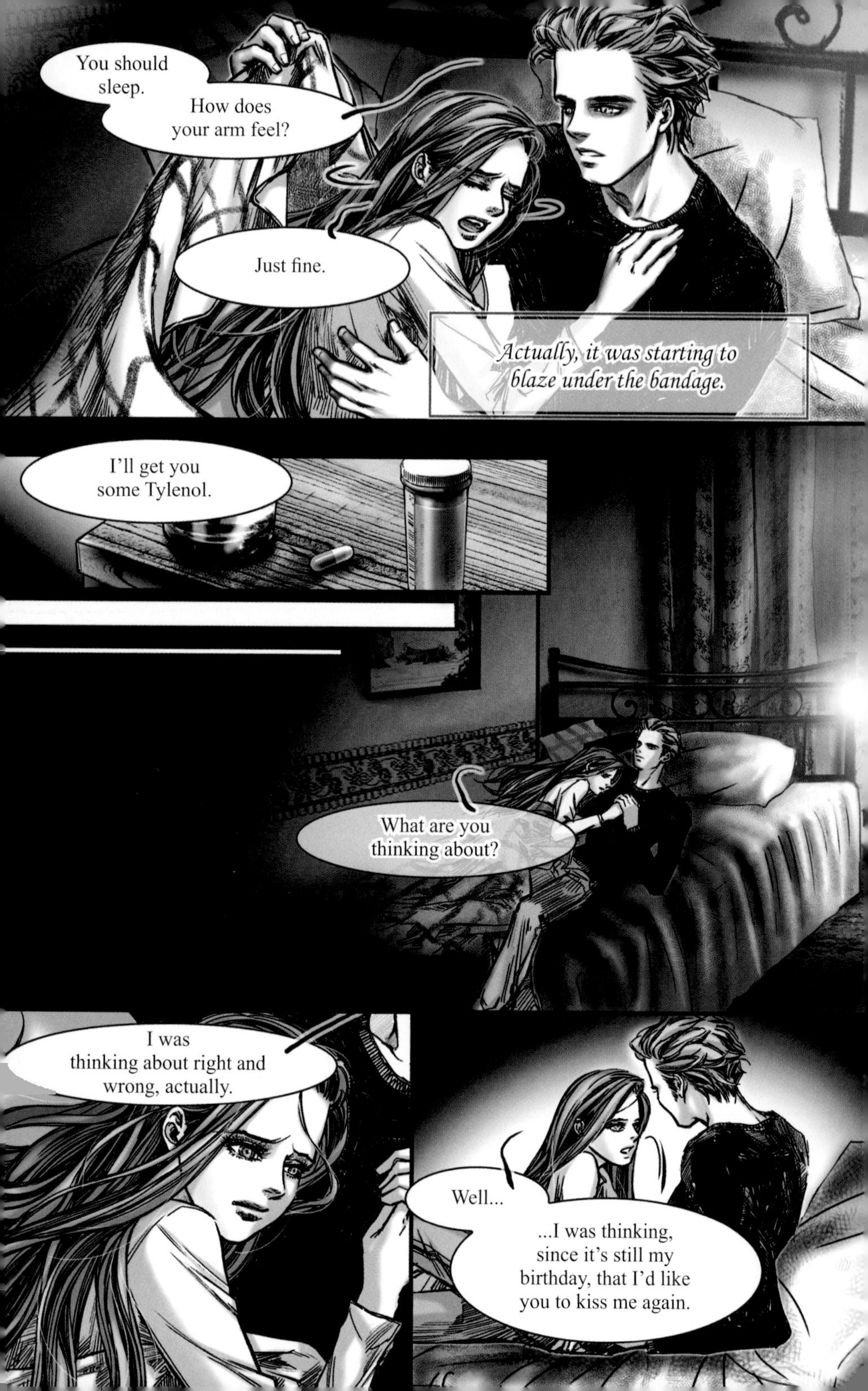
You should sleep.
How does your arm feel?
Just fine.
Actually, it was starting to blaze under the bandage.
I'll get you some Tylenol.
What are you thinking about?
I was thinking about right and wrong, actually.
Well...
...I was thinking, since it's still my birthday, that I'd like you to kiss me again.

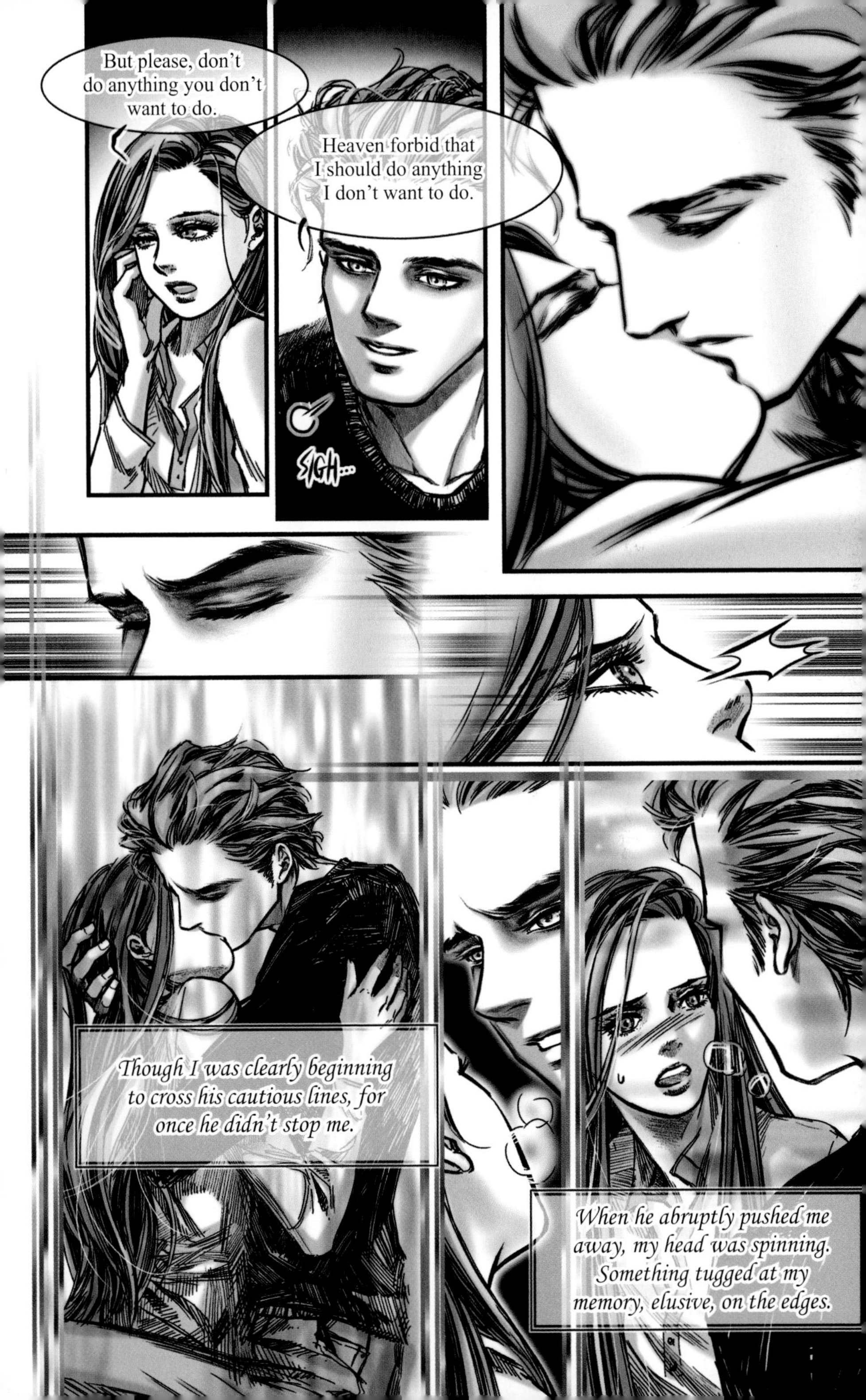
But please, don't do anything you don't want to do.
Heaven forbid that I should do anything I don't want to do.
SIGH...
Though I was clearly beginning to cross his cautious lines, for once he didn't stop me.
When he abruptly pushed me away, my head was spinning. Something tugged at my memory, elusive, on the edges.

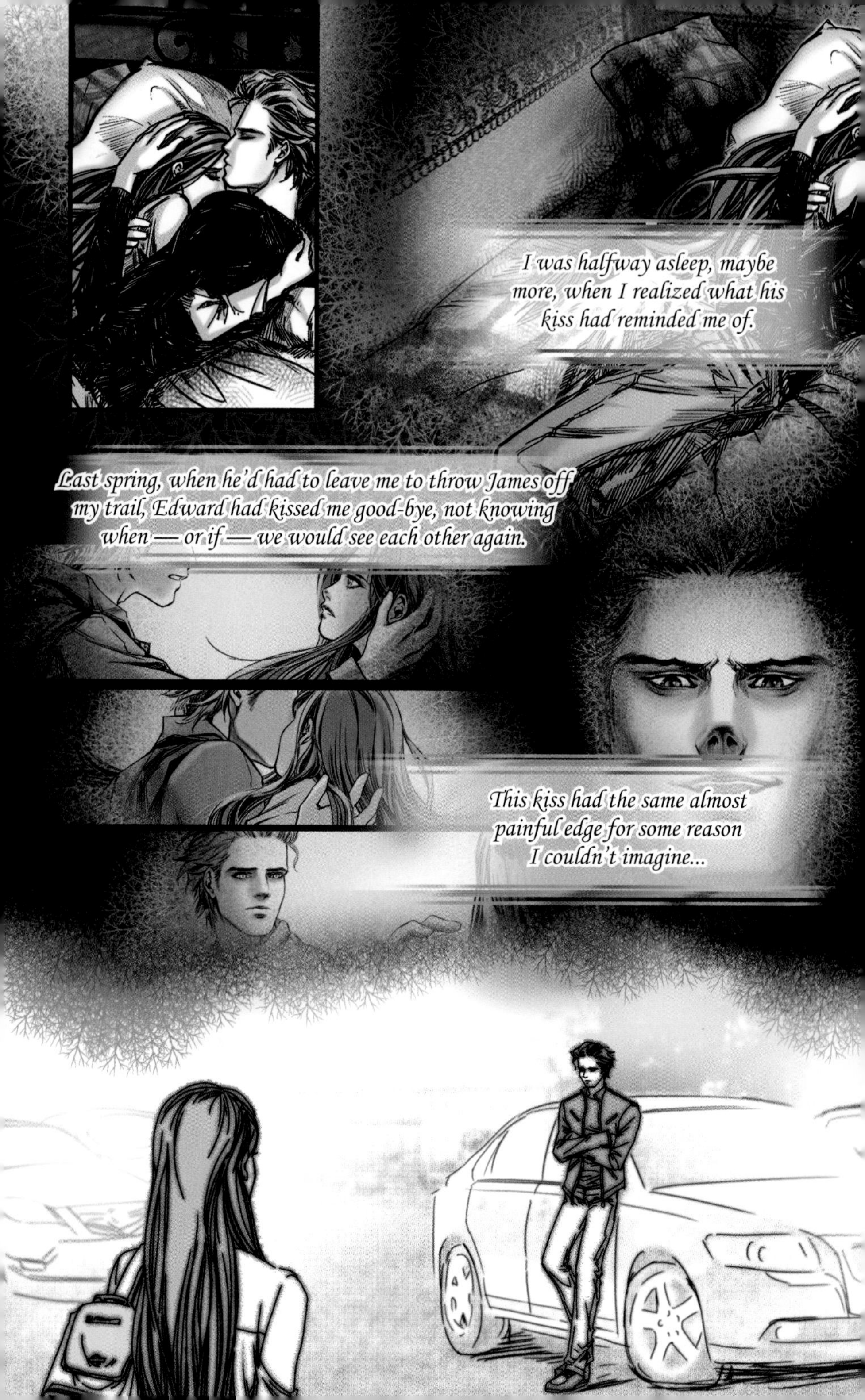
I was halfway asleep, maybe more, when I realized what his kiss had reminded me of.
Last spring, when he'd had to leave me to throw James off my trail, Edward had kissed me good-bye, not knowing when — or if — we would see each other again.
This kiss had the same almost painful edge for some reason I couldn't imagine...

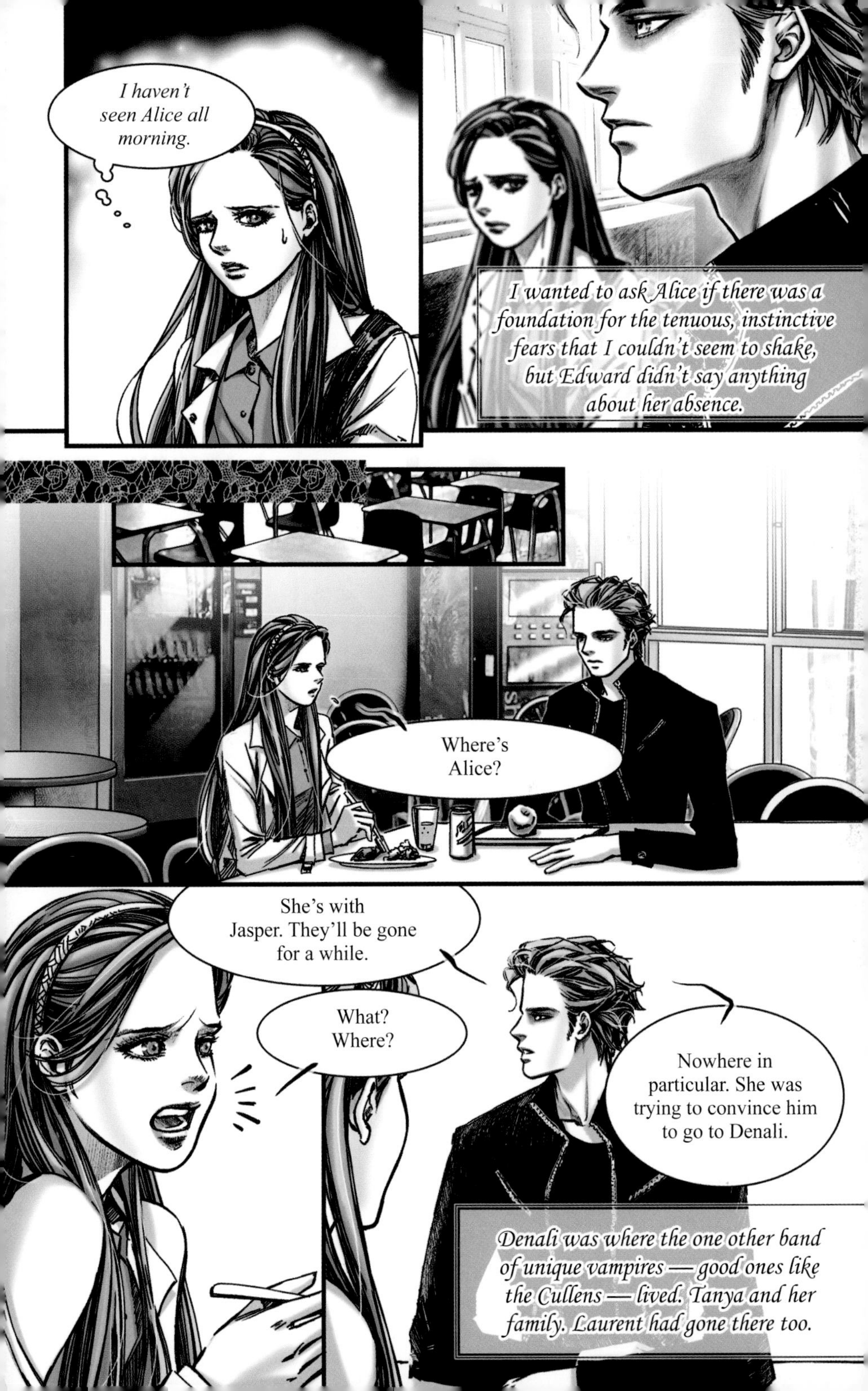
I haven't seen Alice all morning.
I wanted to ask Alice if there was a foundation for the tenuous, instinctive fears that I couldn't seem to shake, but Edward didn't say anything about her absence.
Where's Alice?
She's with Jasper. They'll be gone for a while.
What? Where?
Nowhere in particular. She was trying to convince him to go to Denali.
Denali was where the one other band of unique vampires — good ones like the Cullens — lived. Tanya and her family. Laurent had gone there too.

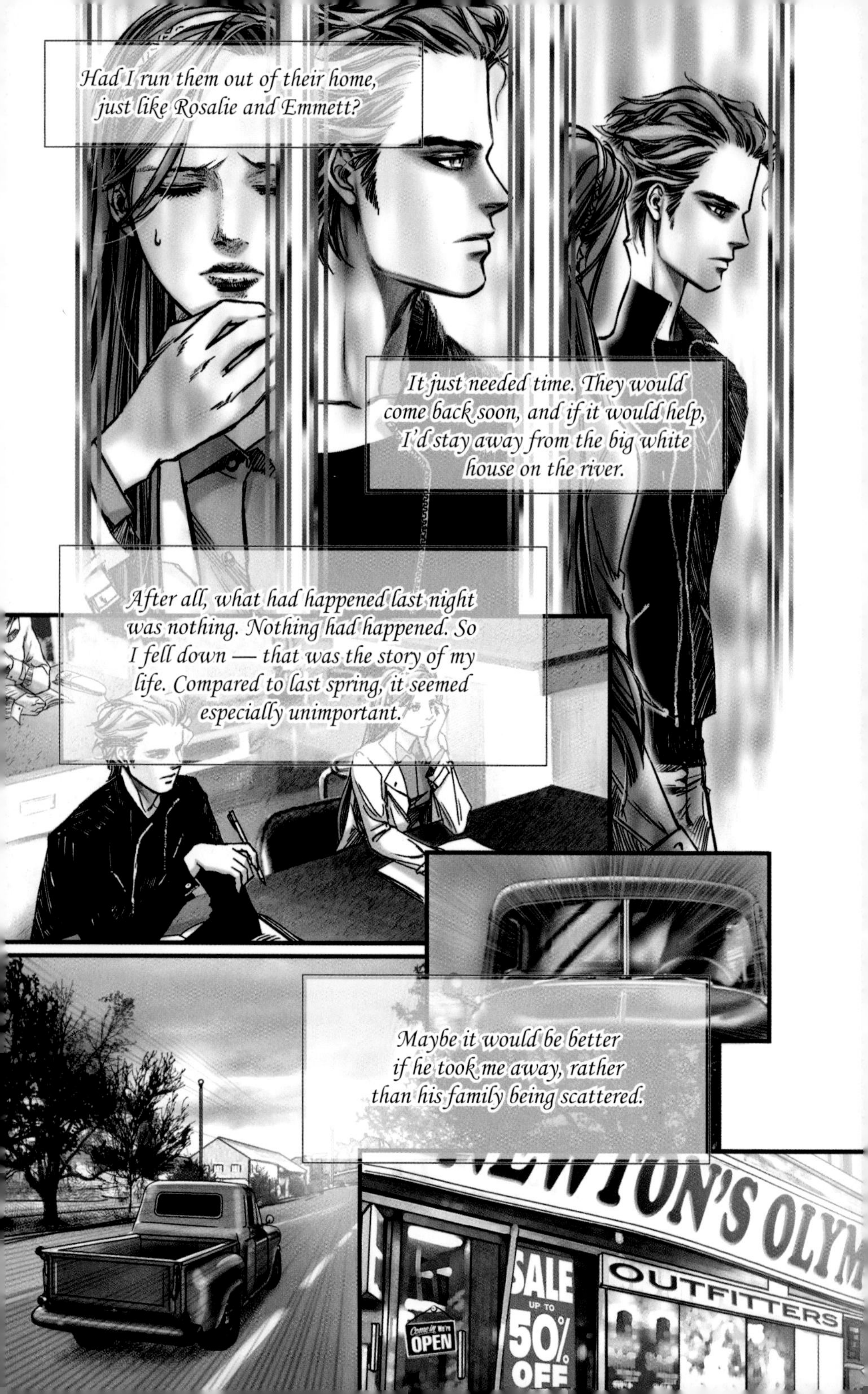
Had I run them out of their home,
just like Rosalie and Emmett?
It just needed time. They would
come back soon, and if it would help,
I'd stay away from the big white
house on the river.
After all, what had happened last night
was nothing. Nothing had happened. So
I fell down — that was the story of my
life. Compared to last spring, it seemed
especially unimportant.
Maybe it would be better
if he took me away, rather
than his family being scattered.
NEWTON'S OLYM
OUTFITTERS
SALE
UP TO
50%
OFF
Come in WE'RE
OPEN

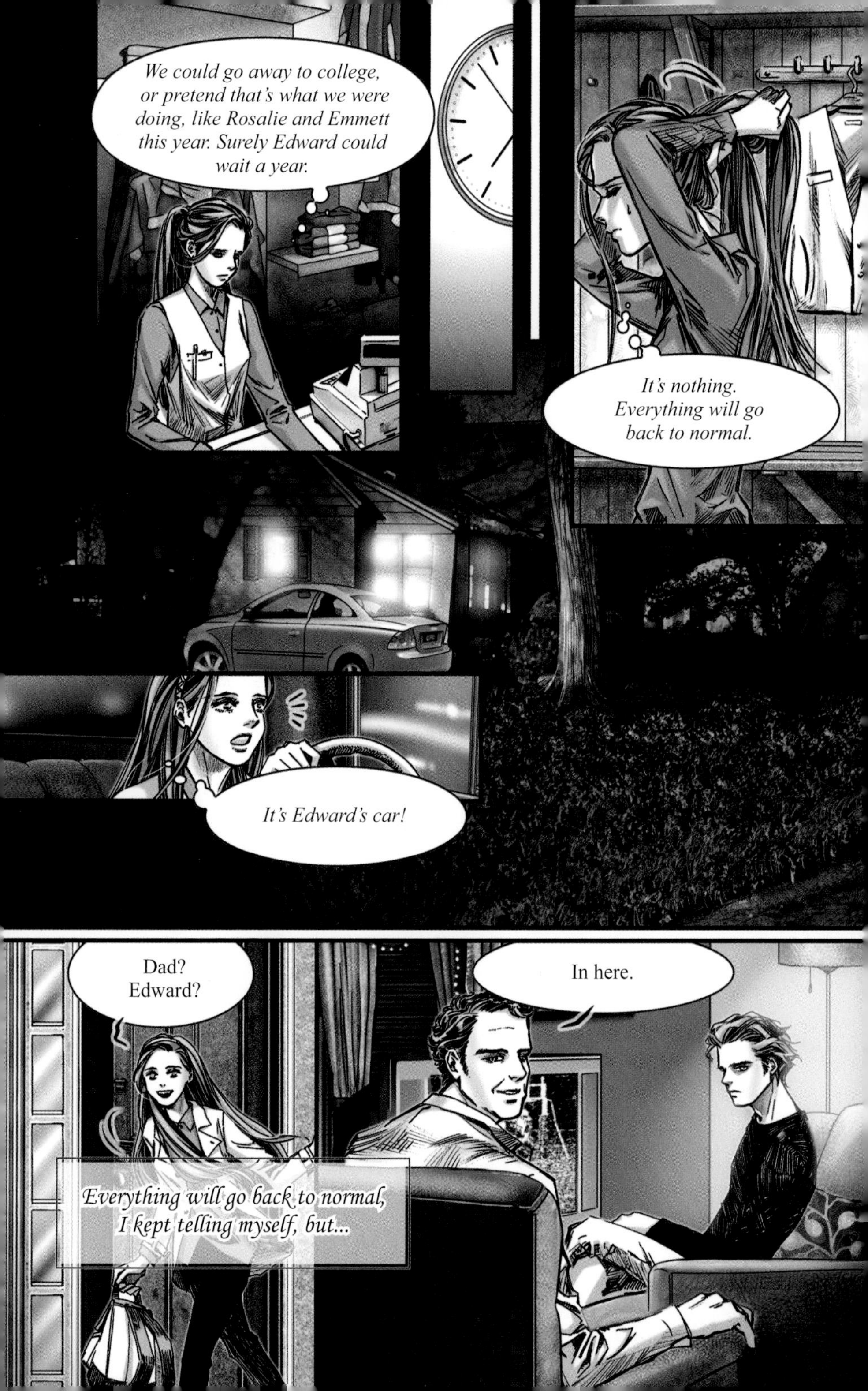
We could go away to college, or pretend that's what we were doing, like Rosalie and Emmett this year. Surely Edward could wait a year.
It's nothing. Everything will go back to normal.
It's Edward's car!
Dad? Edward?
In here.
Everything will go back to normal, I kept telling myself, but...

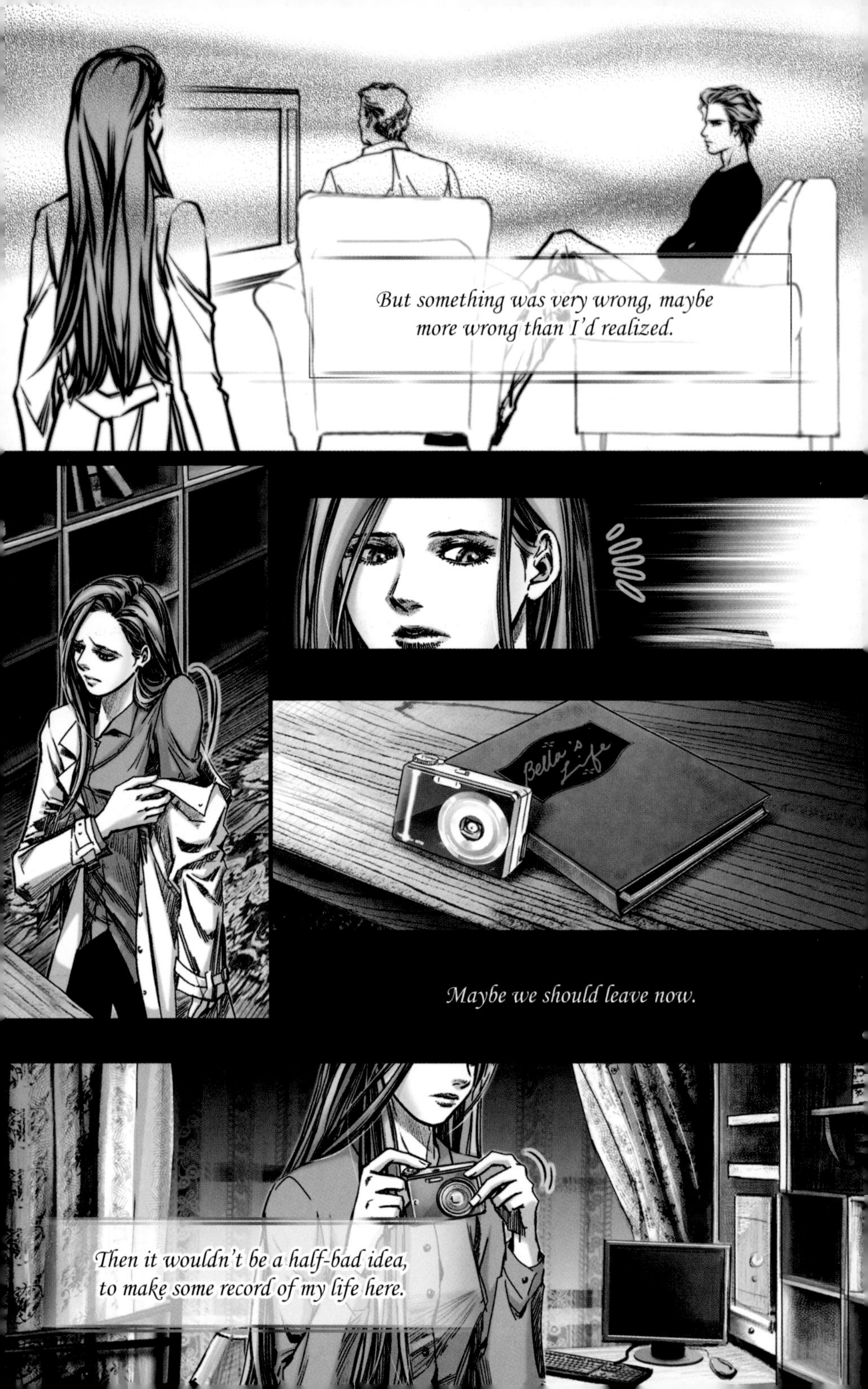
But something was very wrong, maybe more wrong than I'd realized.
Bella's Life
Maybe we should leave now.
Then it wouldn't be a half-bad idea, to make some record of my life here.

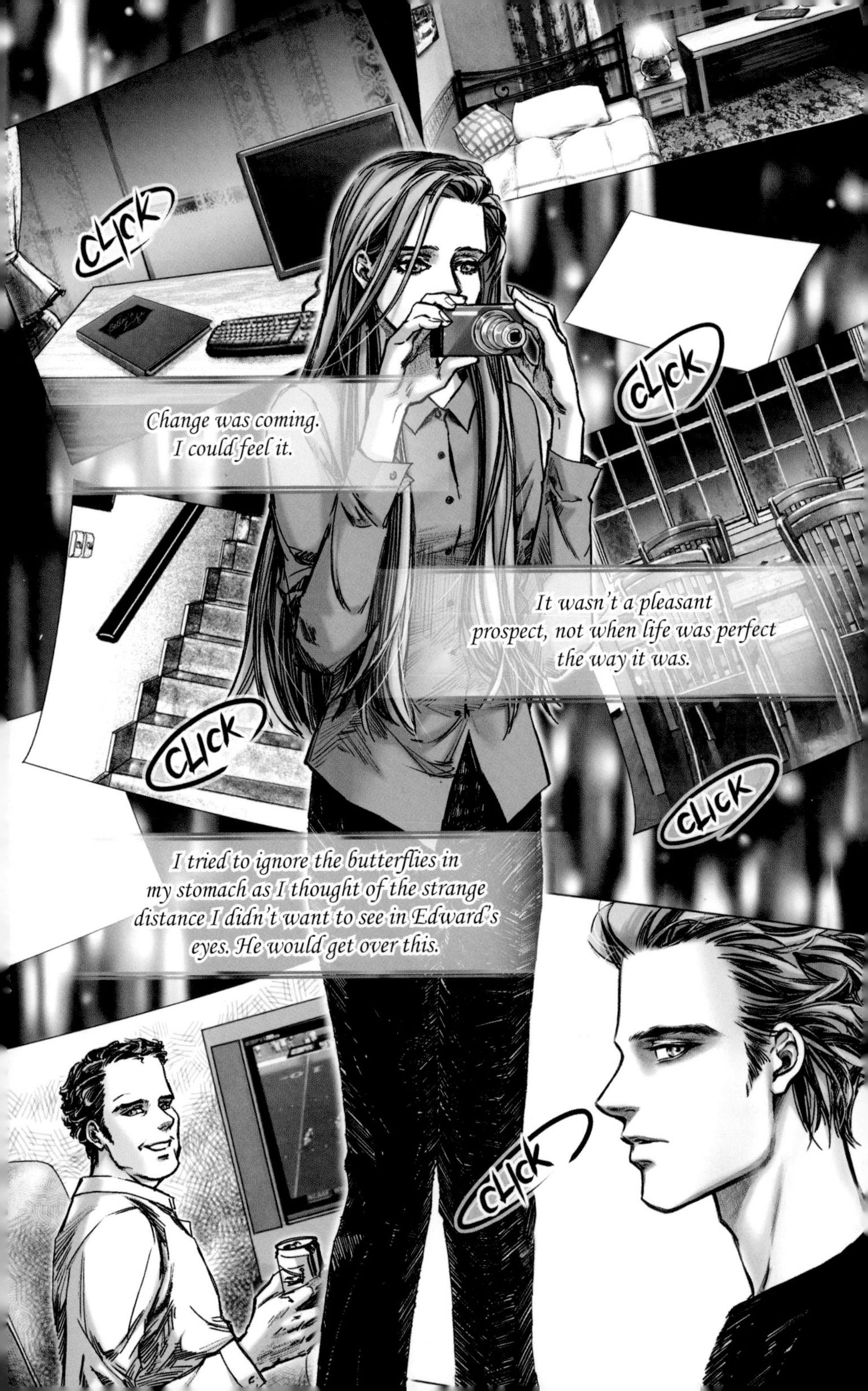
CLICK
Change was coming.
I could feel it.
CLICK
It wasn't a pleasant prospect, not when life was perfect the way it was.
CLICK
CLICK
I tried to ignore the butterflies in my stomach as I thought of the strange distance I didn't want to see in Edward's eyes. He would get over this.
CLICK

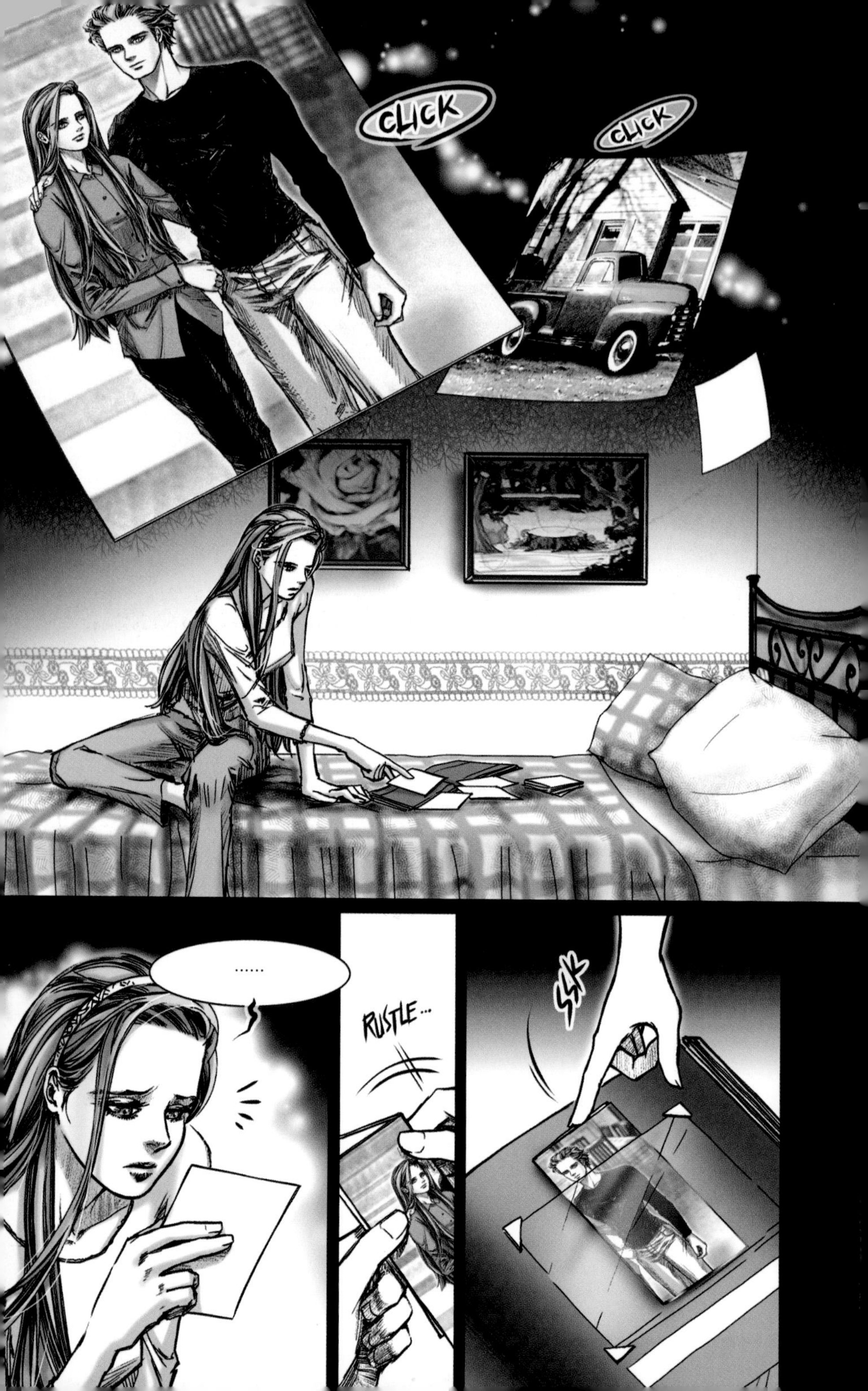
CLICK
CLICK
......
RUSTLE...
SSK

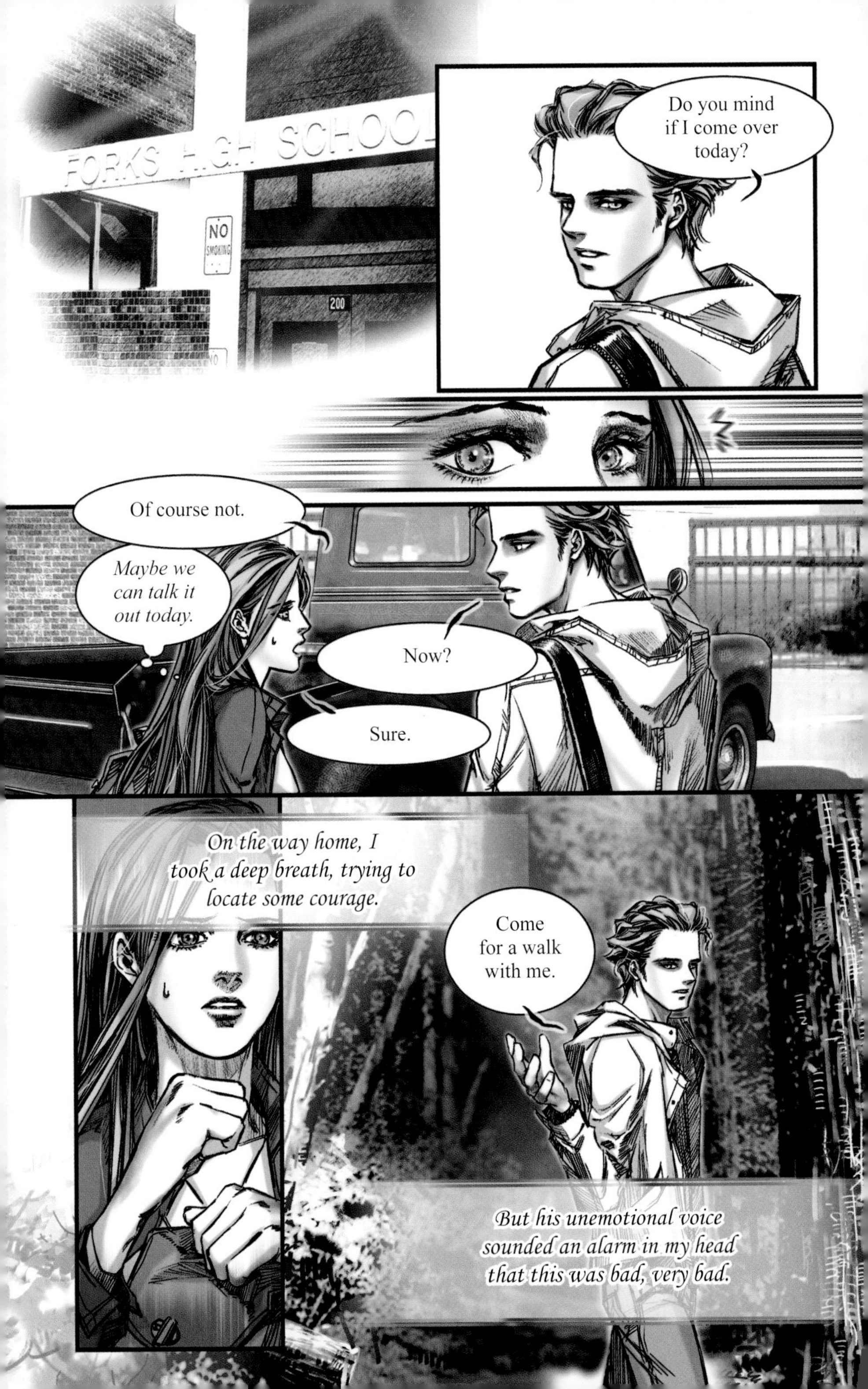
FORKS HIGH SCHOOL
NO SMOKING
200
Do you mind if I come over today?
Of course not.
Maybe we can talk it out today.
Now?
Sure.
On the way home, I took a deep breath, trying to locate some courage.
Come for a walk with me.
But his unemotional voice sounded an alarm in my head that this was bad, very bad.

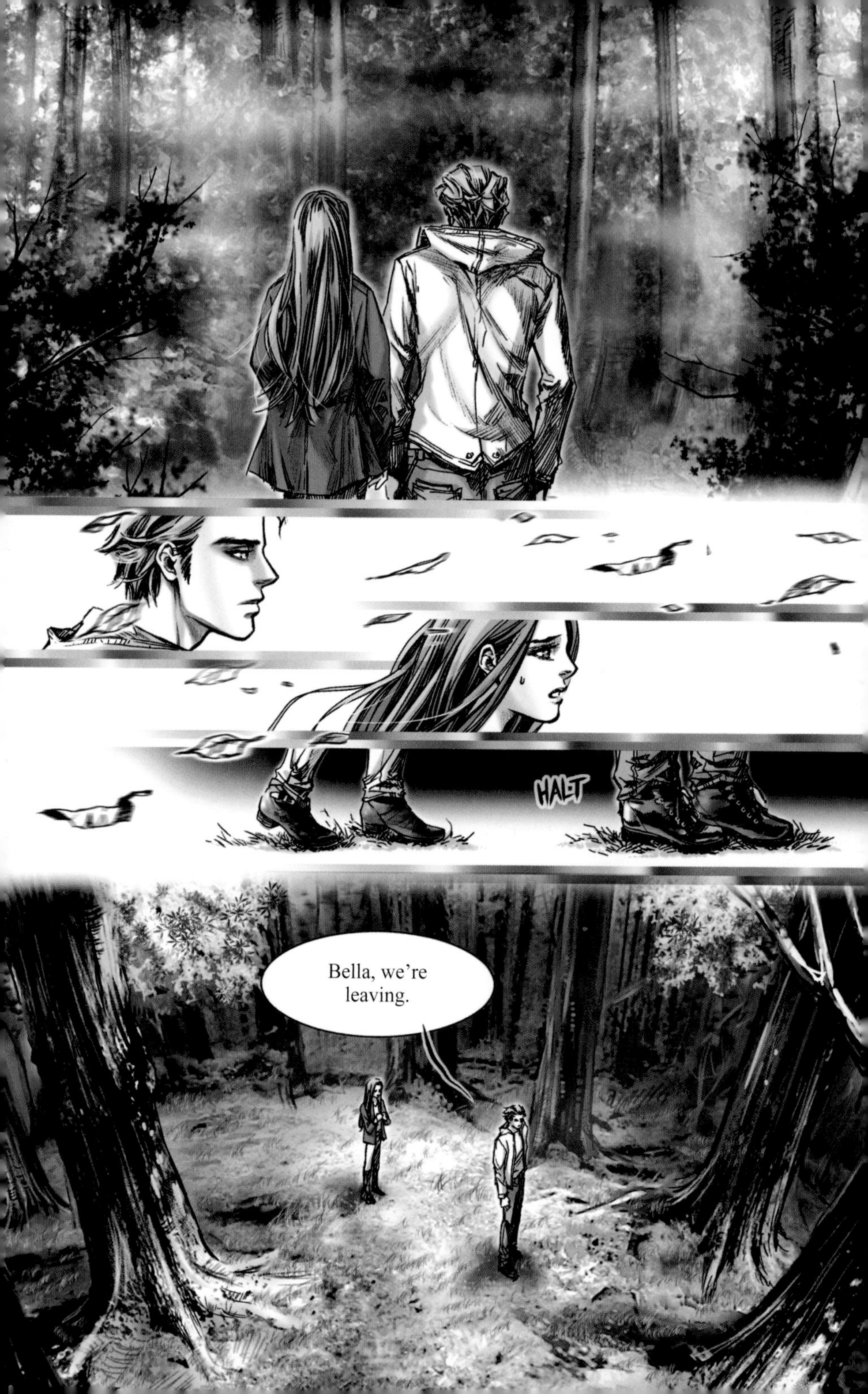
HALT
Bella, we're leaving.

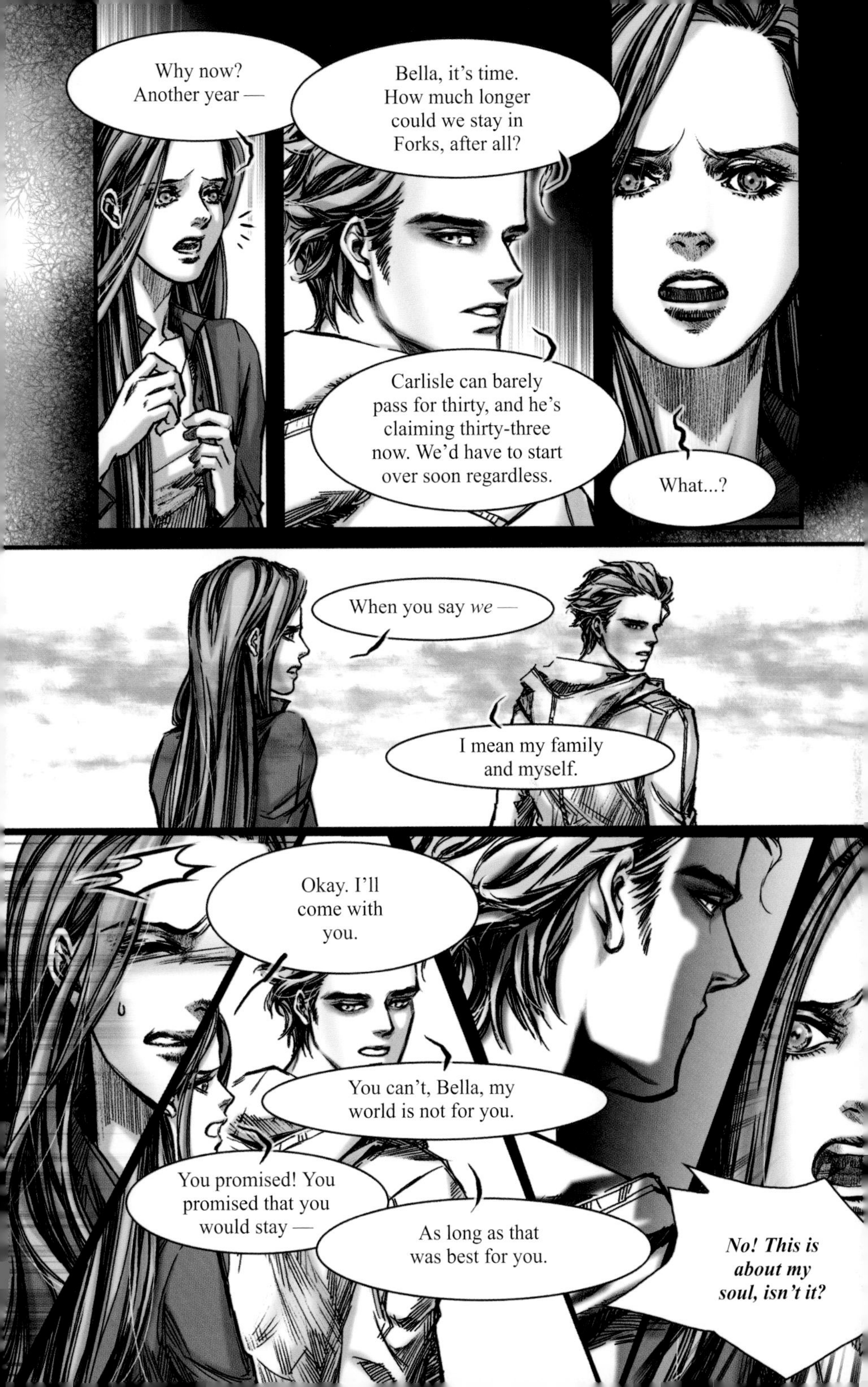
Why now? Another year —
Bella, it's time. How much longer could we stay in Forks, after all?
Carlisle can barely pass for thirty, and he's claiming thirty-three now. We'd have to start over soon regardless.
What...?
When you say *we* —
I mean my family and myself.
Okay. I'll come with you.
You can't, Bella, my world is not for you.
You promised! You promised that you would stay —
As long as that was best for you.
No! This is about my soul, isn't it?

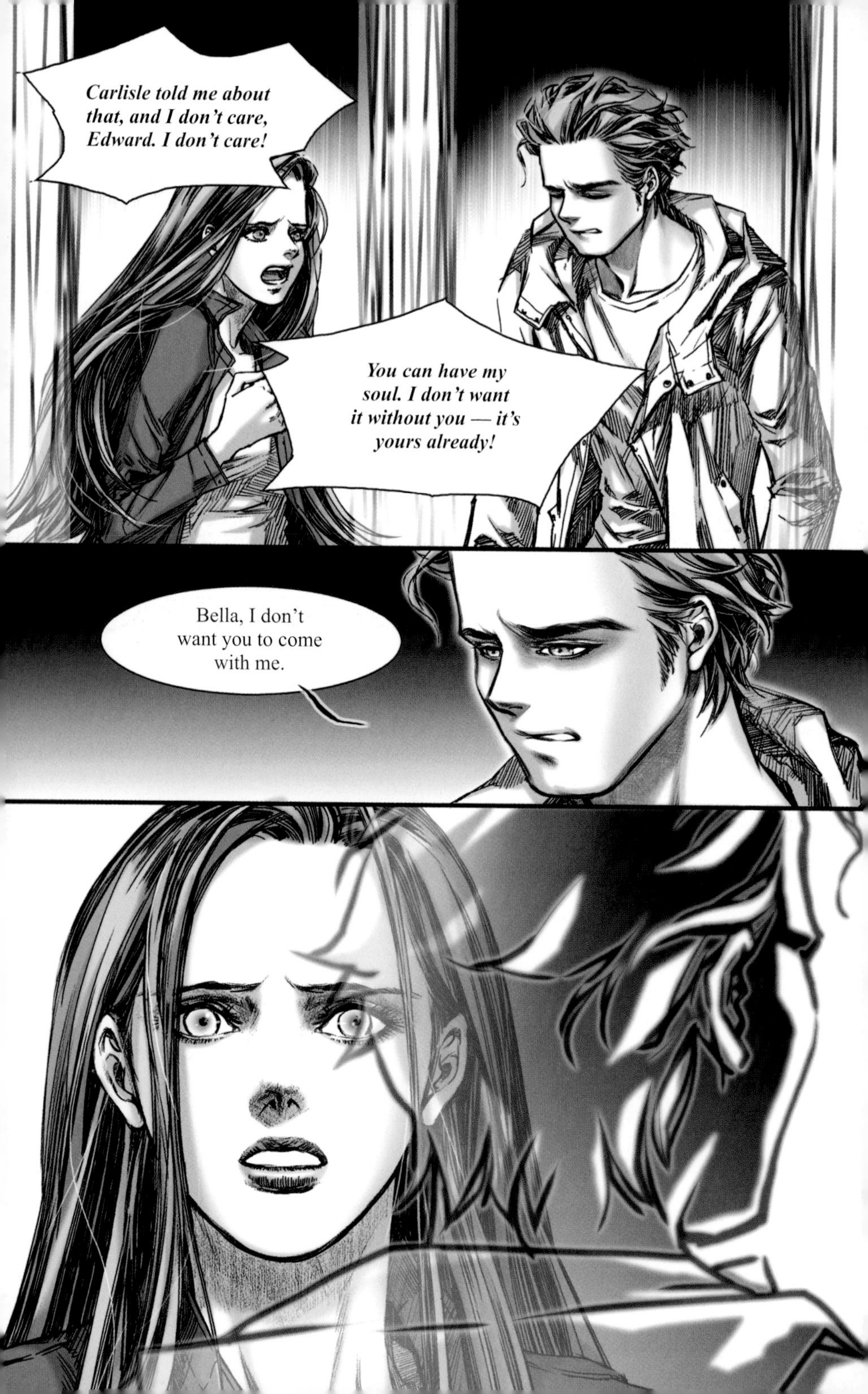
Carlisle told me about that, and I don't care, Edward. I don't care!
You can have my soul. I don't want it without you — it's yours already!
Bella, I don't want you to come with me.

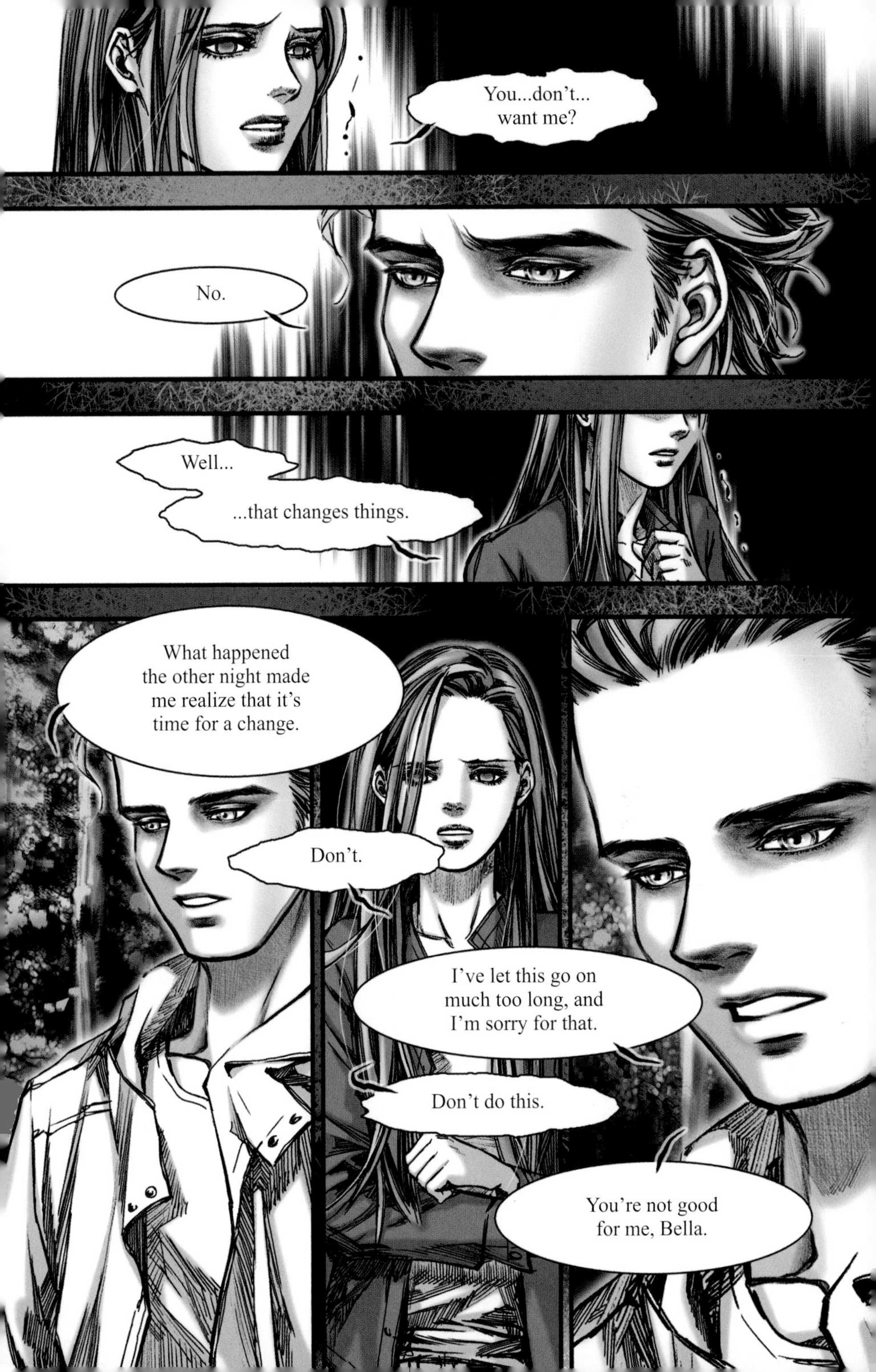
You...don't...
want me?
No.
Well...
...that changes things.
What happened the other night made me realize that it's time for a change.
Don't.
I've let this go on much too long, and I'm sorry for that.
Don't do this.
You're not good for me, Bella.

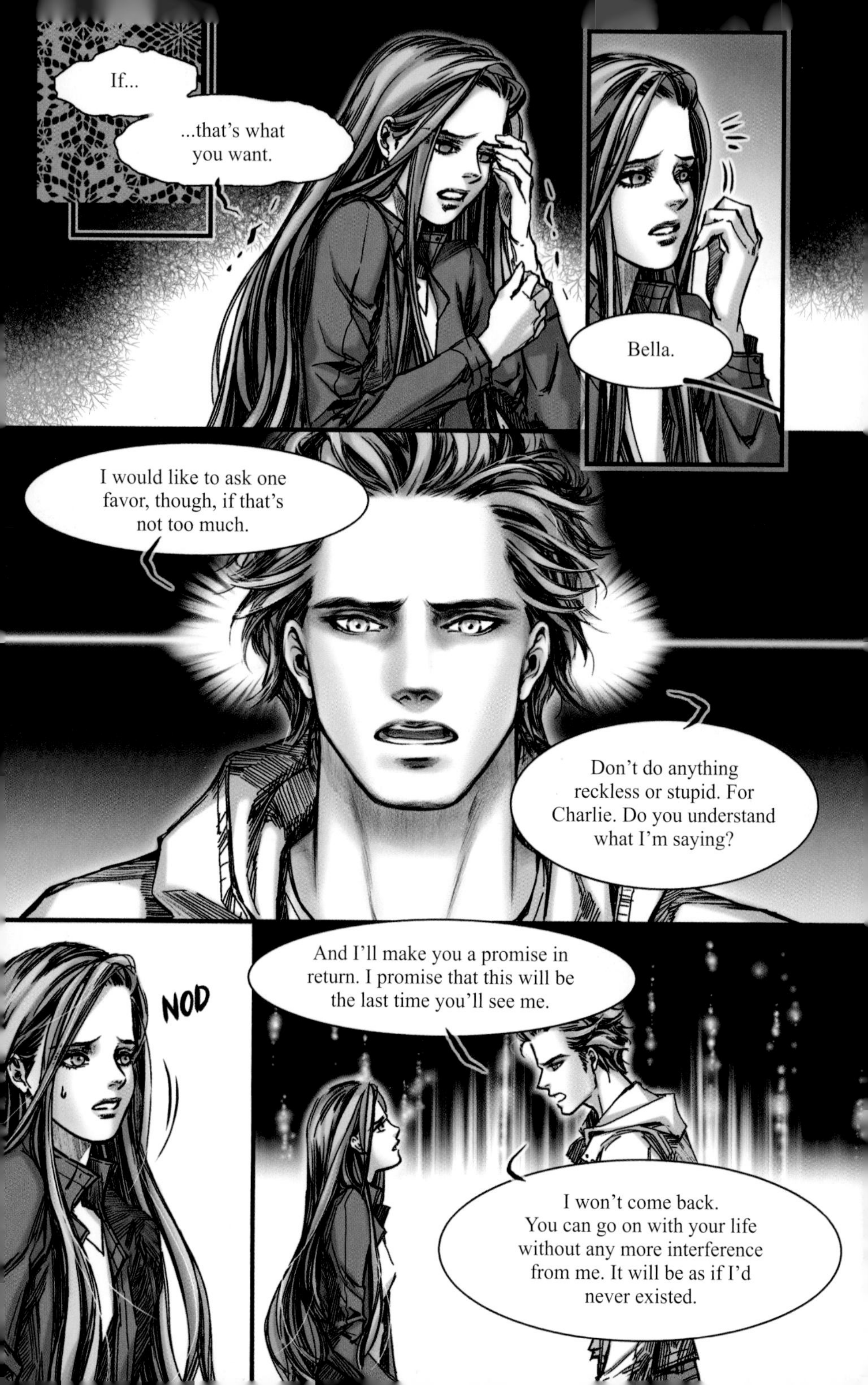
If...
...that's what you want.
Bella.
I would like to ask one favor, though, if that's not too much.
Don't do anything reckless or stupid. For Charlie. Do you understand what I'm saying?
NOD
And I'll make you a promise in return. I promise that this will be the last time you'll see me.
I won't come back.
You can go on with your life without any more interference from me. It will be as if I'd never existed.

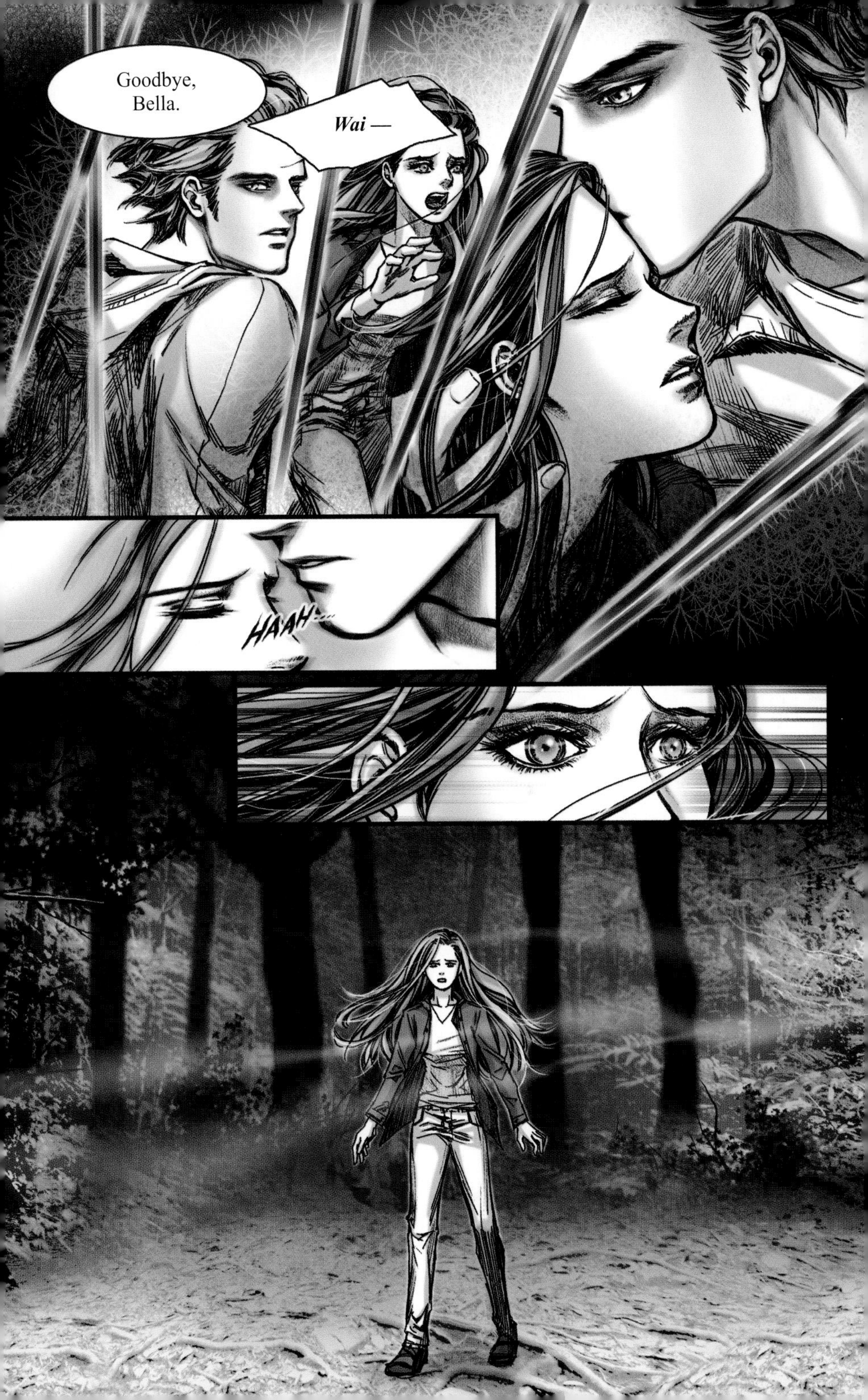
Goodbye, Bella.
Wai —
HAAH...

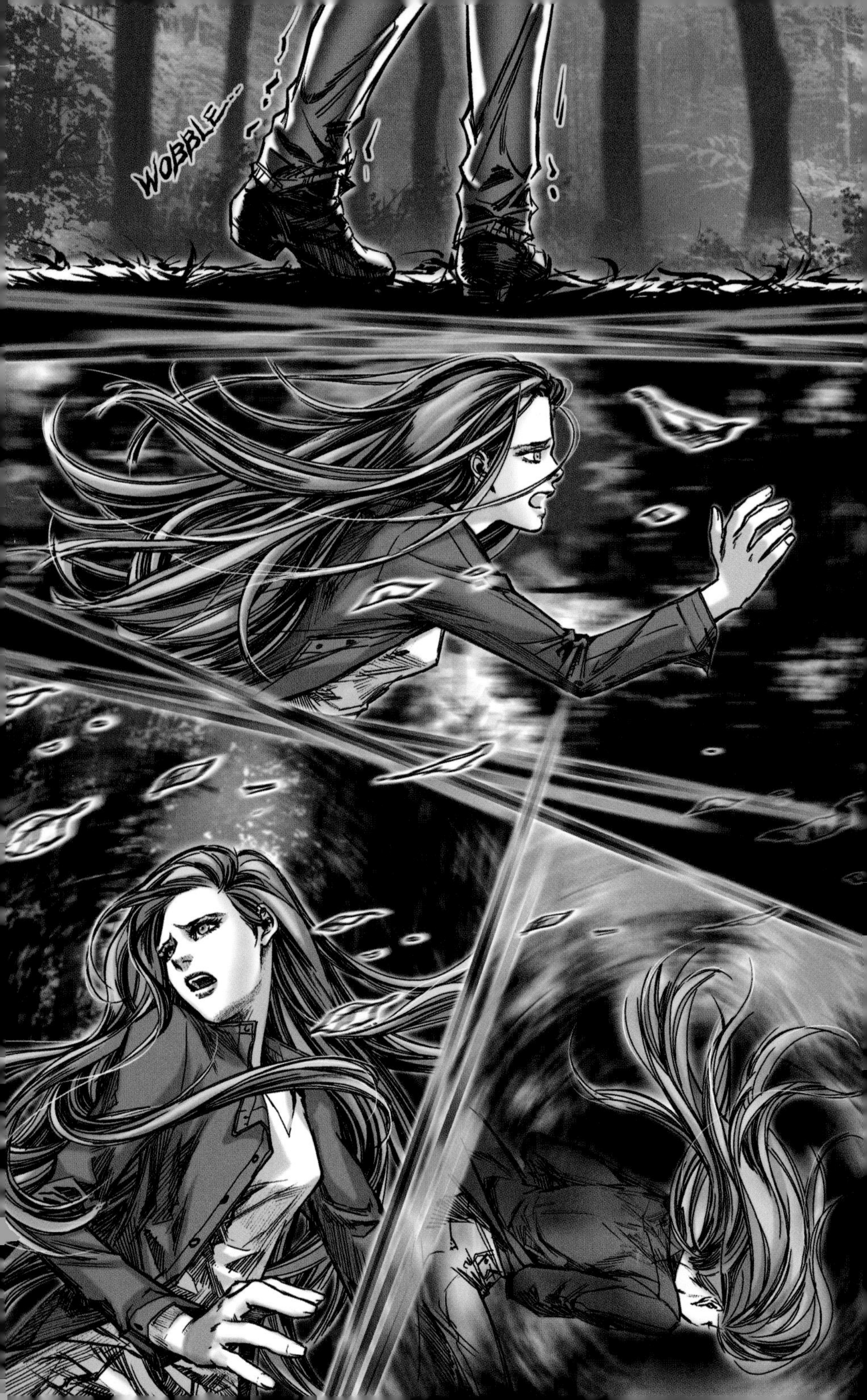
WOBBLE...

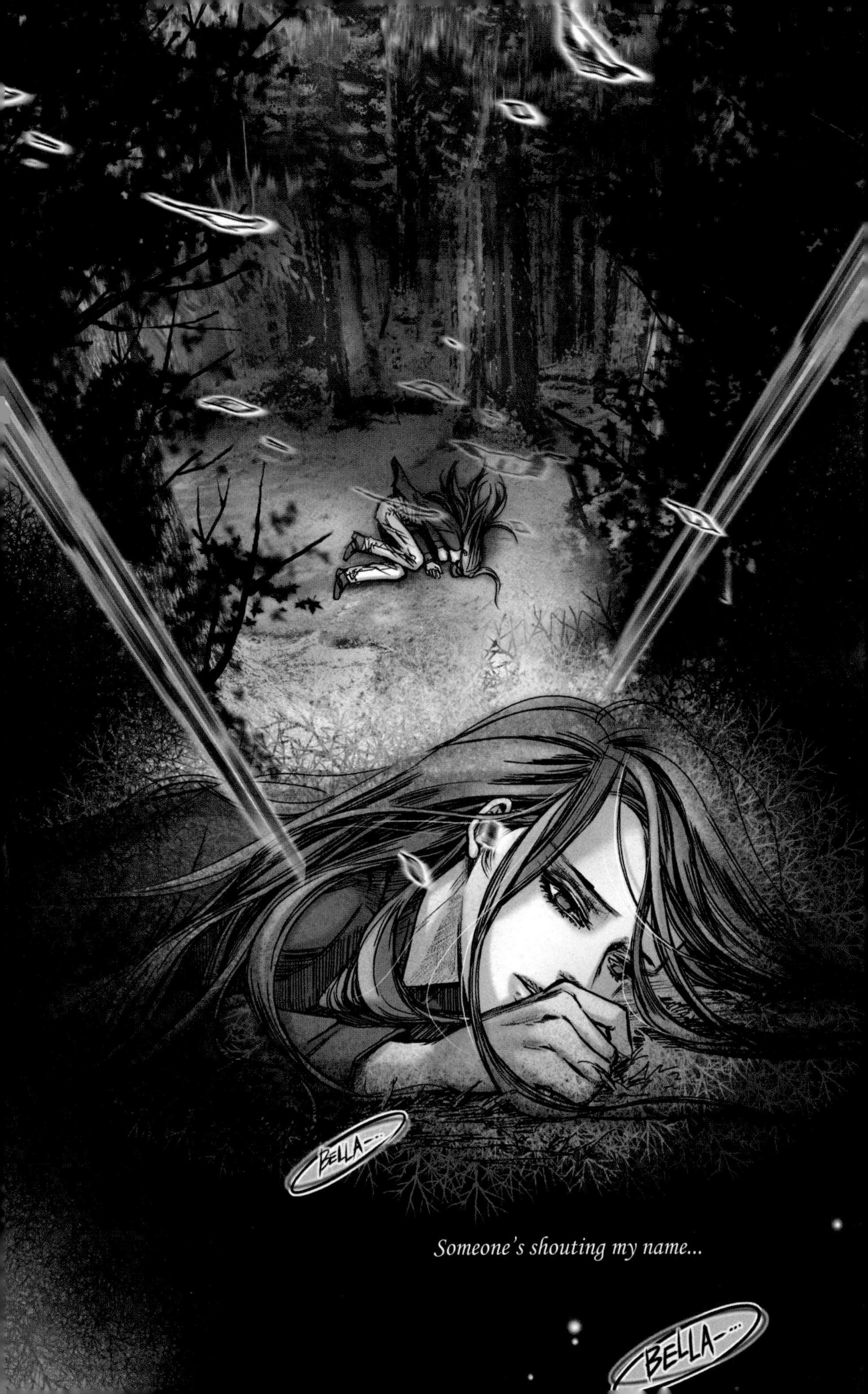
BELLA-...
Someone's shouting my name...
BELLA-...

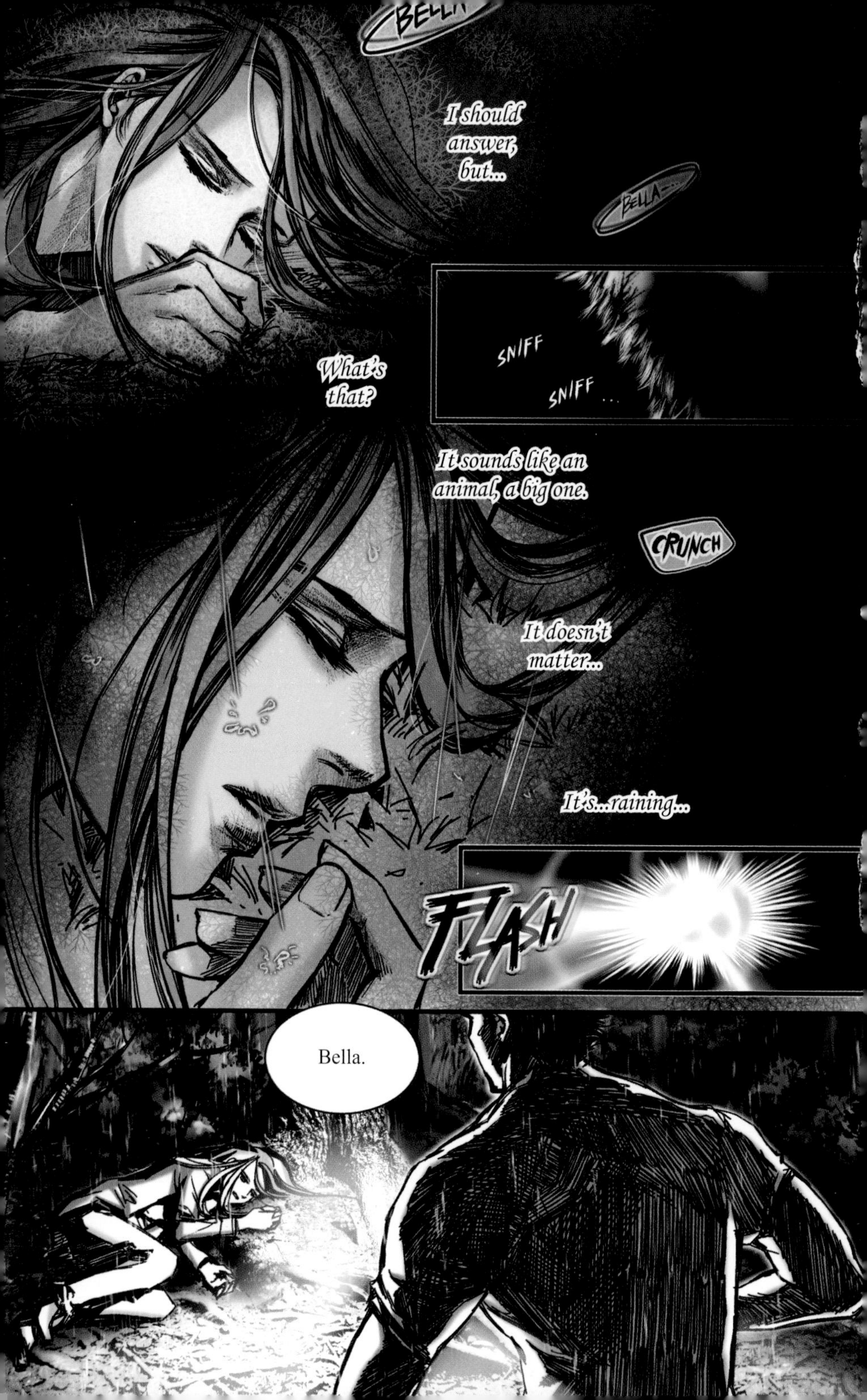
BELLA
I should answer, but...
BELLA—...
SNIFF
SNIFF...
What's that?
It sounds like an animal, a big one.
CRUNCH
It doesn't matter...
It's...raining...
FLASH
Bella.

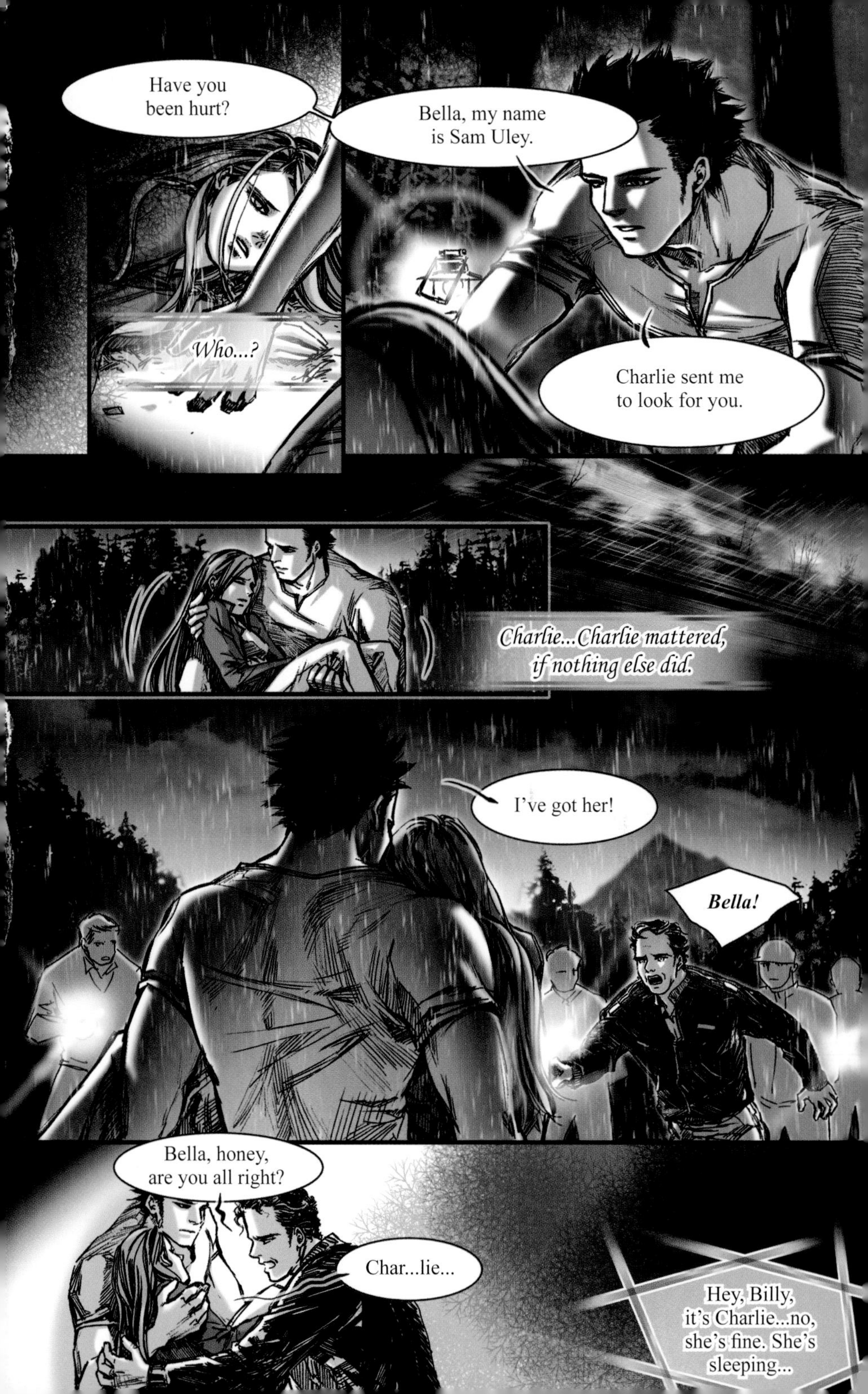
Have you been hurt?
Who...?
Bella, my name is Sam Uley.
Charlie sent me to look for you.
Charlie...Charlie mattered, if nothing else did.
I've got her!
Bella!
Bella, honey, are you all right?
Char...lie...
Hey, Billy, it's Charlie...no, she's fine. She's sleeping...

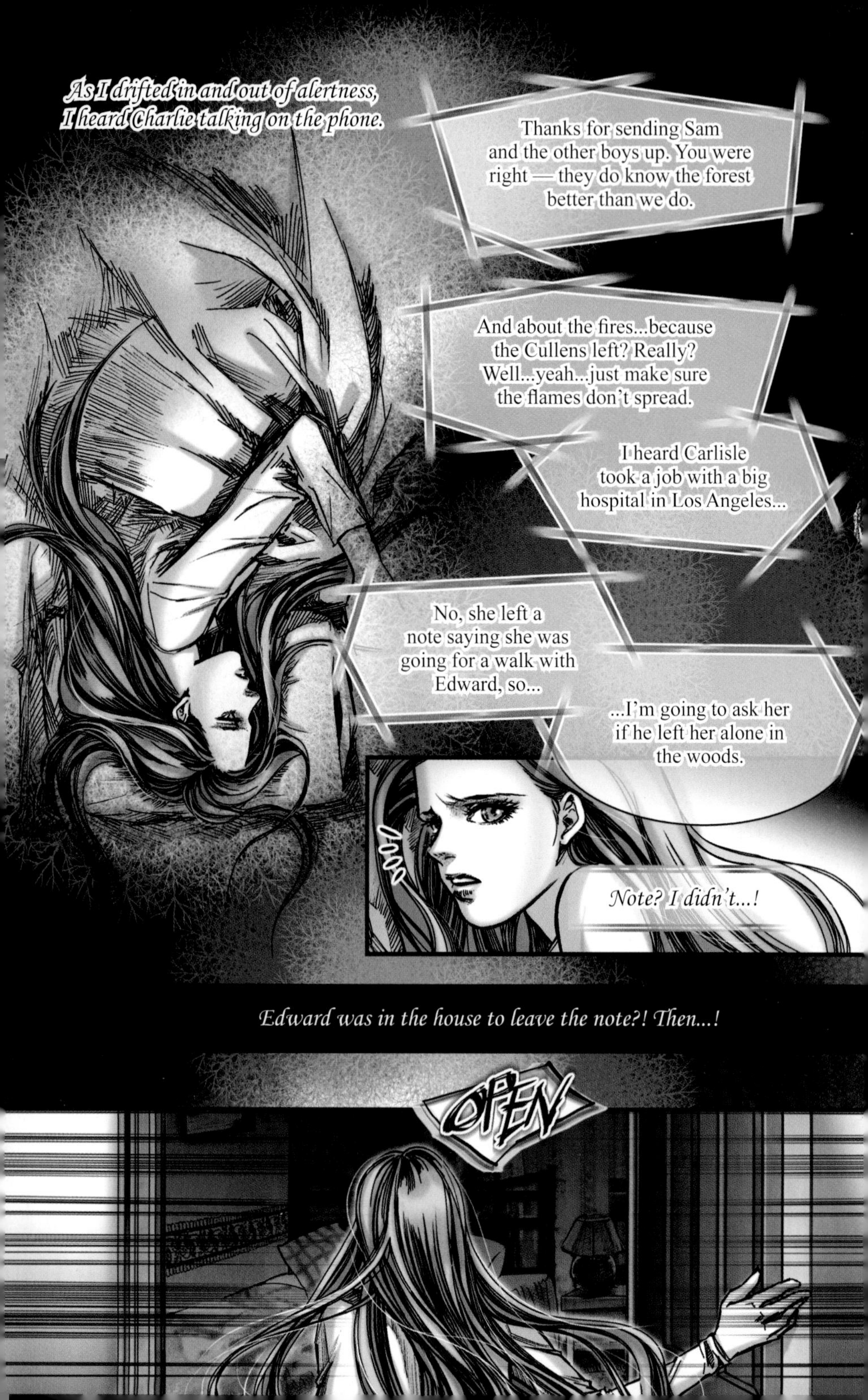
As I drifted in and out of alertness, I heard Charlie talking on the phone.
Thanks for sending Sam and the other boys up. You were right — they do know the forest better than we do.
And about the fires...because the Cullens left? Really? Well...yeah...just make sure the flames don't spread.
I heard Carlisle took a job with a big hospital in Los Angeles...
No, she left a note saying she was going for a walk with Edward, so...
...I'm going to ask her if he left her alone in the woods.
Note? I didn't...!
Edward was in the house to leave the note?! Then...!
OPEN

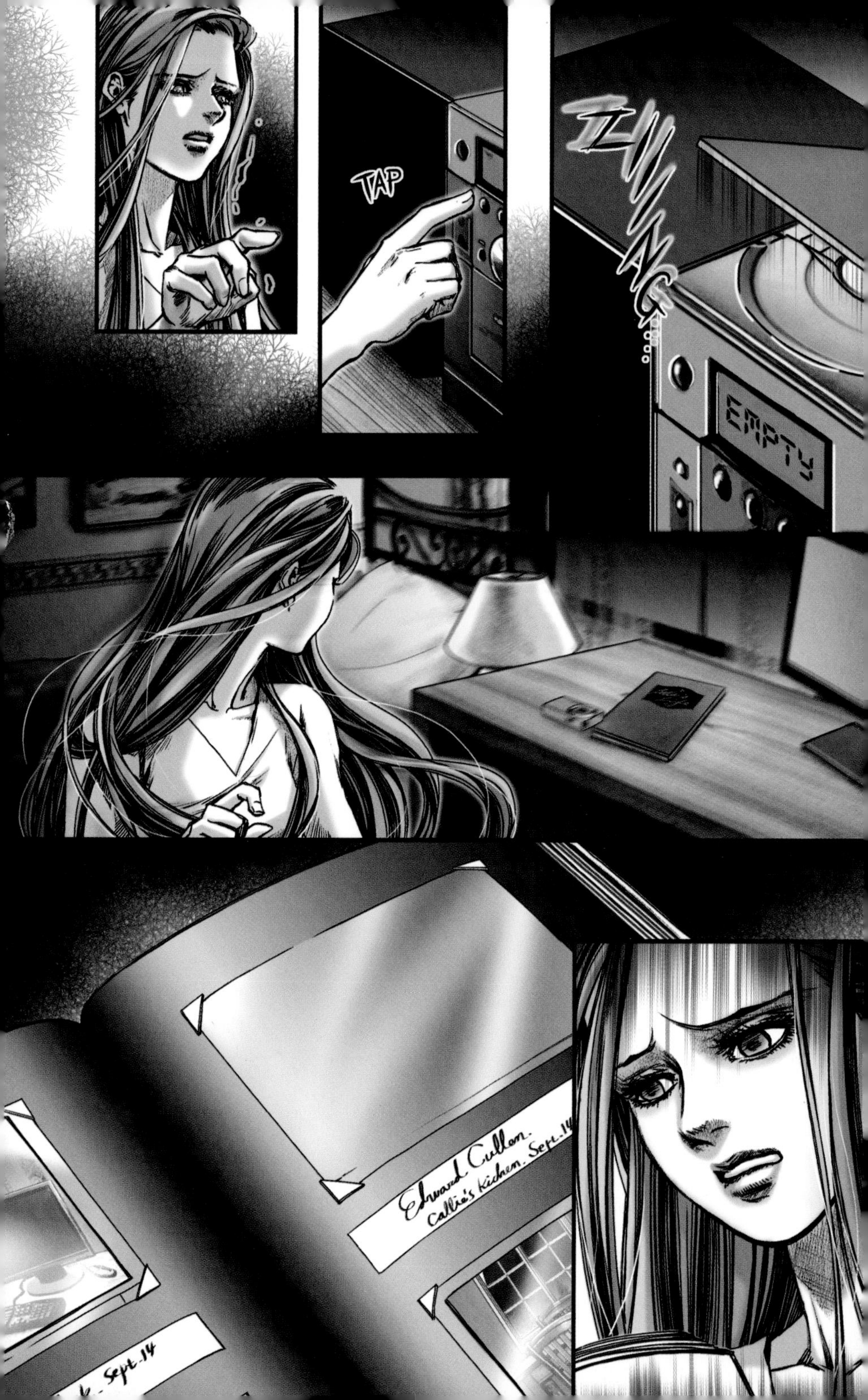
TAP
ZHUNG...
EMPTY
Edward Cullen
Callie's Kitchen, Sept. 14
Sept. 14

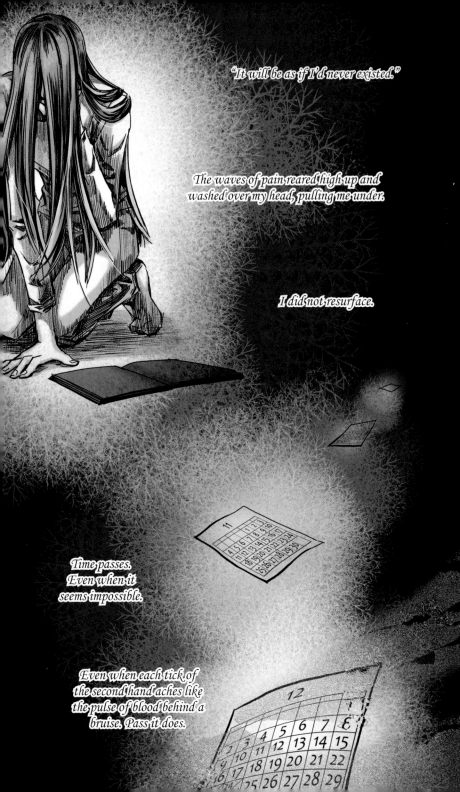

"It will be as if I'd never existed."

The waves of pain reared high up and washed over my head, pulling me under.

I did not resurface.

Time passes. Even when it seems impossible.

Even when each tick of the second hand aches like the pulse of blood behind a bruise. Pass it does.

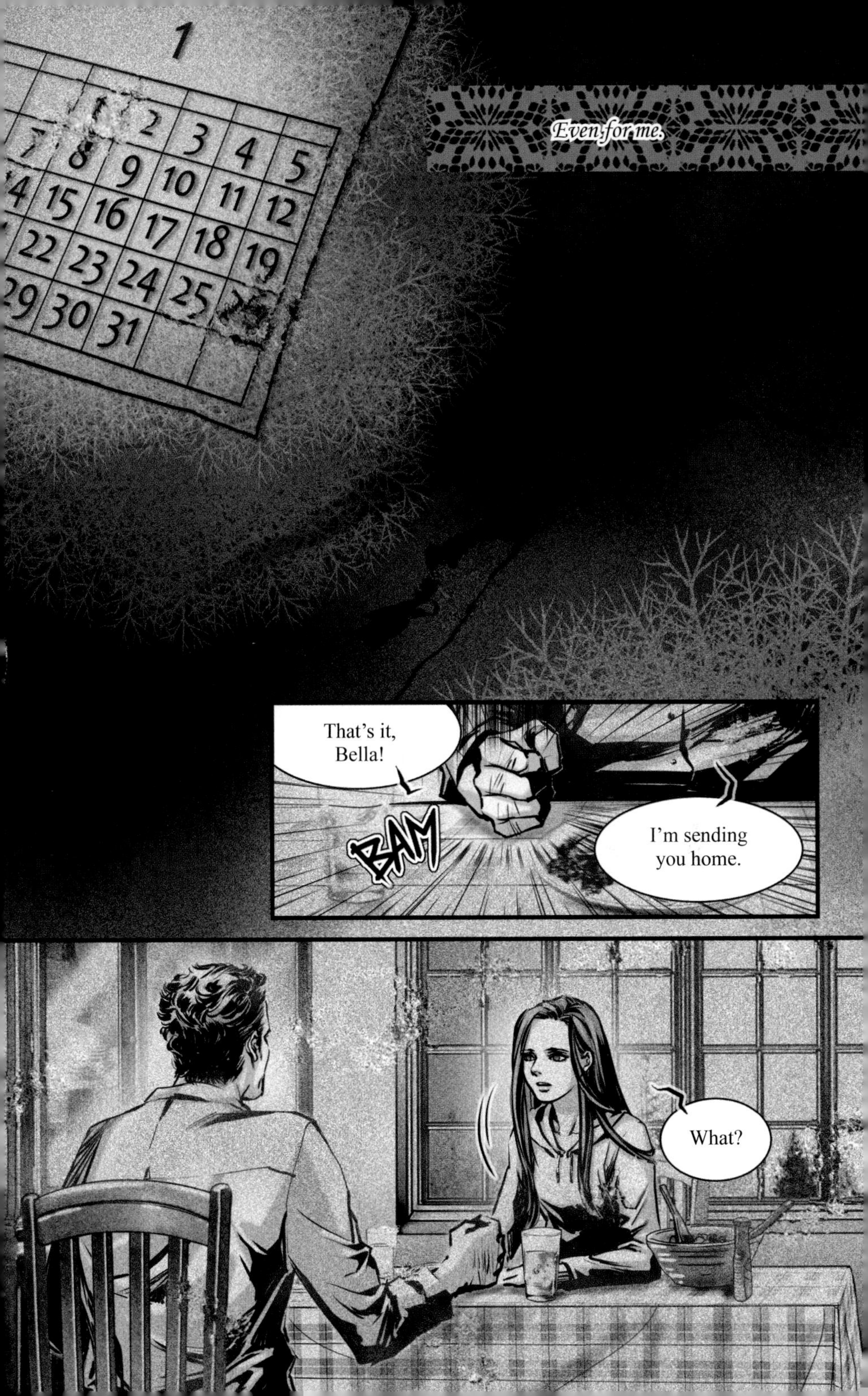
Even for me.
That's it, Bella!
BAM
I'm sending you home.
What?

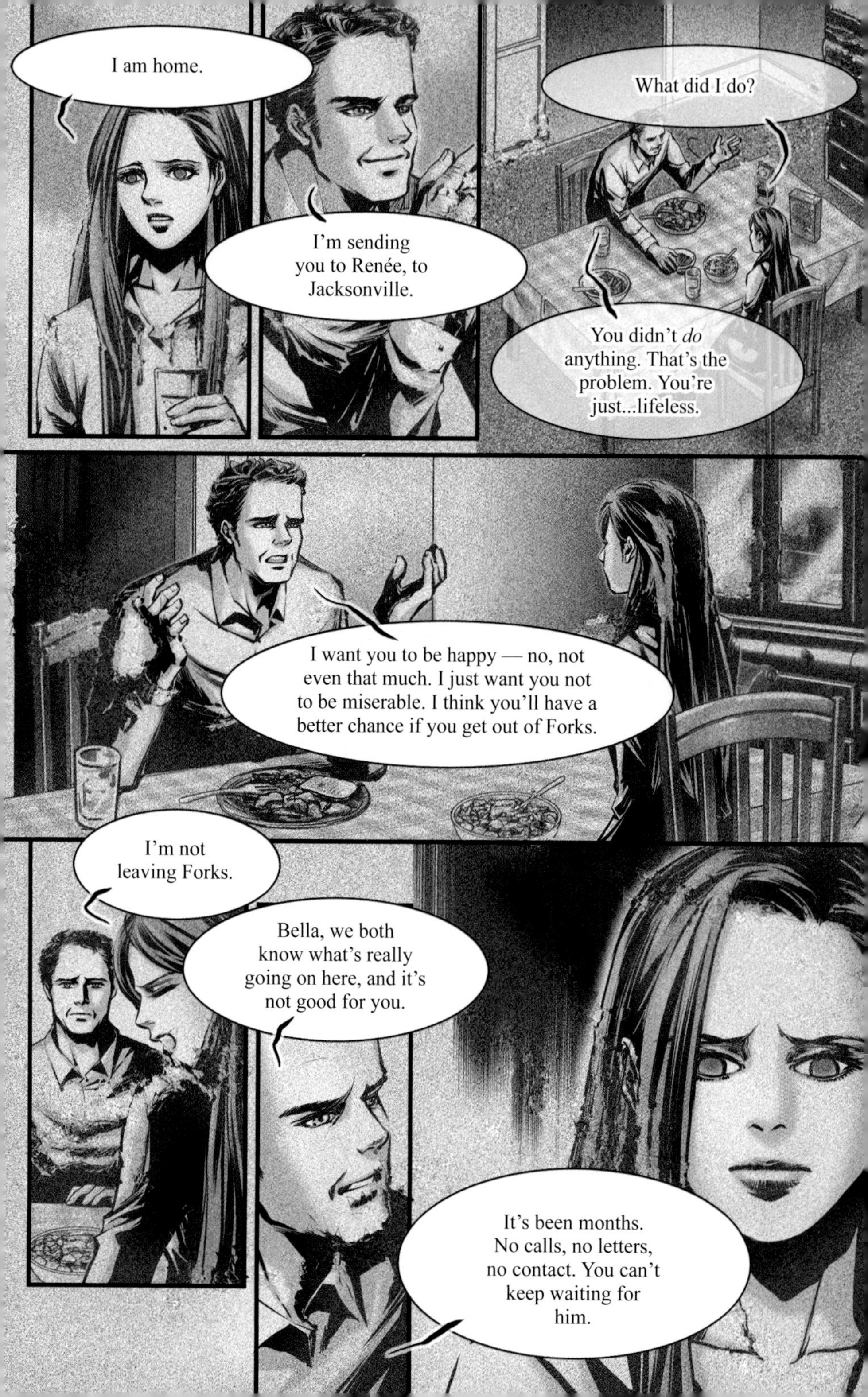
I am home.
I'm sending you to Renée, to Jacksonville.
What did I do?
You didn't *do* anything. That's the problem. You're just...lifeless.
I want you to be happy — no, not even that much. I just want you not to be miserable. I think you'll have a better chance if you get out of Forks.
I'm not leaving Forks.
Bella, we both know what's really going on here, and it's not good for you.
It's been months. No calls, no letters, no contact. You can't keep waiting for him.

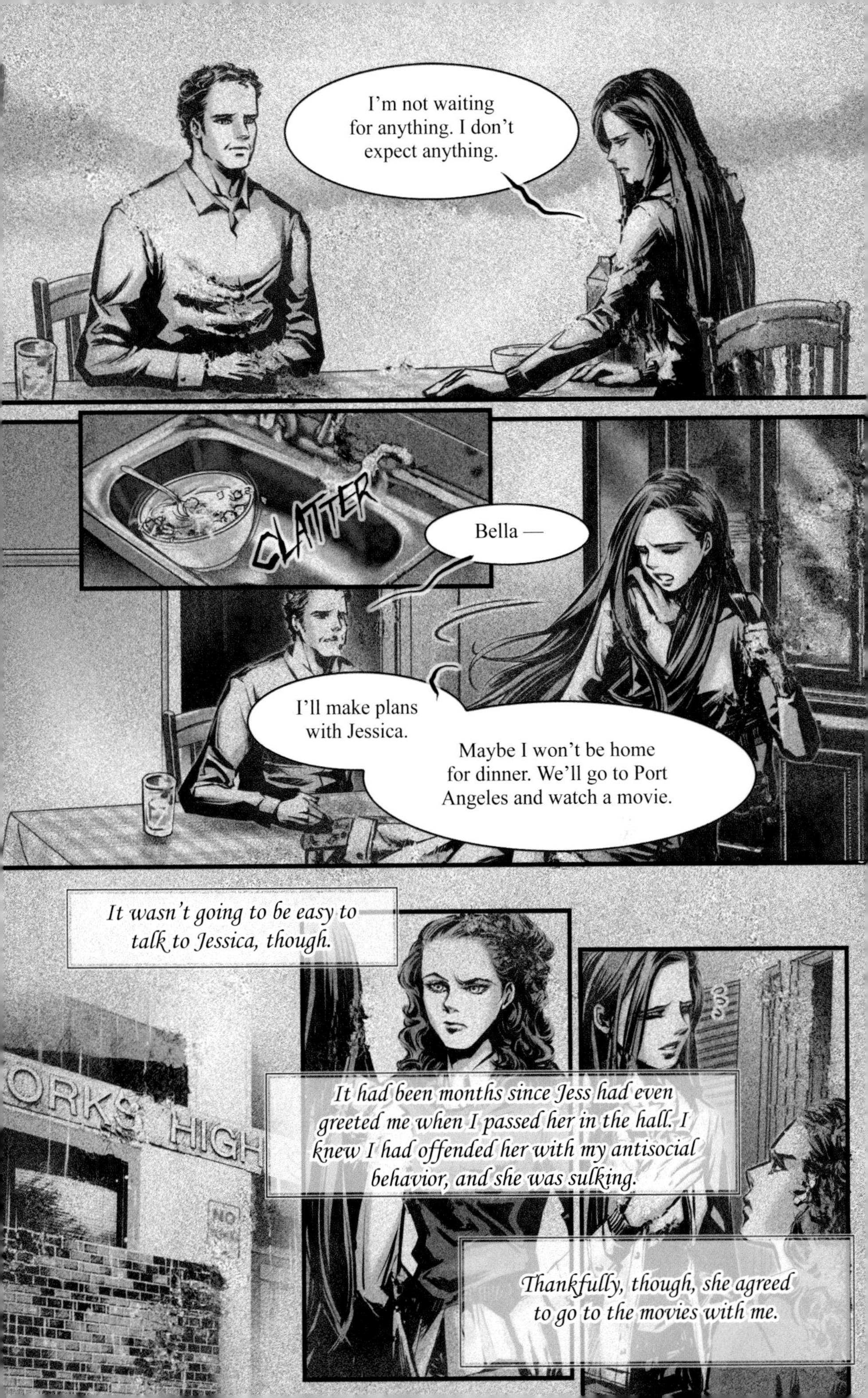
I'm not waiting for anything. I don't expect anything.
CLATTER
Bella —
I'll make plans with Jessica.
Maybe I won't be home for dinner. We'll go to Port Angeles and watch a movie.
It wasn't going to be easy to talk to Jessica, though.
ORKS HIGH
It had been months since Jess had even greeted me when I passed her in the hall. I knew I had offended her with my antisocial behavior, and she was sulking.
Thankfully, though, she agreed to go to the movies with me.

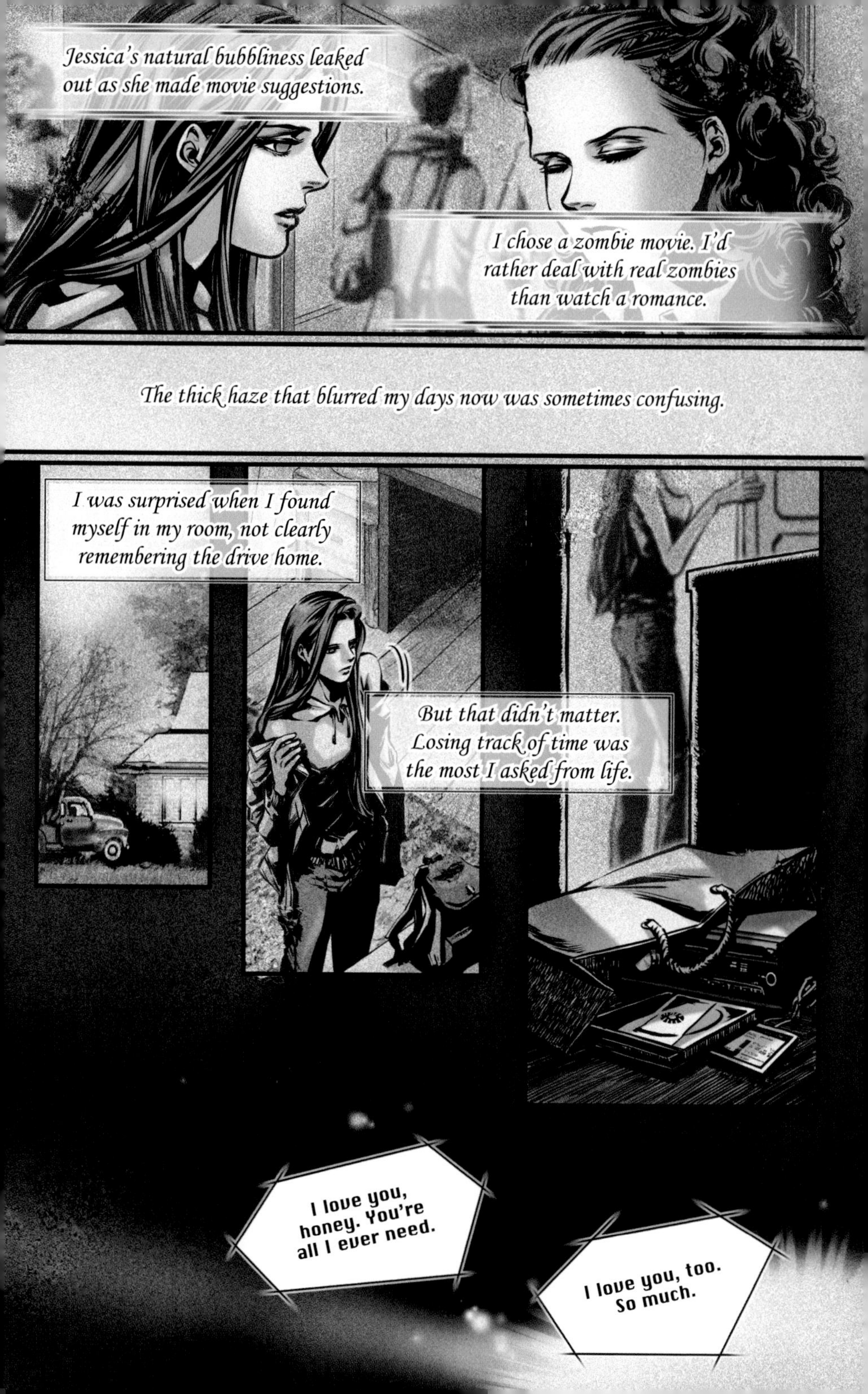
Jessica's natural bubbliness leaked out as she made movie suggestions.
I chose a zombie movie. I'd rather deal with real zombies than watch a romance.
The thick haze that blurred my days now was sometimes confusing.
I was surprised when I found myself in my room, not clearly remembering the drive home.
But that didn't matter. Losing track of time was the most I asked from life.
I love you, honey. You're all I ever need.
I love you, too. So much.

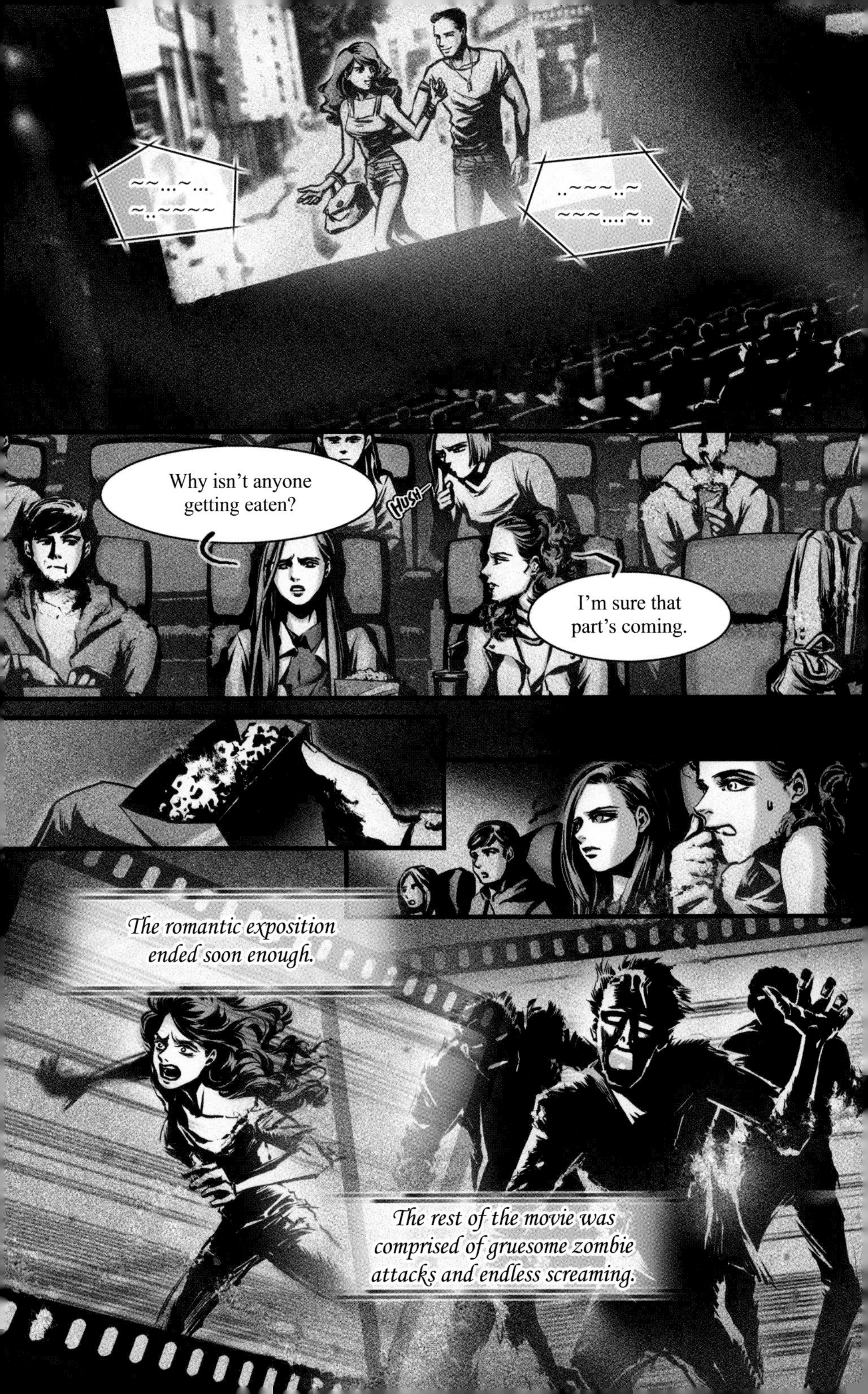
~~...~...
~..~~~~
..~~~..~
~~~....~..
Why isn't anyone getting eaten?
HUSH—
I'm sure that part's coming.
The romantic exposition ended soon enough.
The rest of the movie was comprised of gruesome zombie attacks and endless screaming.
~~~

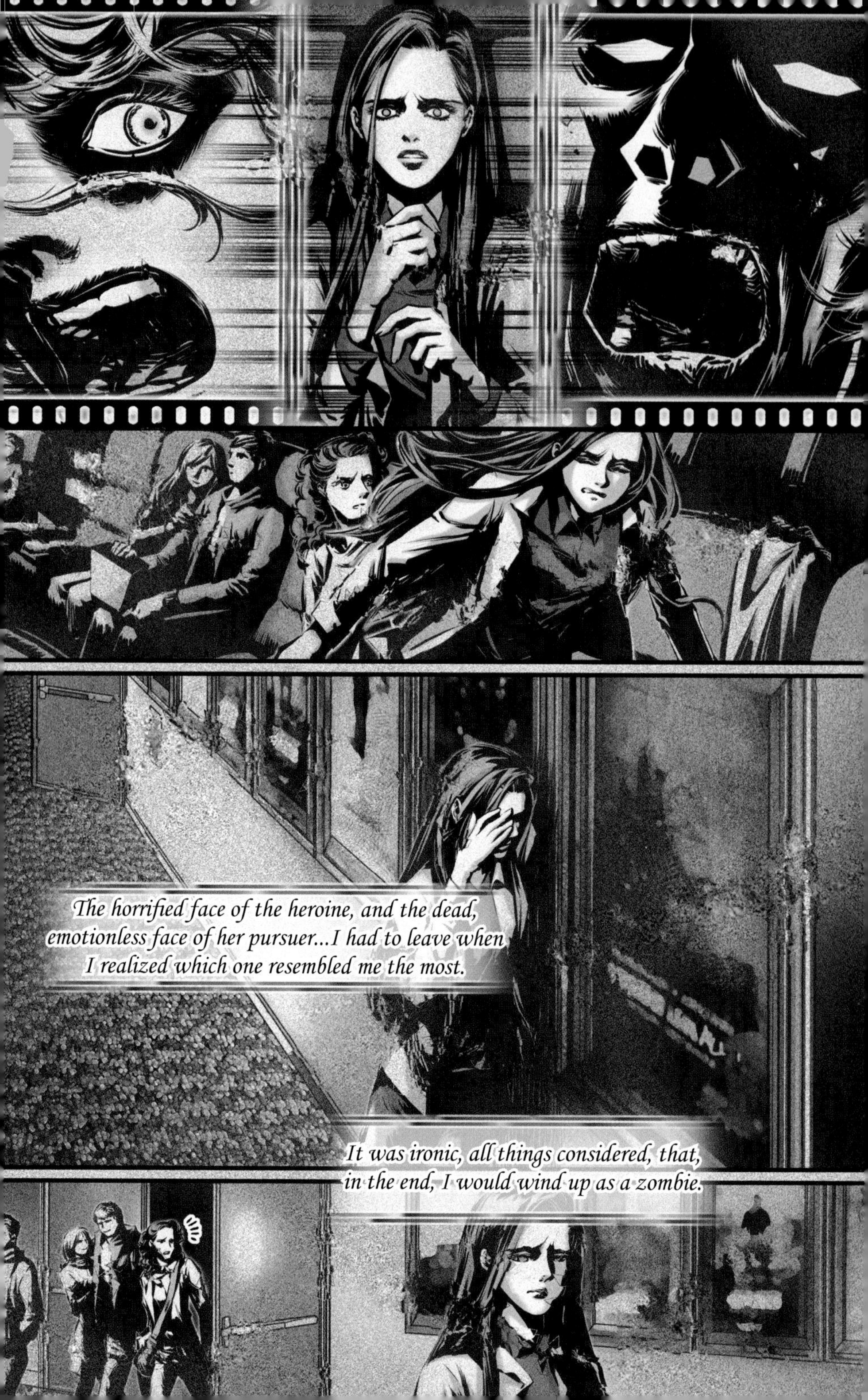
The horrified face of the heroine, and the dead, emotionless face of her pursuer...I had to leave when I realized which one resembled me the most.
It was ironic, all things considered, that, in the end, I would wind up as a zombie.

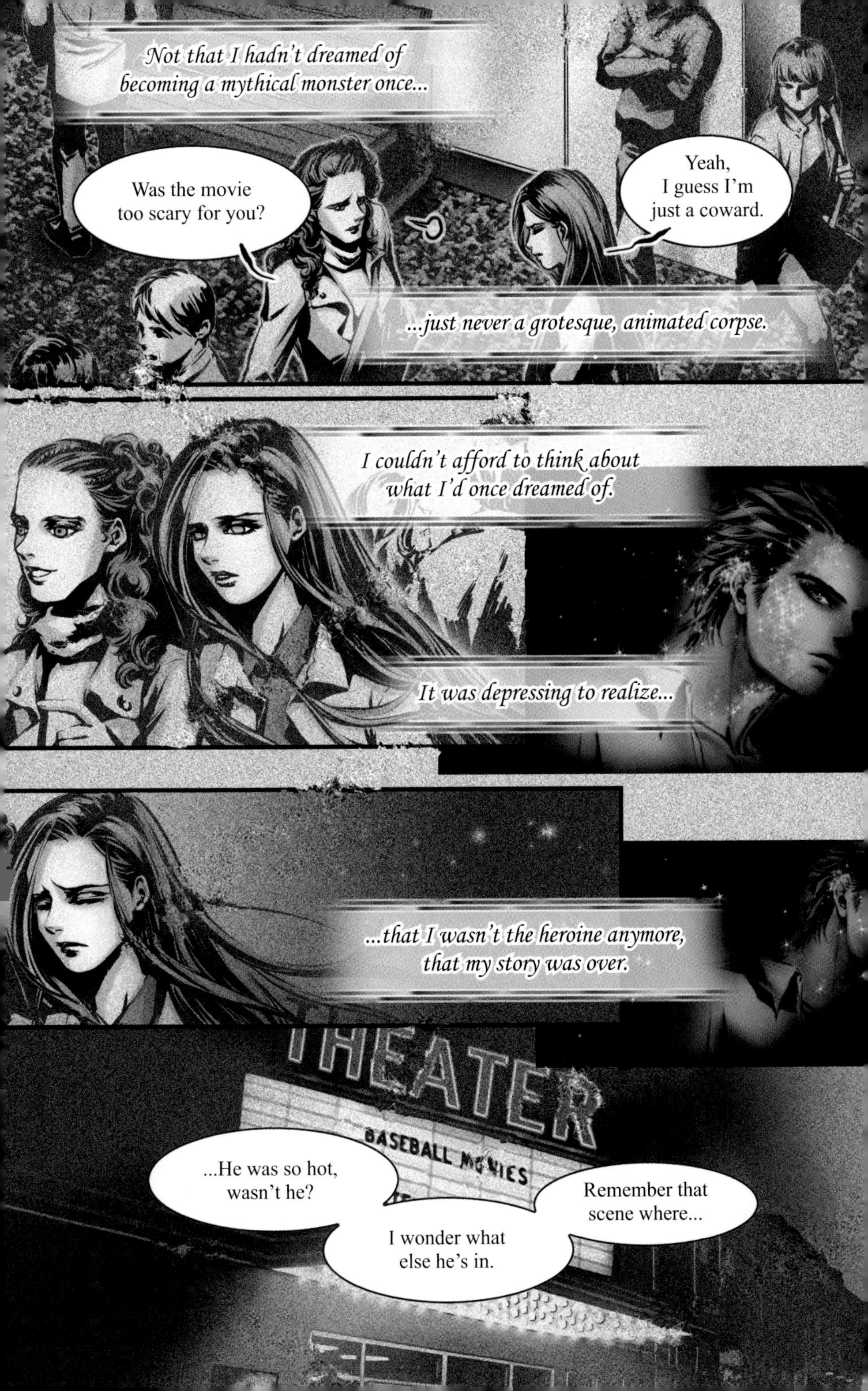
Not that I hadn't dreamed of becoming a mythical monster once...
Was the movie too scary for you?
Yeah, I guess I'm just a coward.
...just never a grotesque, animated corpse.
I couldn't afford to think about what I'd once dreamed of.
It was depressing to realize...
...that I wasn't the heroine anymore, that my story was over.
THEATER
BASEBALL MOVIES
...He was so hot, wasn't he?
Remember that scene where...
I wonder what else he's in.

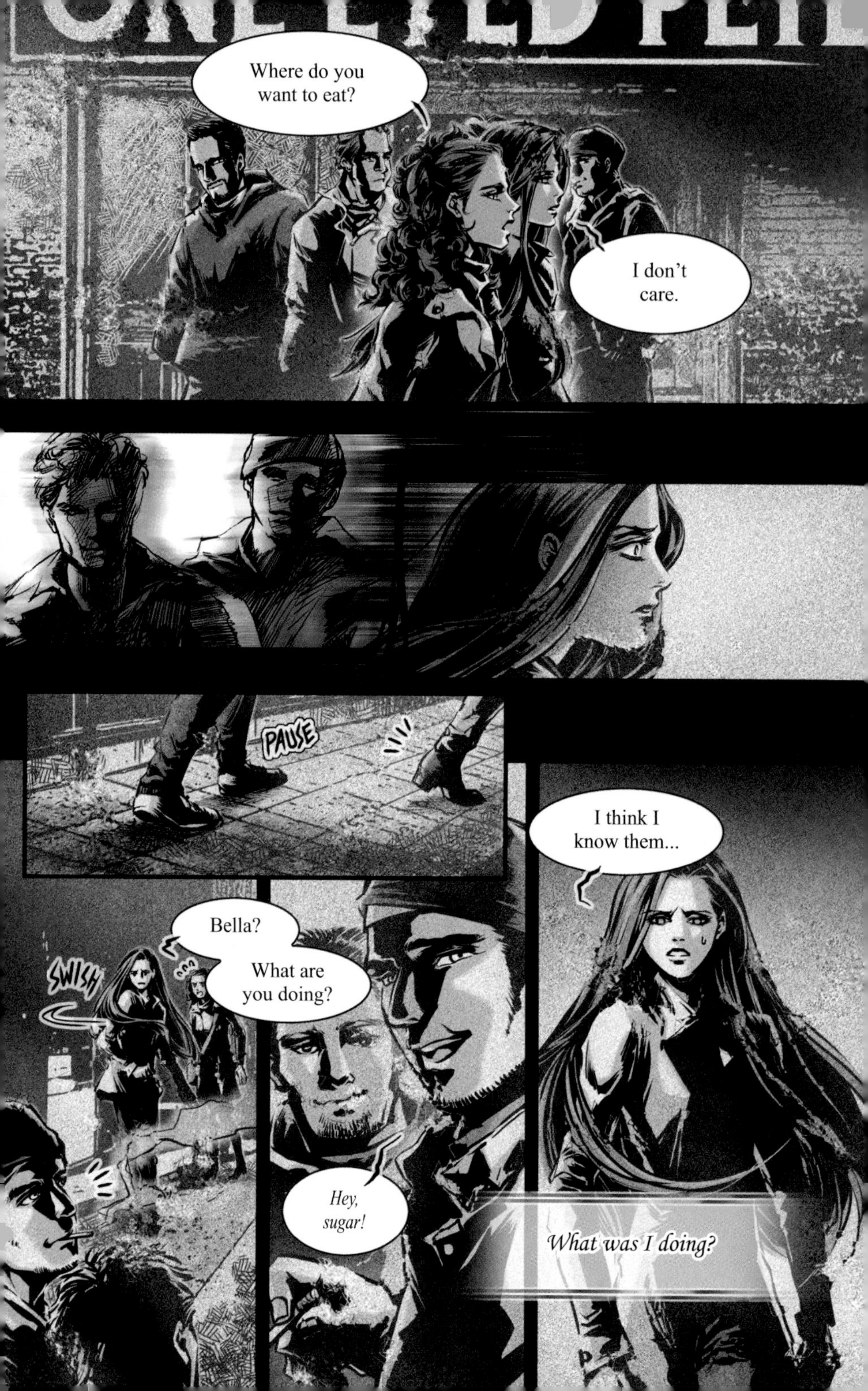
Where do you want to eat?
I don't care.
PAUSE
I think I know them...
Bella?
What are you doing?
SWISH
Hey, sugar!
What was I doing?

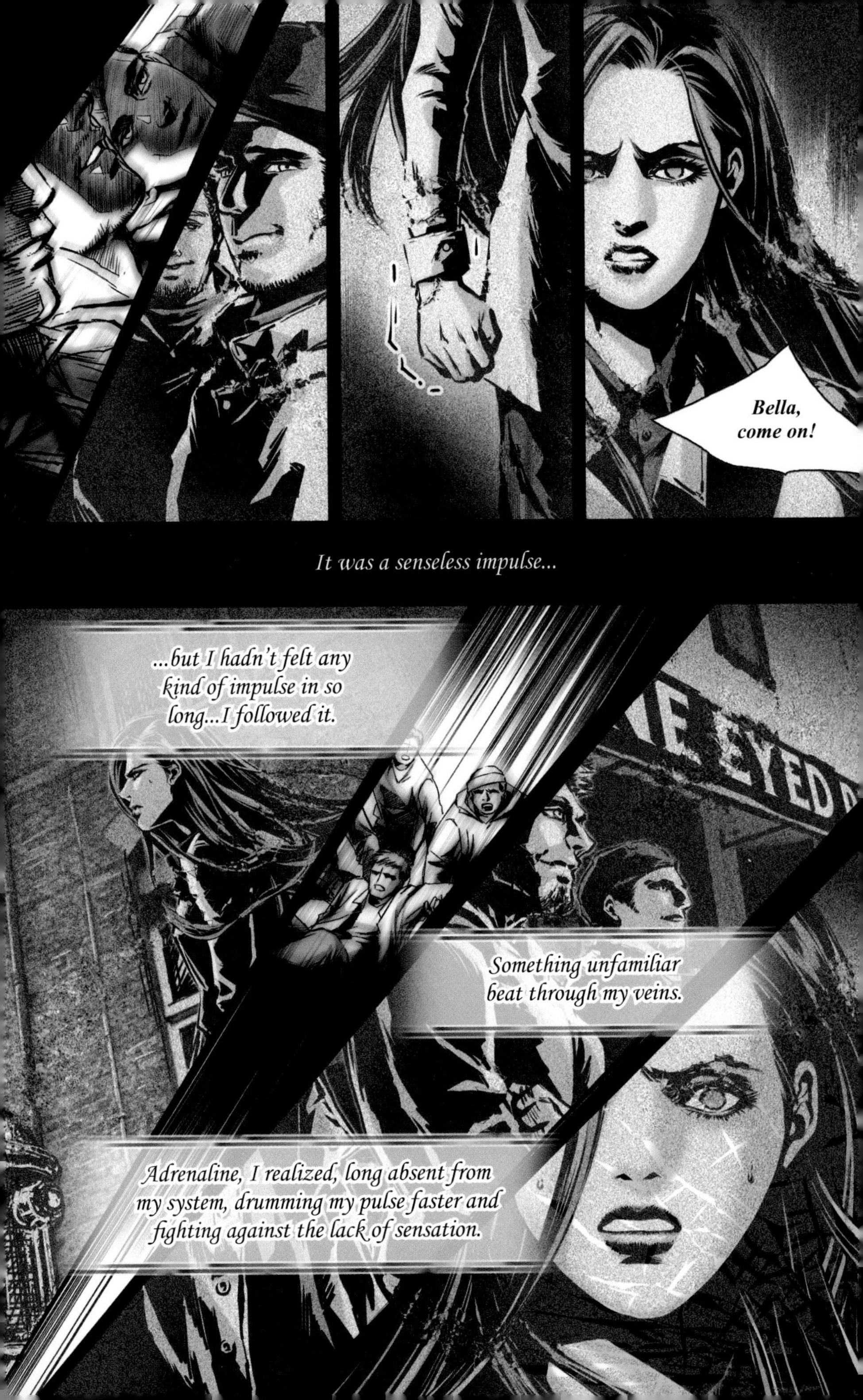
Bella, come on!
It was a senseless impulse...
...but I hadn't felt any kind of impulse in so long...I followed it.
Something unfamiliar beat through my veins.
Adrenaline, I realized, long absent from my system, drumming my pulse faster and fighting against the lack of sensation.

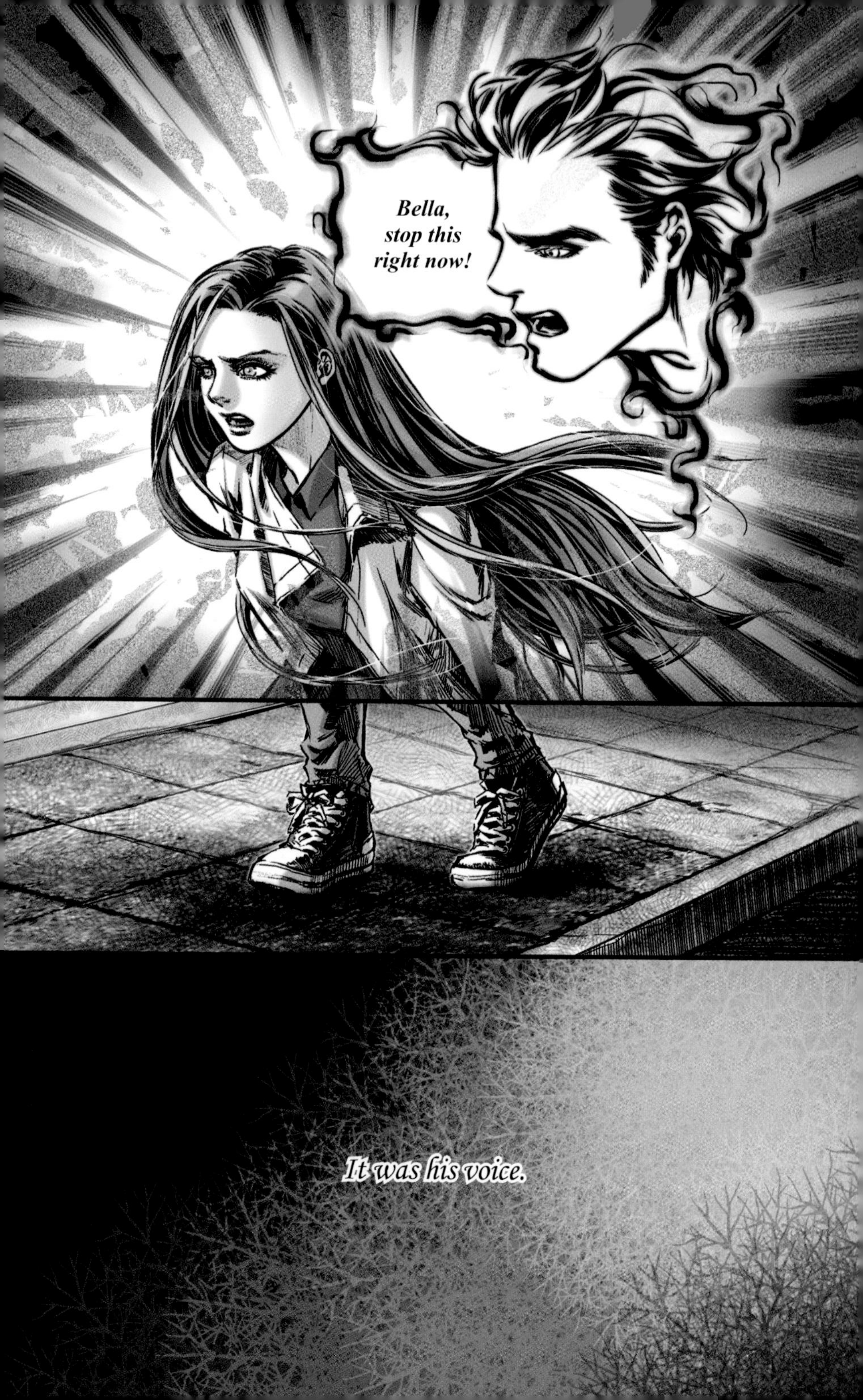
Bella, stop this right now!
It was his voice.

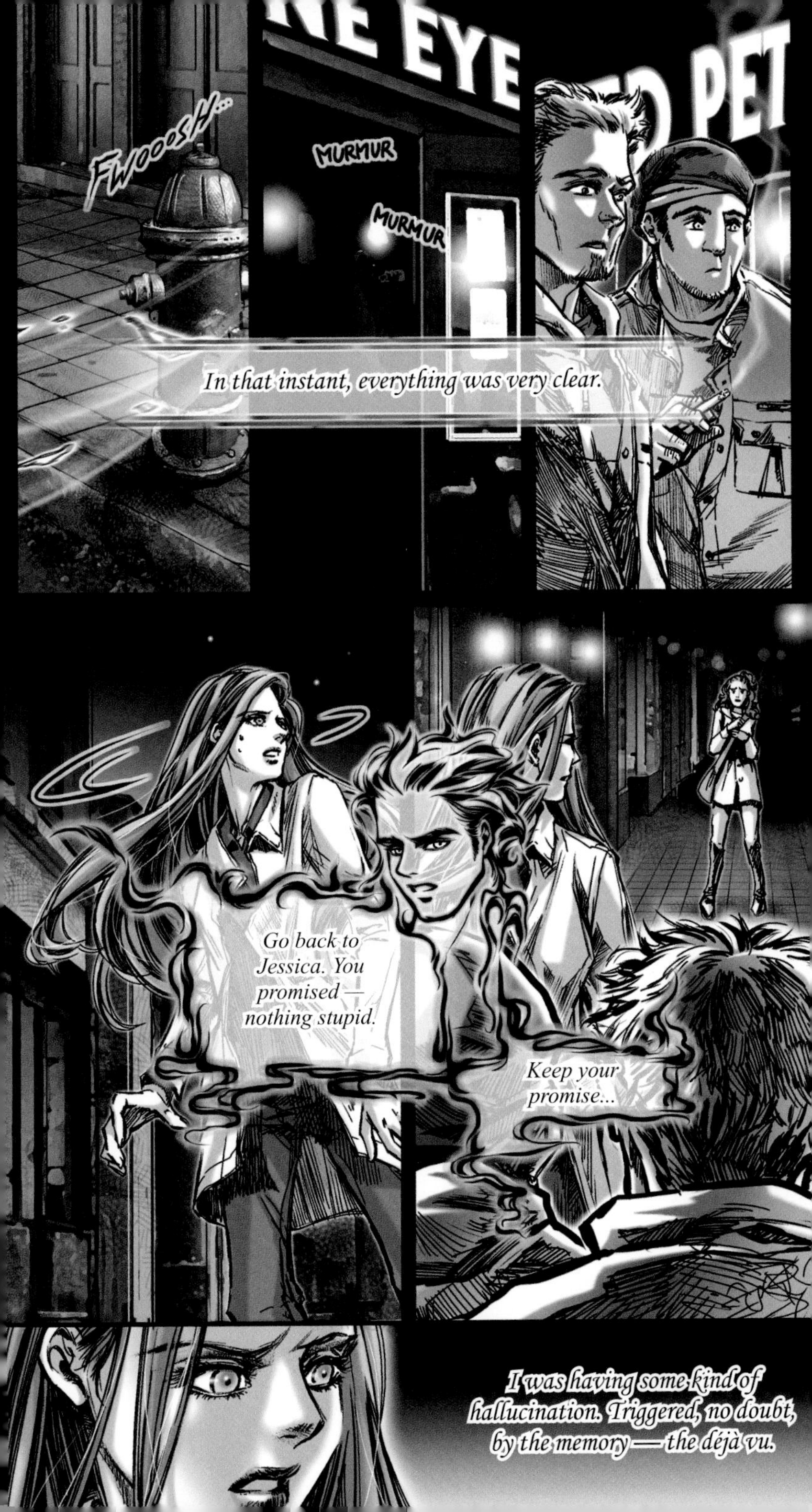
NE EYE
ED PET
FWOOOSH...
MURMUR
MURMUR
In that instant, everything was very clear.
Go back to Jessica. You promised — nothing stupid.
Keep your promise...
I was having some kind of hallucination. Triggered, no doubt, by the memory — the déjà vu.

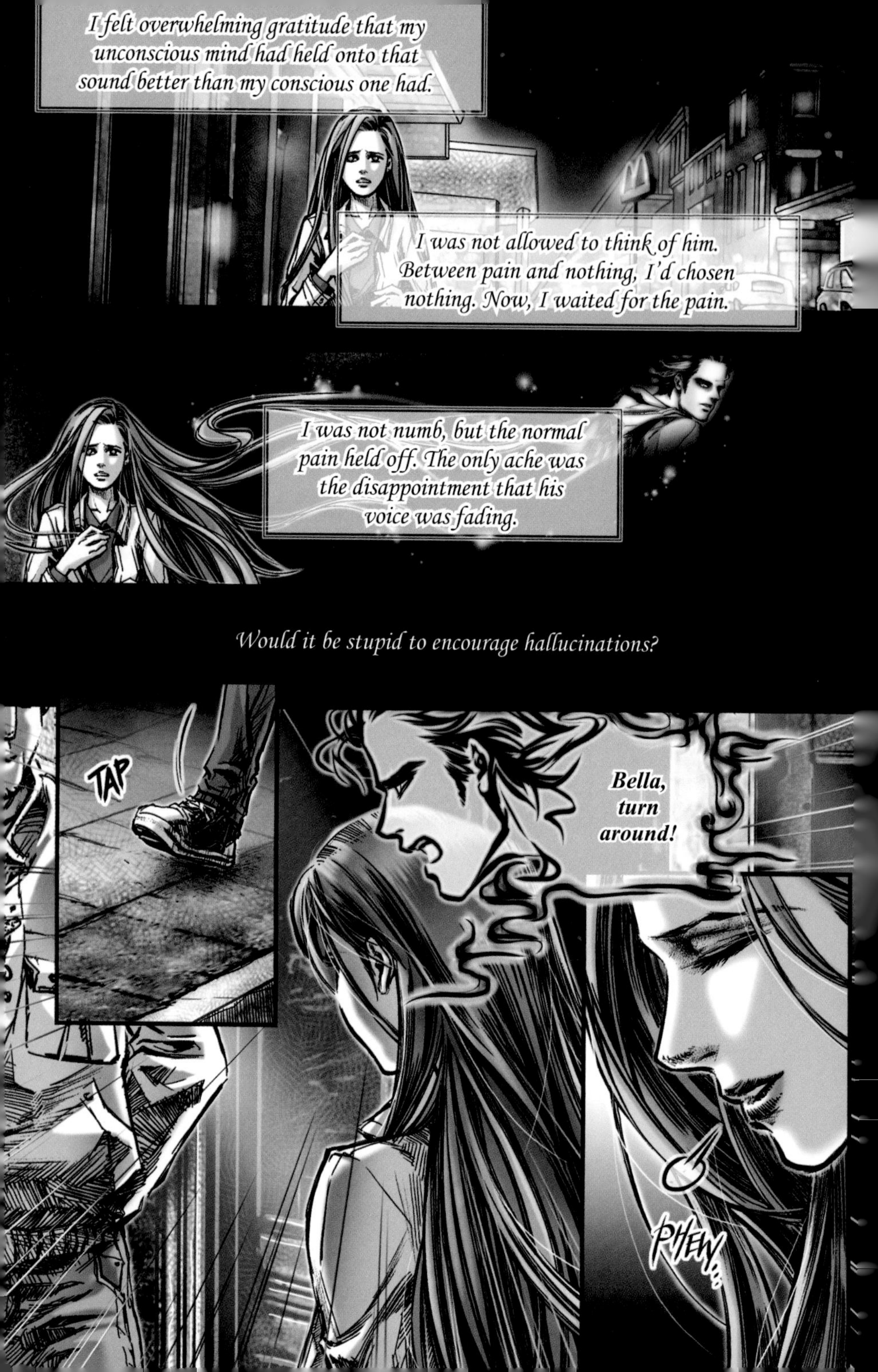
I felt overwhelming gratitude that my unconscious mind had held onto that sound better than my conscious one had.
I was not allowed to think of him. Between pain and nothing, I'd chosen nothing. Now, I waited for the pain.
I was not numb, but the normal pain held off. The only ache was the disappointment that his voice was fading.
Would it be stupid to encourage hallucinations?
TAP
Bella, turn around!
PHEW...

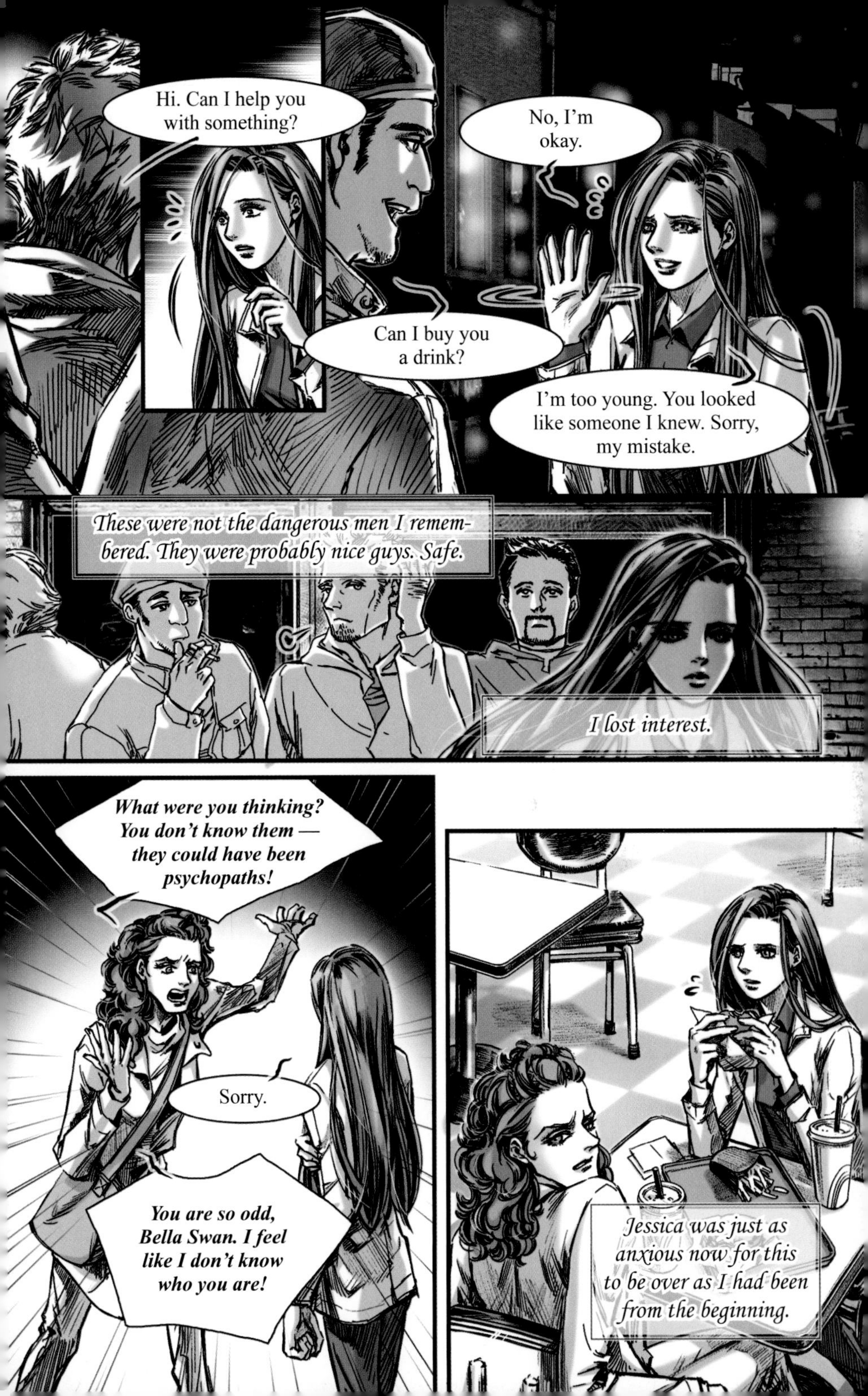
Hi. Can I help you with something?
No, I'm okay.
Can I buy you a drink?
I'm too young. You looked like someone I knew. Sorry, my mistake.
These were not the dangerous men I remembered. They were probably nice guys. Safe.
I lost interest.
What were you thinking? You don't know them — they could have been psychopaths!
Sorry.
You are so odd, Bella Swan. I feel like I don't know who you are!
Jessica was just as anxious now for this to be over as I had been from the beginning.

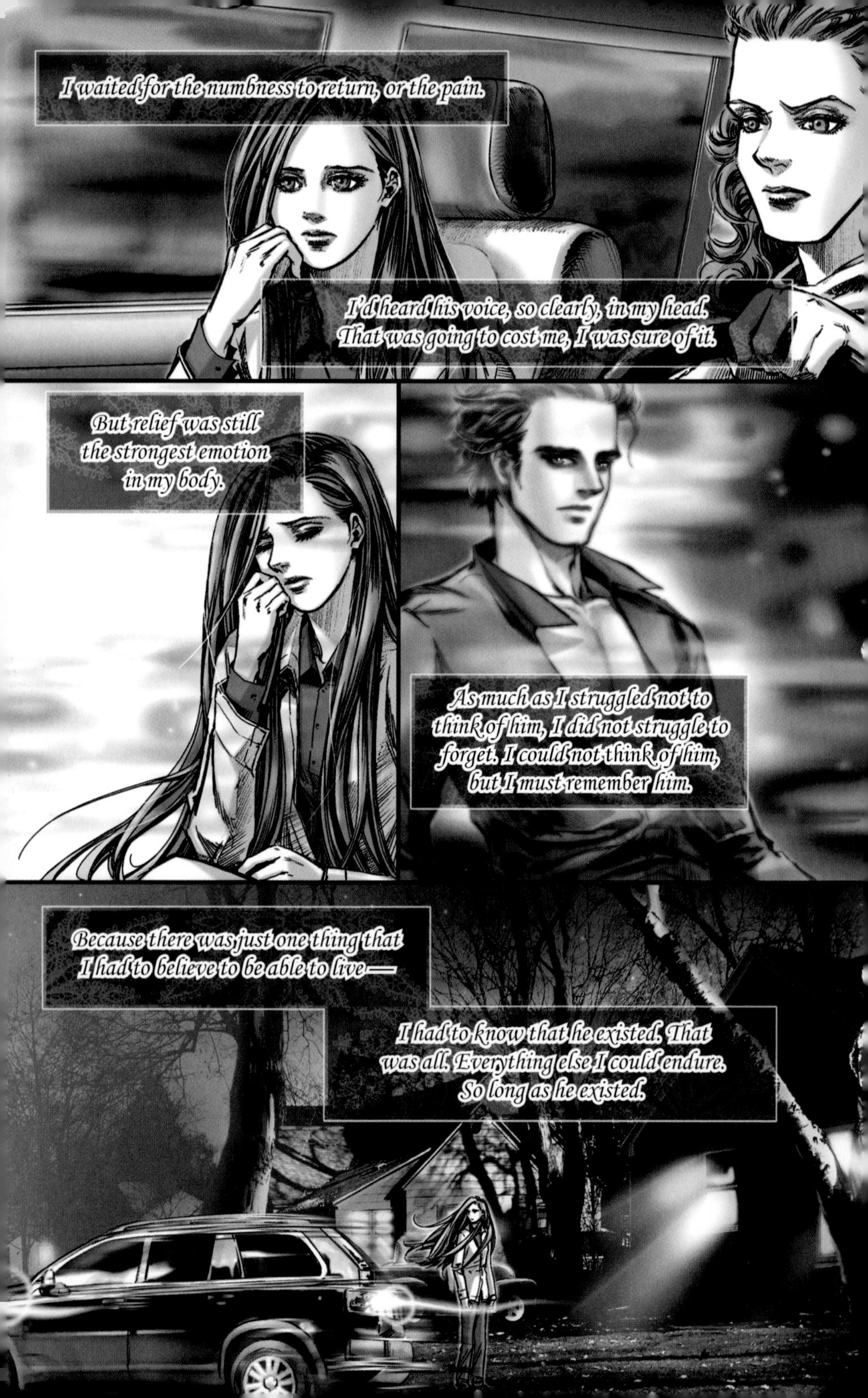
I waited for the numbness to return, or the pain.
I'd heard his voice, so clearly, in my head. That was going to cost me, I was sure of it.
But relief was still the strongest emotion in my body.
As much as I struggled not to think of him, I did not struggle to forget. I could not think of him, but I must remember him.
Because there was just one thing that I had to believe to be able to live—
I had to know that he existed. That was all. Everything else I could endure. So long as he existed.

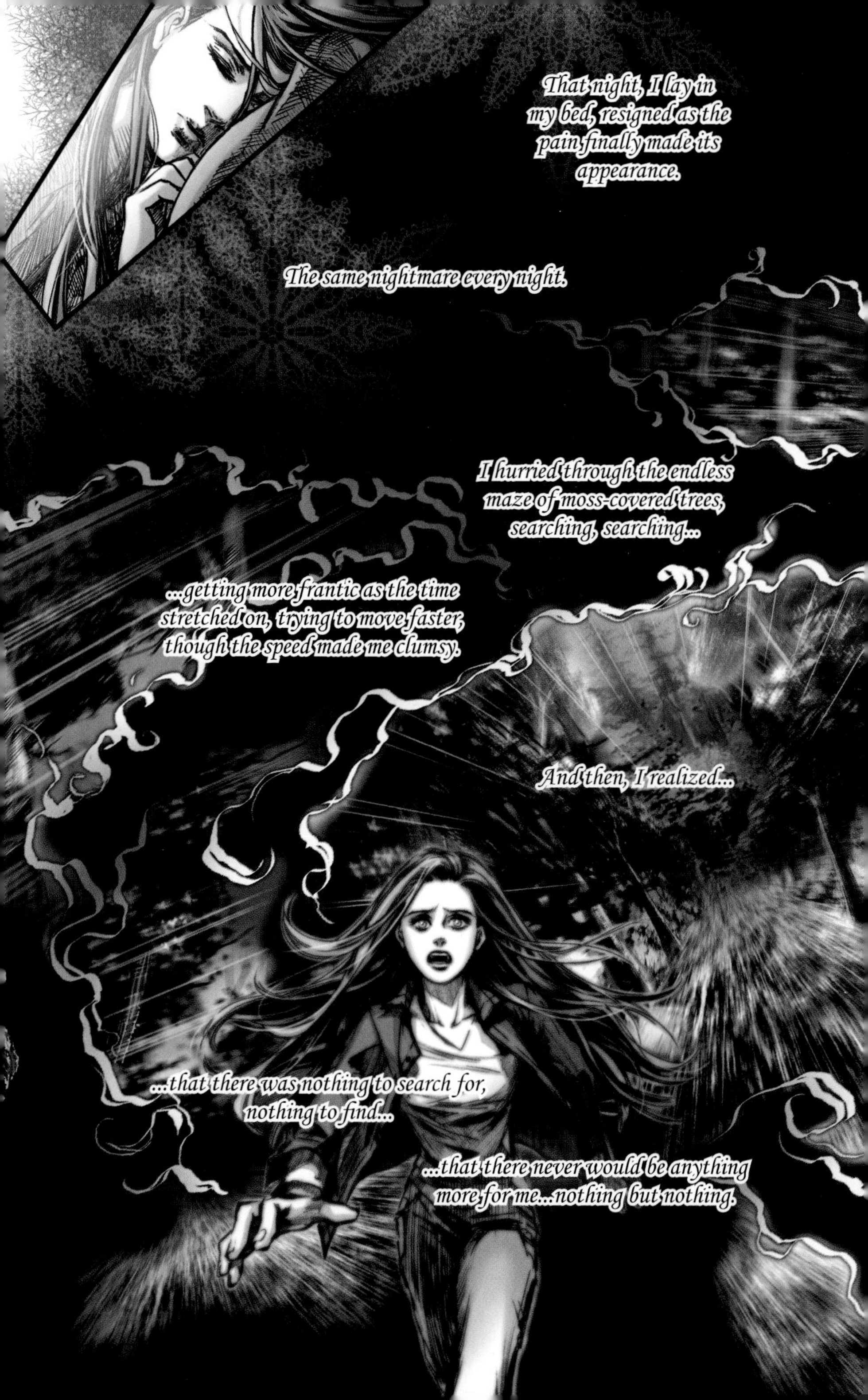
That night, I lay in my bed, resigned as the pain finally made its appearance.
The same nightmare every night.
I hurried through the endless maze of moss-covered trees, searching, searching...
...getting more frantic as the time stretched on, trying to move faster, though the speed made me clumsy.
And then, I realized...
...that there was nothing to search for, nothing to find...
...that there never would be anything more for me...nothing but nothing.

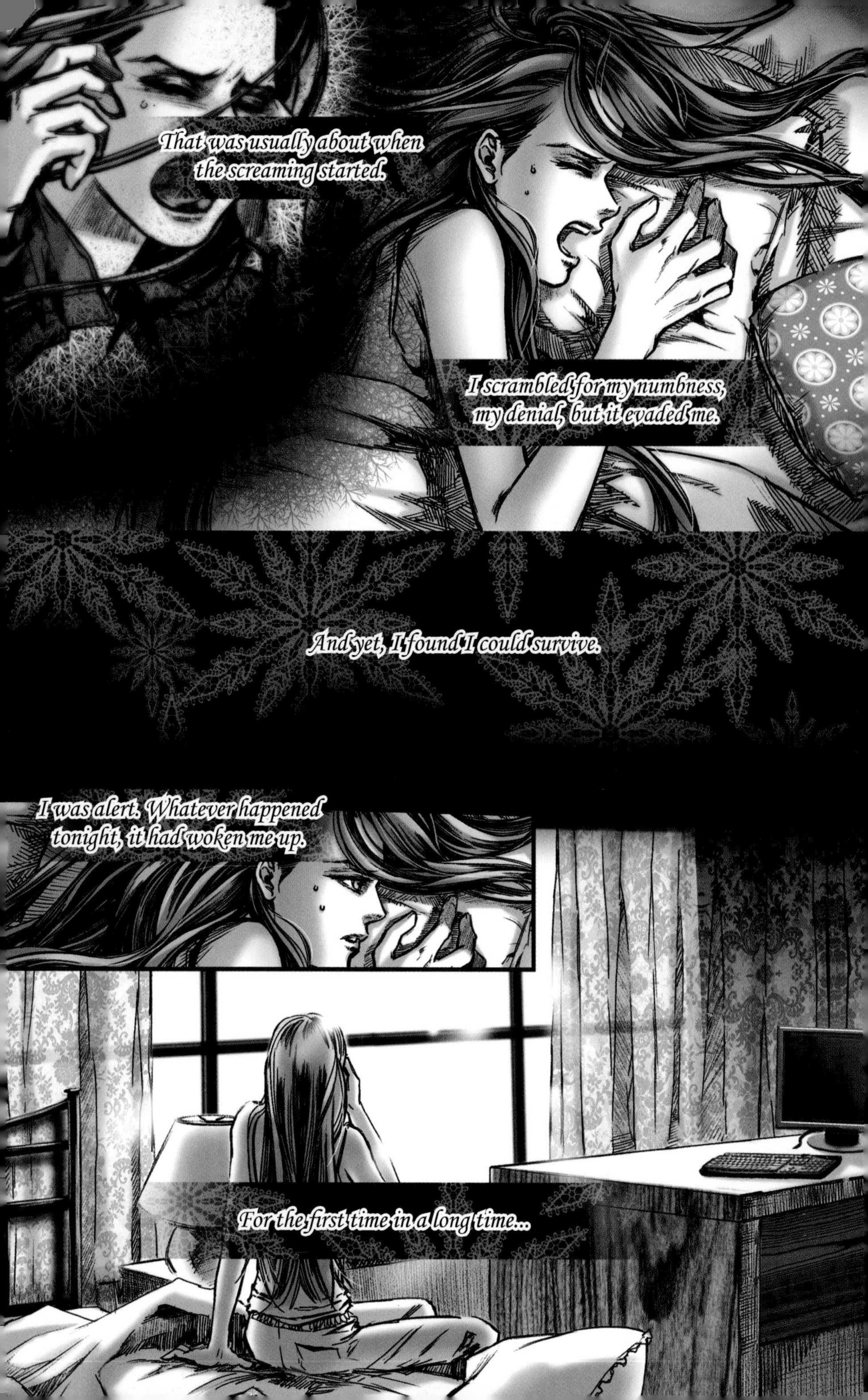

That was usually about when the screaming started.
I scrambled for my numbness, my denial, but it evaded me.
And yet, I found I could survive.
I was alert. Whatever happened tonight, it had woken me up.
For the first time in a long time...

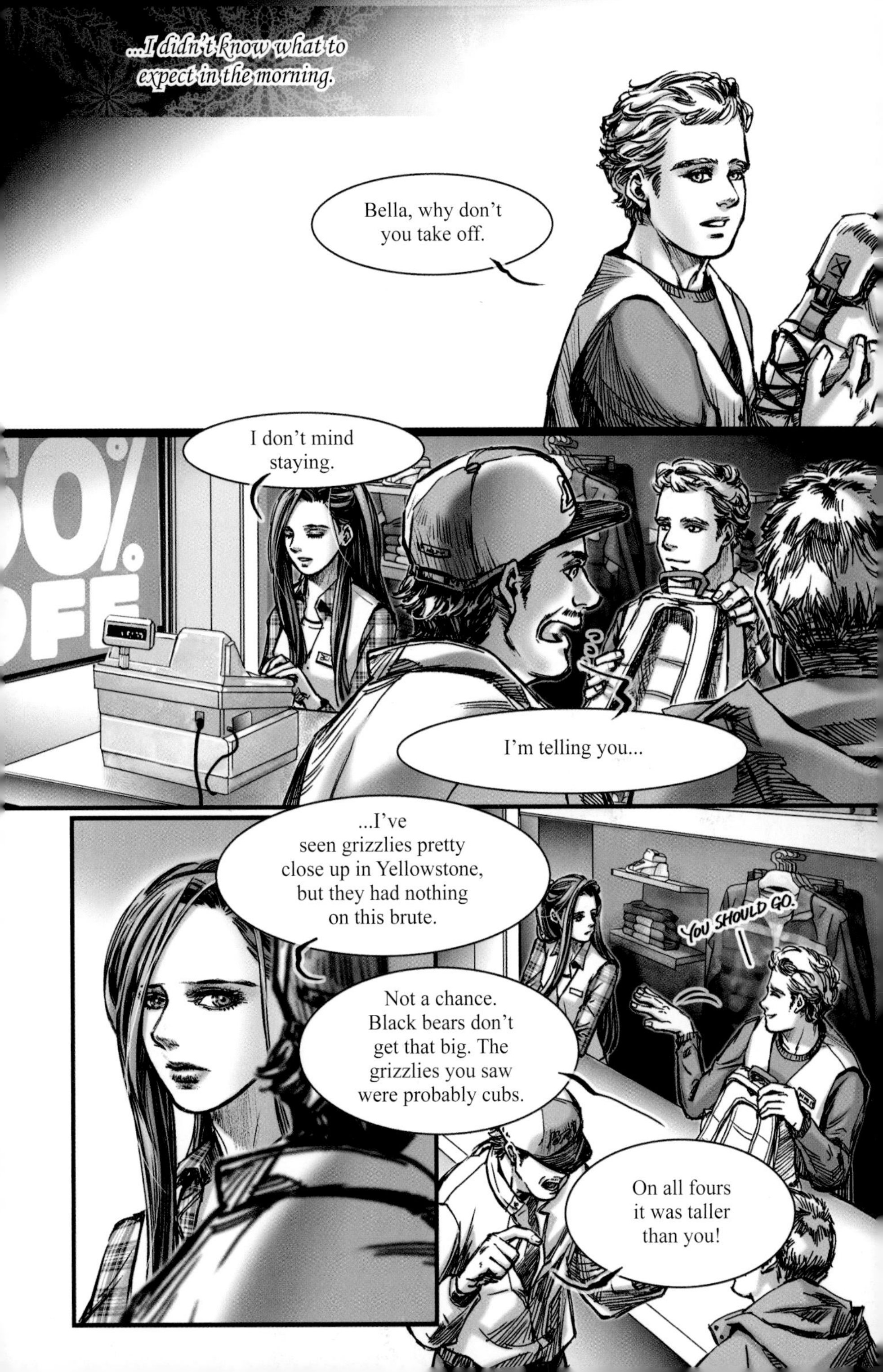
...I didn't know what to expect in the morning.
Bella, why don't you take off.
I don't mind staying.
I'm telling you...
...I've seen grizzlies pretty close up in Yellowstone, but they had nothing on this brute.
YOU SHOULD GO.
Not a chance. Black bears don't get that big. The grizzlies you saw were probably cubs.
On all fours it was taller than you!

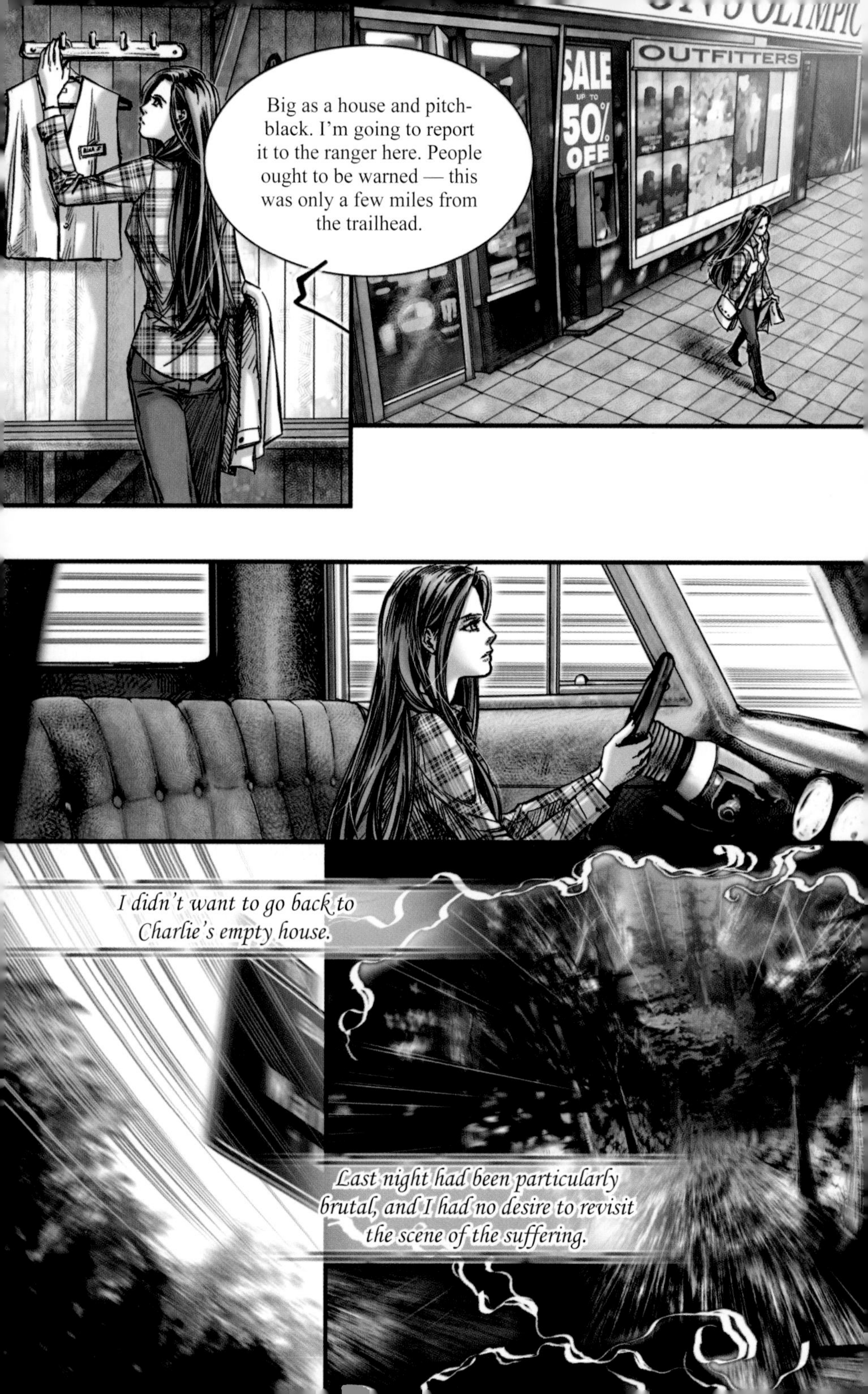
OUTFITTERS
SALE UP TO 50% OFF
Big as a house and pitch-black. I'm going to report it to the ranger here. People ought to be warned — this was only a few miles from the trailhead.
I didn't want to go back to Charlie's empty house.
Last night had been particularly brutal, and I had no desire to revisit the scene of the suffering.

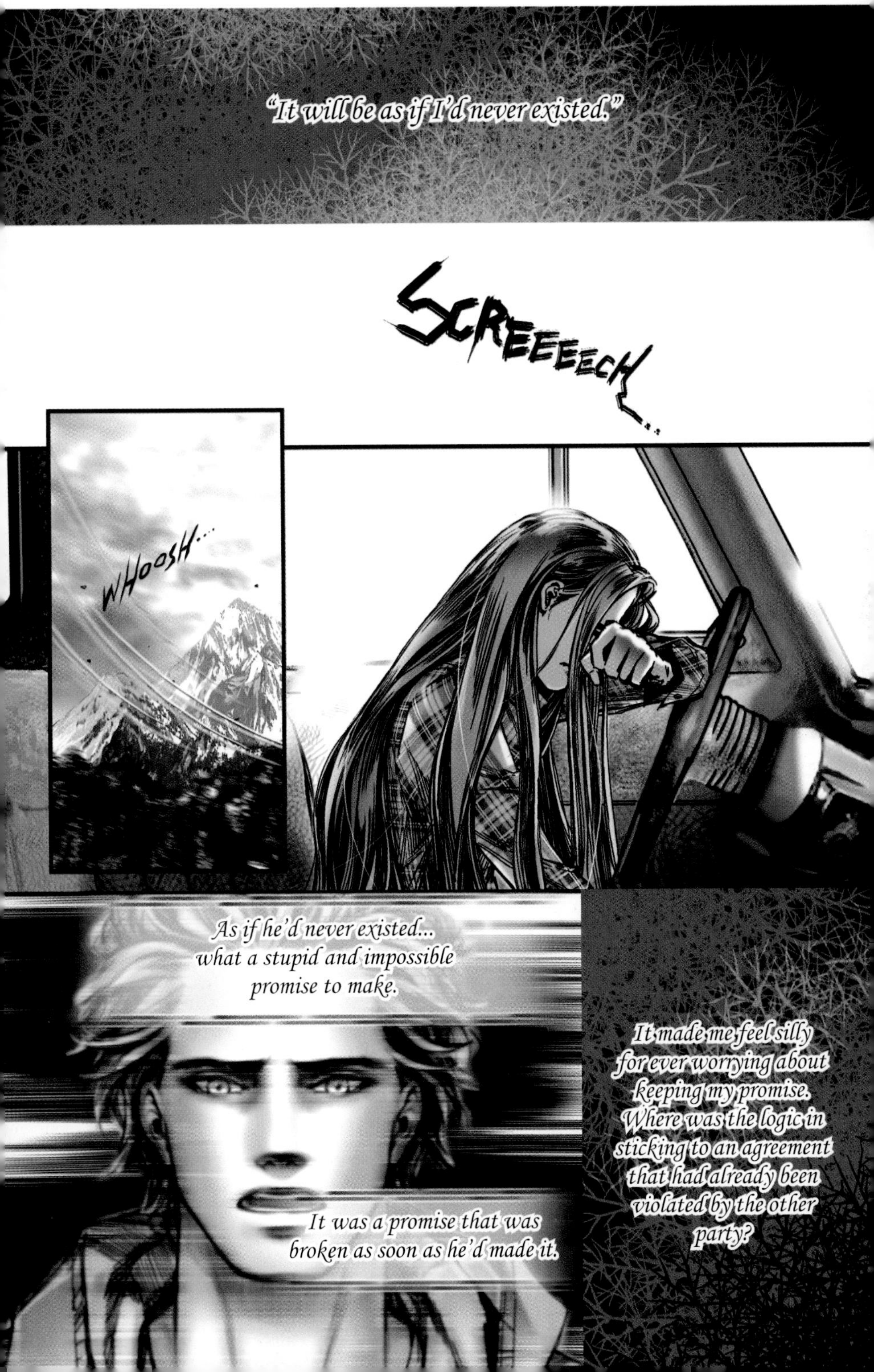
"It will be as if I'd never existed."
SCREEEEECH...
WHOOSH...
As if he'd never existed... what a stupid and impossible promise to make.
It was a promise that was broken as soon as he'd made it.
It made me feel silly for ever worrying about keeping my promise. Where was the logic in sticking to an agreement that had already been violated by the other party?

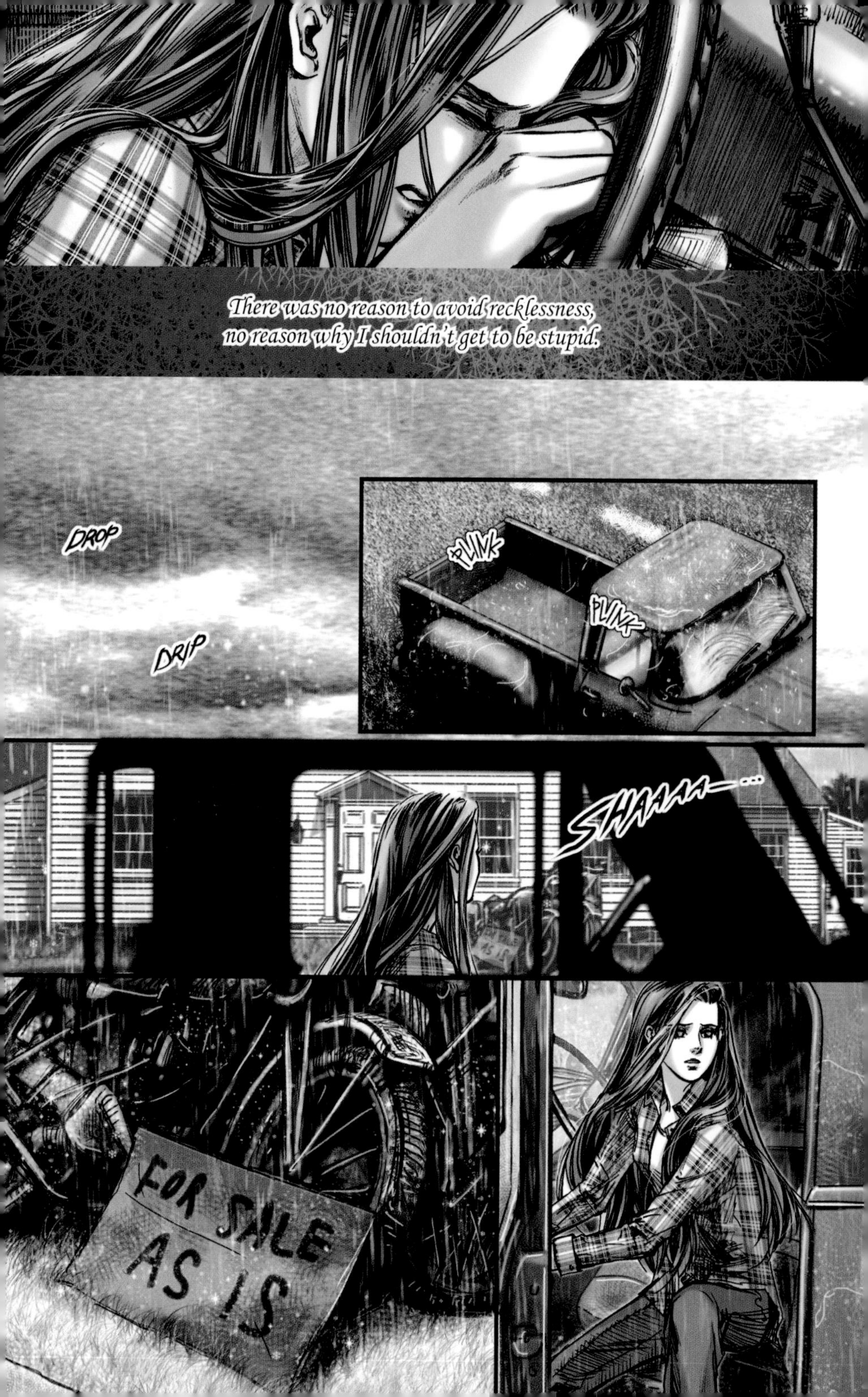
There was no reason to avoid recklessness,
no reason why I shouldn't get to be stupid.
DROP
DRIP
PLINK
PLINK
SHAAAA—...
FOR SALE
AS IS

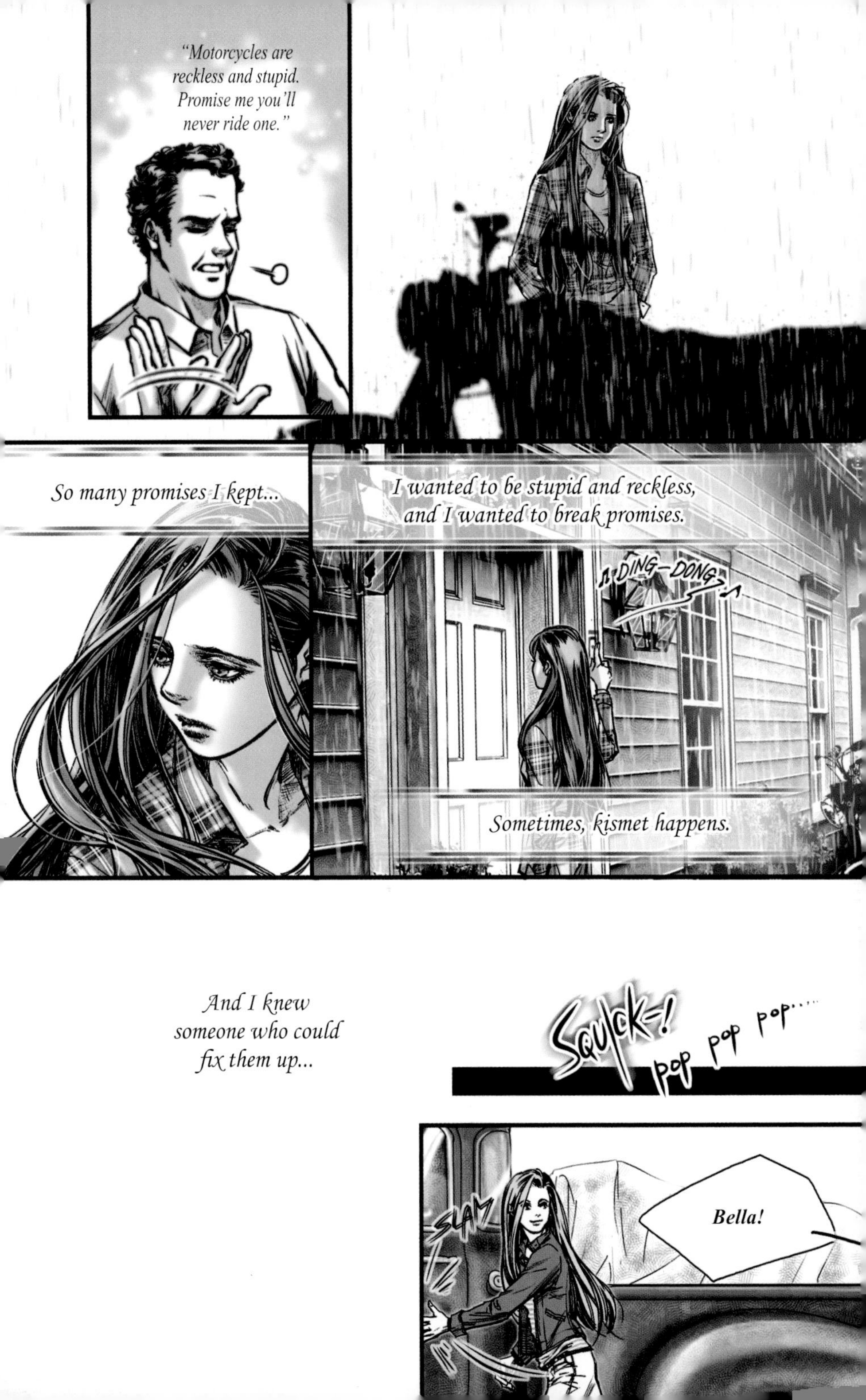
"Motorcycles are reckless and stupid. Promise me you'll never ride one."
So many promises I kept...
I wanted to be stupid and reckless, and I wanted to break promises.
DING-DONG
Sometimes, kismet happens.
And I knew someone who could fix them up...
SQUICK-!
pop pop pop.....
SLAM
Bella!

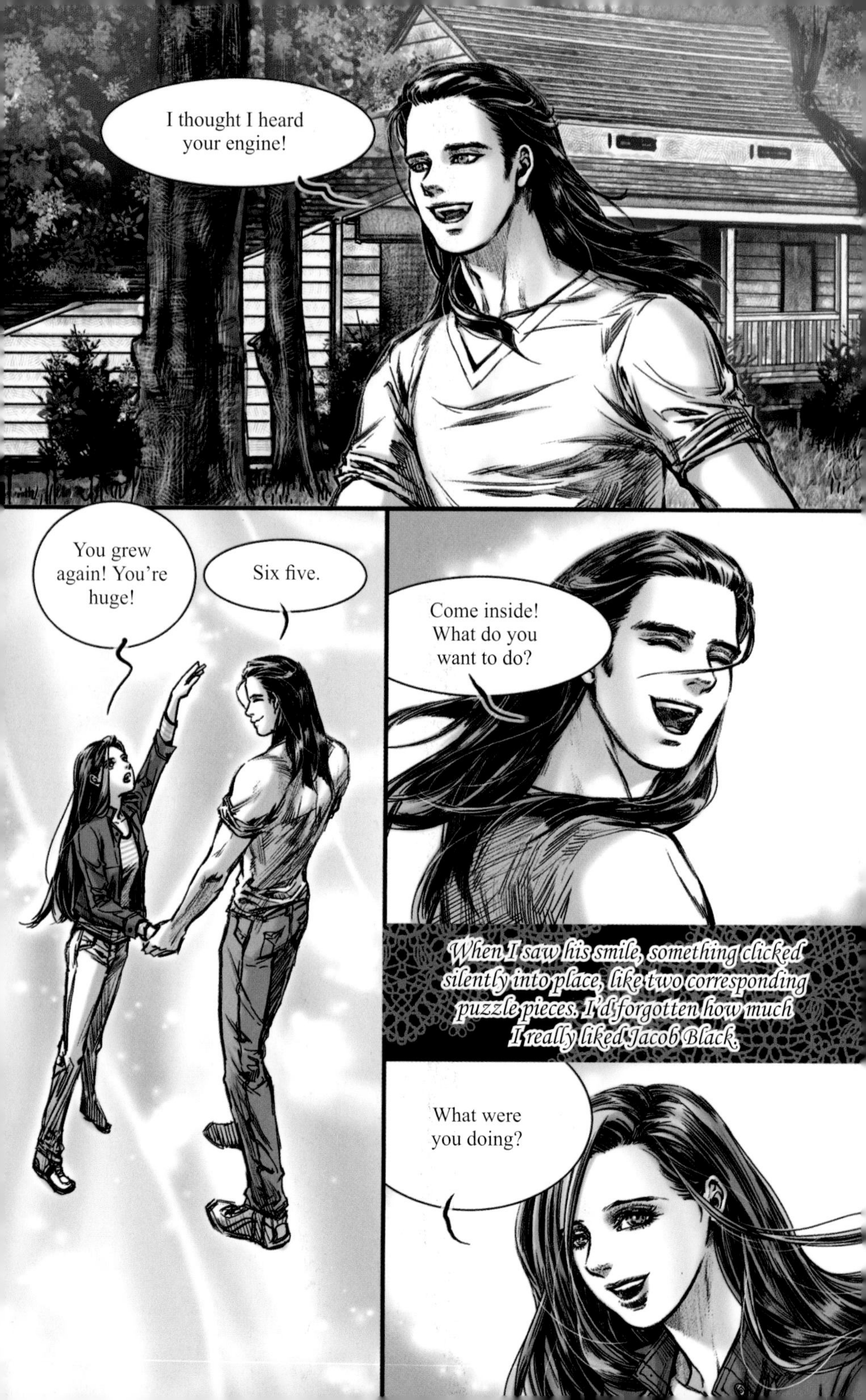
I thought I heard your engine!
You grew again! You're huge!
Six five.
Come inside! What do you want to do?
When I saw his smile, something clicked silently into place, like two corresponding puzzle pieces. I'd forgotten how much I really liked Jacob Black.
What were you doing?

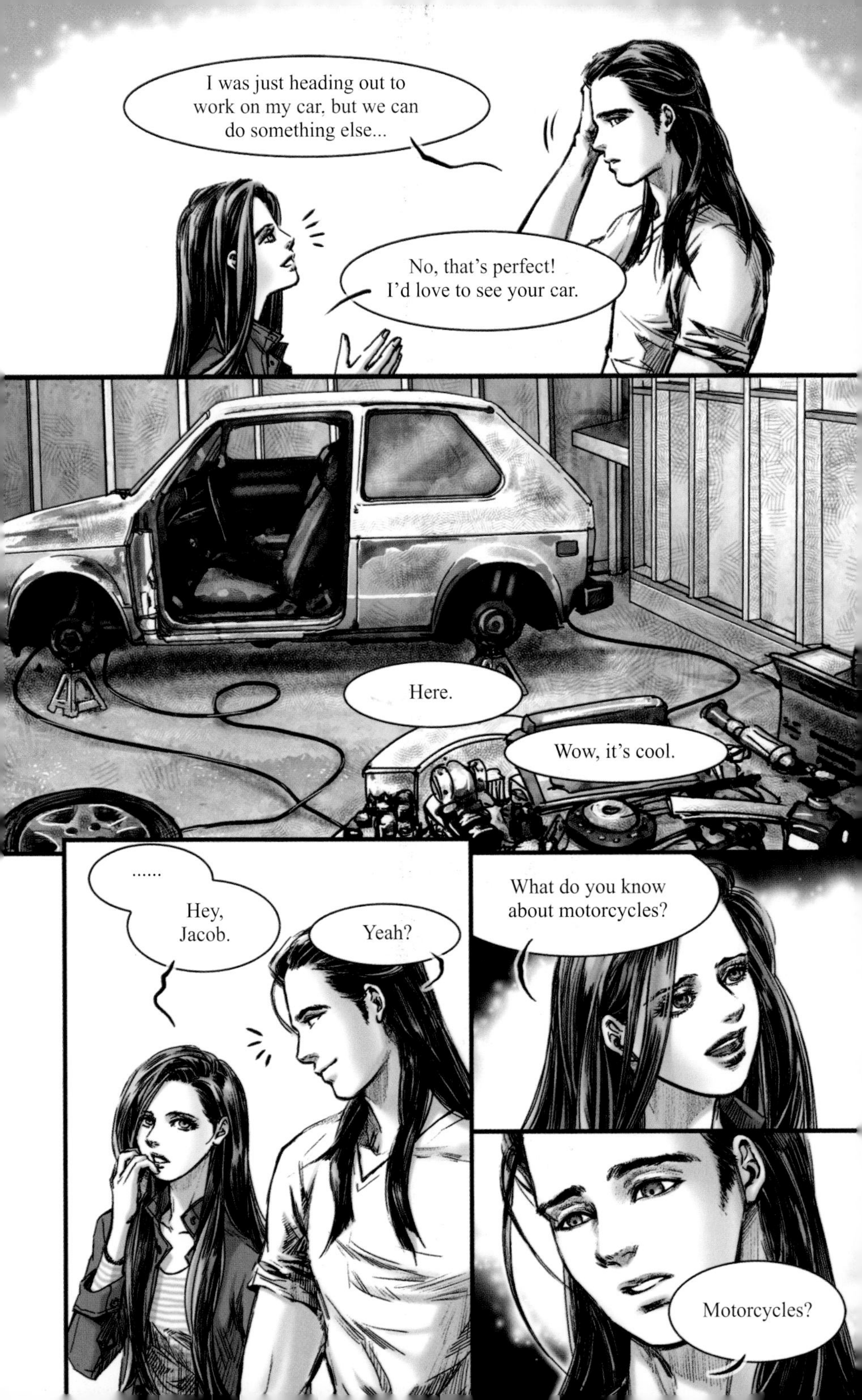
I was just heading out to work on my car, but we can do something else...
No, that's perfect! I'd love to see your car.
Here.
Wow, it's cool.
......
Hey, Jacob.
Yeah?
What do you know about motorcycles?
Motorcycles?

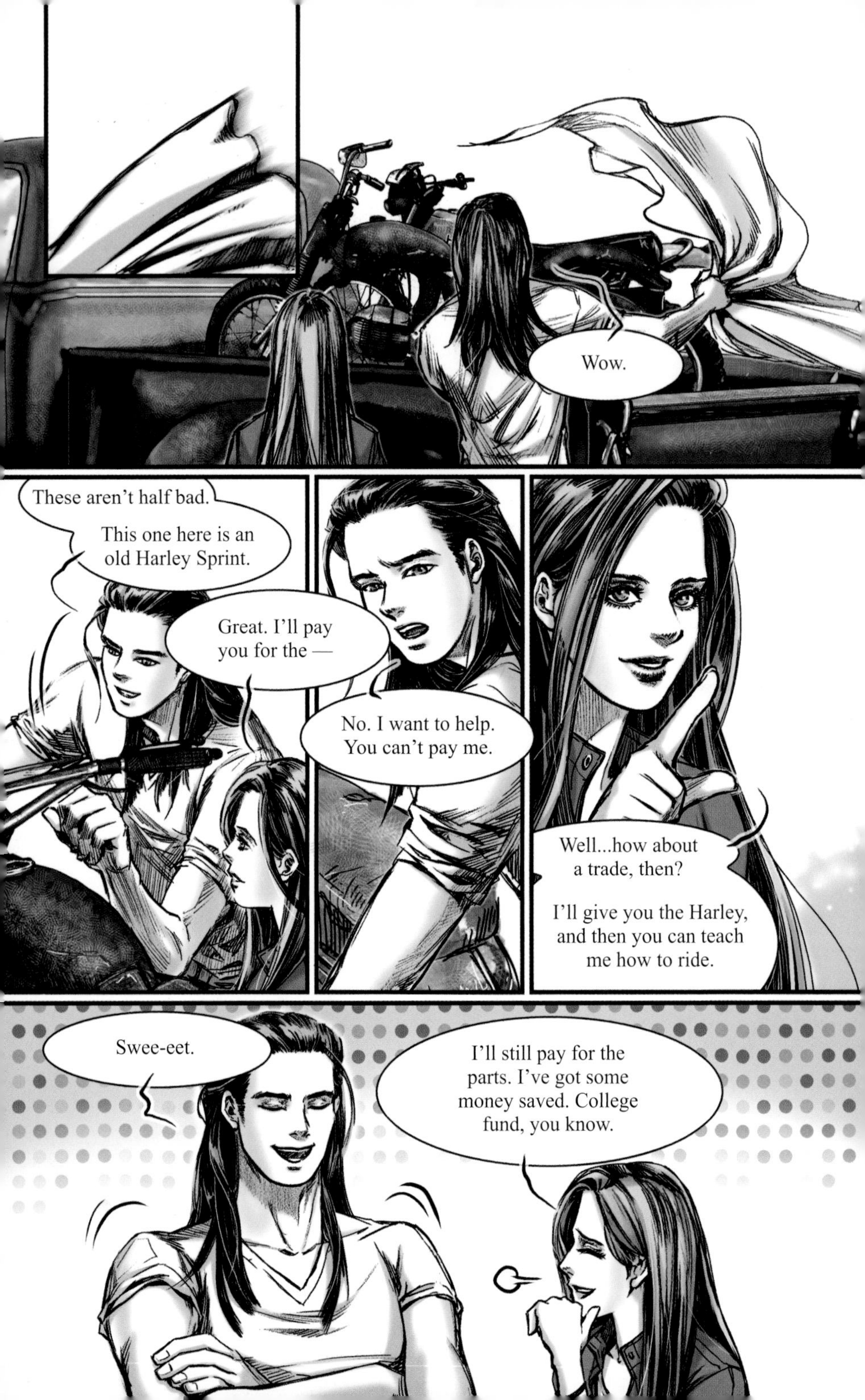
Wow.
These aren't half bad.
This one here is an old Harley Sprint.
Great. I'll pay you for the —
No. I want to help. You can't pay me.
Well...how about a trade, then?
I'll give you the Harley, and then you can teach me how to ride.
Swee-eet.
I'll still pay for the parts. I've got some money saved. College fund, you know.

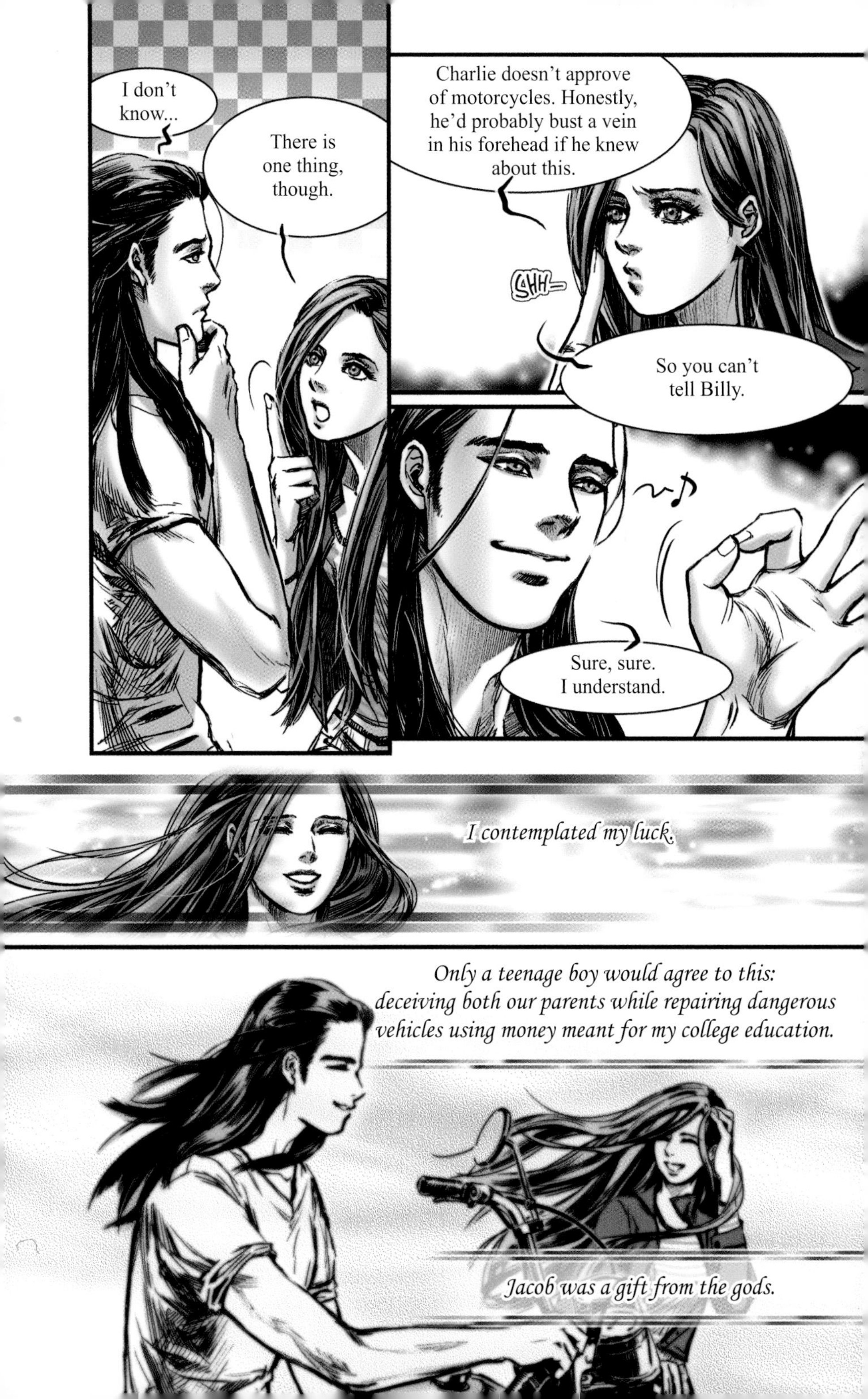
I don't know...
There is one thing, though.
Charlie doesn't approve of motorcycles. Honestly, he'd probably bust a vein in his forehead if he knew about this.
SHH—
So you can't tell Billy.
Sure, sure. I understand.
I contemplated my luck.
Only a teenage boy would agree to this: deceiving both our parents while repairing dangerous vehicles using money meant for my college education.
Jacob was a gift from the gods.

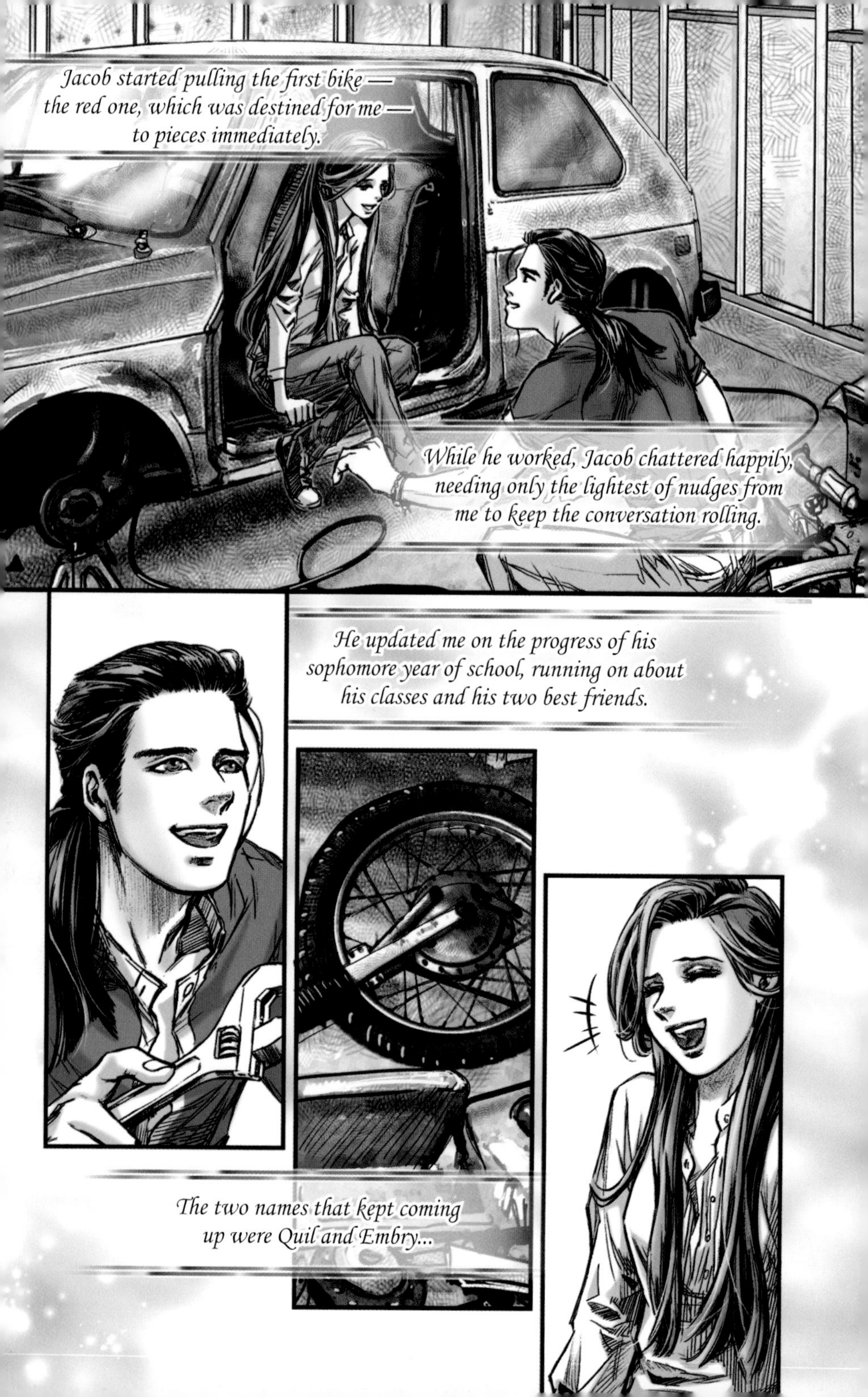
Jacob started pulling the first bike — the red one, which was destined for me — to pieces immediately.
While he worked, Jacob chattered happily, needing only the lightest of nudges from me to keep the conversation rolling.
He updated me on the progress of his sophomore year of school, running on about his classes and his two best friends.
The two names that kept coming up were Quil and Embry...

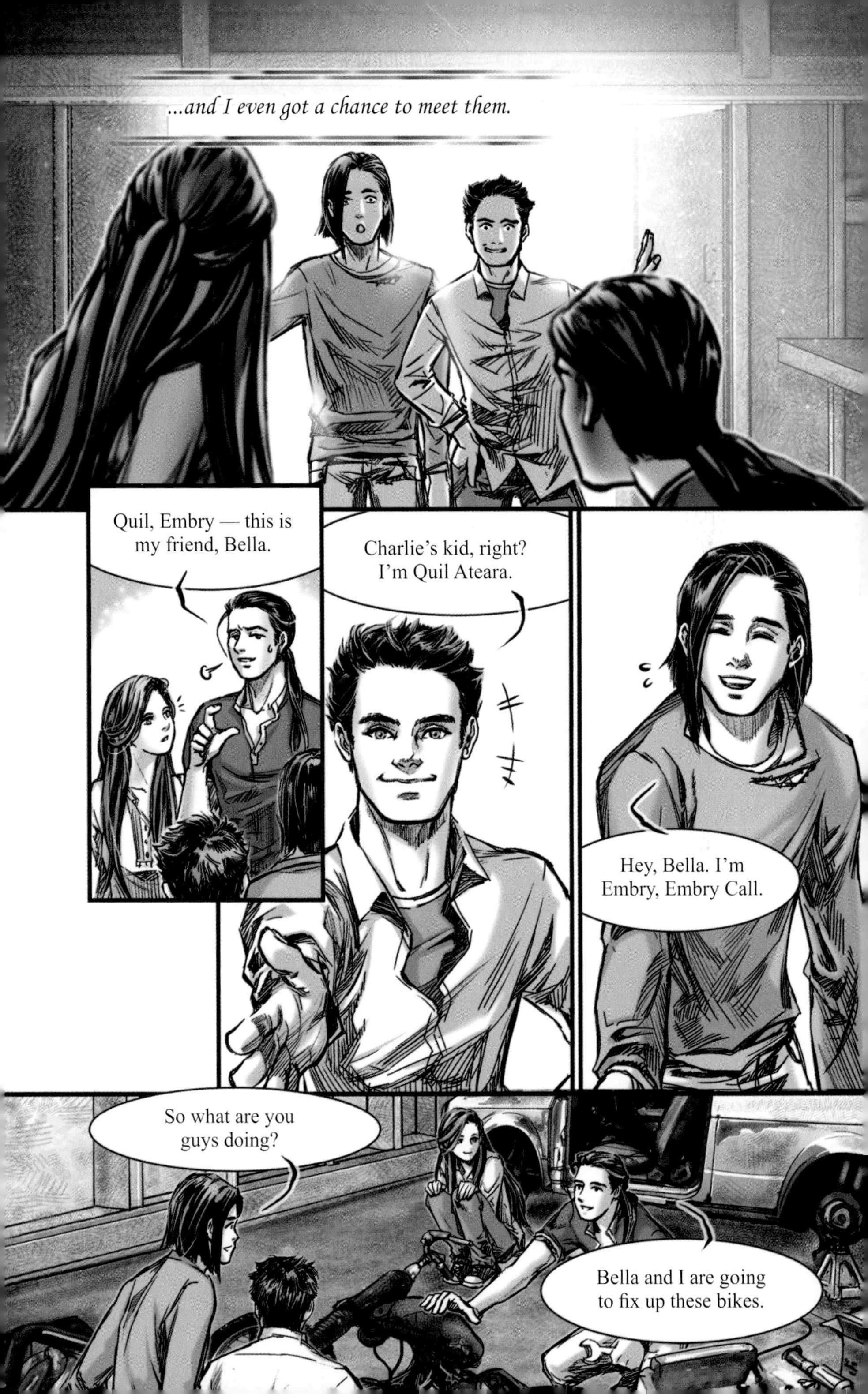
...and I even got a chance to meet them.
Quil, Embry — this is my friend, Bella.
Charlie's kid, right? I'm Quil Ateara.
Hey, Bella. I'm Embry, Embry Call.
So what are you guys doing?
Bella and I are going to fix up these bikes.

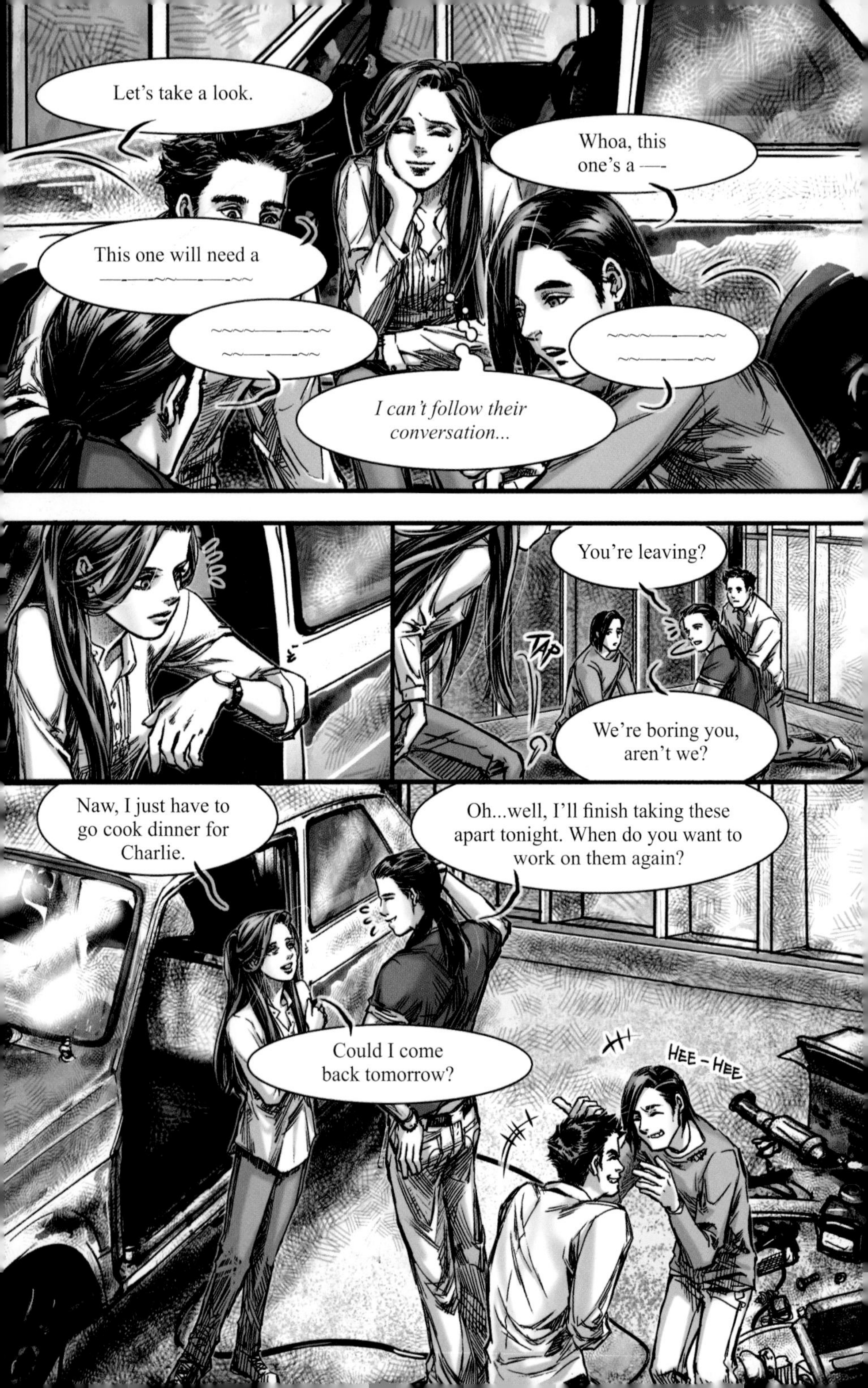
Let's take a look.
Whoa, this one's a —-
This one will need a
I can't follow their conversation...
You're leaving?
TAP
We're boring you, aren't we?
Naw, I just have to go cook dinner for Charlie.
Oh...well, I'll finish taking these apart tonight. When do you want to work on them again?
Could I come back tomorrow?
HEE-HEE

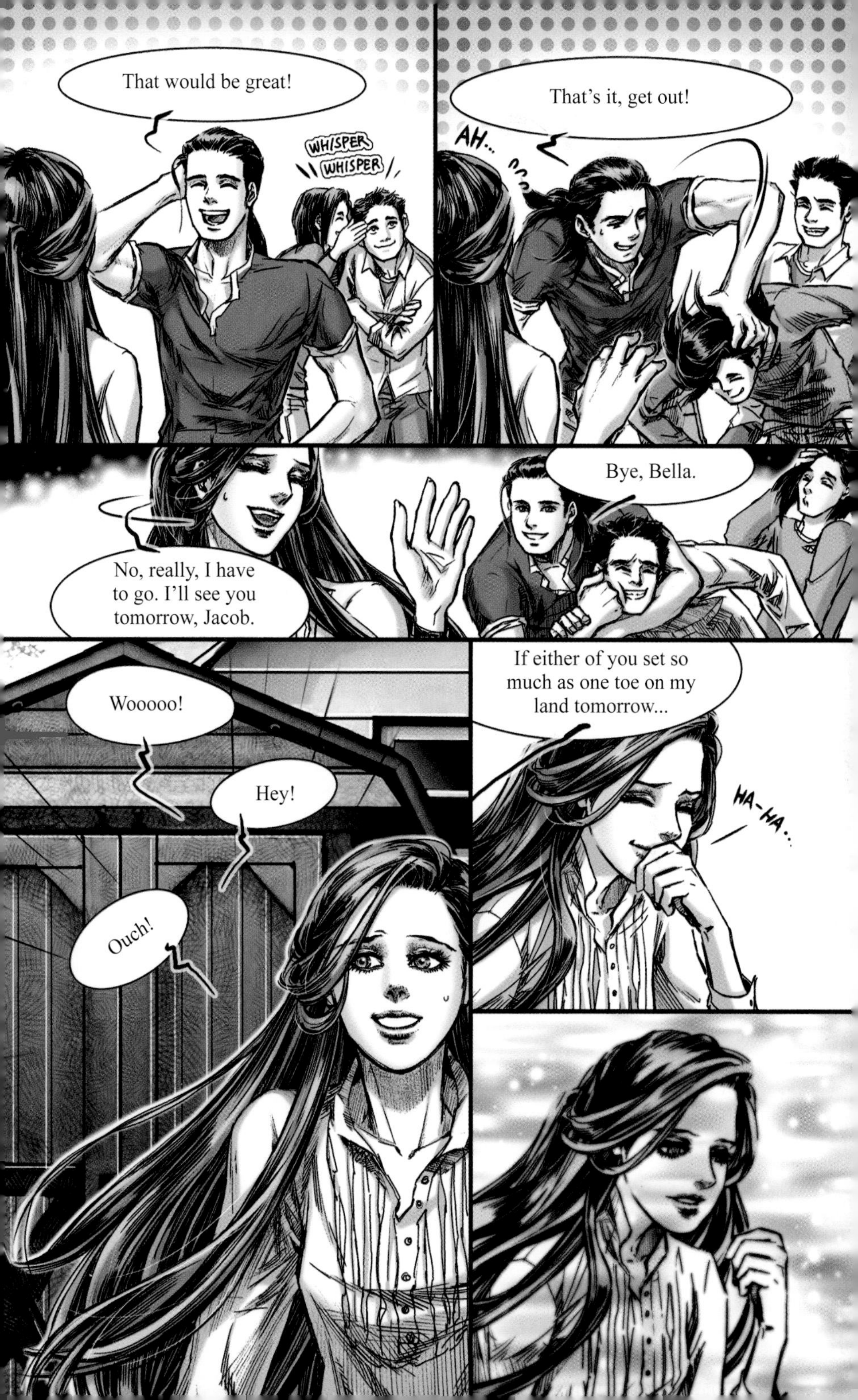
That would be great!
WHISPER
WHISPER
That's it, get out!
AH...
No, really, I have to go. I'll see you tomorrow, Jacob.
Bye, Bella.
Wooooo!
Hey!
Ouch!
If either of you set so much as one toe on my land tomorrow...
HA-HA...

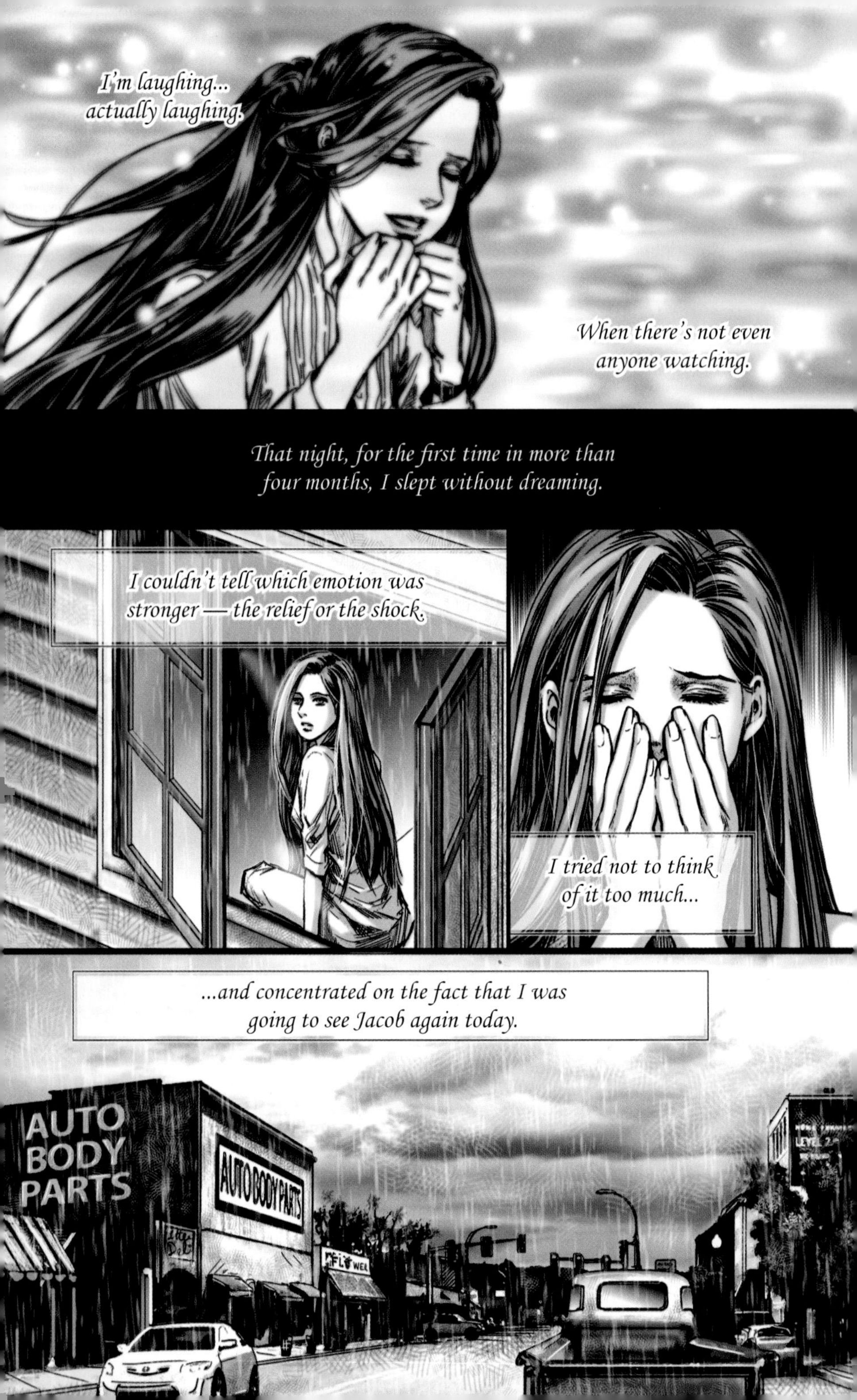
I'm laughing...
actually laughing.
When there's not even anyone watching.
That night, for the first time in more than four months, I slept without dreaming.
I couldn't tell which emotion was stronger — the relief or the shock.
I tried not to think of it too much...
...and concentrated on the fact that I was going to see Jacob again today.
AUTO BODY PARTS
AUTO BODY PARTS

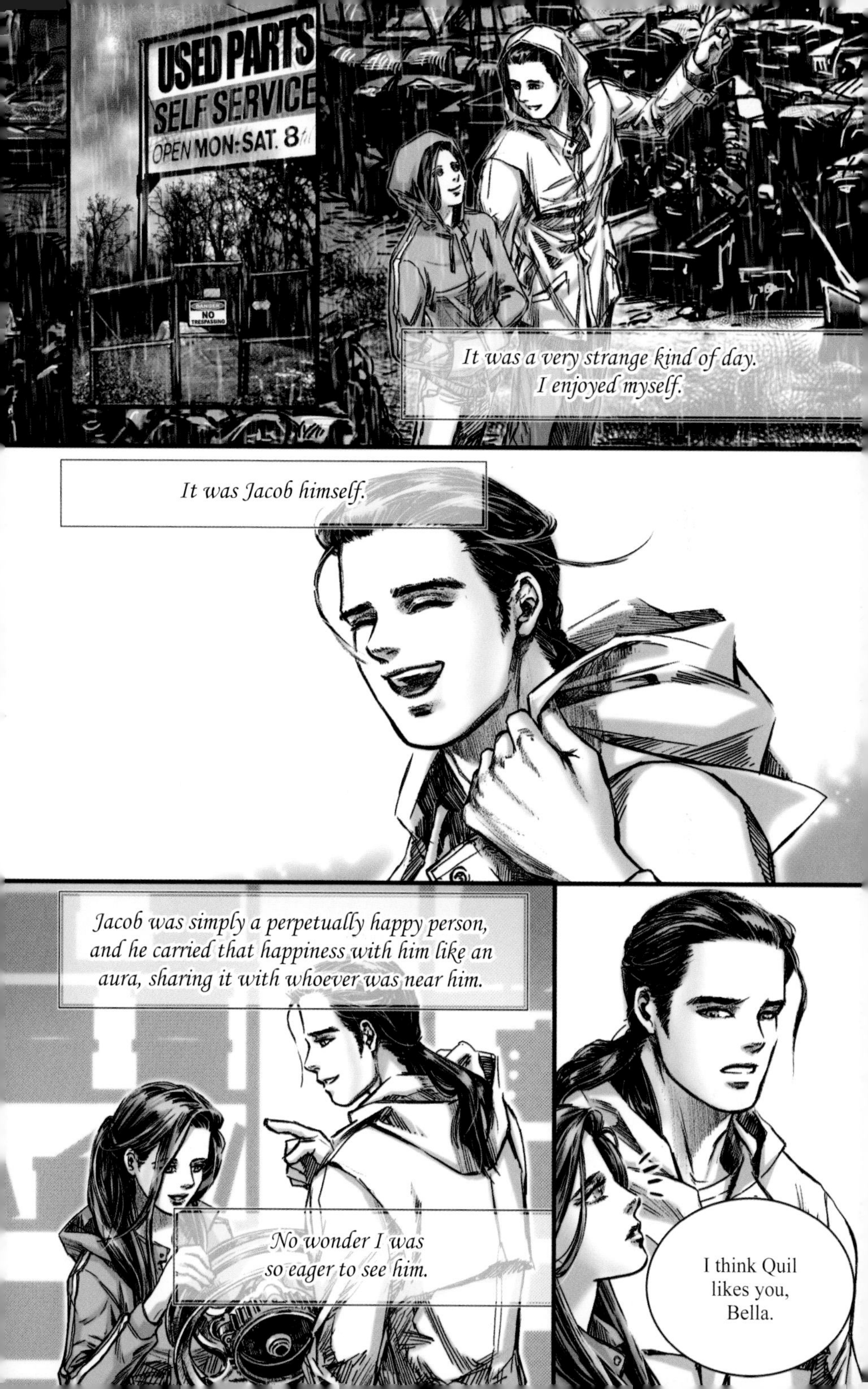
USED PARTS
SELF SERVICE
OPEN MON-SAT. 8
DANGER
NO TRESPASSING
It was a very strange kind of day. I enjoyed myself.
It was Jacob himself.
Jacob was simply a perpetually happy person, and he carried that happiness with him like an aura, sharing it with whoever was near him.
No wonder I was so eager to see him.
I think Quil likes you, Bella.

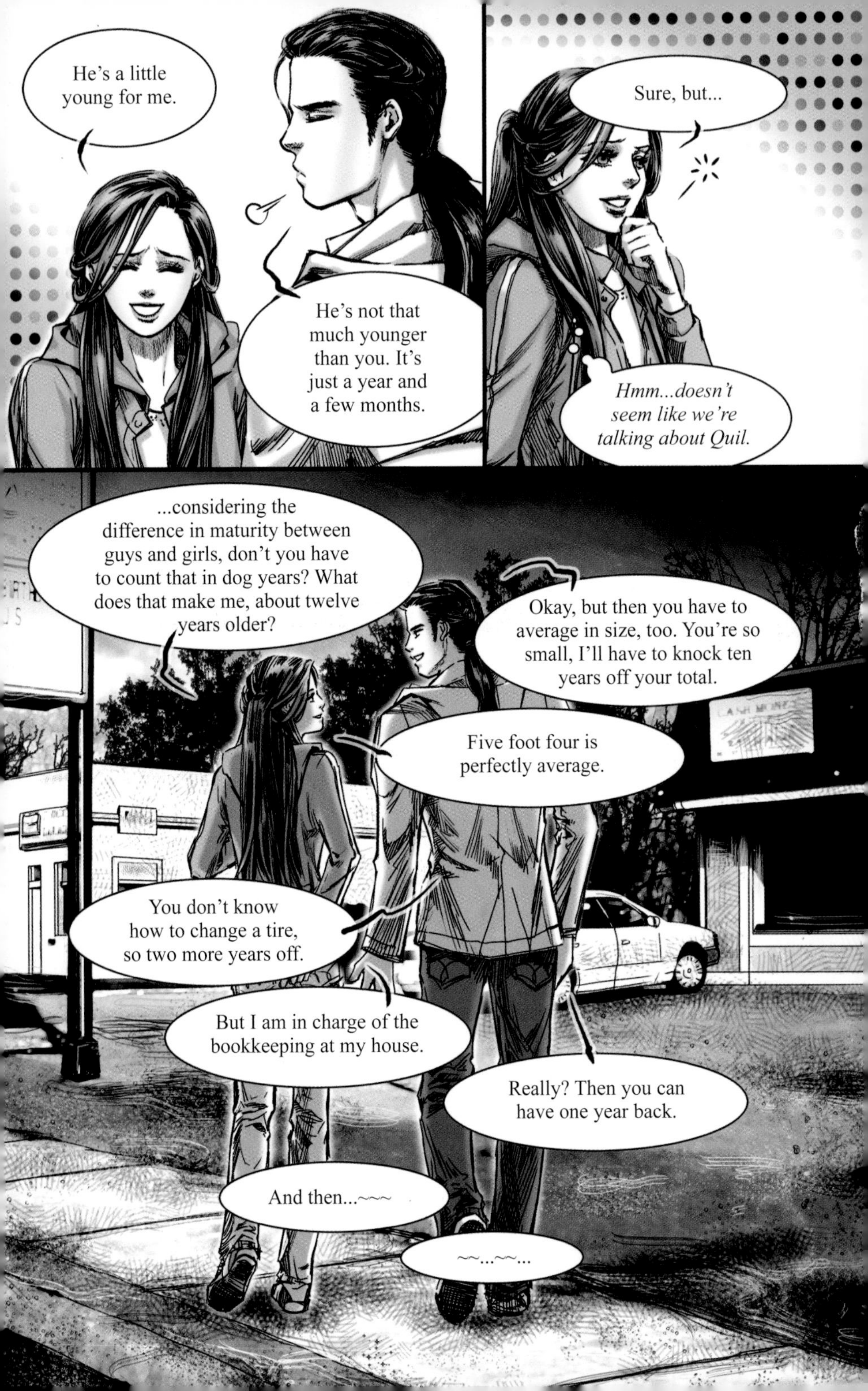
He's a little young for me.
He's not that much younger than you. It's just a year and a few months.
Sure, but...
Hmm...doesn't seem like we're talking about Quil.
...considering the difference in maturity between guys and girls, don't you have to count that in dog years? What does that make me, about twelve years older?
Okay, but then you have to average in size, too. You're so small, I'll have to knock ten years off your total.
Five foot four is perfectly average.
You don't know how to change a tire, so two more years off.
But I am in charge of the bookkeeping at my house.
Really? Then you can have one year back.
And then...~~~
~~...~~...

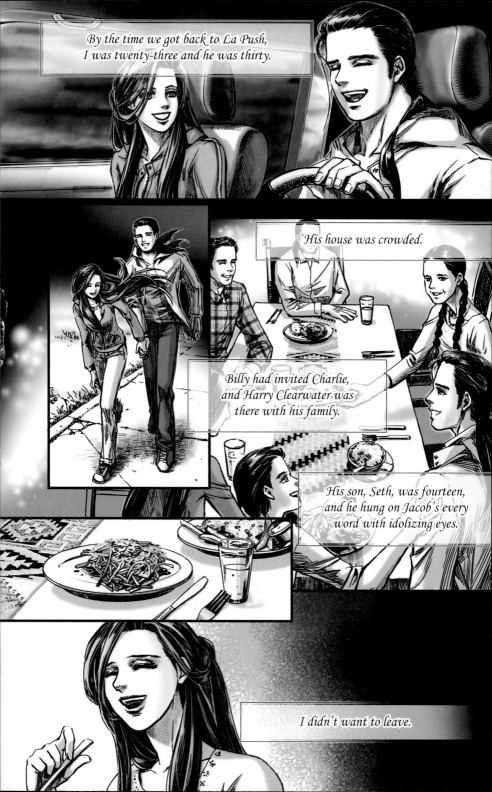

By the time we got back to La Push,
I was twenty-three and he was thirty.

His house was crowded.

Billy had invited Charlie,
and Harry Clearwater was
there with his family.

His son, Seth, was fourteen,
and he hung on Jacob's every
word with idolizing eyes.

I didn't want to leave.

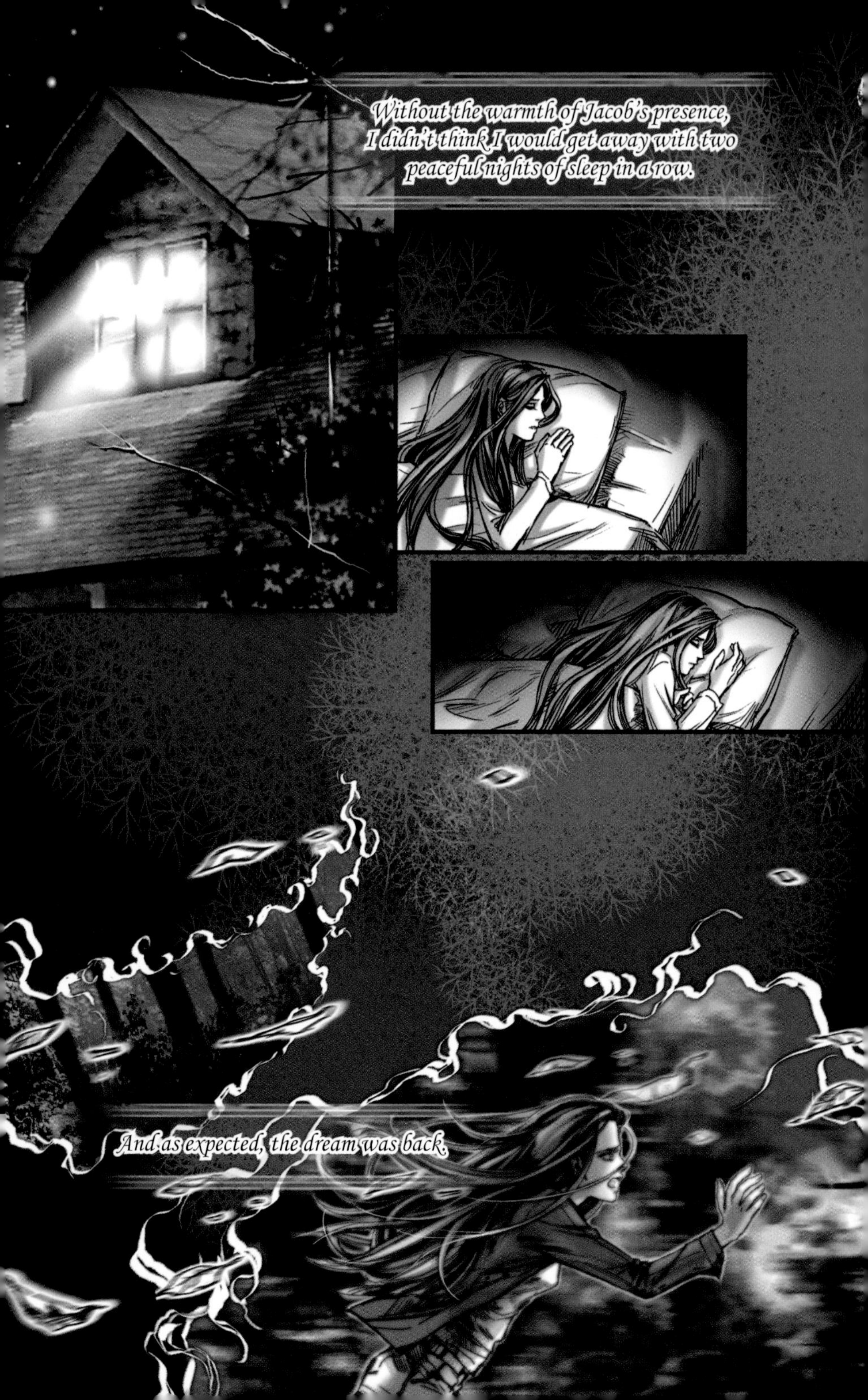
Without the warmth of Jacob's presence, I didn't think I would get away with two peaceful nights of sleep in a row.
And as expected, the dream was back.

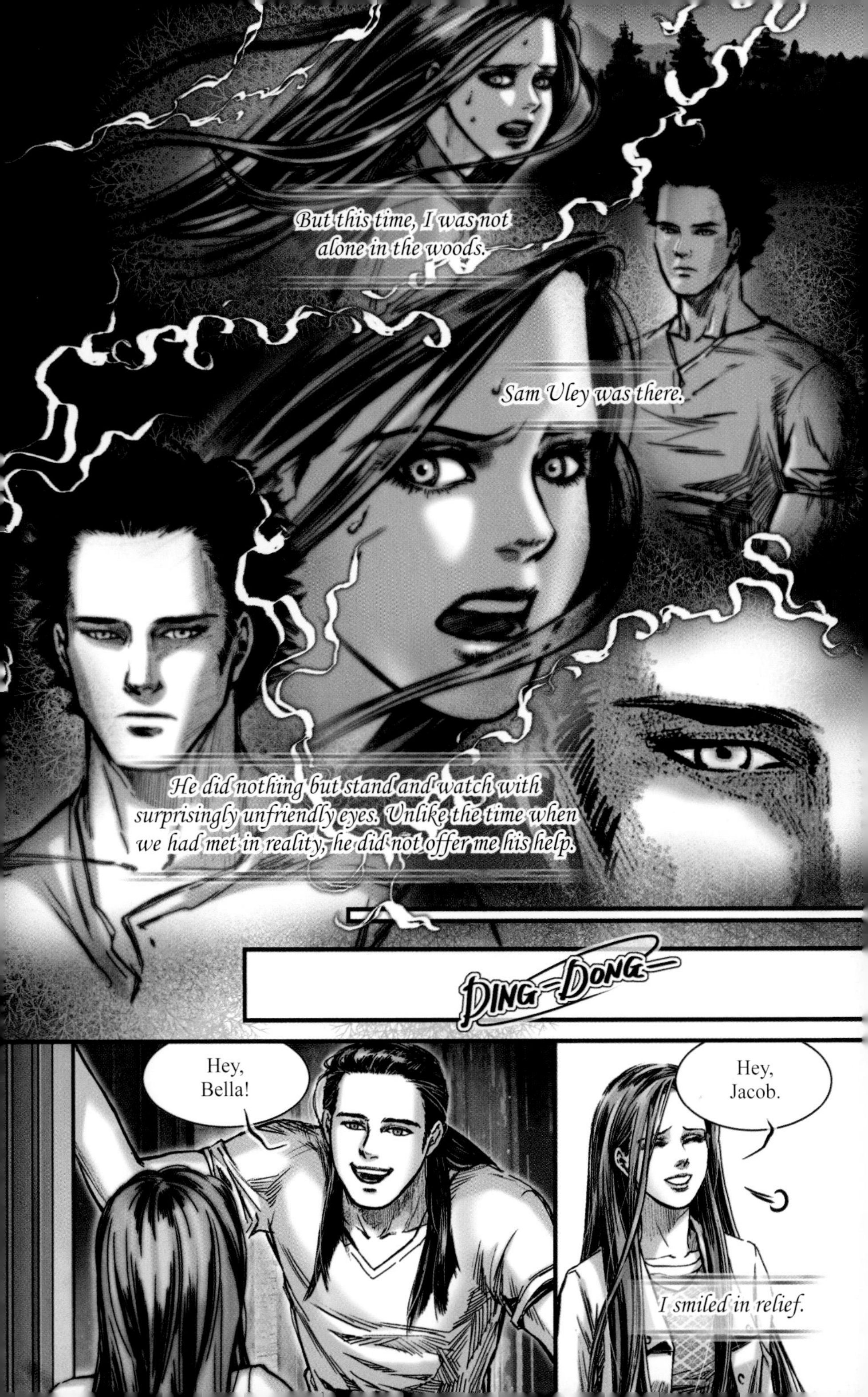
But this time, I was not alone in the woods.
Sam Uley was there.
He did nothing but stand and watch with surprisingly unfriendly eyes. Unlike the time when we had met in reality, he did not offer me his help.
DING-DONG
Hey, Bella!
Hey, Jacob.
I smiled in relief.

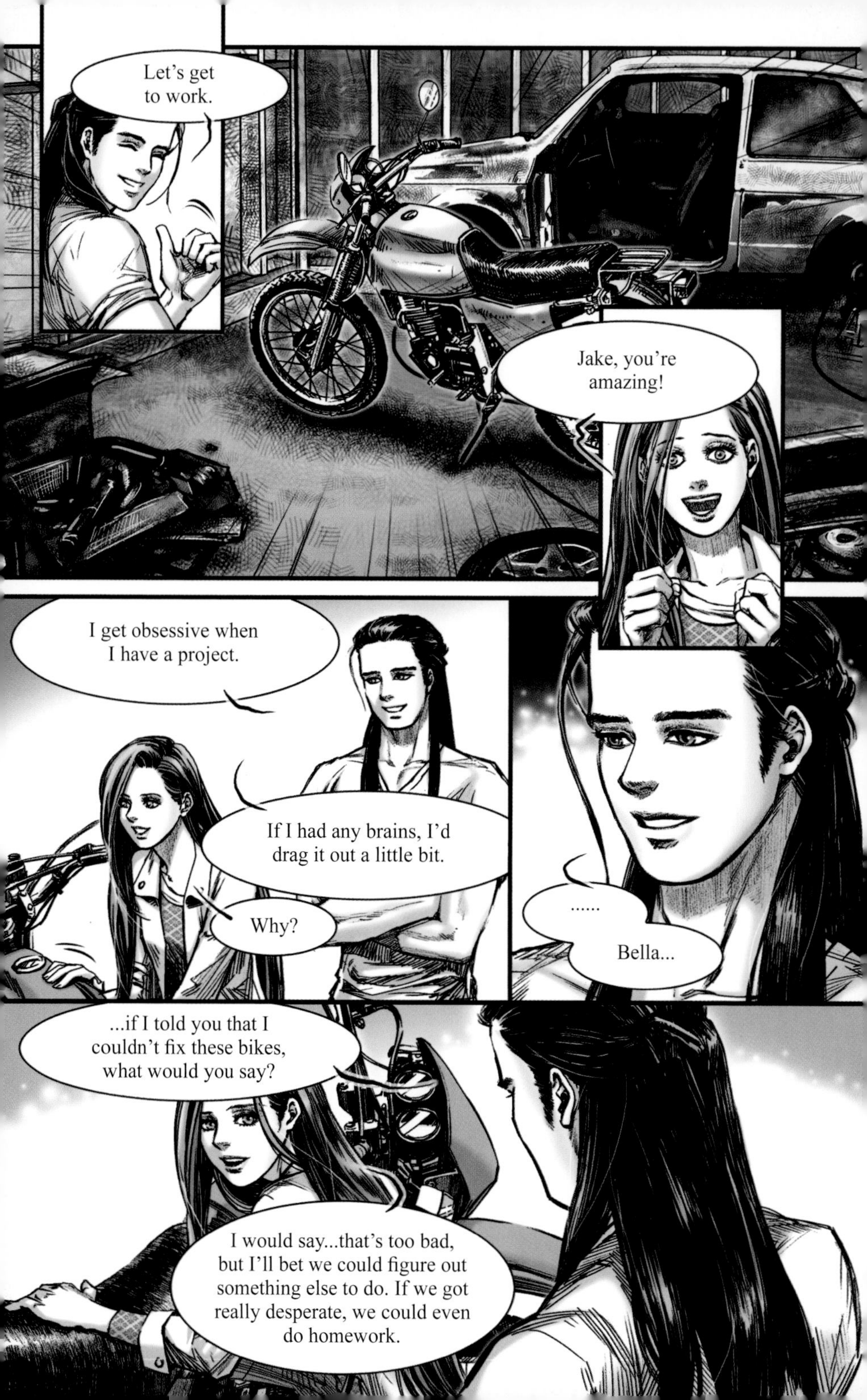

Let's get to work.
Jake, you're amazing!
I get obsessive when I have a project.
If I had any brains, I'd drag it out a little bit.
Why?
......
Bella...
...if I told you that I couldn't fix these bikes, what would you say?
I would say...that's too bad, but I'll bet we could figure out something else to do. If we got really desperate, we could even do homework.

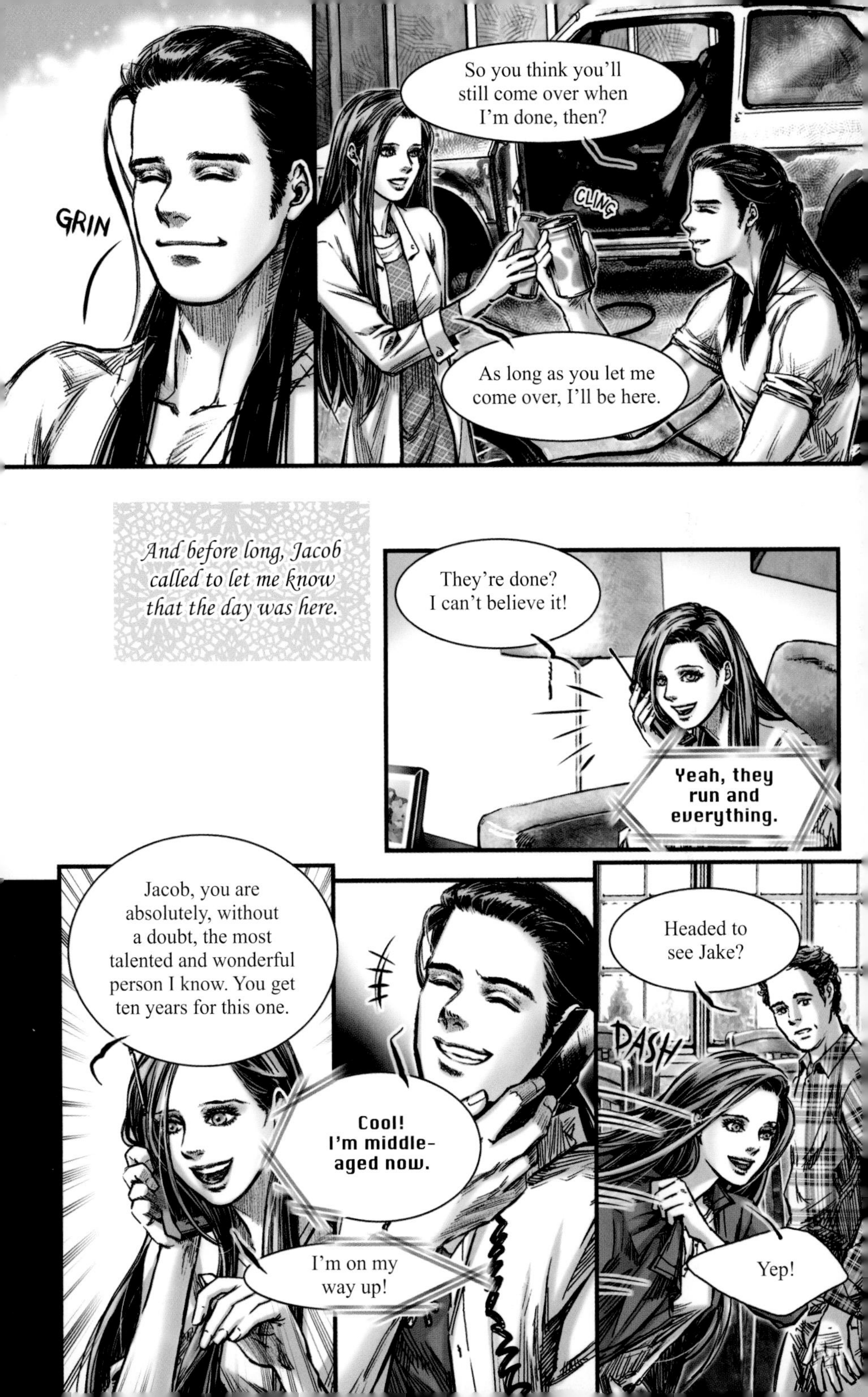
GRIN
So you think you'll still come over when I'm done, then?
CLING
As long as you let me come over, I'll be here.
And before long, Jacob called to let me know that the day was here.
They're done? I can't believe it!
Yeah, they run and everything.
Jacob, you are absolutely, without a doubt, the most talented and wonderful person I know. You get ten years for this one.
Cool! I'm middle-aged now.
I'm on my way up!
Headed to see Jake?
DASH
Yep!

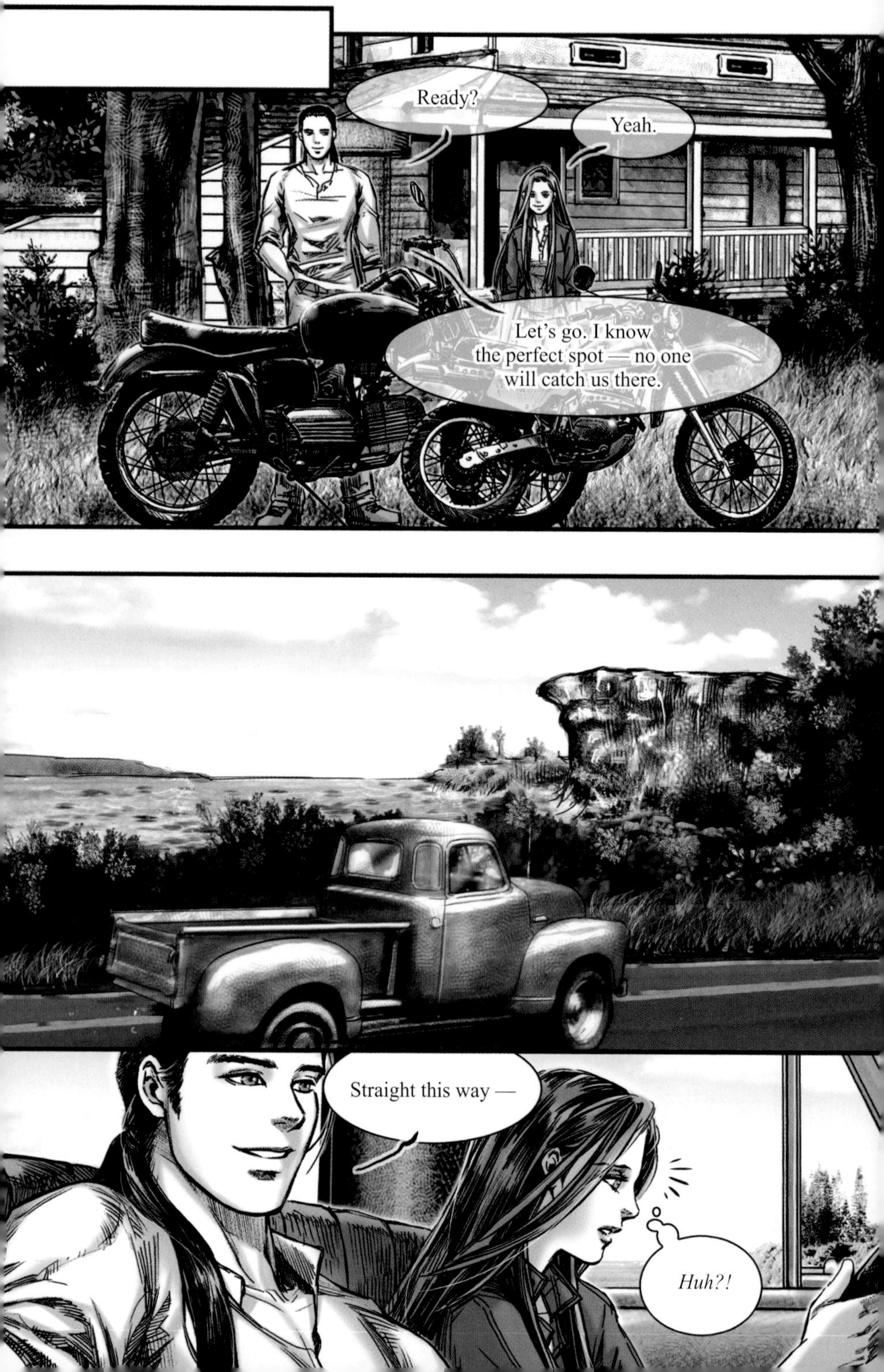
Ready?
Yeah.
Let's go. I know the perfect spot — no one will catch us there.
Straight this way —
Huh?!

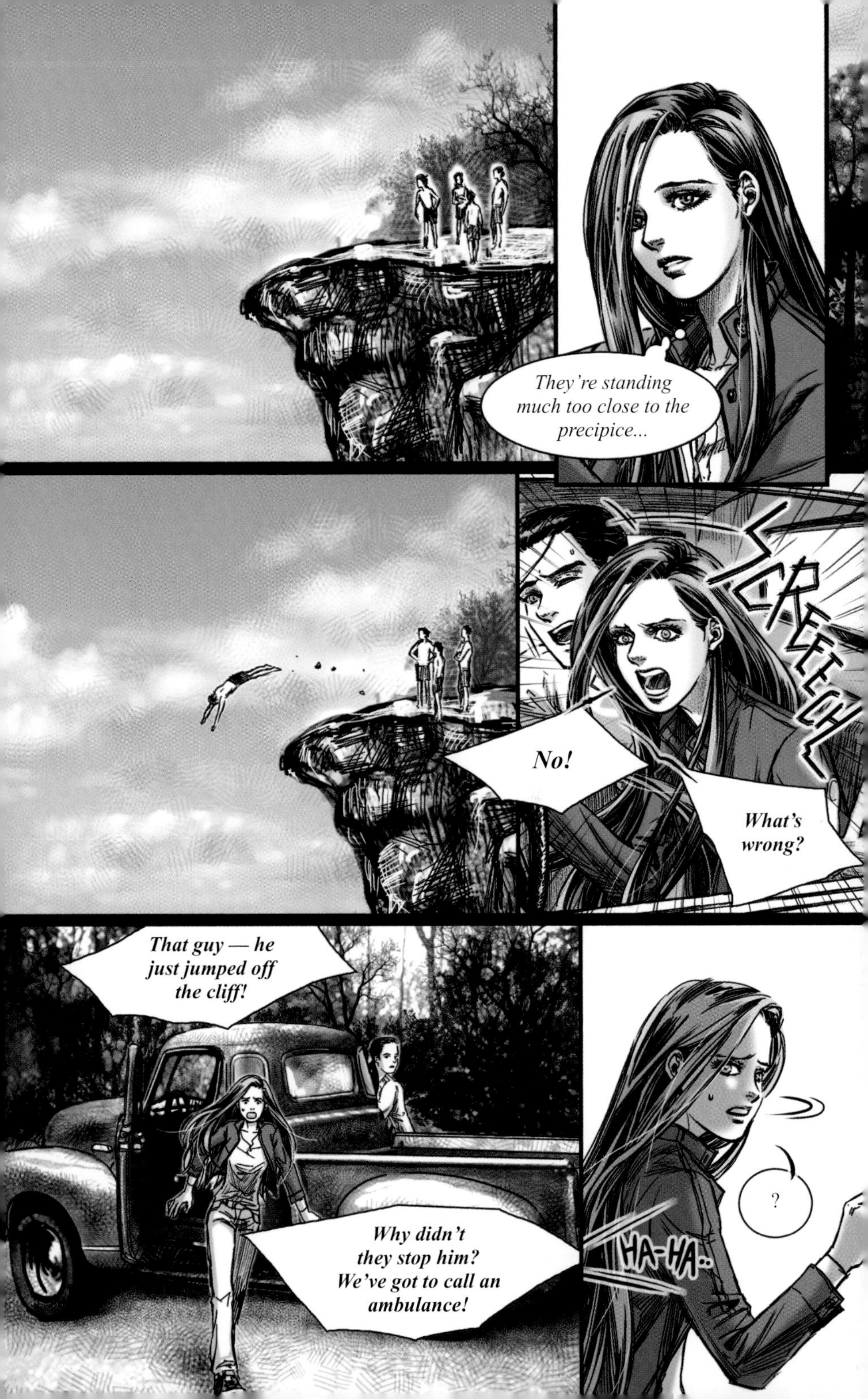
They're standing much too close to the precipice...
SCREECH
No!
What's wrong?
That guy — he just jumped off the cliff!
Why didn't they stop him? We've got to call an ambulance!
HA-HA..
?

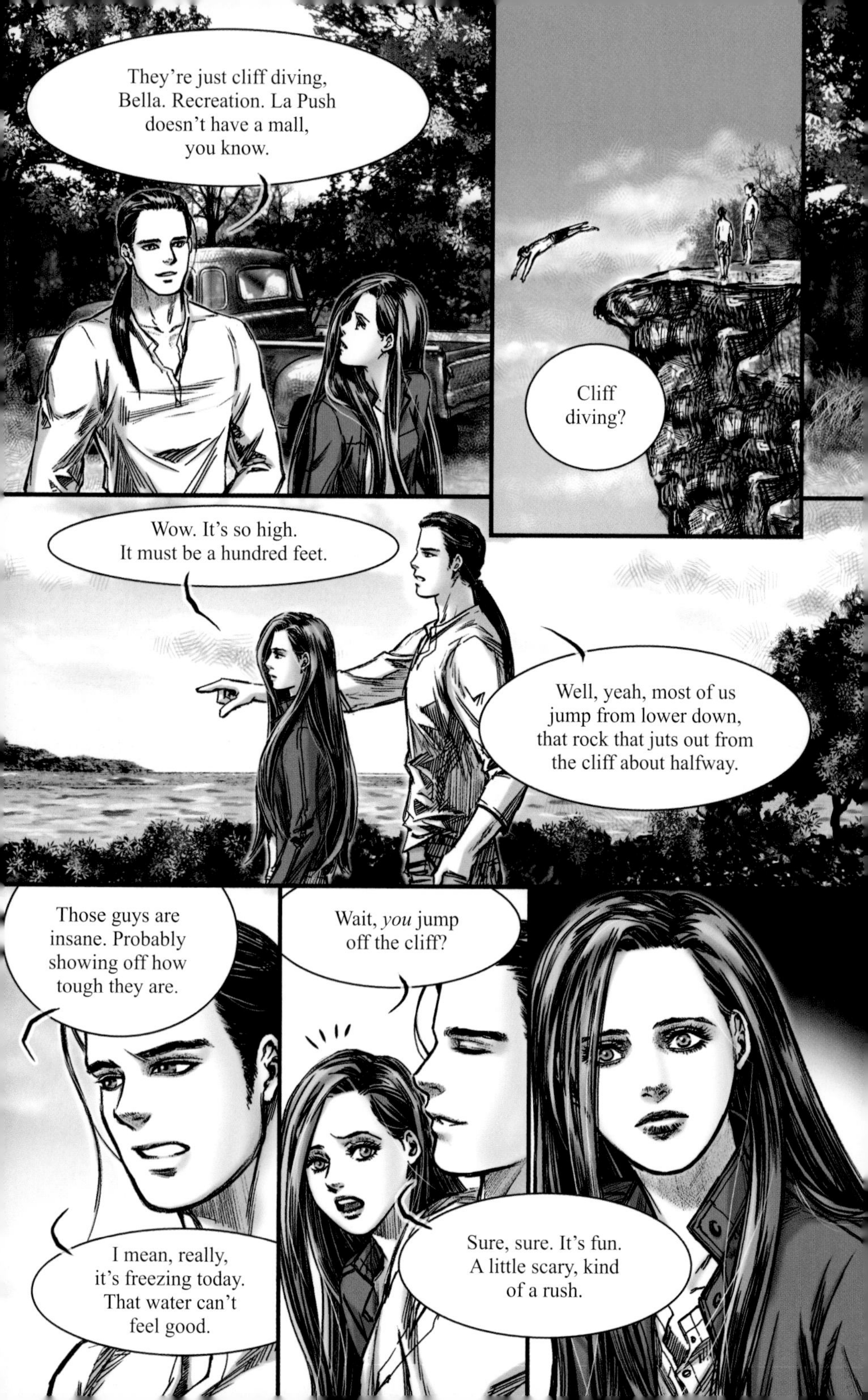
They're just cliff diving, Bella. Recreation. La Push doesn't have a mall, you know.
Cliff diving?
Wow. It's so high. It must be a hundred feet.
Well, yeah, most of us jump from lower down, that rock that juts out from the cliff about halfway.
Those guys are insane. Probably showing off how tough they are.
I mean, really, it's freezing today. That water can't feel good.
Wait, *you* jump off the cliff?
Sure, sure. It's fun. A little scary, kind of a rush.

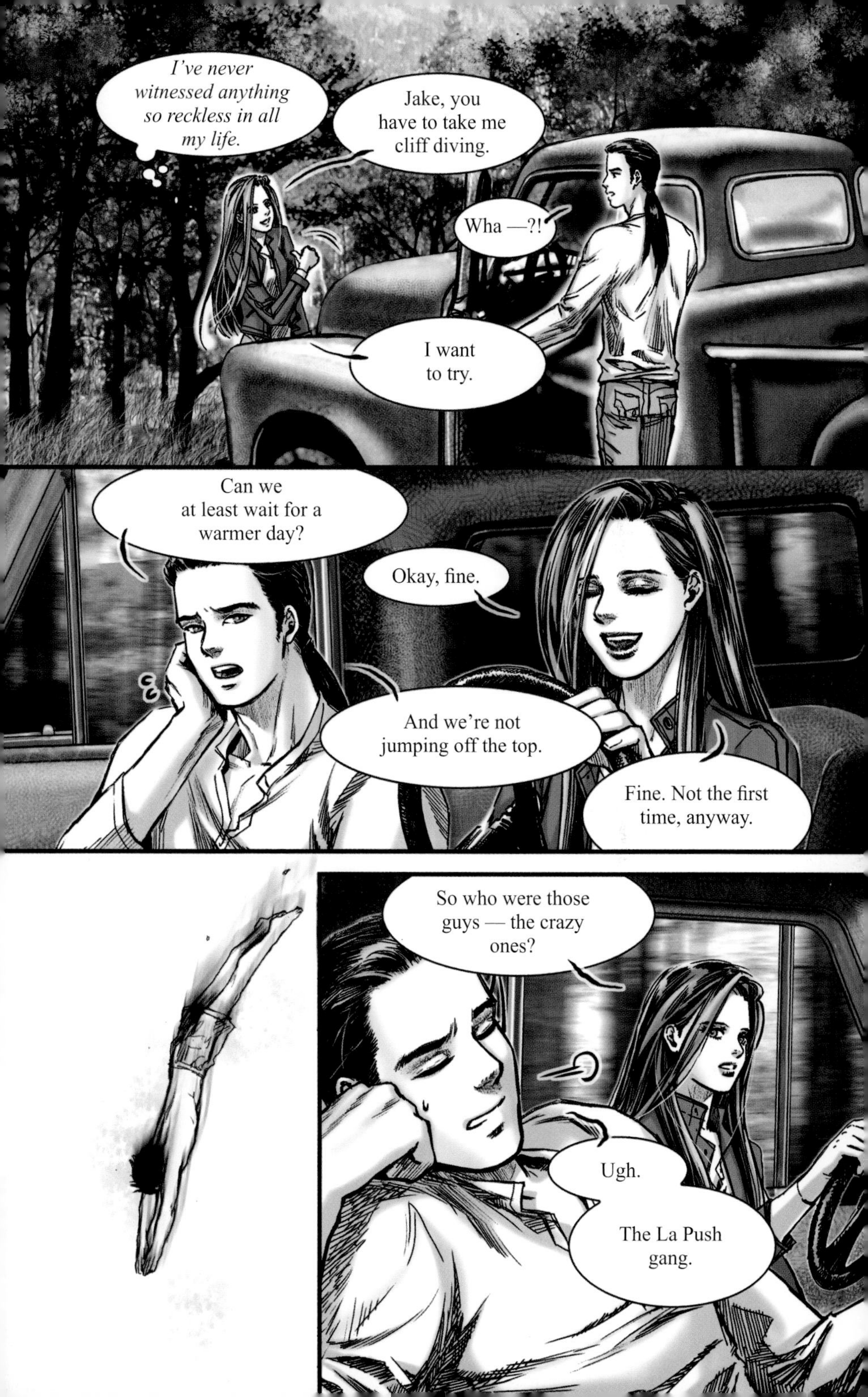
I've never witnessed anything so reckless in all my life.
Jake, you have to take me cliff diving.
Wha —?!
I want to try.
Can we at least wait for a warmer day?
Okay, fine.
And we're not jumping off the top.
Fine. Not the first time, anyway.
So who were those guys — the crazy ones?
Ugh.
The La Push gang.

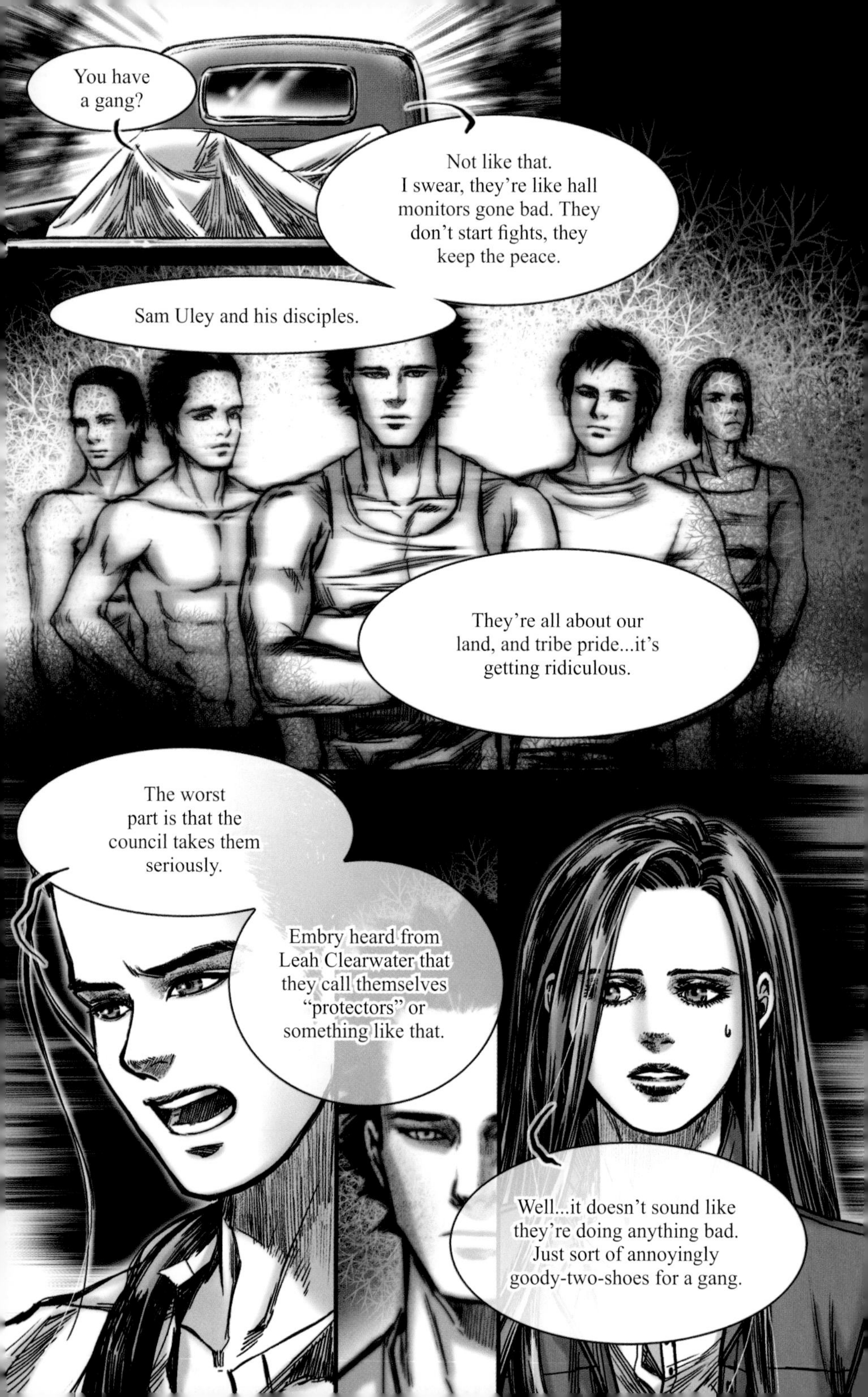
You have a gang?
Not like that. I swear, they're like hall monitors gone bad. They don't start fights, they keep the peace.
Sam Uley and his disciples.
They're all about our land, and tribe pride...it's getting ridiculous.
The worst part is that the council takes them seriously.
Embry heard from Leah Clearwater that they call themselves "protectors" or something like that.
Well...it doesn't sound like they're doing anything bad. Just sort of annoyingly goody-two-shoes for a gang.

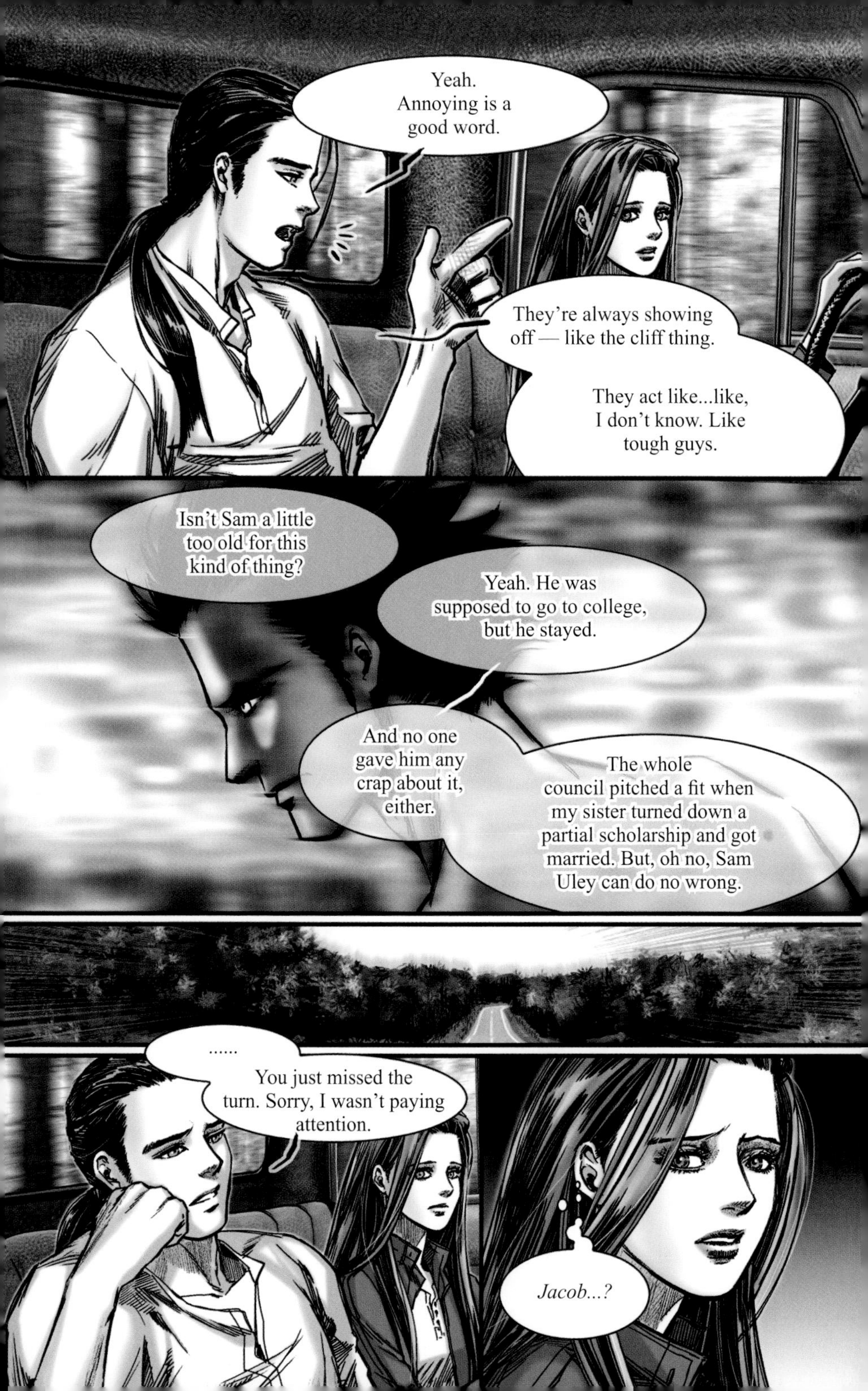
Yeah. Annoying is a good word.
They're always showing off — like the cliff thing.
They act like...like, I don't know. Like tough guys.
Isn't Sam a little too old for this kind of thing?
Yeah. He was supposed to go to college, but he stayed.
And no one gave him any crap about it, either.
The whole council pitched a fit when my sister turned down a partial scholarship and got married. But, oh no, Sam Uley can do no wrong.
......
You just missed the turn. Sorry, I wasn't paying attention.
Jacob...?

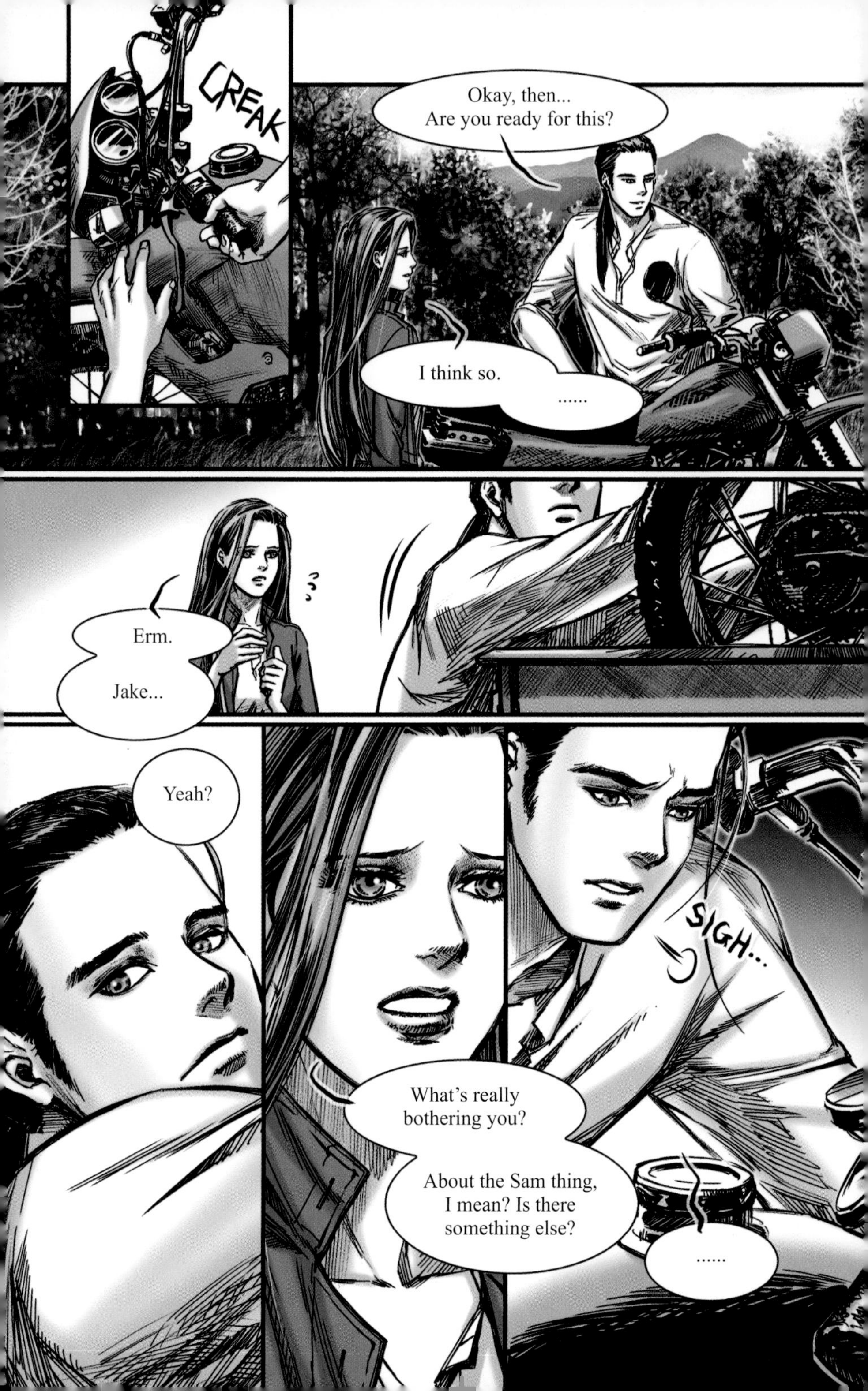
CREAK
Okay, then... Are you ready for this?
I think so.
......
Erm.
Jake...
Yeah?
SIGH...
What's really bothering you?
About the Sam thing, I mean? Is there something else?
......

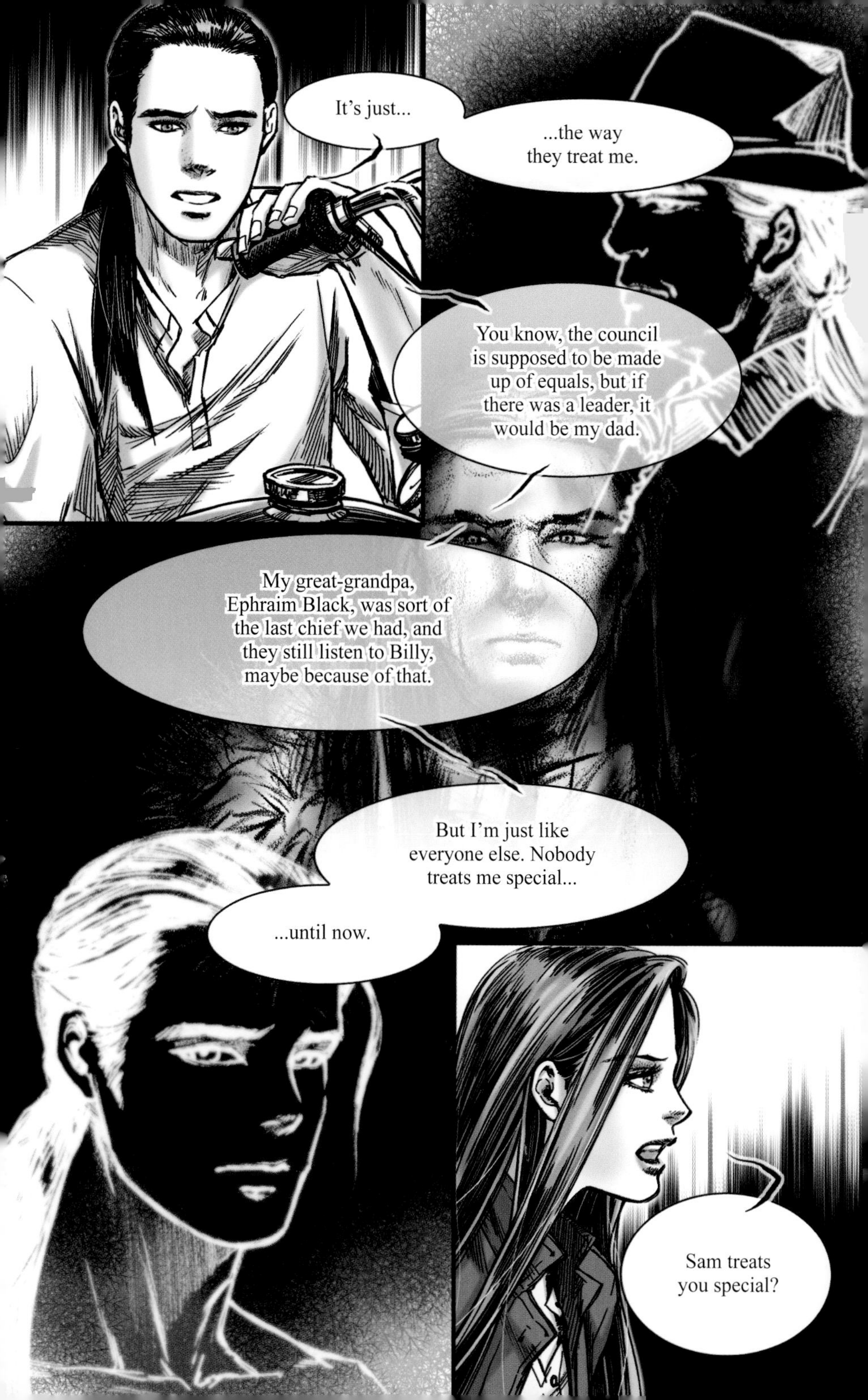
It's just...
...the way they treat me.
You know, the council is supposed to be made up of equals, but if there was a leader, it would be my dad.
My great-grandpa, Ephraim Black, was sort of the last chief we had, and they still listen to Billy, maybe because of that.
But I'm just like everyone else. Nobody treats me special...
...until now.
Sam treats you special?

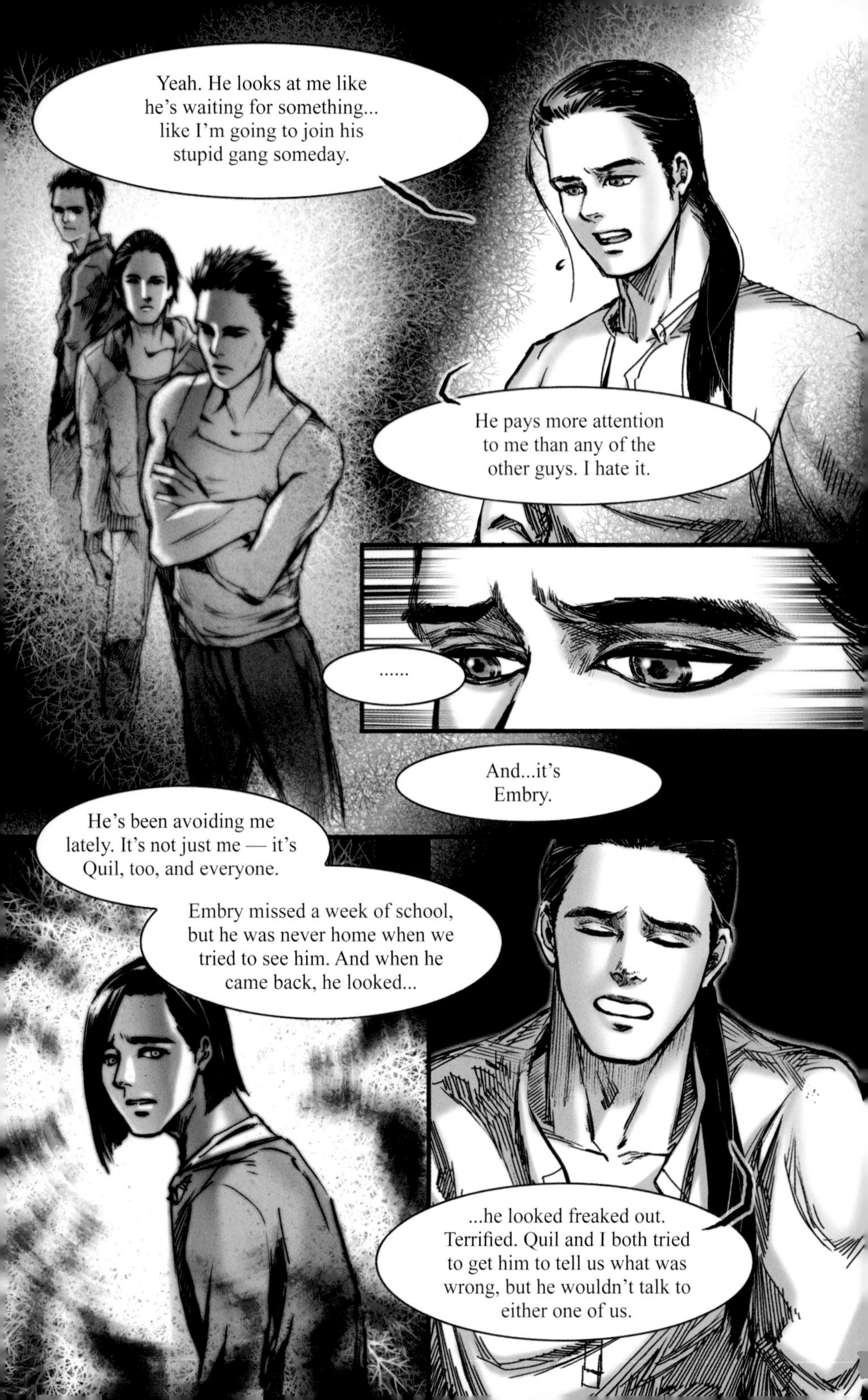
Yeah. He looks at me like he's waiting for something... like I'm going to join his stupid gang someday.
He pays more attention to me than any of the other guys. I hate it.
......
And...it's Embry.
He's been avoiding me lately. It's not just me — it's Quil, too, and everyone.
Embry missed a week of school, but he was never home when we tried to see him. And when he came back, he looked...
...he looked freaked out. Terrified. Quil and I both tried to get him to tell us what was wrong, but he wouldn't talk to either one of us.

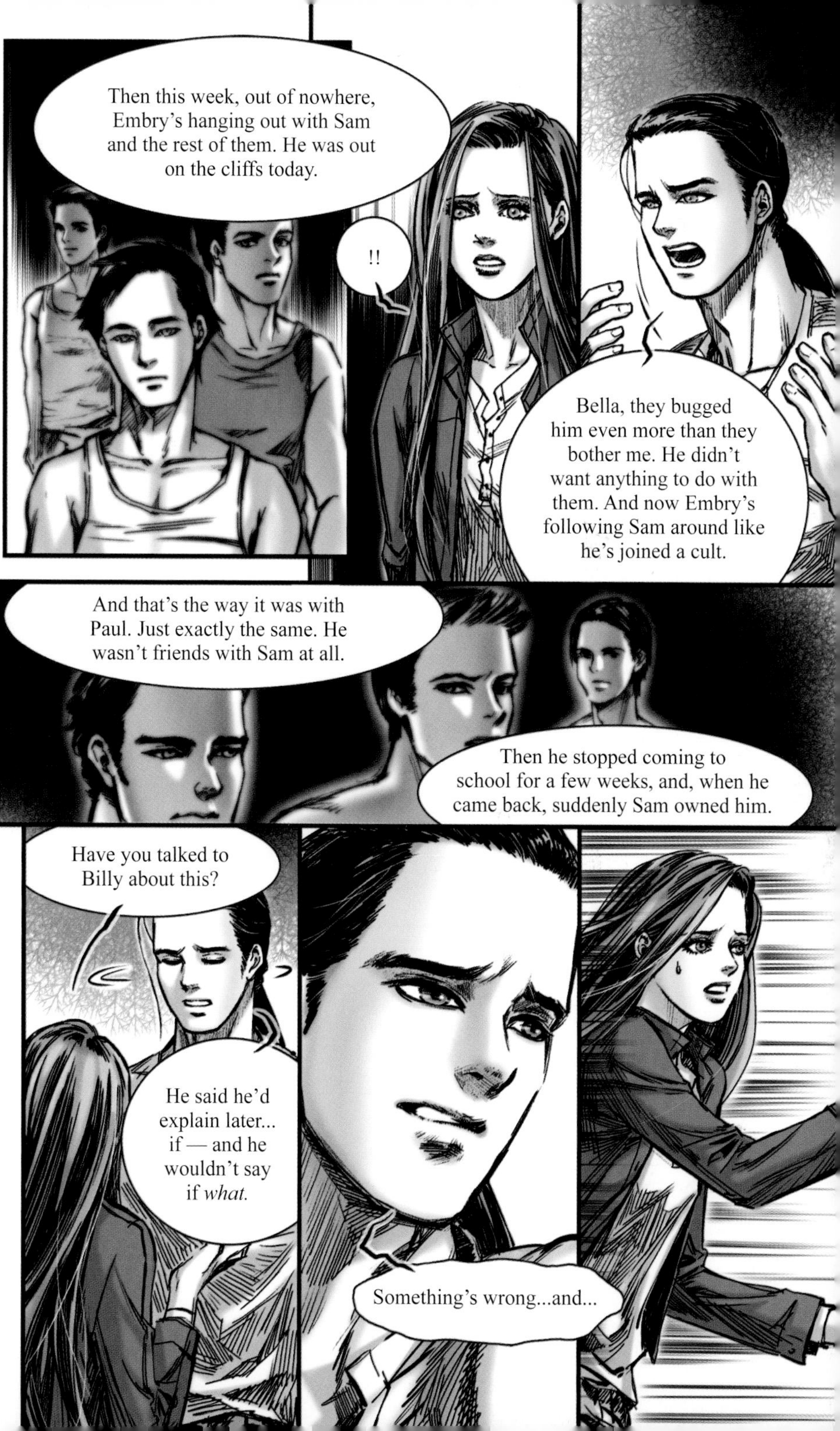
Then this week, out of nowhere, Embry's hanging out with Sam and the rest of them. He was out on the cliffs today.
!!
Bella, they bugged him even more than they bother me. He didn't want anything to do with them. And now Embry's following Sam around like he's joined a cult.
And that's the way it was with Paul. Just exactly the same. He wasn't friends with Sam at all.
Then he stopped coming to school for a few weeks, and, when he came back, suddenly Sam owned him.
Have you talked to Billy about this?
He said he'd explain later... if — and he wouldn't say if *what.*
Something's wrong...and...

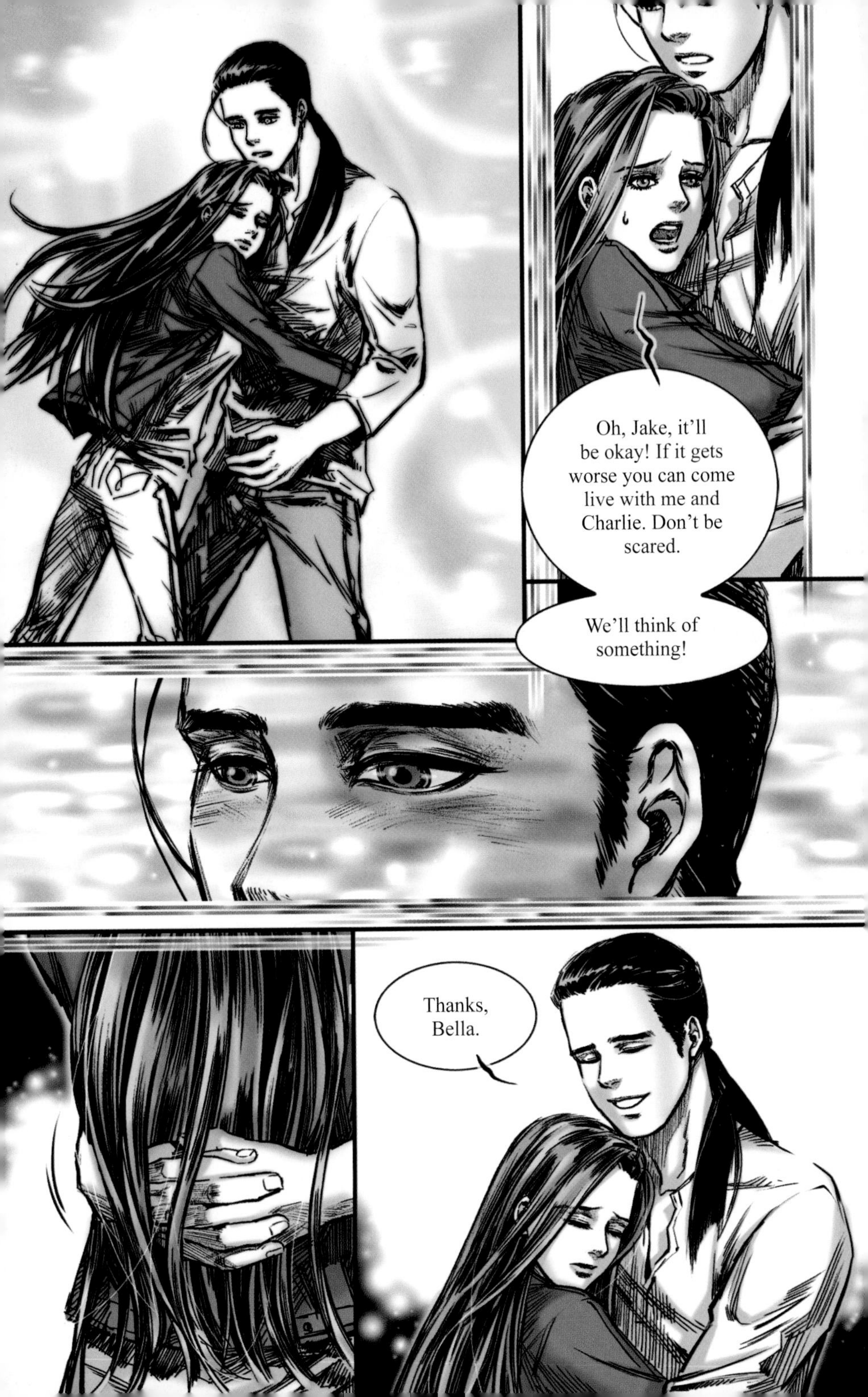
Oh, Jake, it'll be okay! If it gets worse you can come live with me and Charlie. Don't be scared.
We'll think of something!
Thanks, Bella.

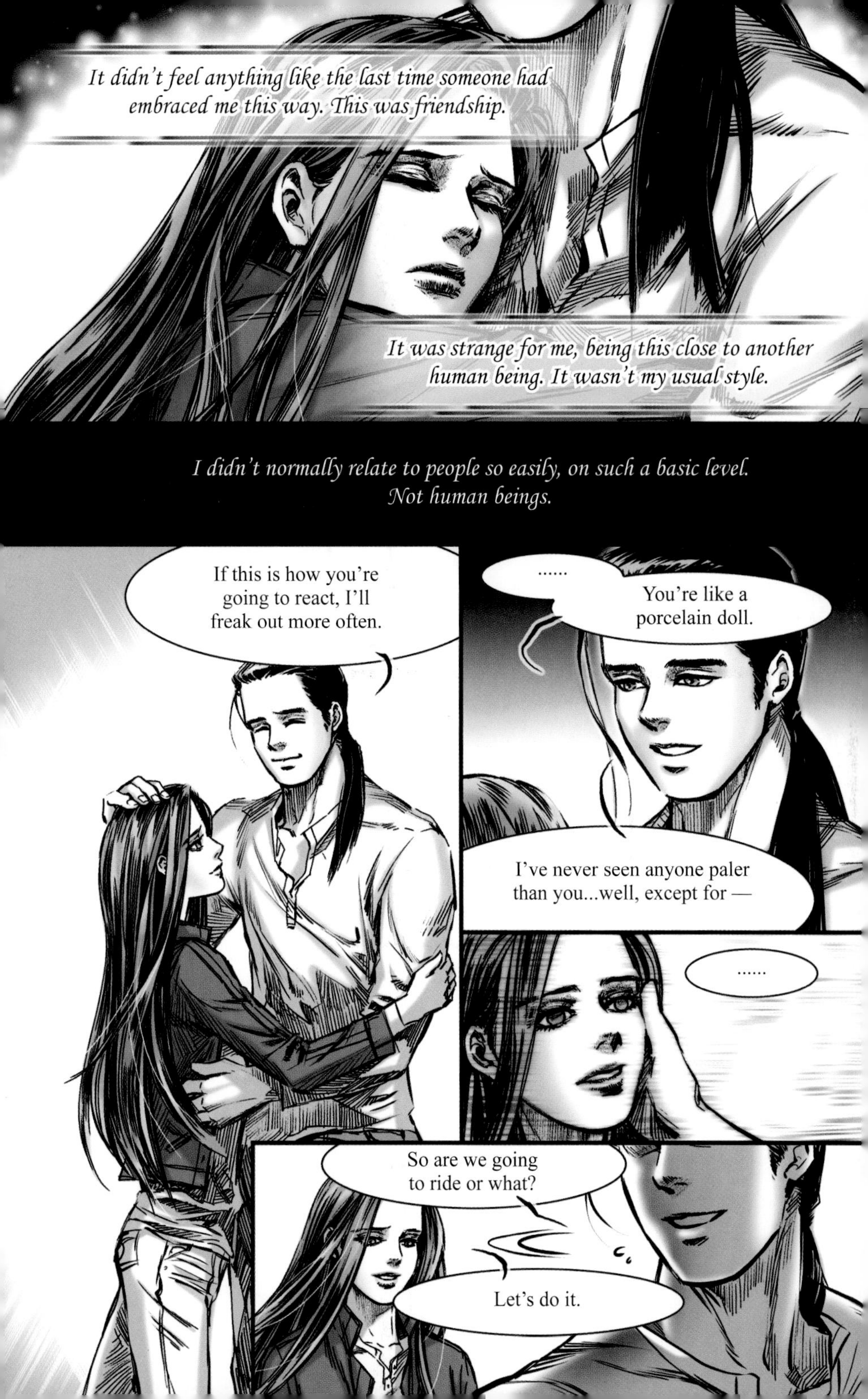
It didn't feel anything like the last time someone had embraced me this way. This was friendship.
It was strange for me, being this close to another human being. It wasn't my usual style.
I didn't normally relate to people so easily, on such a basic level. Not human beings.
If this is how you're going to react, I'll freak out more often.
......
You're like a porcelain doll.
I've never seen anyone paler than you...well, except for —
......
So are we going to ride or what?
Let's do it.

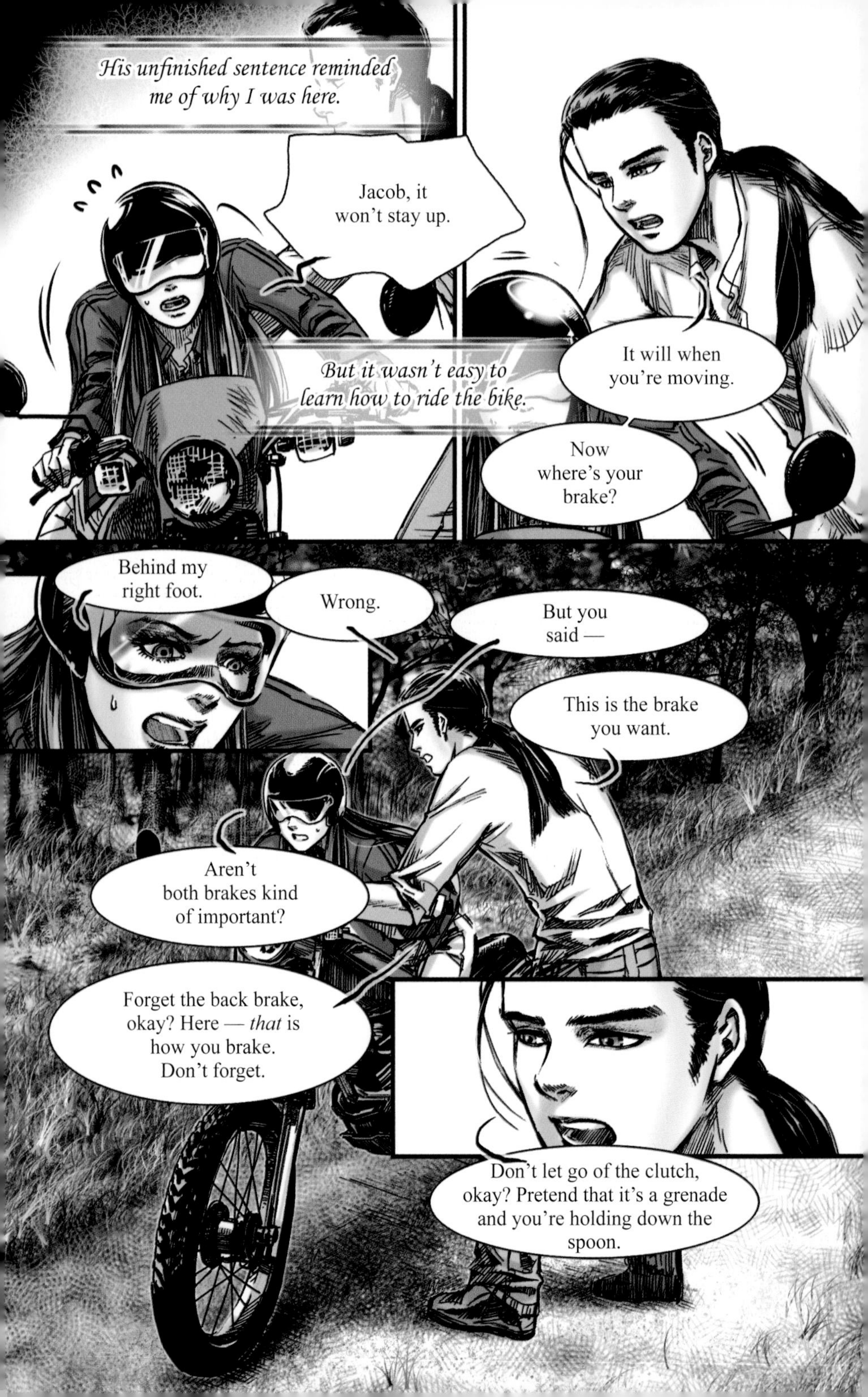
His unfinished sentence reminded me of why I was here.
Jacob, it won't stay up.
But it wasn't easy to learn how to ride the bike.
It will when you're moving.
Now where's your brake?
Behind my right foot.
Wrong.
But you said —
This is the brake you want.
Aren't both brakes kind of important?
Forget the back brake, okay? Here — *that* is how you brake. Don't forget.
Don't let go of the clutch, okay? Pretend that it's a grenade and you're holding down the spoon.

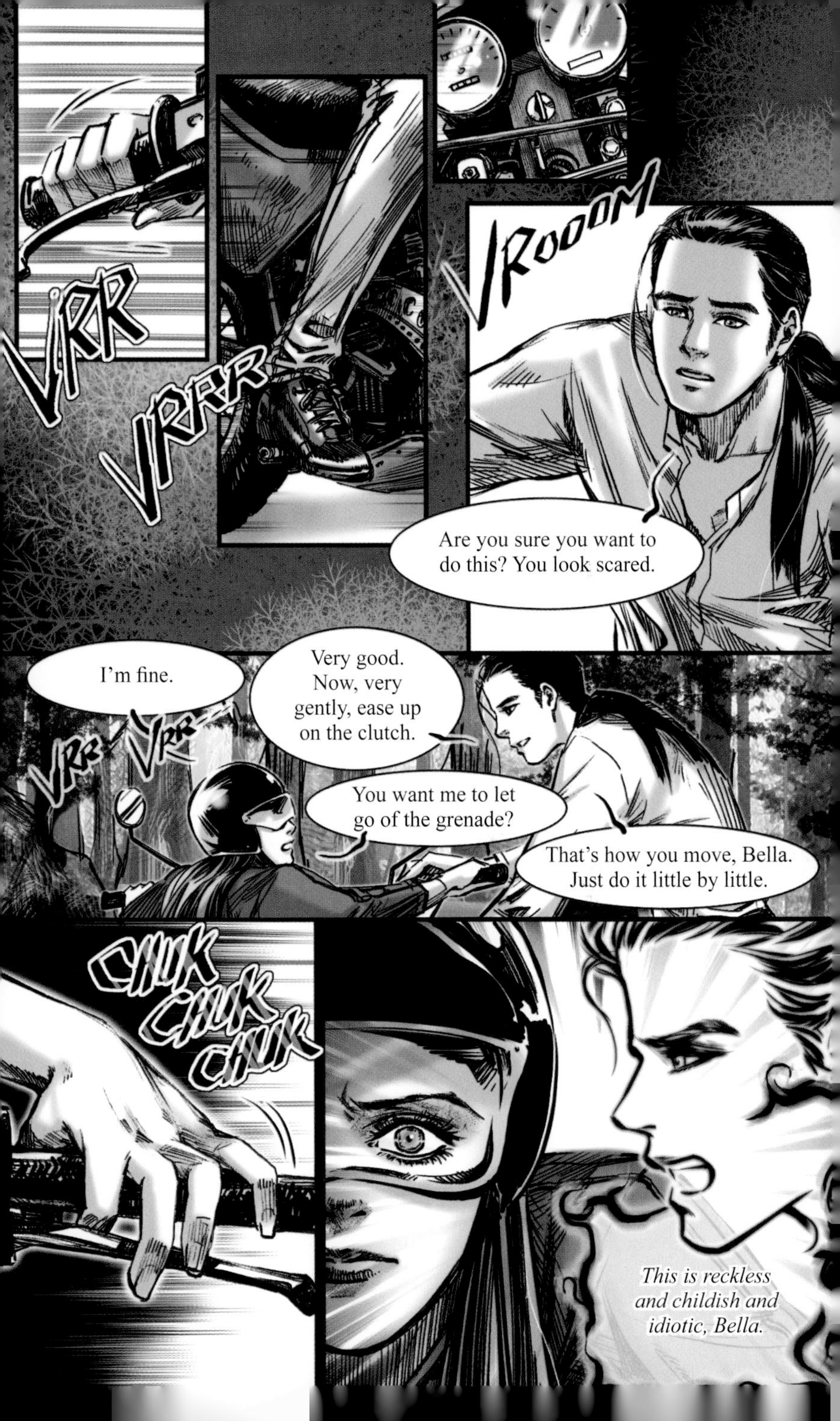
VRR
VRRR
VROOOM
Are you sure you want to do this? You look scared.
I'm fine.
VRR VRR
Very good. Now, very gently, ease up on the clutch.
You want me to let go of the grenade?
That's how you move, Bella. Just do it little by little.
CHUK CHUK CHUK
This is reckless and childish and idiotic, Bella.

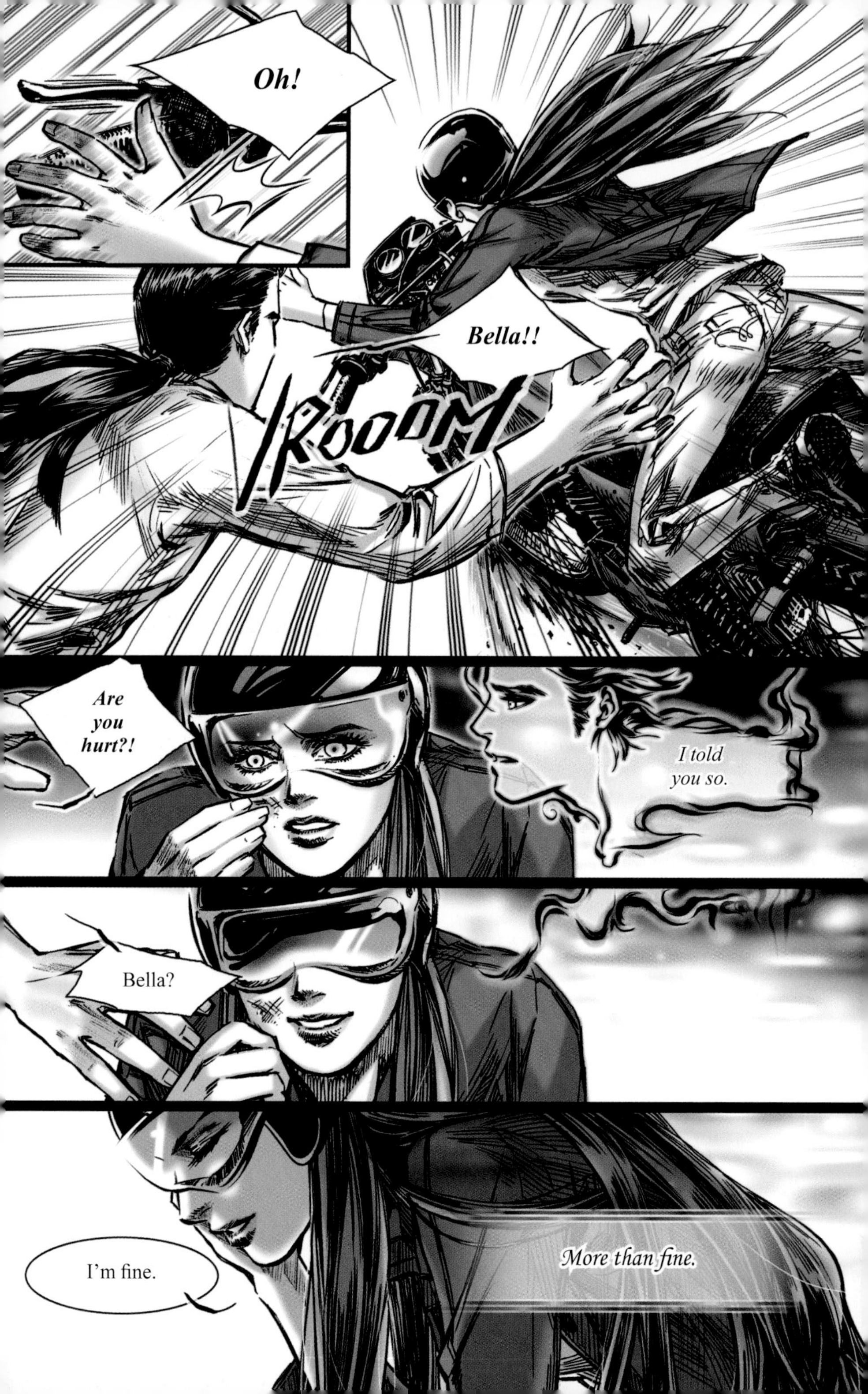
Oh!
Bella!!
ROOOM
Are you hurt?!
I told you so.
Bella?
I'm fine.
More than fine.

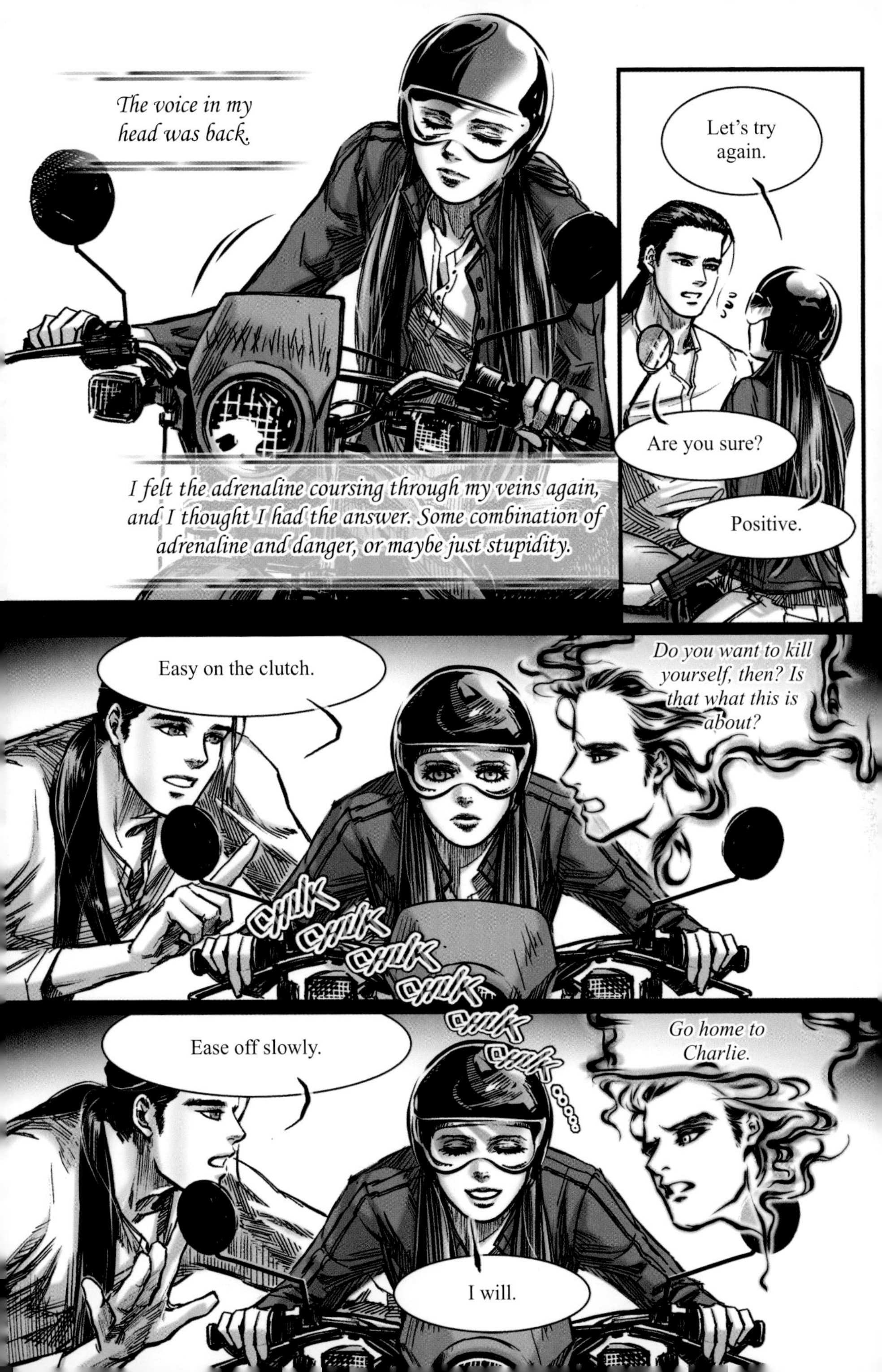
The voice in my head was back.
Let's try again.
Are you sure?
Positive.
I felt the adrenaline coursing through my veins again, and I thought I had the answer. Some combination of adrenaline and danger, or maybe just stupidity.
Easy on the clutch.
Do you want to kill yourself, then? Is that what this is about?
Ease off slowly.
Go home to Charlie.
I will.

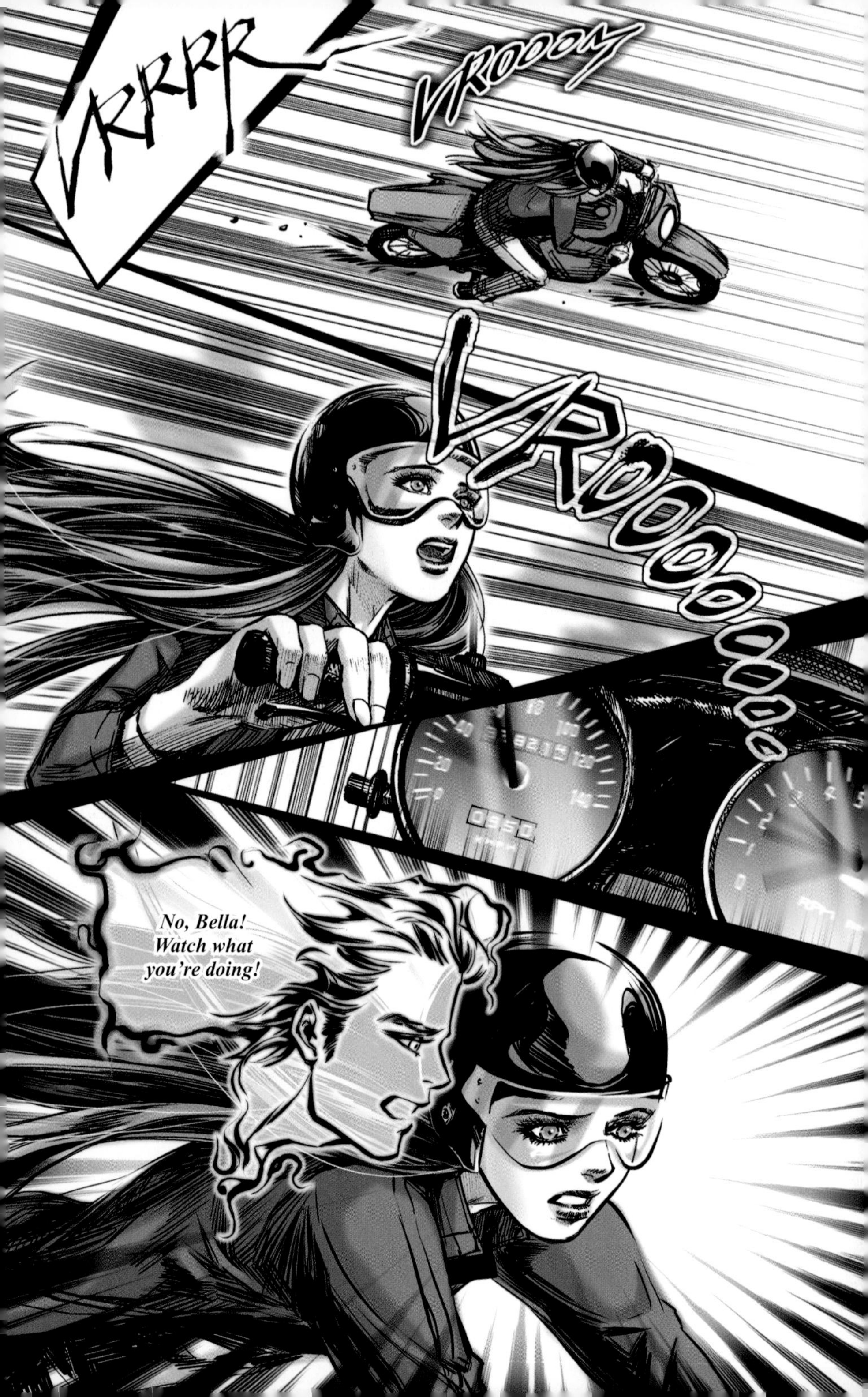
VRRRR
VROOOM
VROOOOOOOOOOOO
No, Bella! Watch what you're doing!

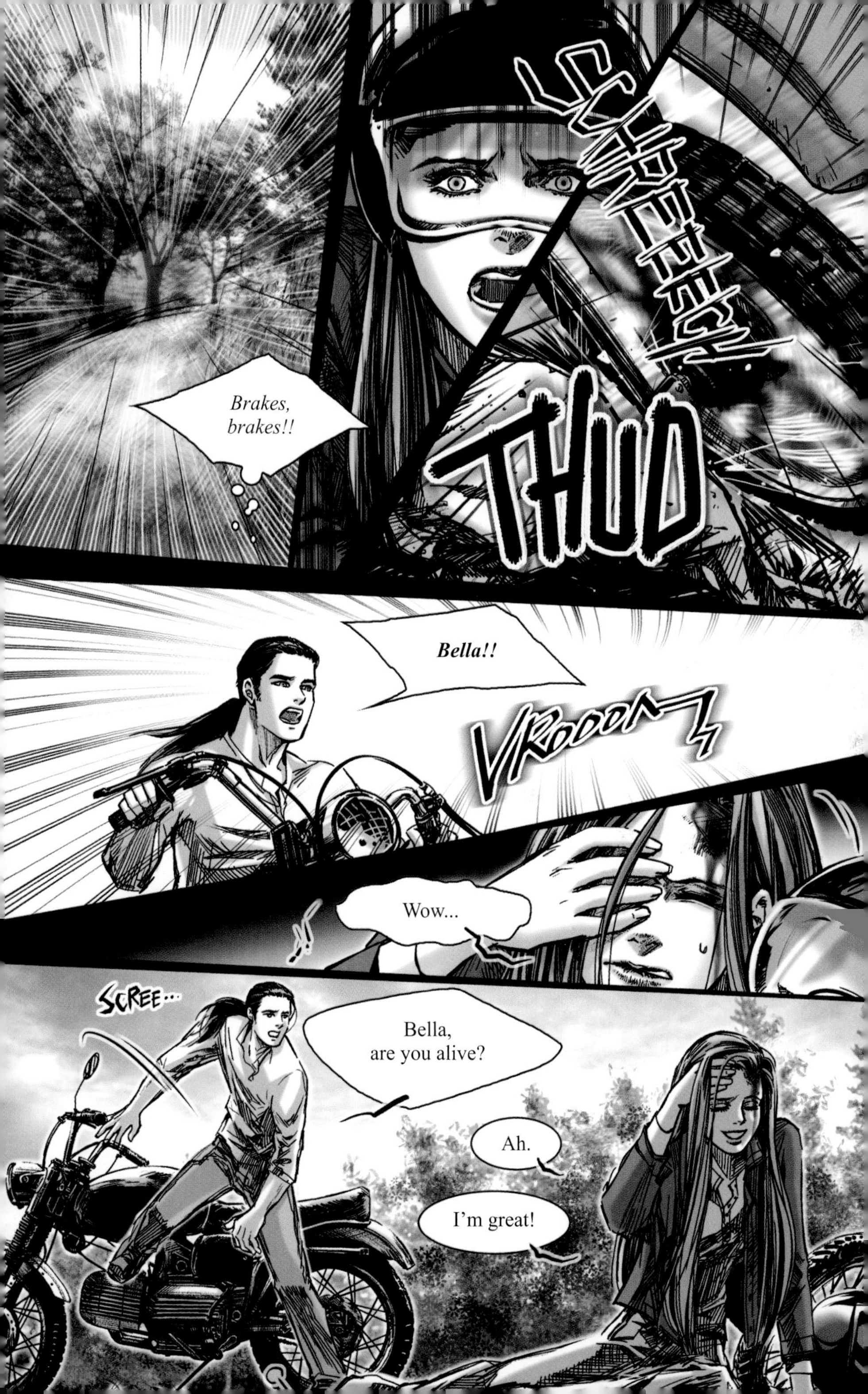
SCREECH!
Brakes, brakes!!
THUD
Bella!!
VROOOM
Wow...
SCREE...
Bella, are you alive?
Ah.
I'm great!

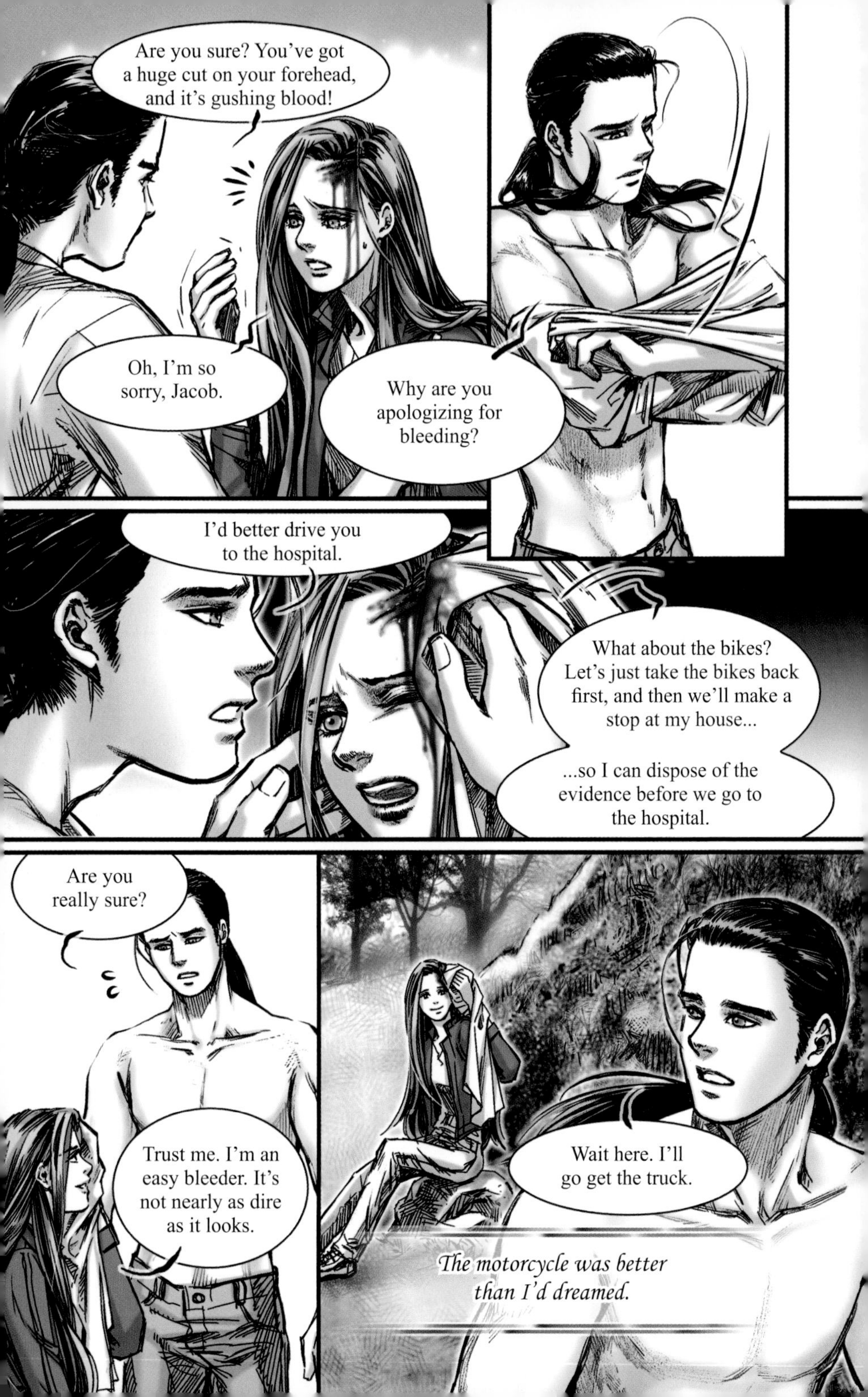
Are you sure? You've got a huge cut on your forehead, and it's gushing blood!
Oh, I'm so sorry, Jacob.
Why are you apologizing for bleeding?
I'd better drive you to the hospital.
What about the bikes? Let's just take the bikes back first, and then we'll make a stop at my house...
...so I can dispose of the evidence before we go to the hospital.
Are you really sure?
Trust me. I'm an easy bleeder. It's not nearly as dire as it looks.
Wait here. I'll go get the truck.
The motorcycle was better than I'd dreamed.

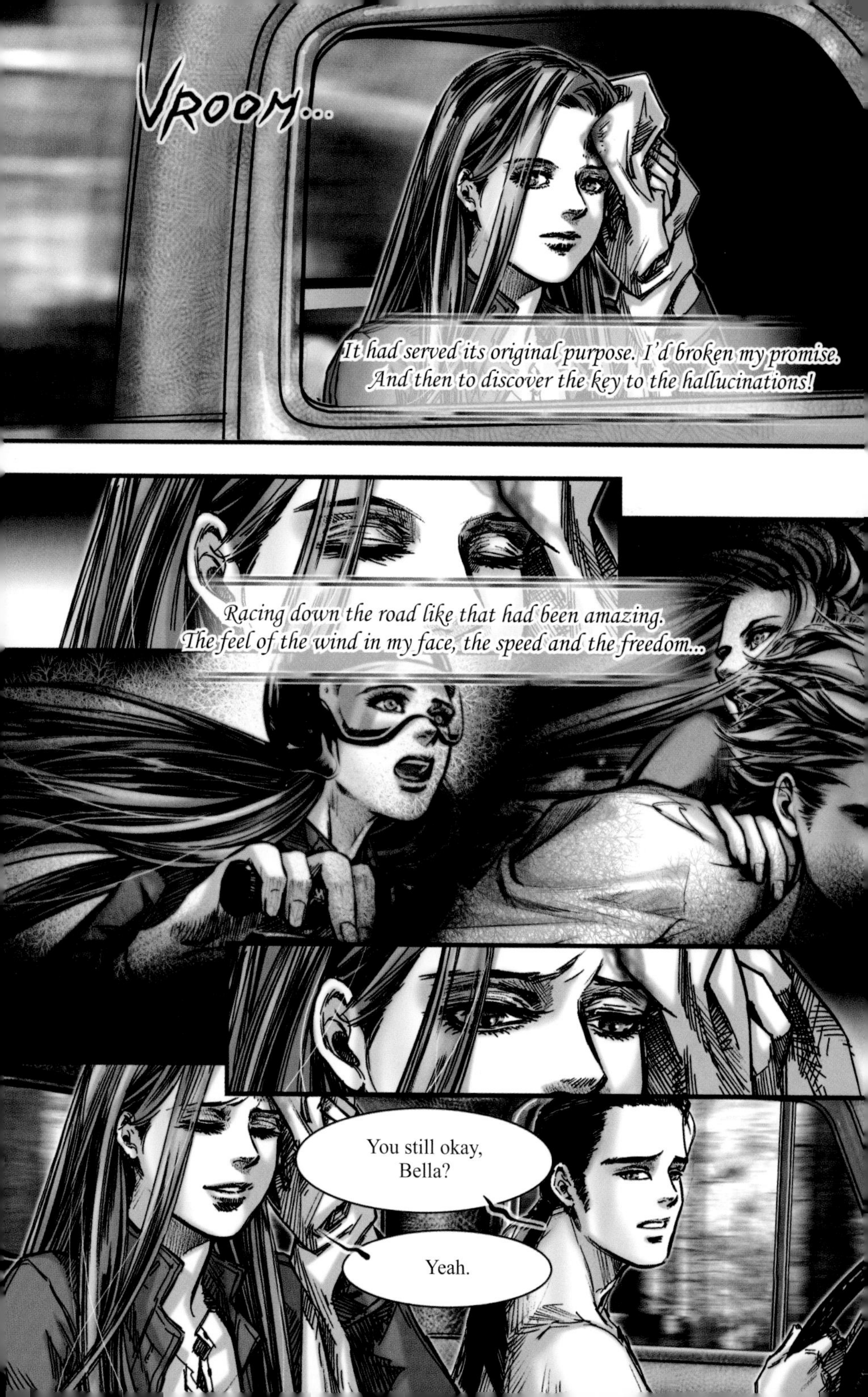
VROOM...
It had served its original purpose. I'd broken my promise.
And then to discover the key to the hallucinations!
Racing down the road like that had been amazing.
The feel of the wind in my face, the speed and the freedom...
You still okay, Bella?
Yeah.

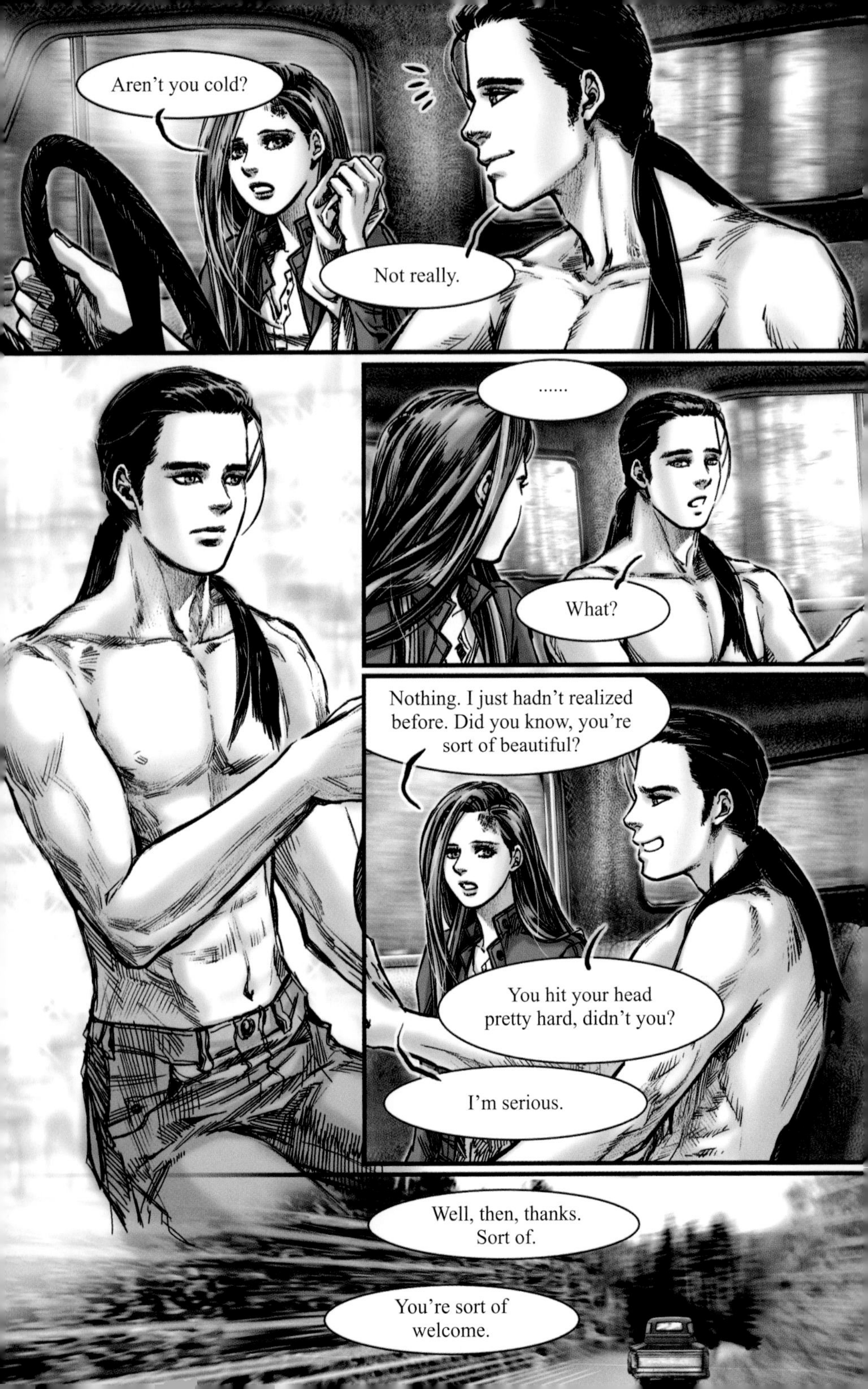
Aren't you cold?
Not really.
......
What?
Nothing. I just hadn't realized before. Did you know, you're sort of beautiful?
You hit your head pretty hard, didn't you?
I'm serious.
Well, then, thanks. Sort of.
You're sort of welcome.

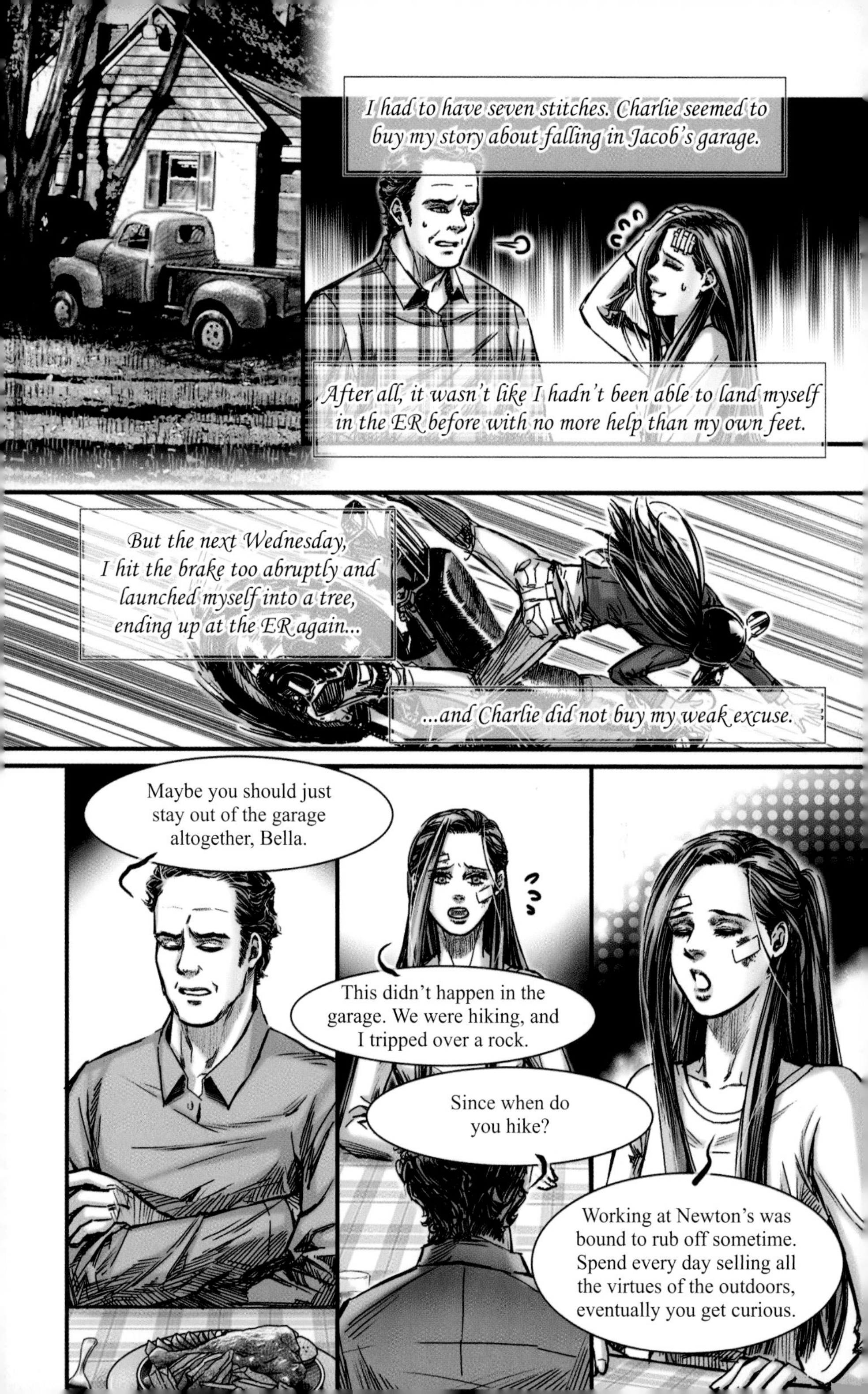
I had to have seven stitches. Charlie seemed to buy my story about falling in Jacob's garage.
After all, it wasn't like I hadn't been able to land myself in the ER before with no more help than my own feet.
But the next Wednesday, I hit the brake too abruptly and launched myself into a tree, ending up at the ER again...
...and Charlie did not buy my weak excuse.
Maybe you should just stay out of the garage altogether, Bella.
This didn't happen in the garage. We were hiking, and I tripped over a rock.
Since when do you hike?
Working at Newton's was bound to rub off sometime. Spend every day selling all the virtues of the outdoors, eventually you get curious.

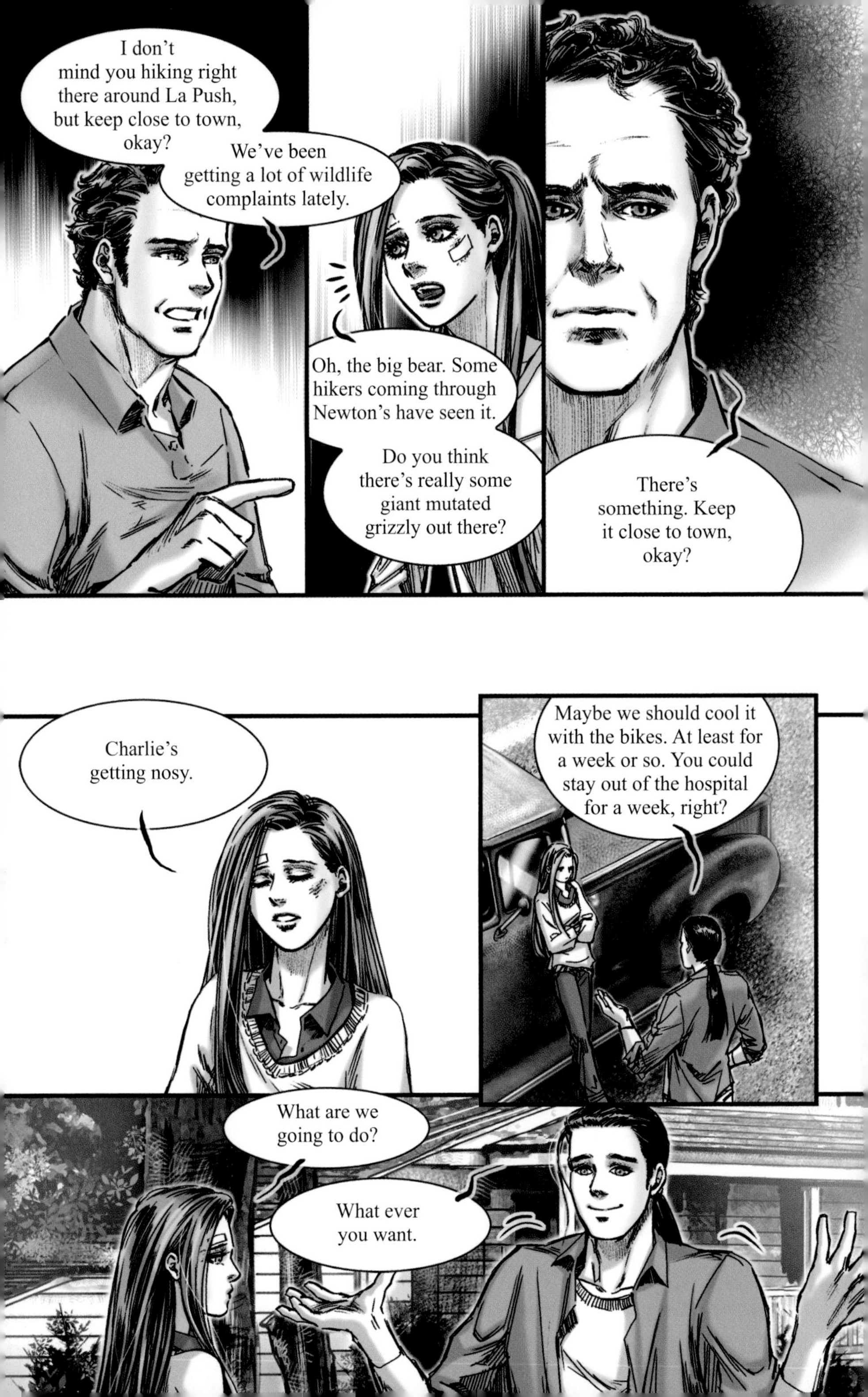
I don't mind you hiking right there around La Push, but keep close to town, okay?
We've been getting a lot of wildlife complaints lately.
Oh, the big bear. Some hikers coming through Newton's have seen it.
Do you think there's really some giant mutated grizzly out there?
There's something. Keep it close to town, okay?
Charlie's getting nosy.
Maybe we should cool it with the bikes. At least for a week or so. You could stay out of the hospital for a week, right?
What are we going to do?
What ever you want.

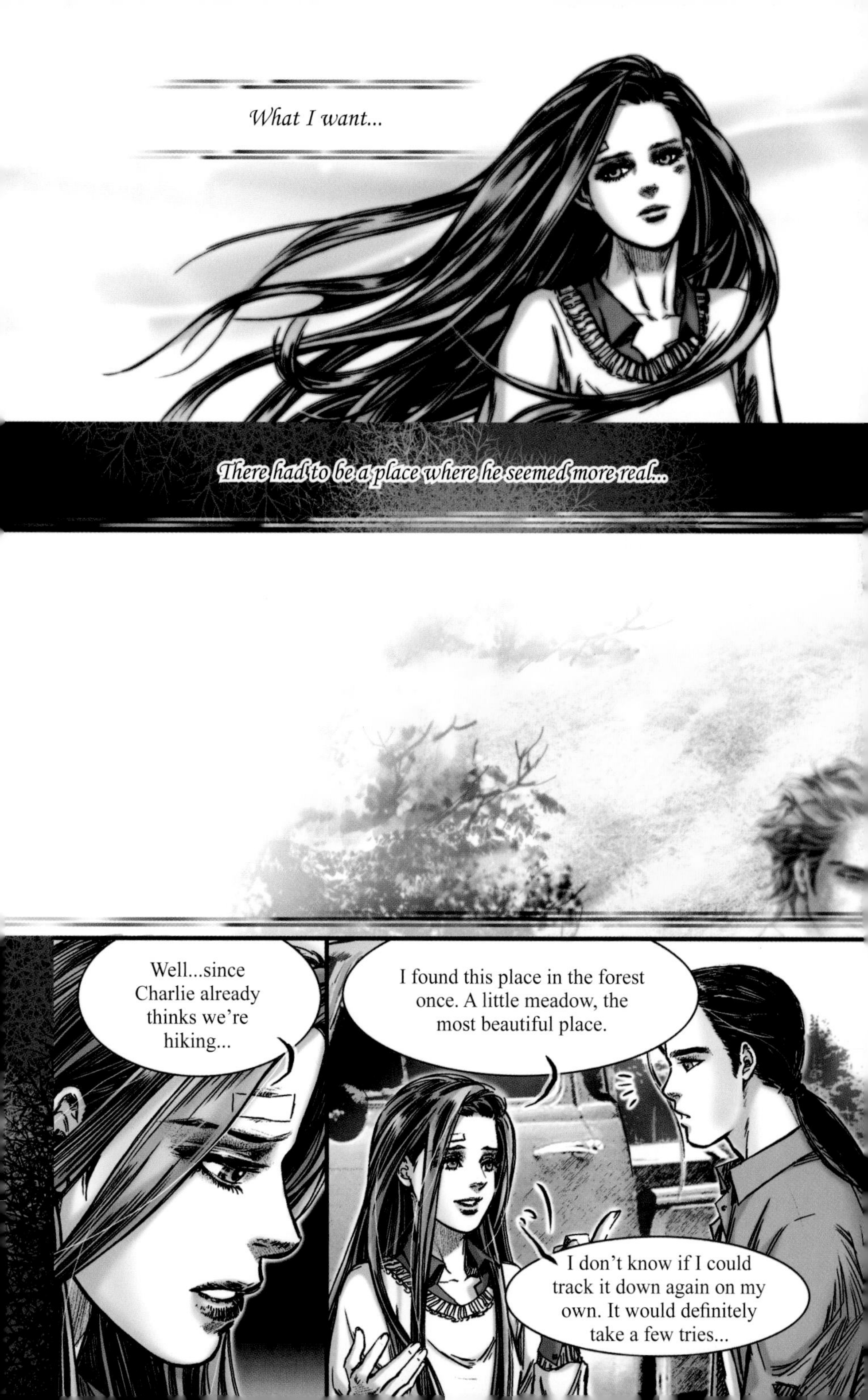

What I want...
There had to be a place where he seemed more real...
Well...since Charlie already thinks we're hiking...
I found this place in the forest once. A little meadow, the most beautiful place.
I don't know if I could track it down again on my own. It would definitely take a few tries...

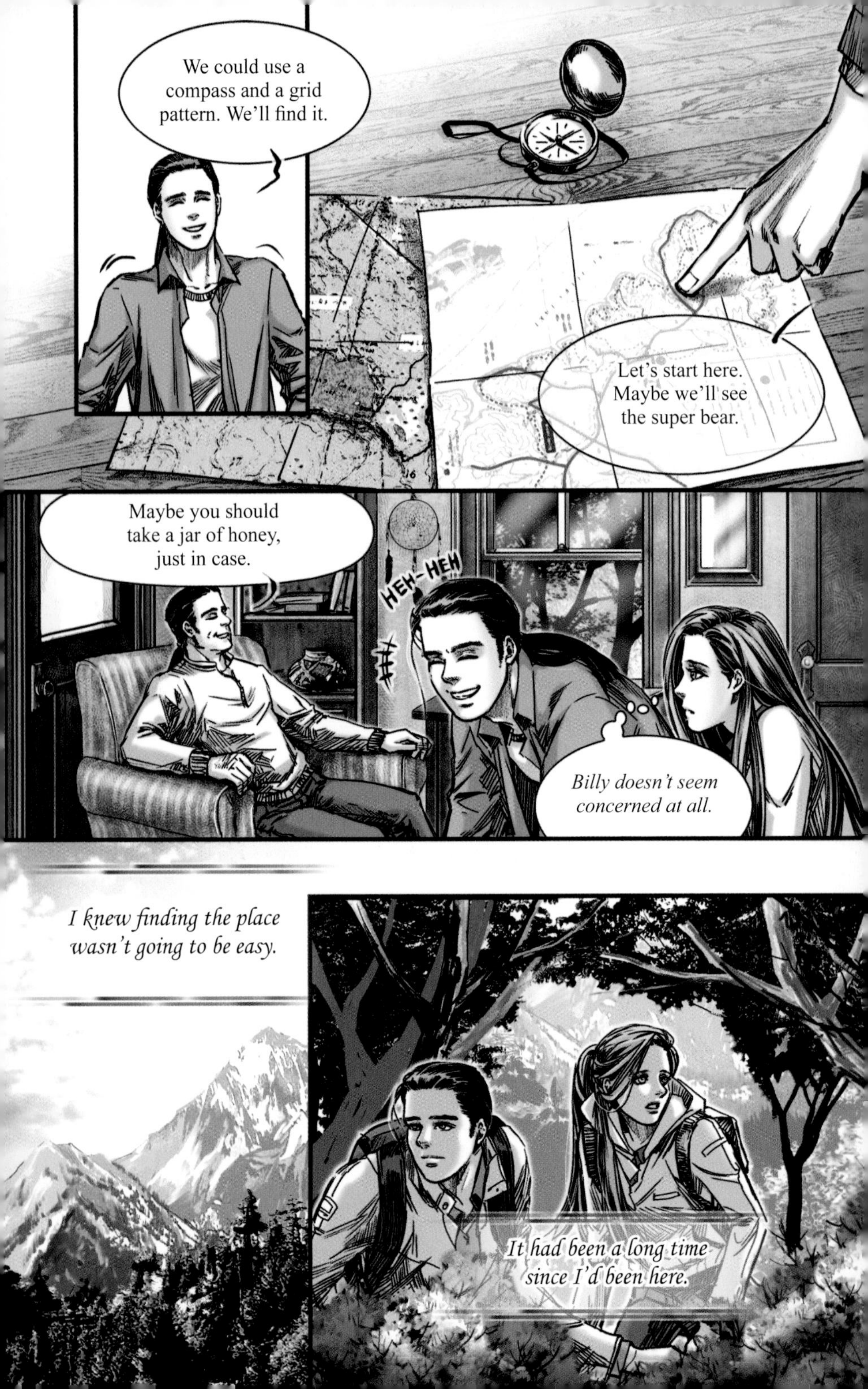

We could use a compass and a grid pattern. We'll find it.
Let's start here. Maybe we'll see the super bear.
Maybe you should take a jar of honey, just in case.
HEH-HEH
Billy doesn't seem concerned at all.
I knew finding the place wasn't going to be easy.
It had been a long time since I'd been here.

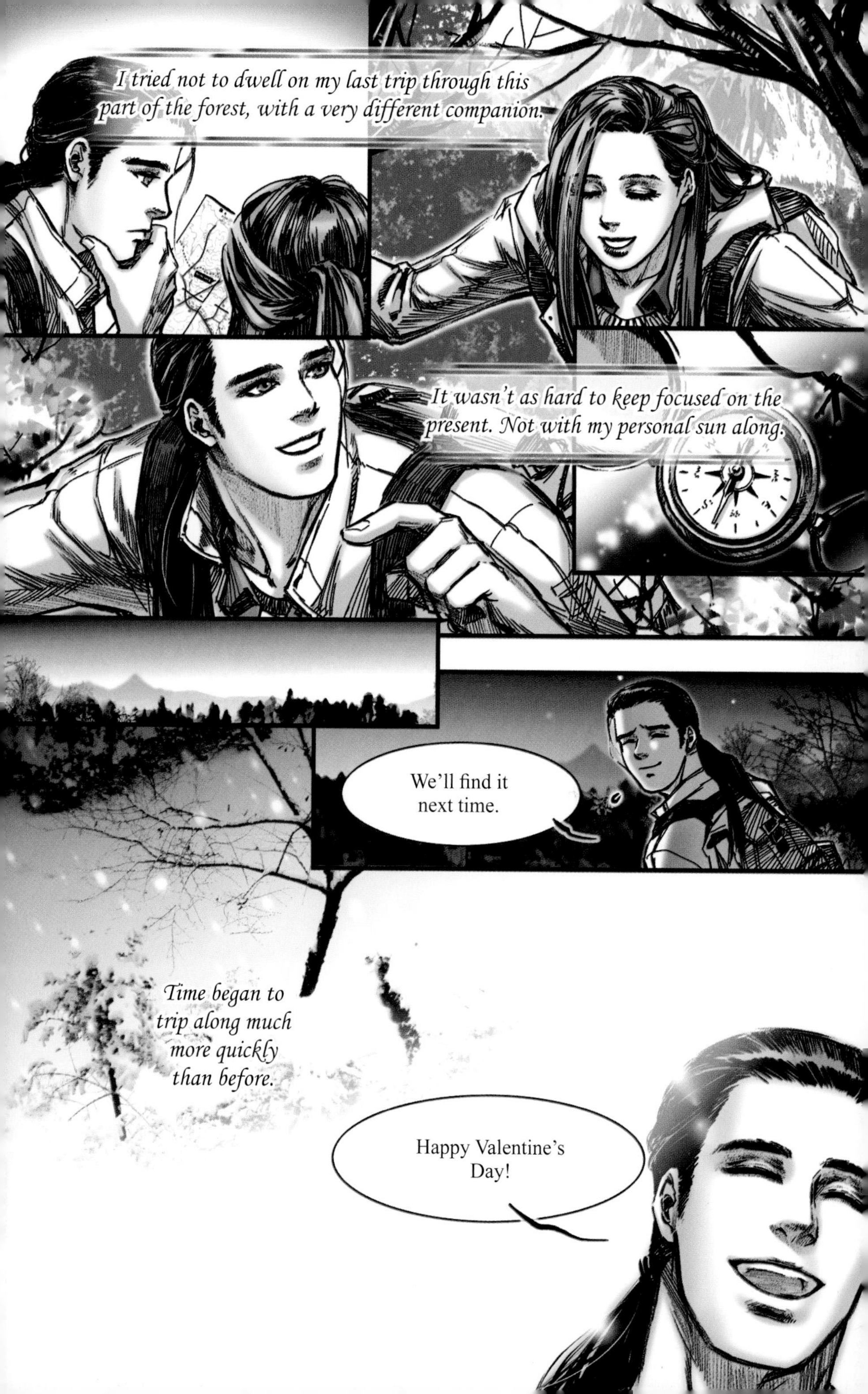
I tried not to dwell on my last trip through this part of the forest, with a very different companion.
It wasn't as hard to keep focused on the present. Not with my personal sun along.
We'll find it next time.
Time began to trip along much more quickly than before.
Happy Valentine's Day!

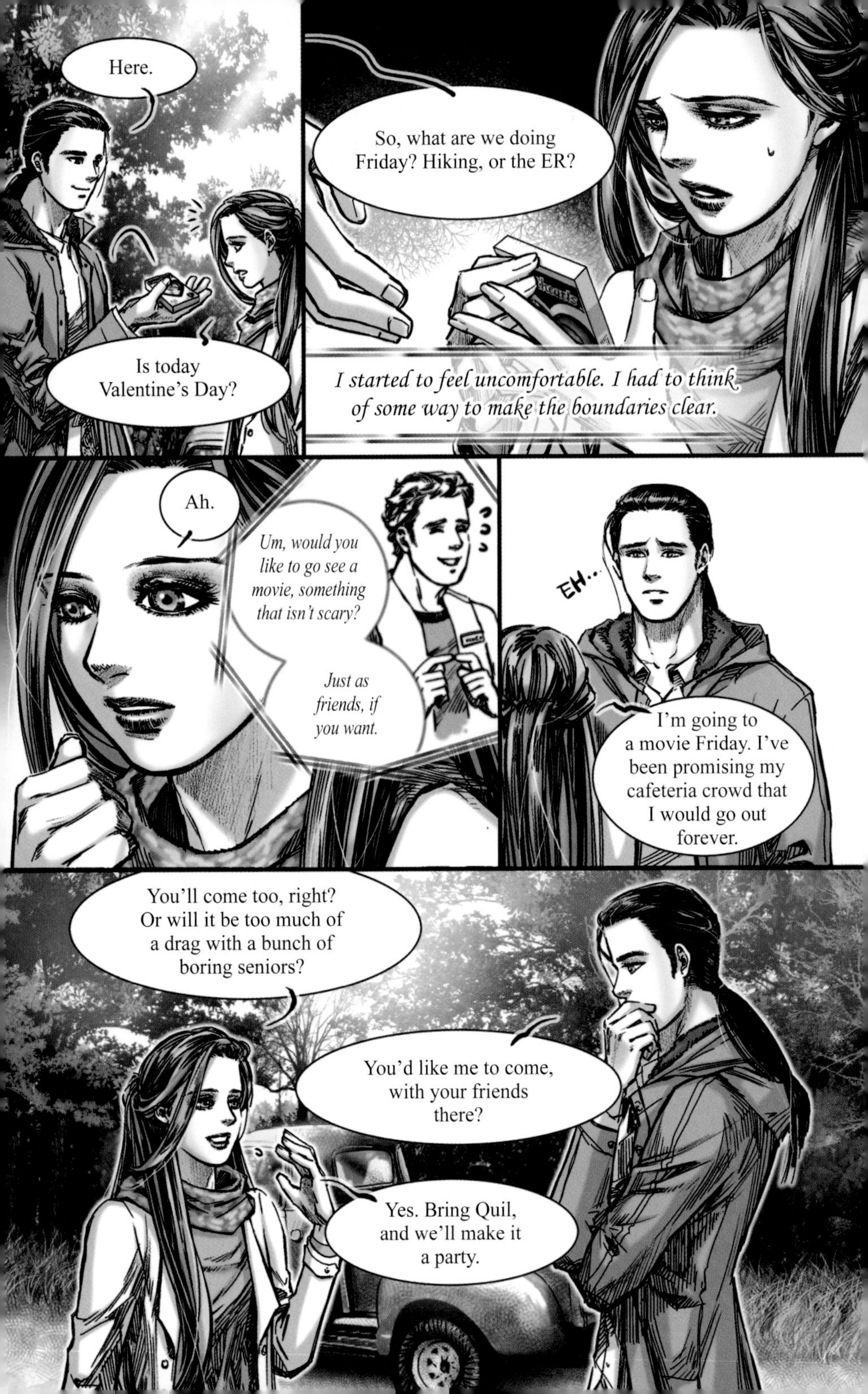
Here.
Is today Valentine's Day?
So, what are we doing Friday? Hiking, or the ER?
I started to feel uncomfortable. I had to think of some way to make the boundaries clear.
Ah.
Um, would you like to go see a movie, something that isn't scary?
Just as friends, if you want.
EH...
I'm going to a movie Friday. I've been promising my cafeteria crowd that I would go out forever.
You'll come too, right? Or will it be too much of a drag with a bunch of boring seniors?
You'd like me to come, with your friends there?
Yes. Bring Quil, and we'll make it a party.

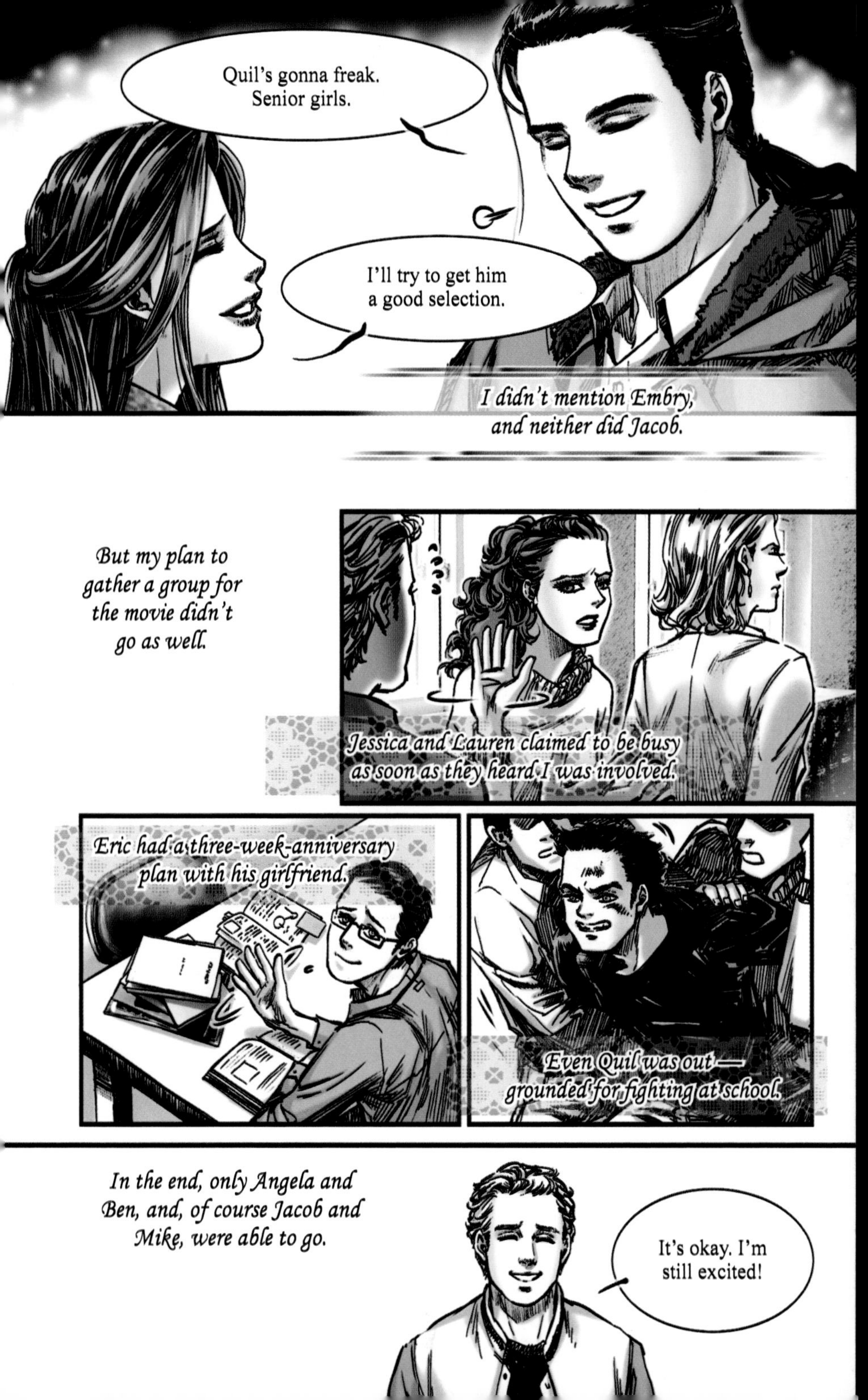
Quil's gonna freak. Senior girls.
I'll try to get him a good selection.
I didn't mention Embry, and neither did Jacob.
But my plan to gather a group for the movie didn't go as well.
Jessica and Lauren claimed to be busy as soon as they heard I was involved.
Eric had a three-week-anniversary plan with his girlfriend.
Even Quil was out—grounded for fighting at school.
In the end, only Angela and Ben, and, of course Jacob and Mike, were able to go.
It's okay. I'm still excited!

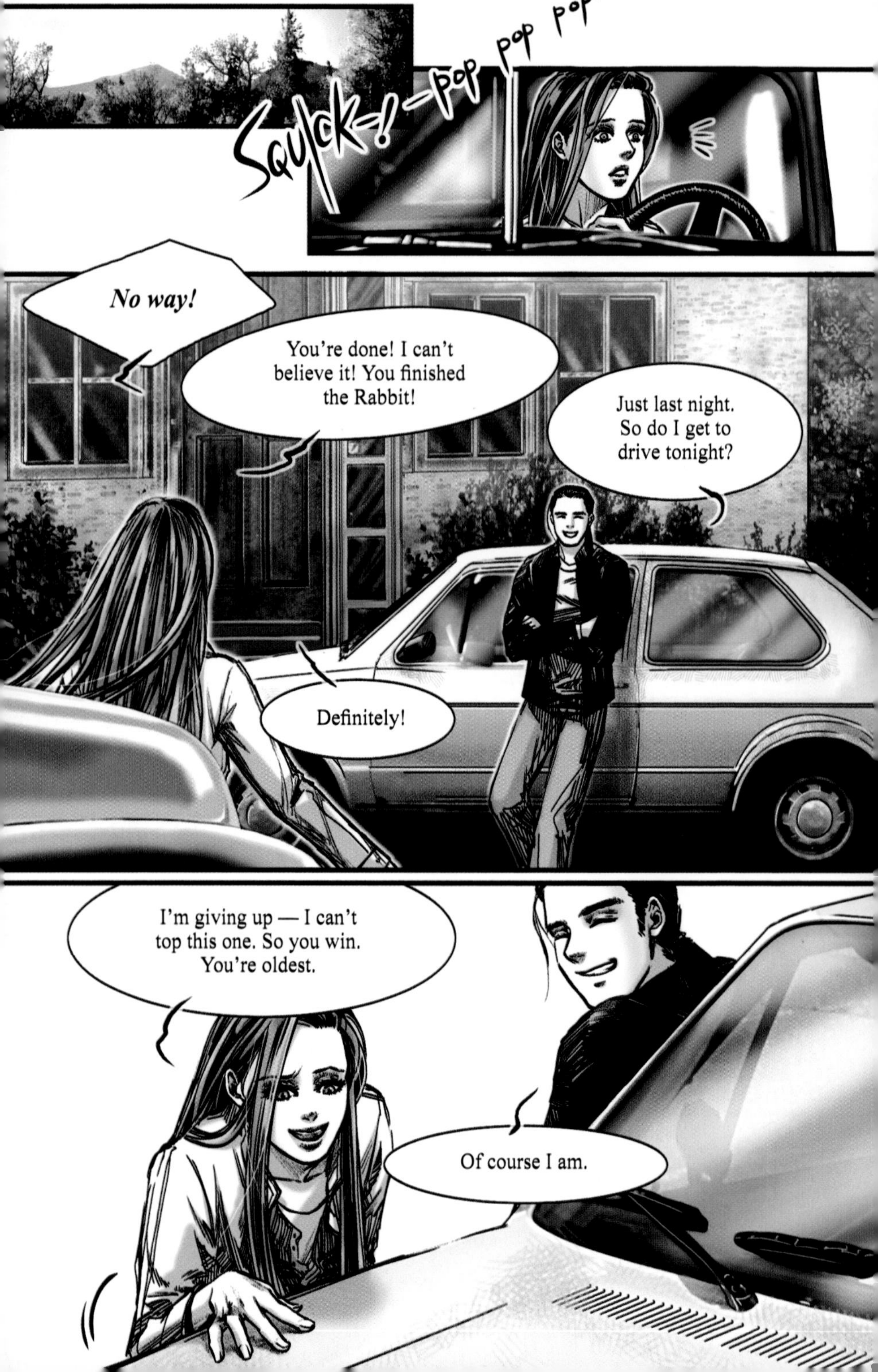
Squick-!-pop pop pop.....
No way!
You're done! I can't believe it! You finished the Rabbit!
Just last night. So do I get to drive tonight?
Definitely!
I'm giving up — I can't top this one. So you win. You're oldest.
Of course I am.

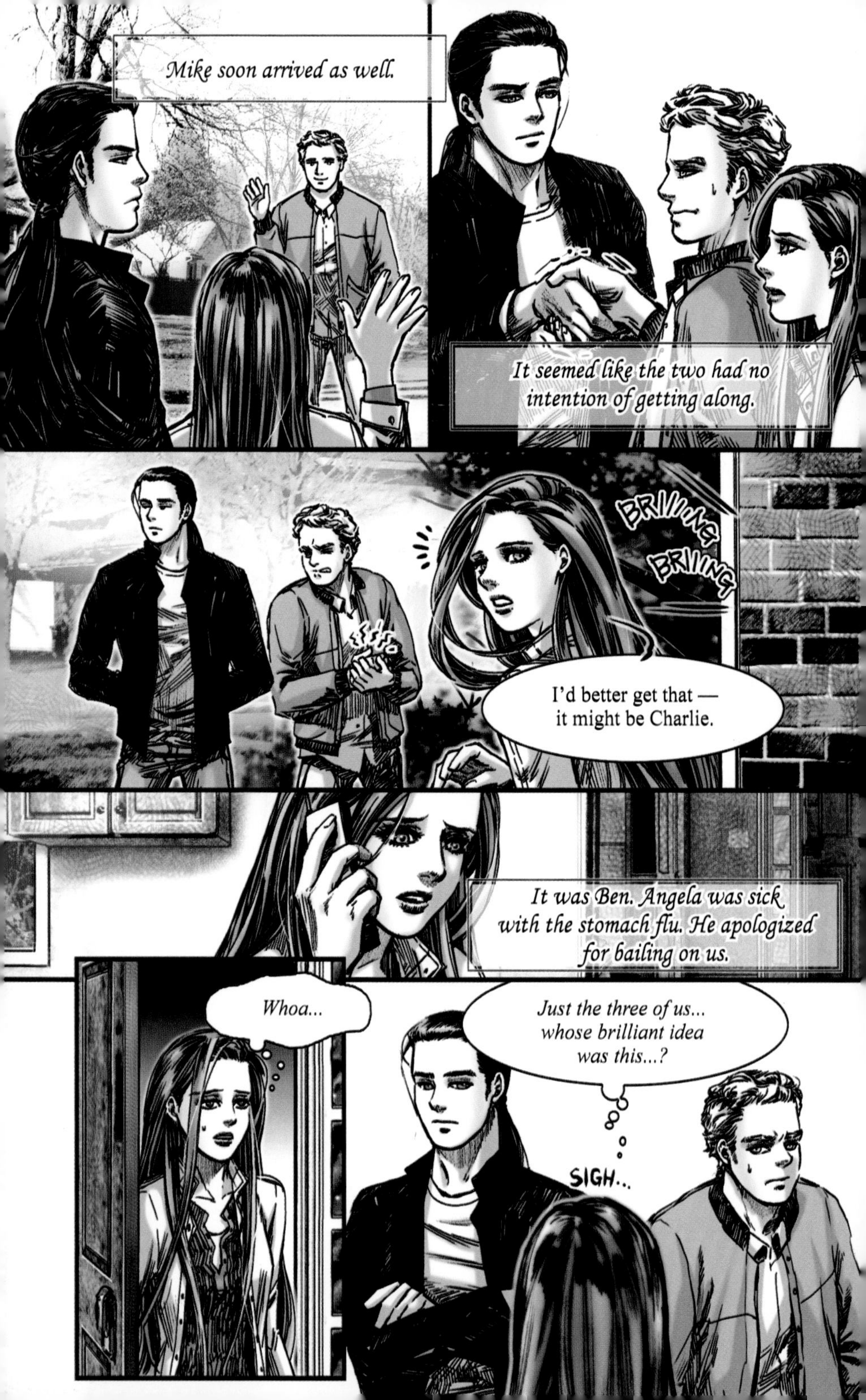
Mike soon arrived as well.
It seemed like the two had no intention of getting along.
BRIIIING
BRIIING
I'd better get that — it might be Charlie.
It was Ben. Angela was sick with the stomach flu. He apologized for bailing on us.
Whoa...
Just the three of us... whose brilliant idea was this...?
SIGH...

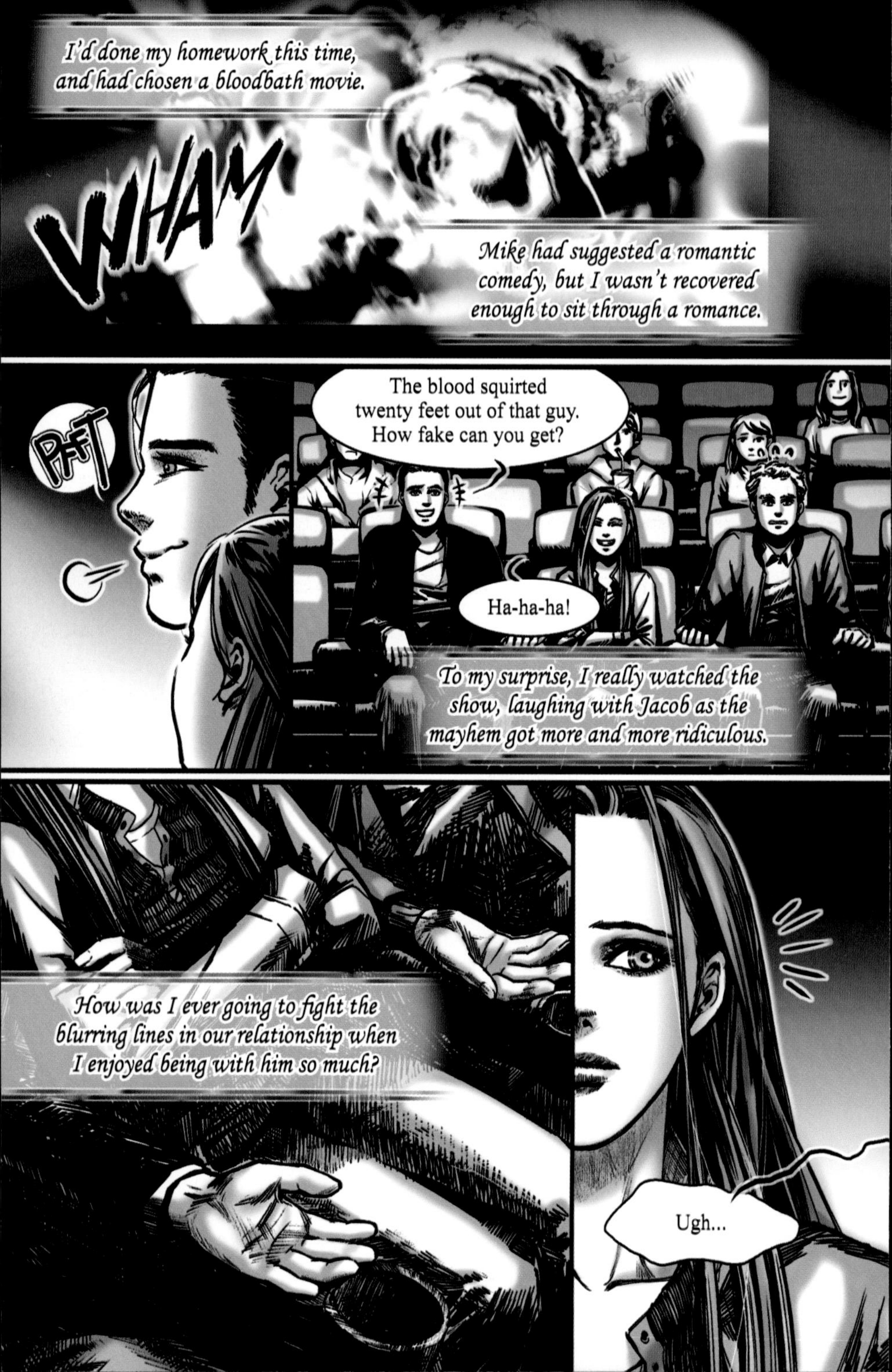
I'd done my homework this time, and had chosen a bloodbath movie.
WHAM
Mike had suggested a romantic comedy, but I wasn't recovered enough to sit through a romance.
PFFT
The blood squirted twenty feet out of that guy. How fake can you get?
Ha-ha-ha!
To my surprise, I really watched the show, laughing with Jacob as the mayhem got more and more ridiculous.
How was I ever going to fight the blurring lines in our relationship when I enjoyed being with him so much?
Ugh...

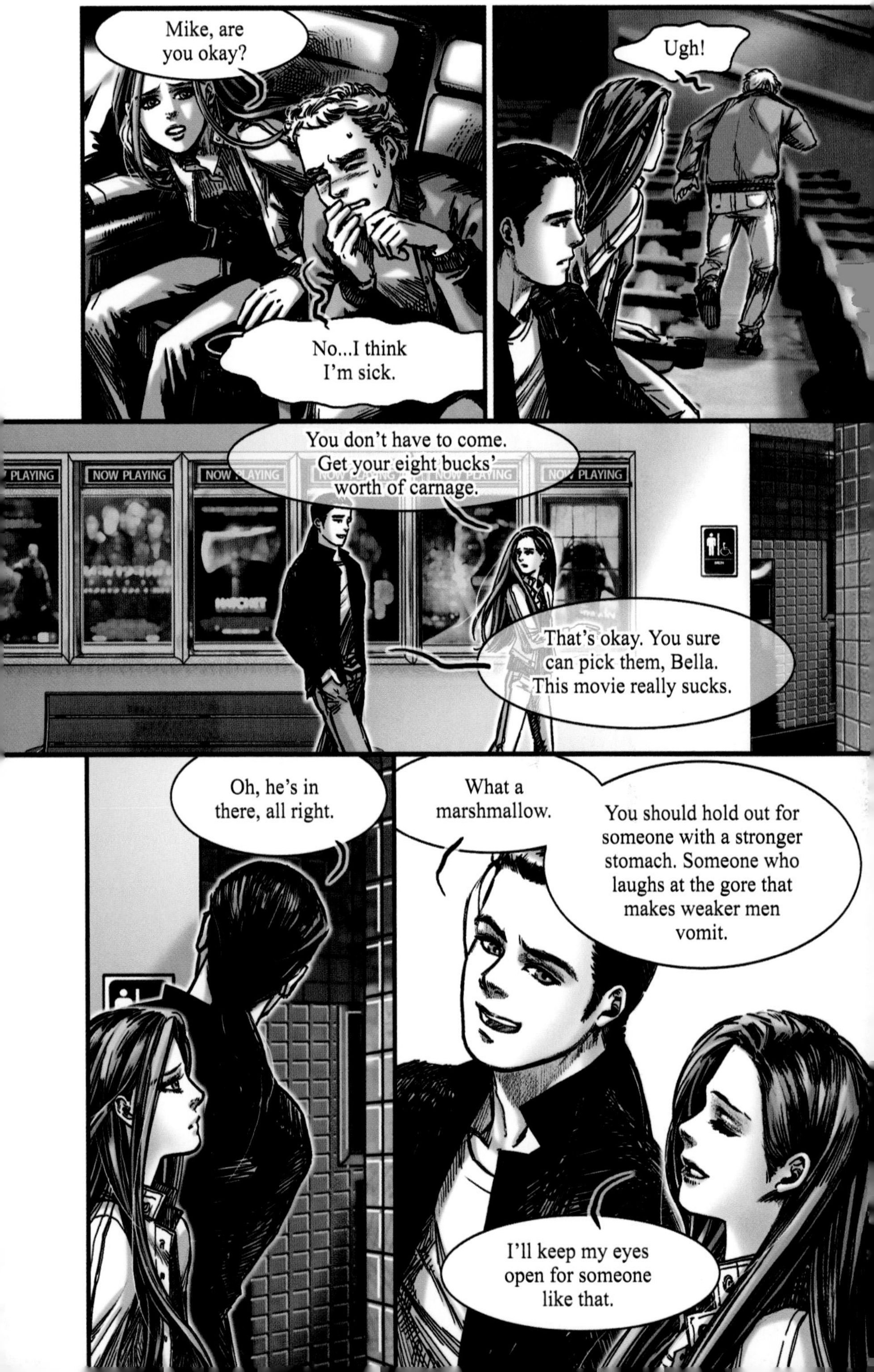

Mike, are you okay?
No...I think I'm sick.
Ugh!
NOW PLAYING
You don't have to come. Get your eight bucks' worth of carnage.
That's okay. You sure can pick them, Bella. This movie really sucks.
Oh, he's in there, all right.
What a marshmallow.
You should hold out for someone with a stronger stomach. Someone who laughs at the gore that makes weaker men vomit.
I'll keep my eyes open for someone like that.

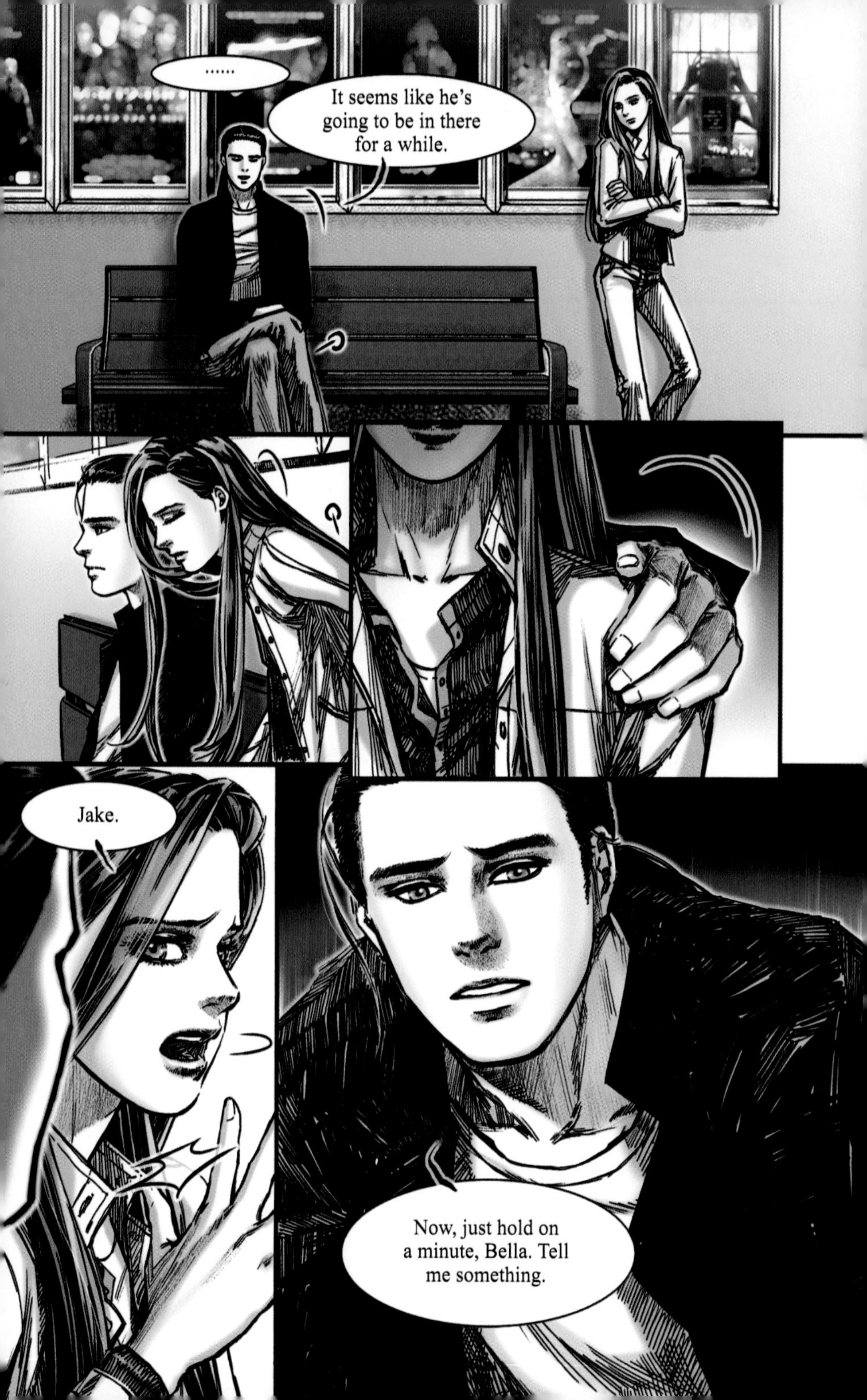
......
It seems like he's going to be in there for a while.
Jake.
Now, just hold on a minute, Bella. Tell me something.

You like me, right?

You know I do.

There was nothing left in my life at this point that was more important than Jacob Black, But he seemed determined to ruin everything.

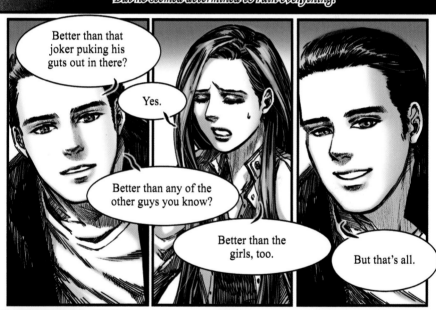

Better than that joker puking his guts out in there?

Yes.

Better than any of the other guys you know?

Better than the girls, too.

But that's all.

...Yes.

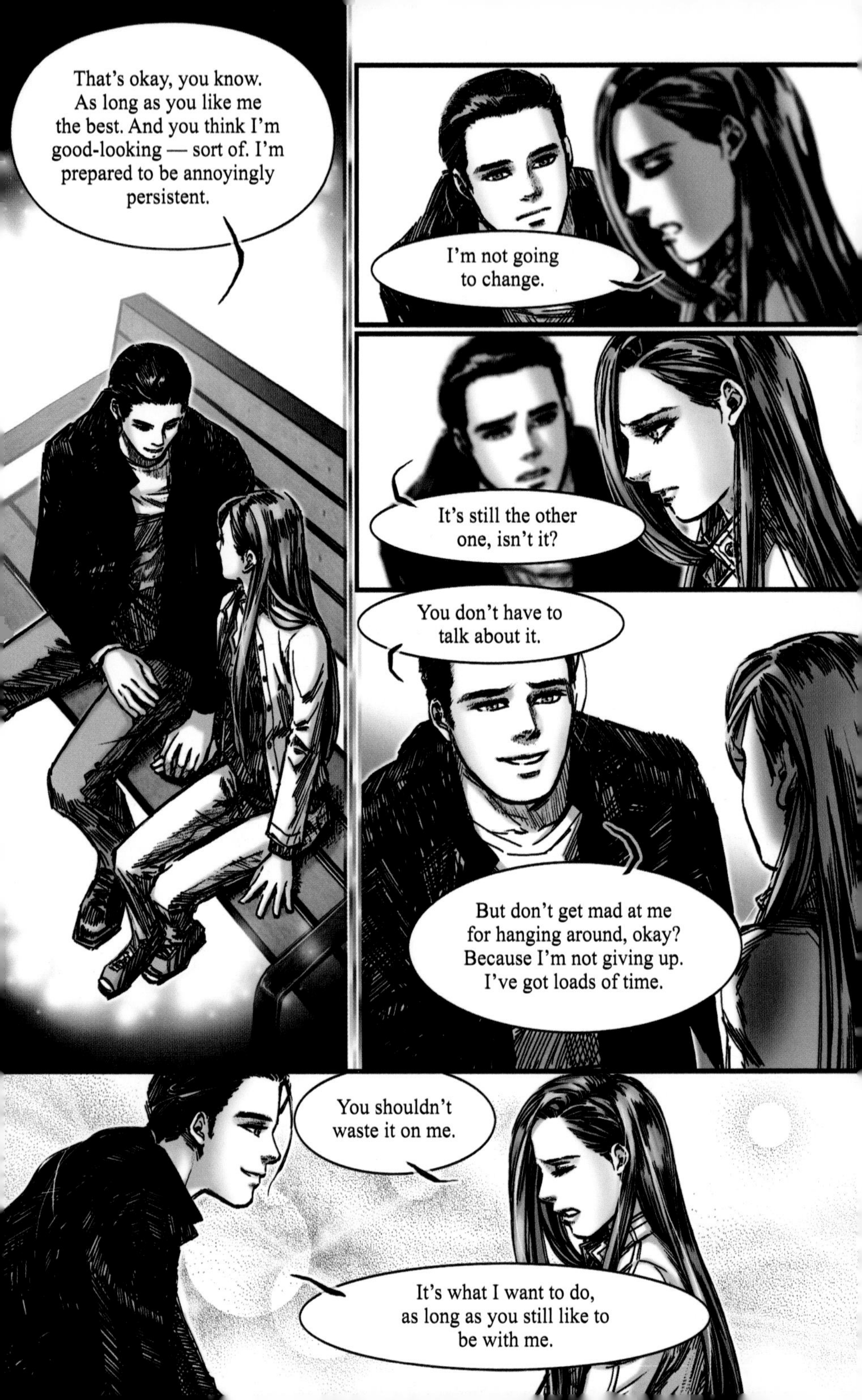
That's okay, you know. As long as you like me the best. And you think I'm good-looking — sort of. I'm prepared to be annoyingly persistent.
I'm not going to change.
It's still the other one, isn't it?
You don't have to talk about it.
But don't get mad at me for hanging around, okay? Because I'm not giving up. I've got loads of time.
You shouldn't waste it on me.
It's what I want to do, as long as you still like to be with me.

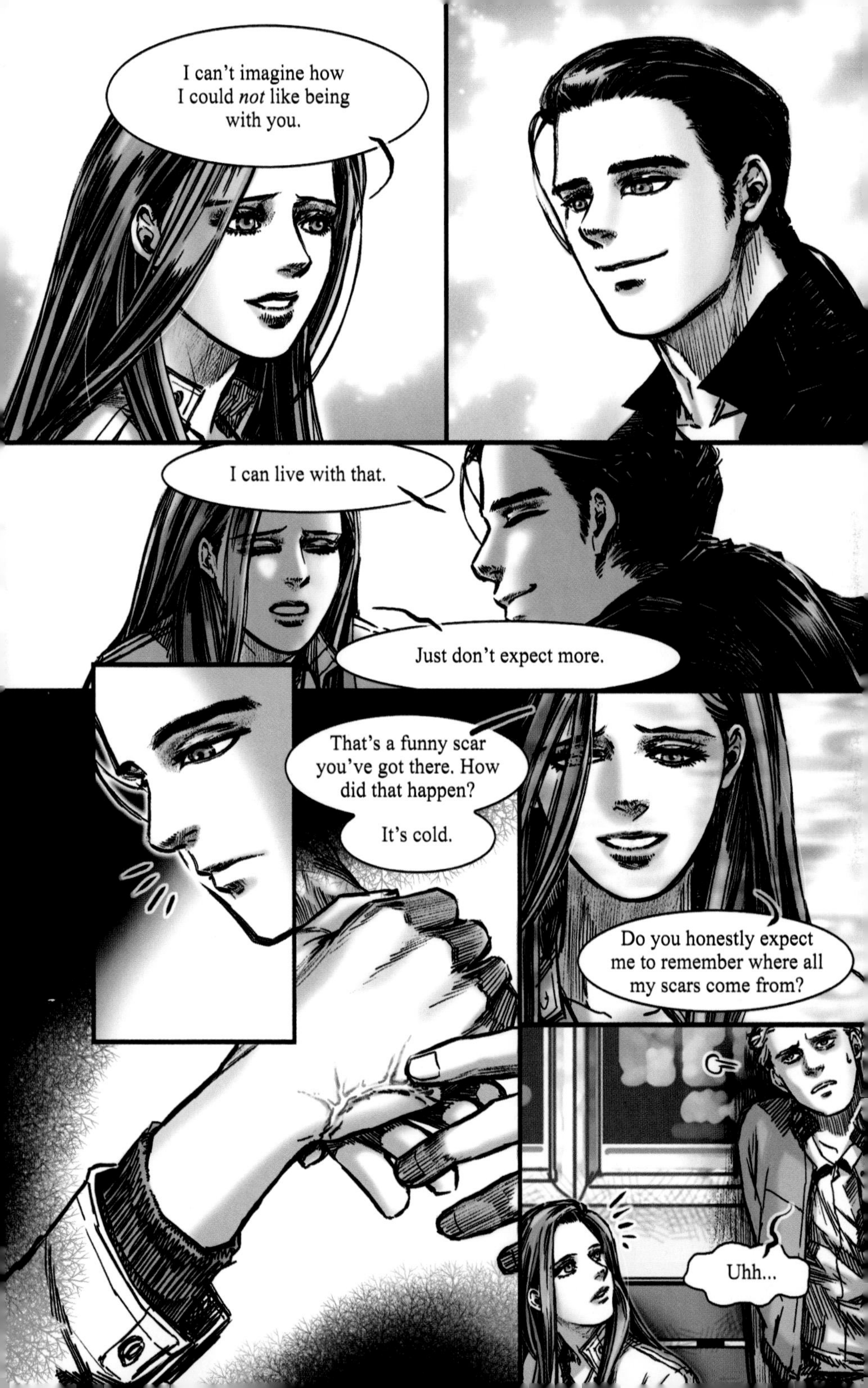
I can't imagine how I could *not* like being with you.
I can live with that.
Just don't expect more.
That's a funny scar you've got there. How did that happen?
It's cold.
Do you honestly expect me to remember where all my scars come from?
Uhh...

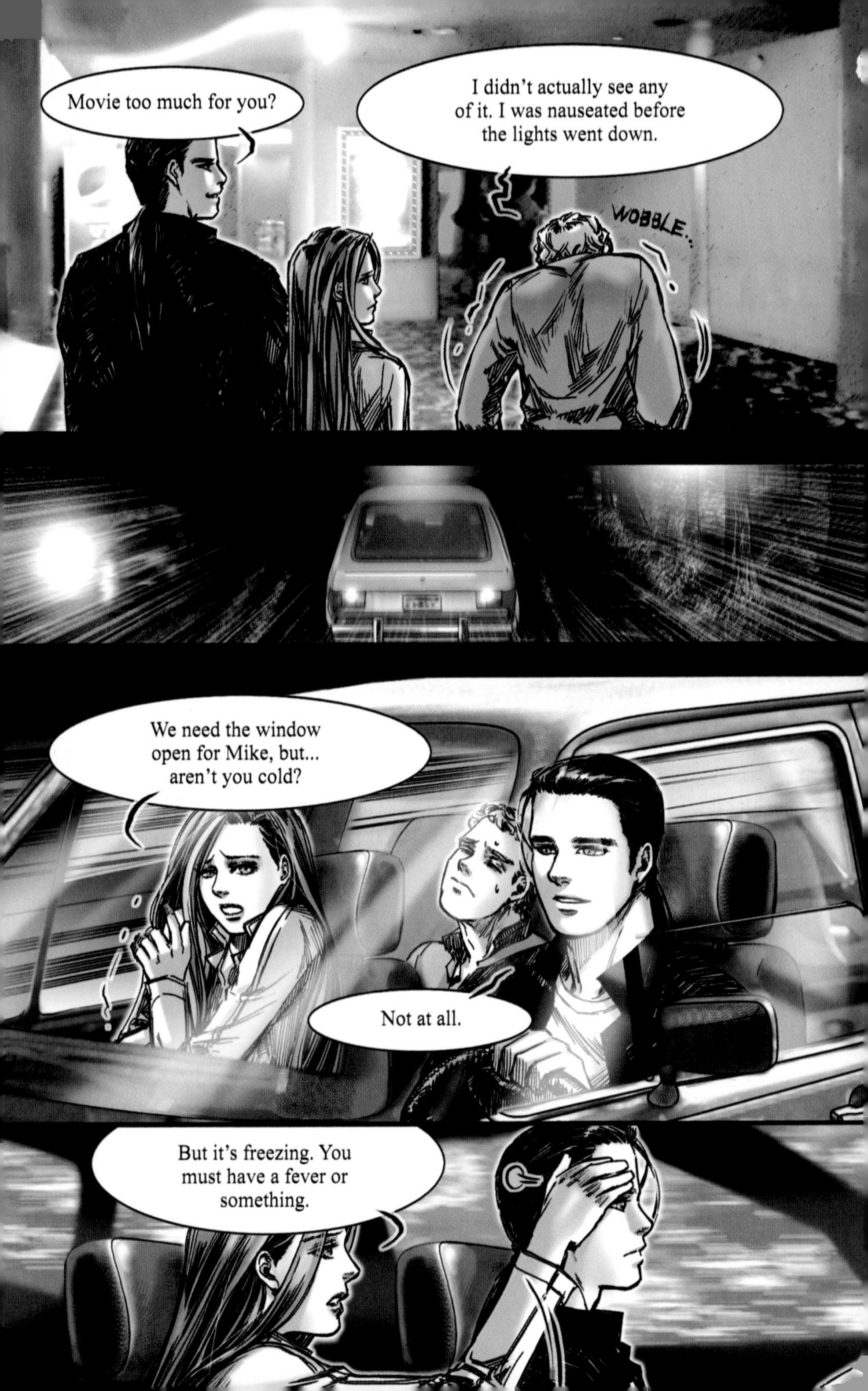
Movie too much for you?
I didn't actually see any of it. I was nauseated before the lights went down.
WOBBLE...
We need the window open for Mike, but... aren't you cold?
Not at all.
But it's freezing. You must have a fever or something.

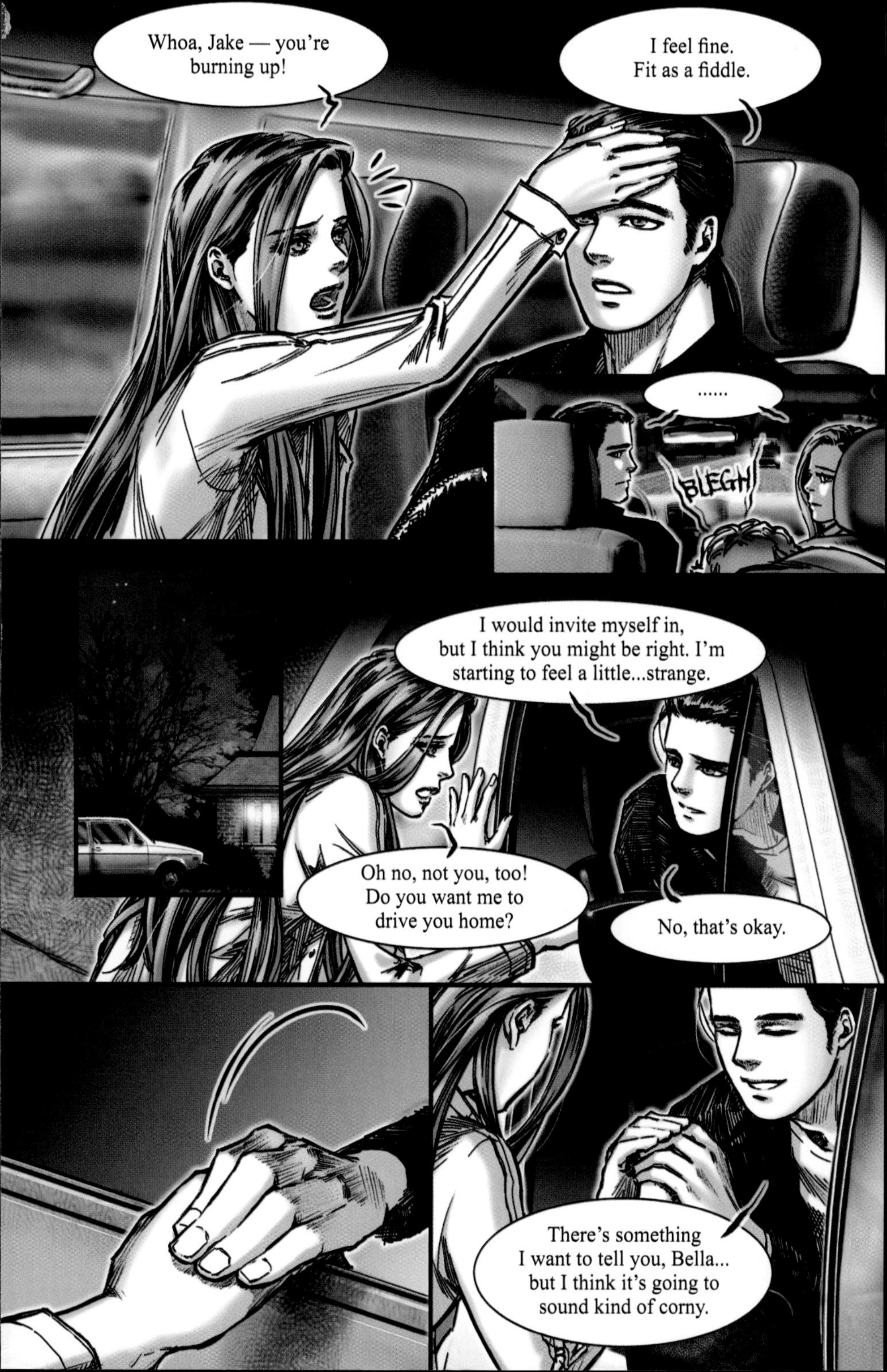
Whoa, Jake — you're burning up!
I feel fine. Fit as a fiddle.
......
BLEGH!
I would invite myself in, but I think you might be right. I'm starting to feel a little...strange.
Oh no, not you, too! Do you want me to drive you home?
No, that's okay.
There's something I want to tell you, Bella... but I think it's going to sound kind of corny.

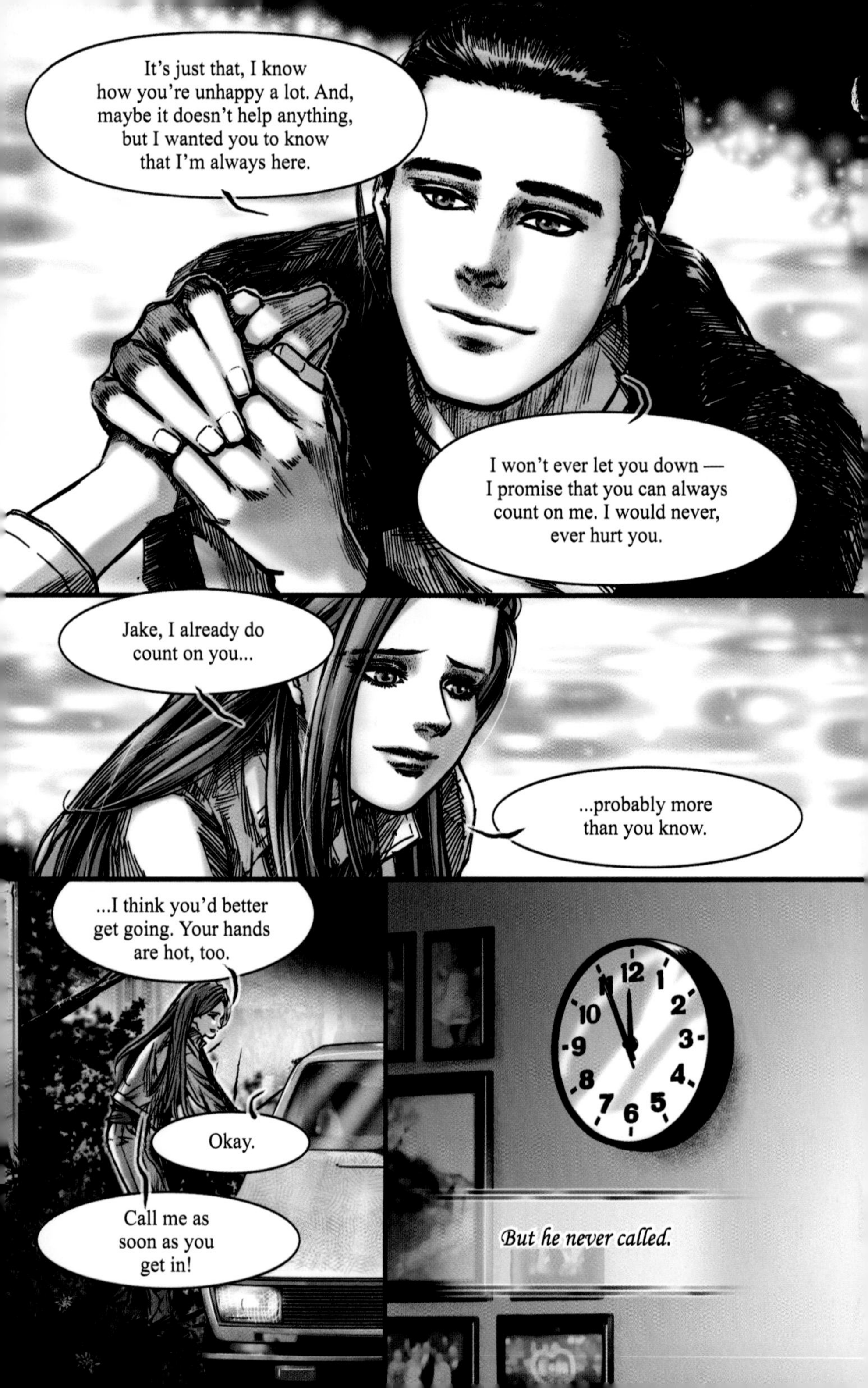
It's just that, I know how you're unhappy a lot. And, maybe it doesn't help anything, but I wanted you to know that I'm always here.
I won't ever let you down — I promise that you can always count on me. I would never, ever hurt you.
Jake, I already do count on you...
...probably more than you know.
...I think you'd better get going. Your hands are hot, too.
Okay.
Call me as soon as you get in!
12 1 2 3 4 5 6 7 8 9 10 11
But he never called.

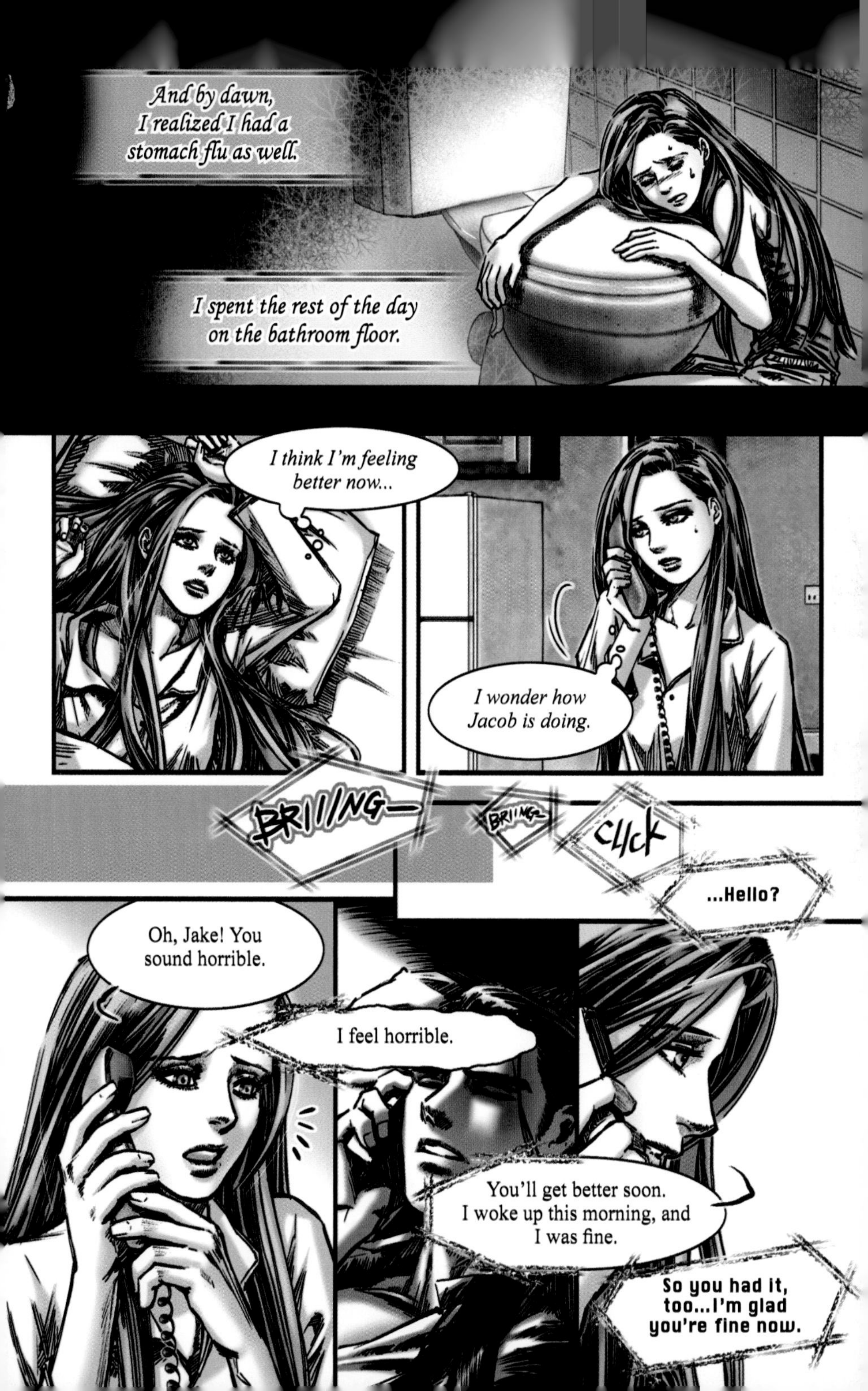
And by dawn, I realized I had a stomach flu as well.
I spent the rest of the day on the bathroom floor.
I think I'm feeling better now...
I wonder how Jacob is doing.
BRIIING—
BRIING
CLICK
...Hello?
Oh, Jake! You sound horrible.
I feel horrible.
You'll get better soon. I woke up this morning, and I was fine.
So you had it, too...I'm glad you're fine now.

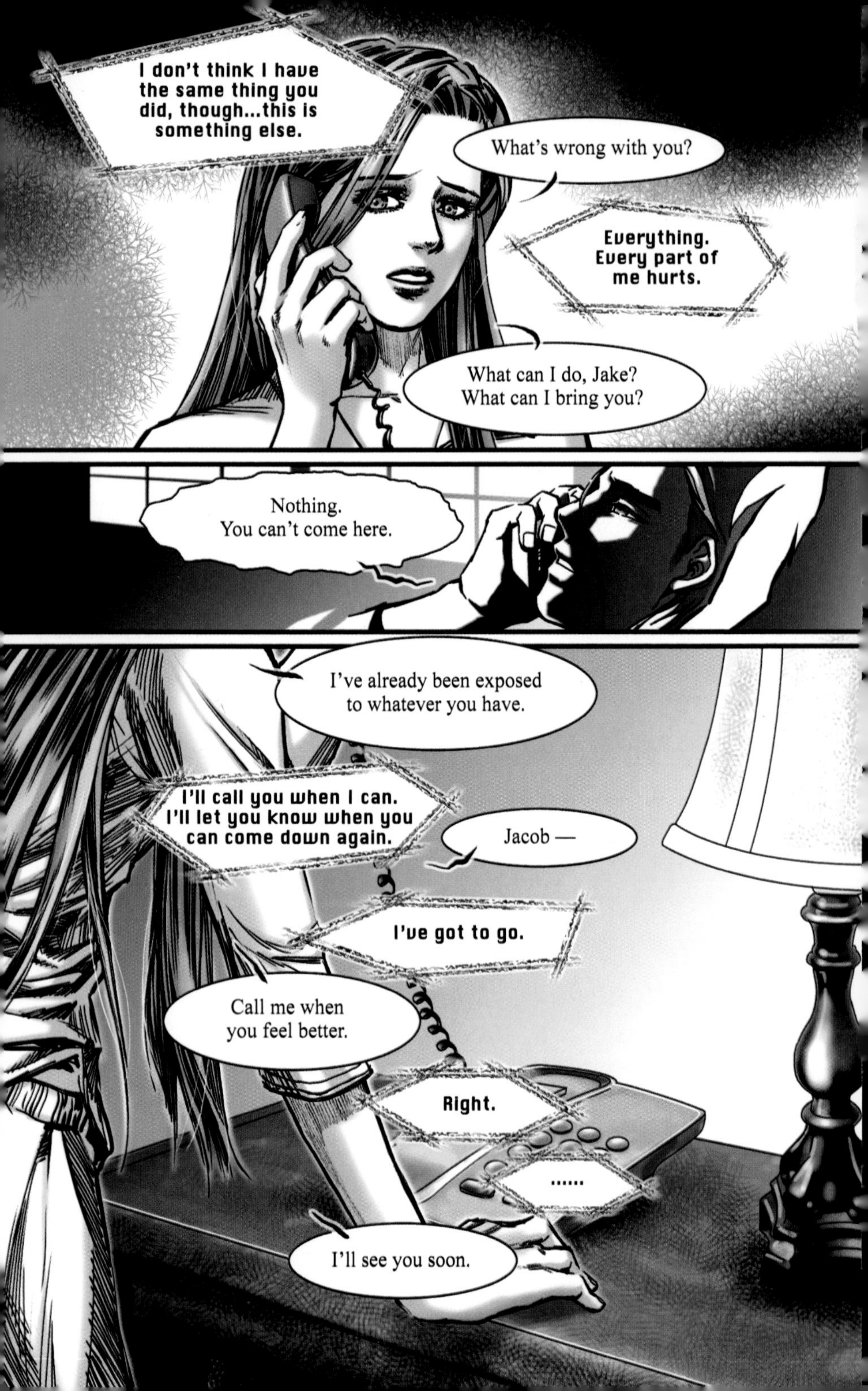
I don't think I have the same thing you did, though...this is something else.
What's wrong with you?
Everything. Every part of me hurts.
What can I do, Jake? What can I bring you?
Nothing. You can't come here.
I've already been exposed to whatever you have.
I'll call you when I can. I'll let you know when you can come down again.
Jacob —
I've got to go.
Call me when you feel better.
Right.
......
I'll see you soon.

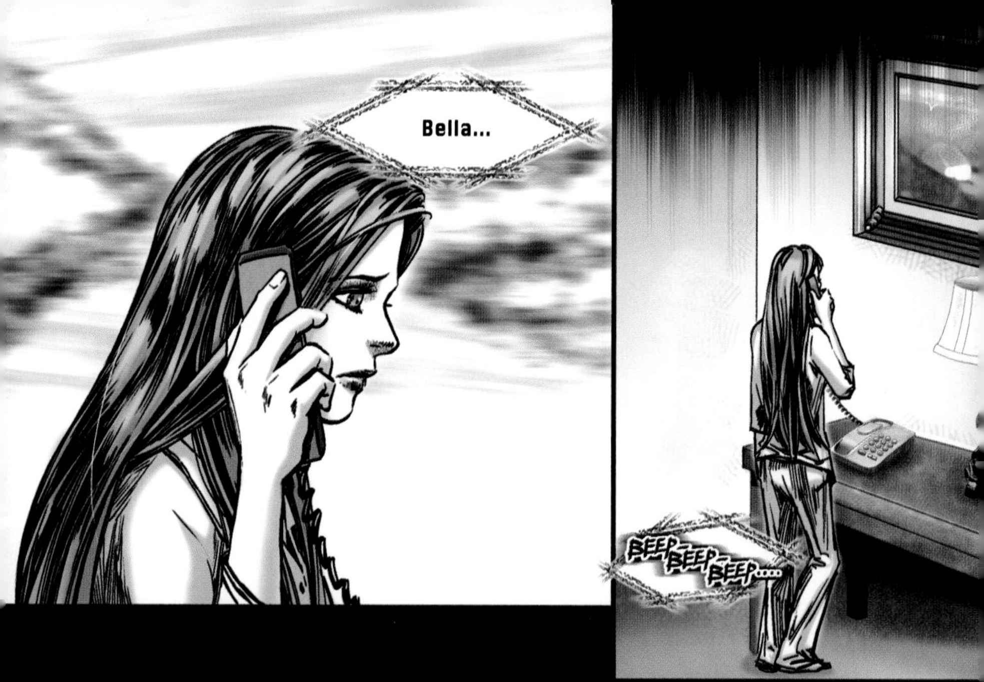
Bella...
BEEP-BEEP-BEEP....

But Jacob didn't call.

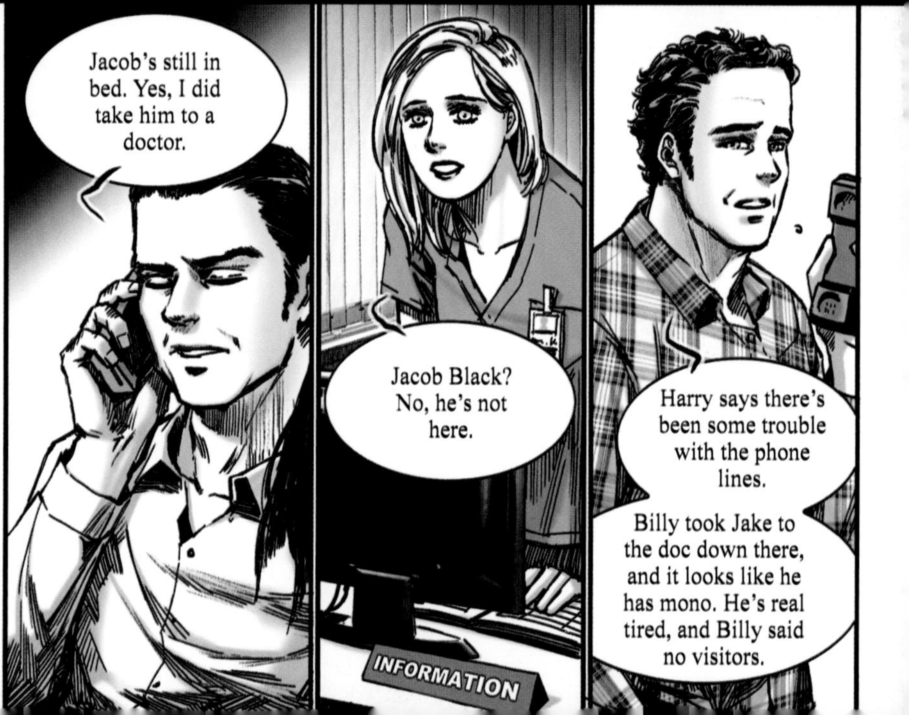
Jacob's still in bed. Yes, I did take him to a doctor.
Jacob Black? No, he's not here.
INFORMATION
Harry says there's been some trouble with the phone lines.
Billy took Jake to the doc down there, and it looks like he has mono. He's real tired, and Billy said no visitors.

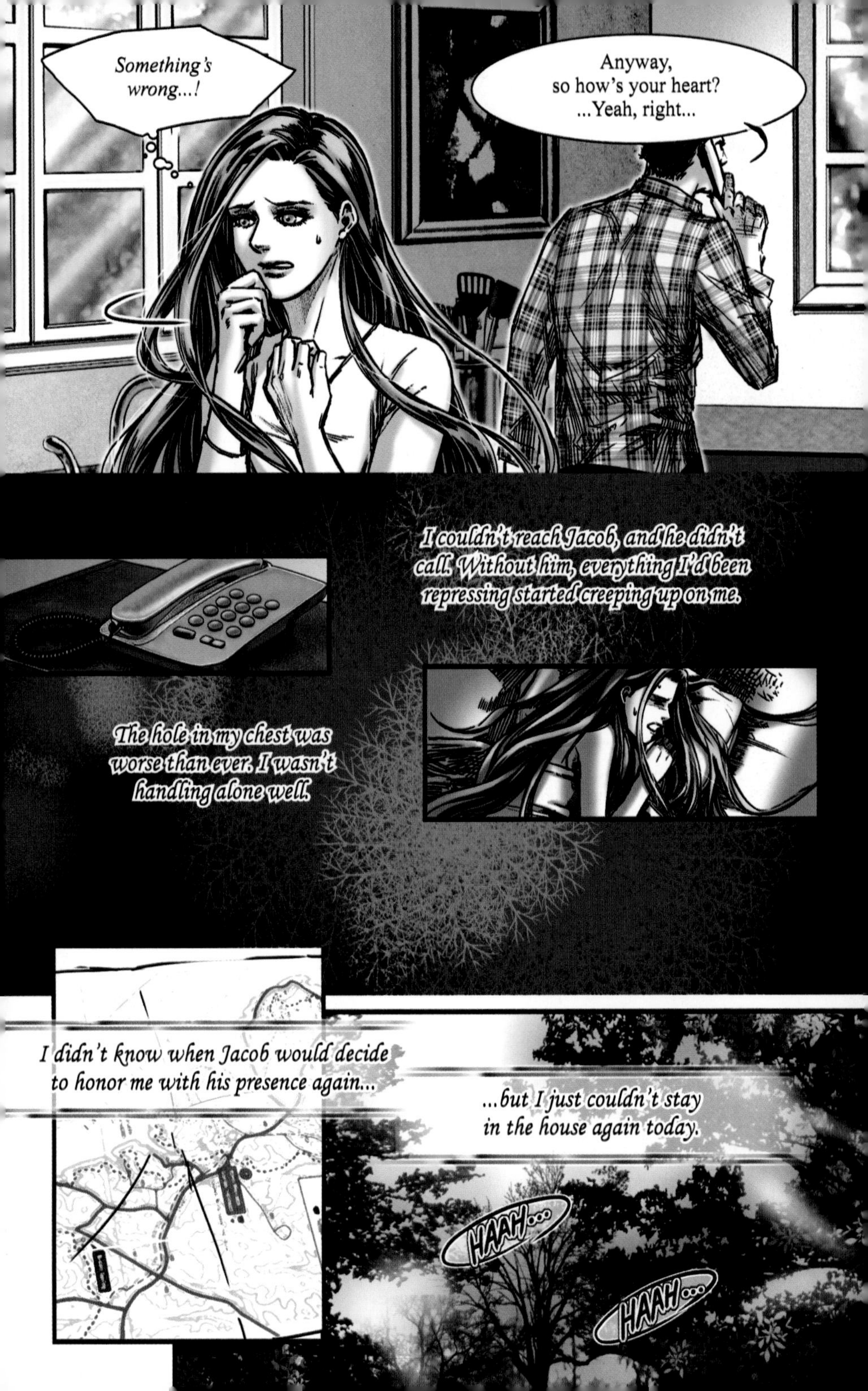
Something's wrong...!
Anyway, so how's your heart? ...Yeah, right...
I couldn't reach Jacob, and he didn't call. Without him, everything I'd been repressing started creeping up on me.
The hole in my chest was worse than ever. I wasn't handling alone well.
I didn't know when Jacob would decide to honor me with his presence again...
...but I just couldn't stay in the house again today.
HAAH...
HAAH...

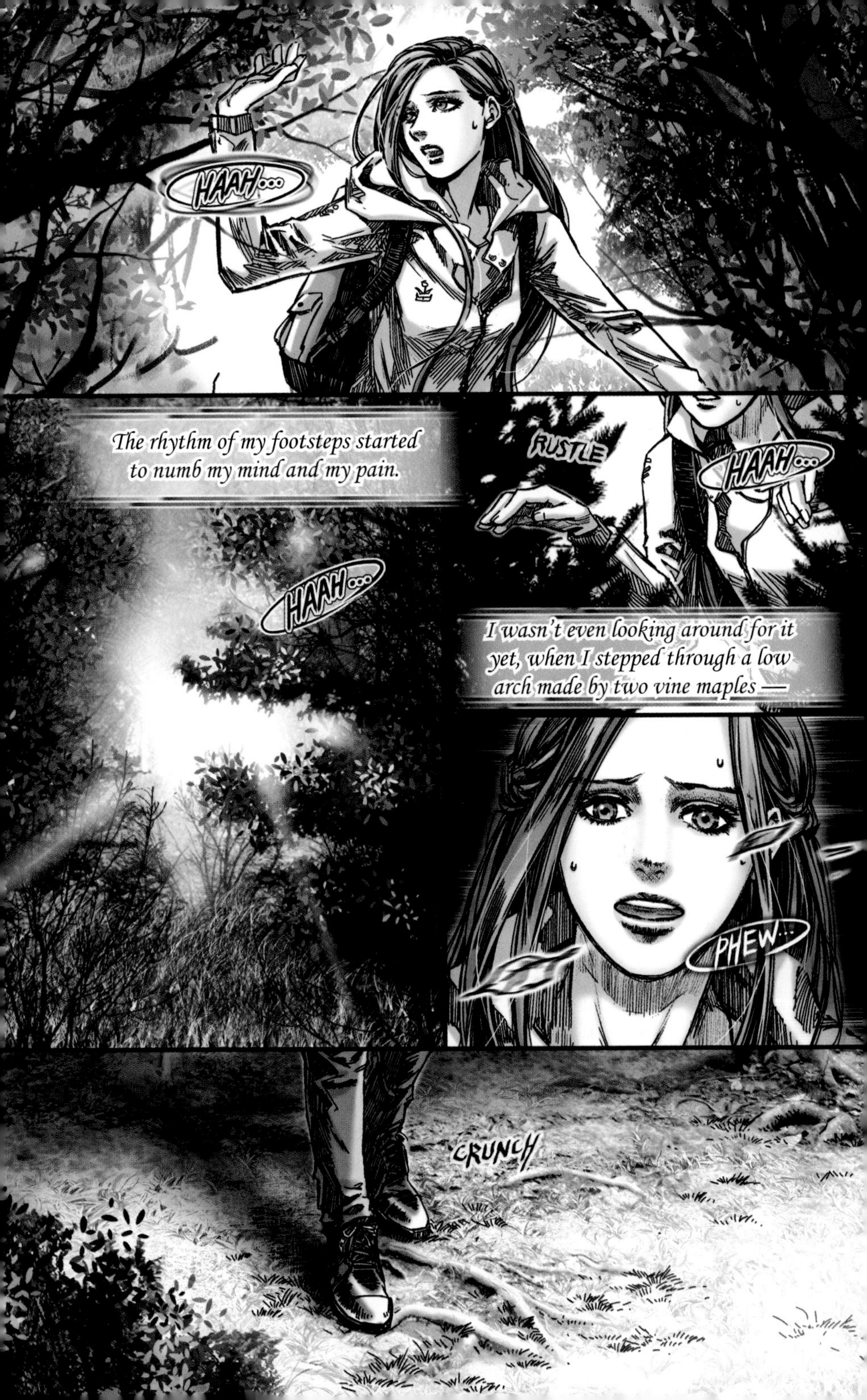
HAAH...
The rhythm of my footsteps started to numb my mind and my pain.
RUSTLE
HAAH...
HAAH...
I wasn't even looking around for it yet, when I stepped through a low arch made by two vine maples —
PHEW...
CRUNCH

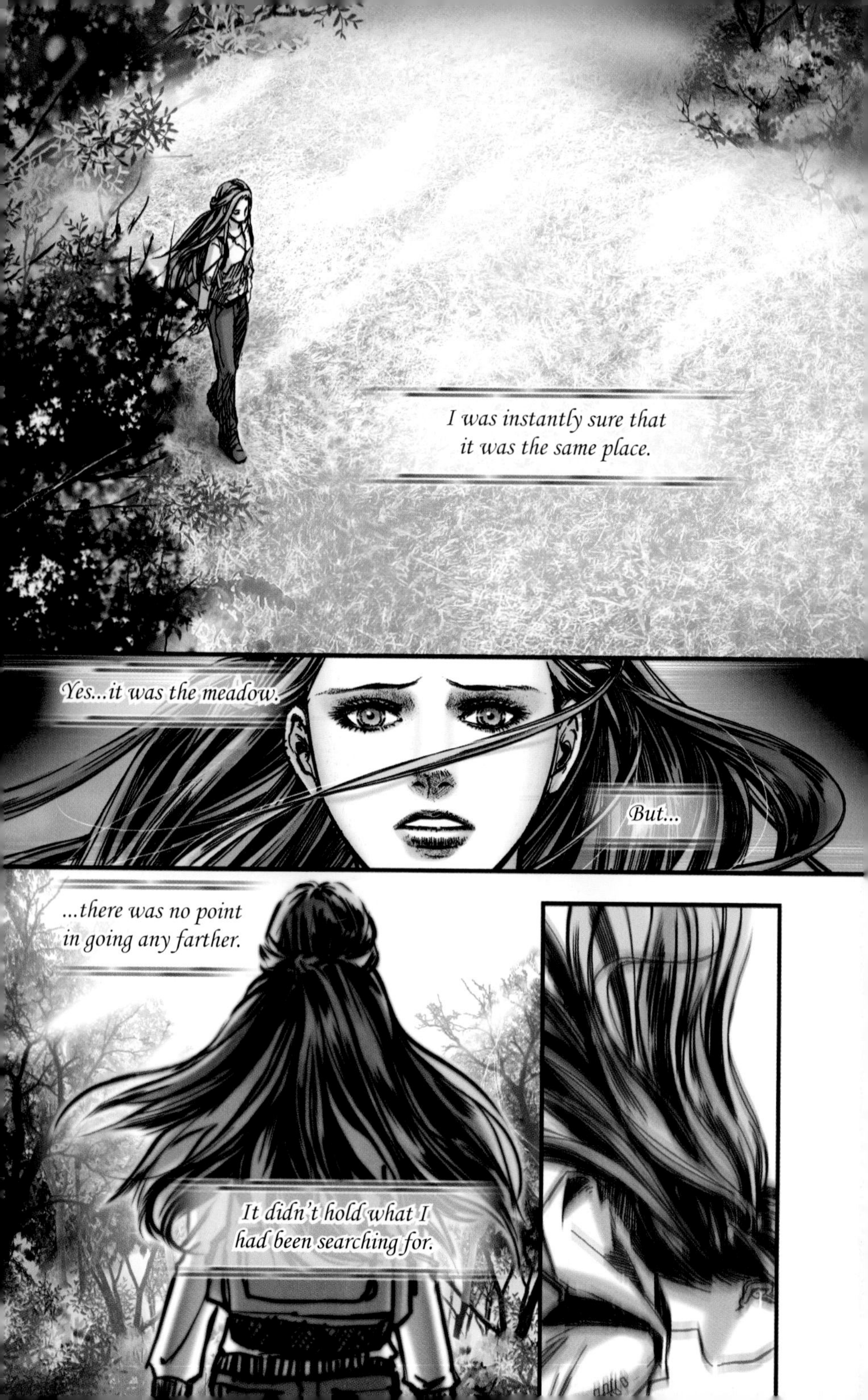
I was instantly sure that
it was the same place.
Yes...it was the meadow.
But...
...there was no point
in going any farther.
It didn't hold what I
had been searching for.

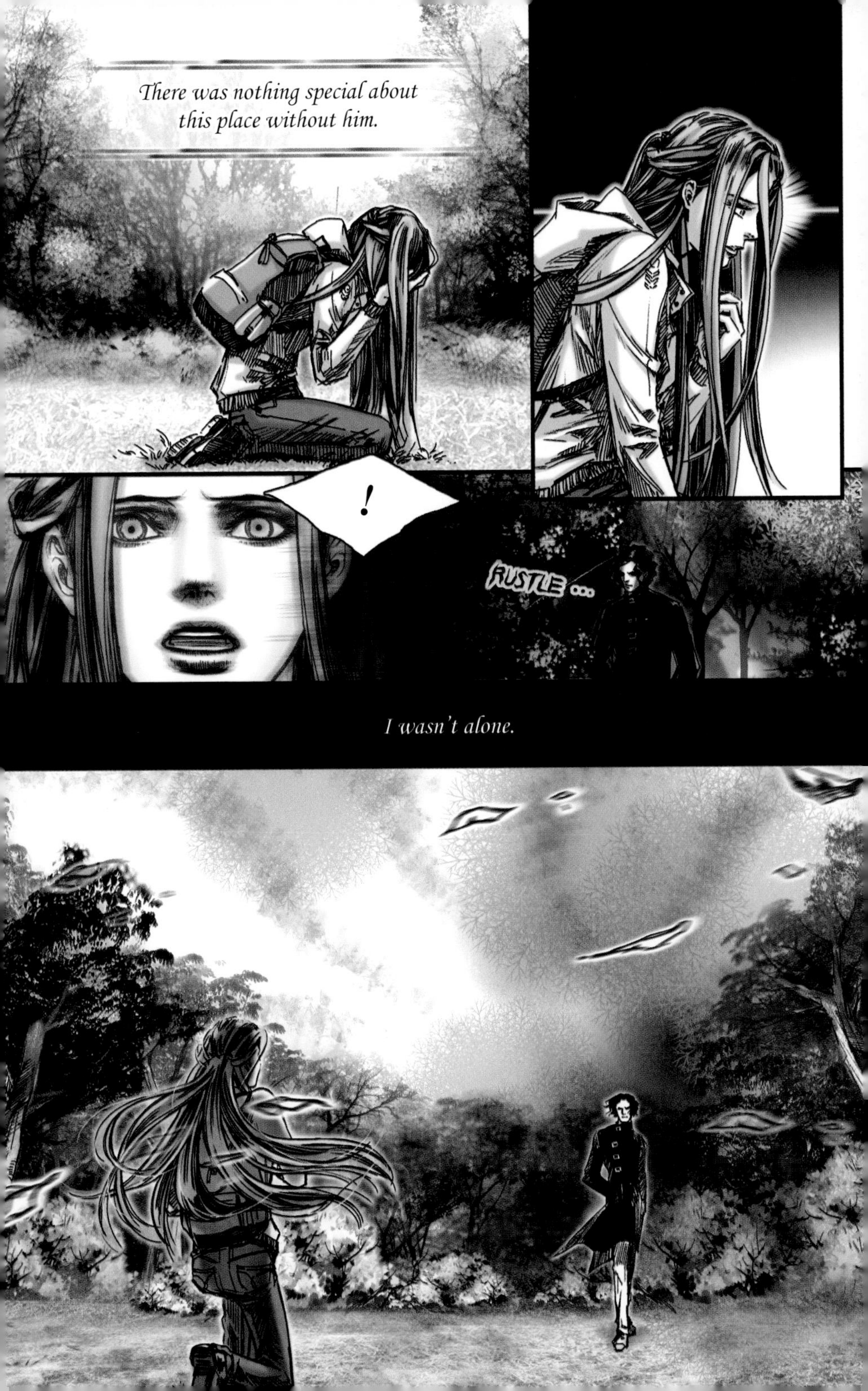
There was nothing special about this place without him.
!
RUSTLE...
I wasn't alone.

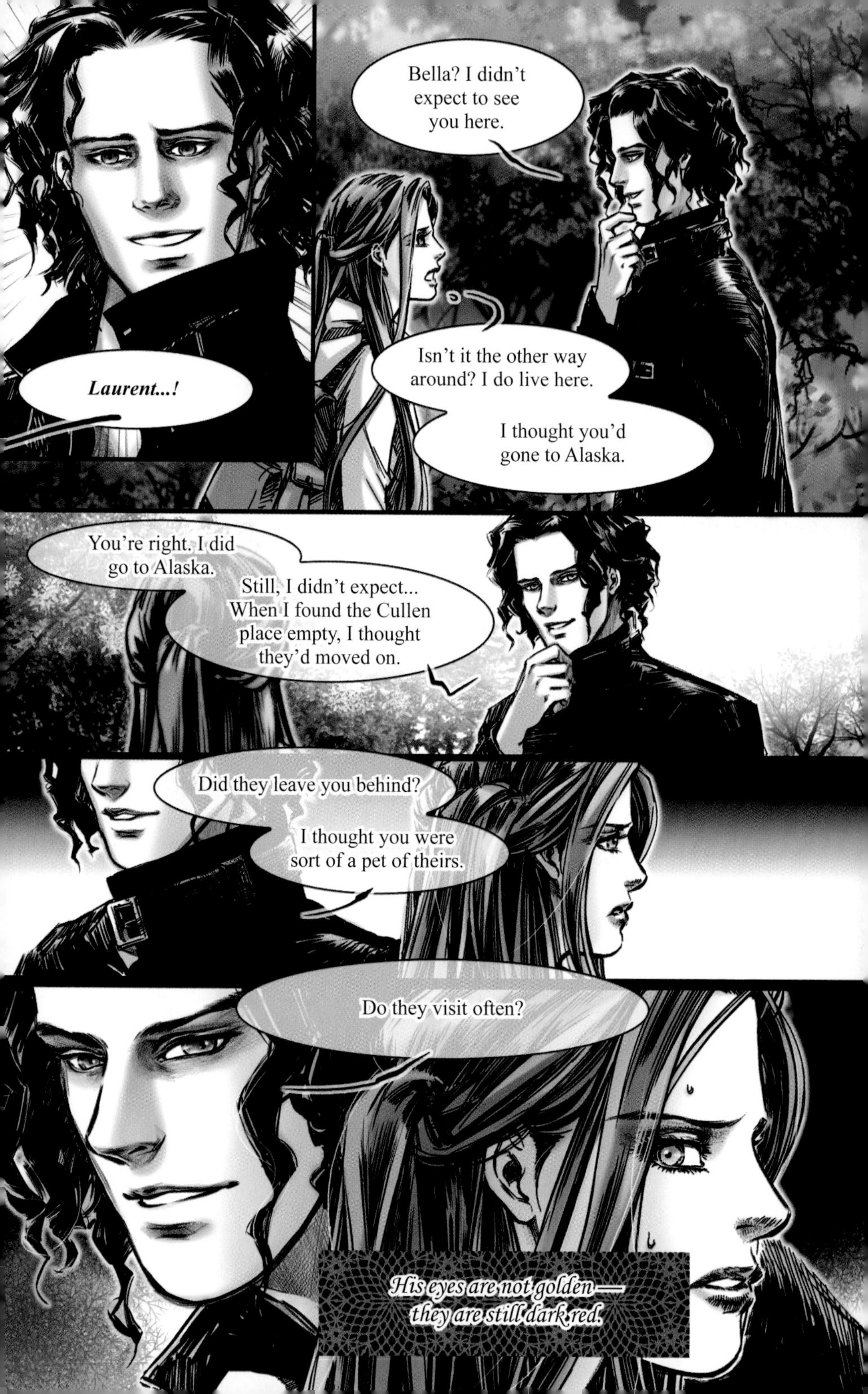
Laurent...!
Bella? I didn't expect to see you here.
Isn't it the other way around? I do live here.
I thought you'd gone to Alaska.
You're right. I did go to Alaska.
Still, I didn't expect... When I found the Cullen place empty, I thought they'd moved on.
Did they leave you behind?
I thought you were sort of a pet of theirs.
Do they visit often?
His eyes are not golden— they are still dark red.

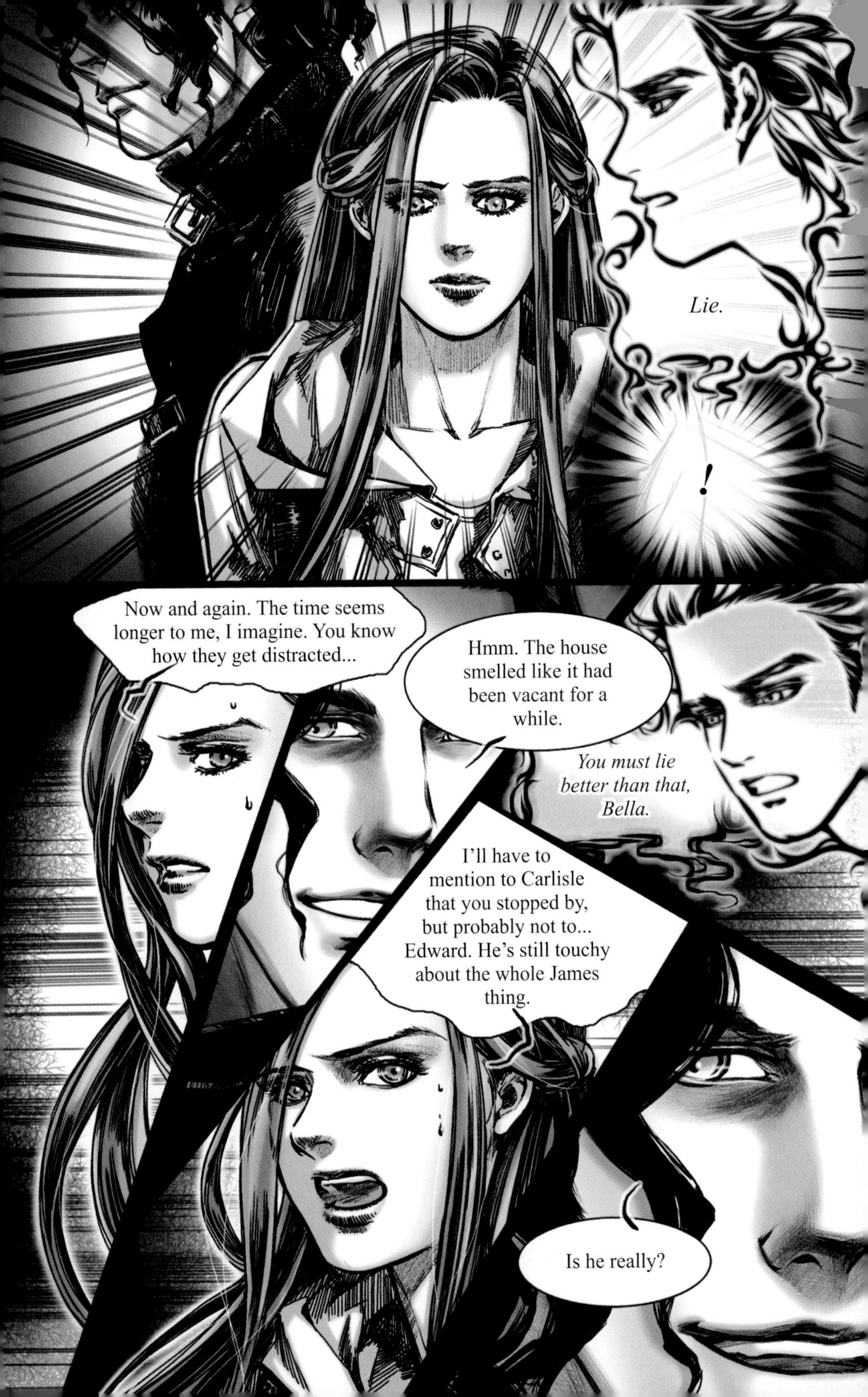
Lie.
!
Now and again. The time seems longer to me, I imagine. You know how they get distracted...
Hmm. The house smelled like it had been vacant for a while.
You must lie better than that, Bella.
I'll have to mention to Carlisle that you stopped by, but probably not to... Edward. He's still touchy about the whole James thing.
Is he really?

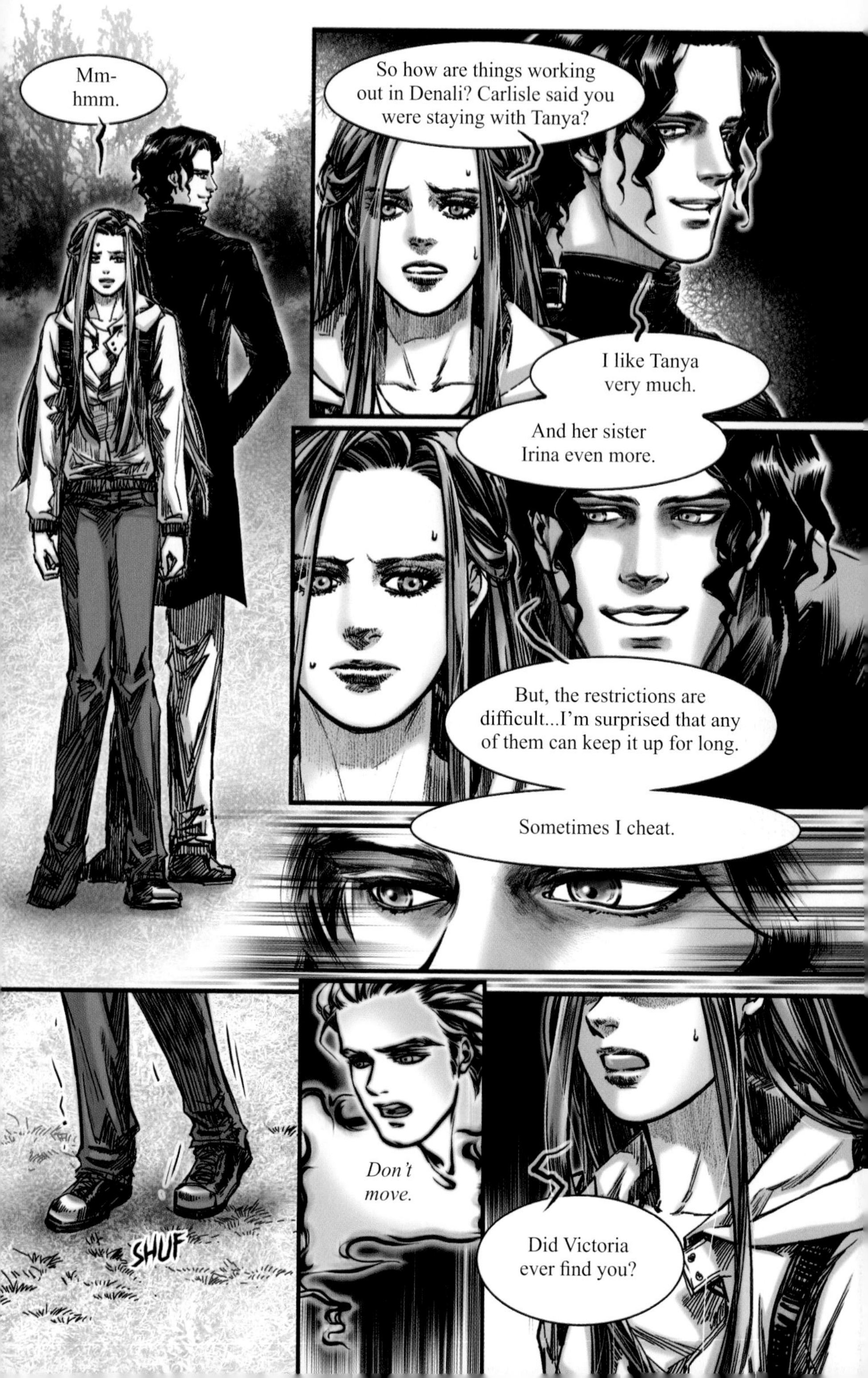
Mm-hmm.
So how are things working out in Denali? Carlisle said you were staying with Tanya?
I like Tanya very much.
And her sister Irina even more.
But, the restrictions are difficult...I'm surprised that any of them can keep it up for long.
Sometimes I cheat.
SHUF
Don't move.
Did Victoria ever find you?

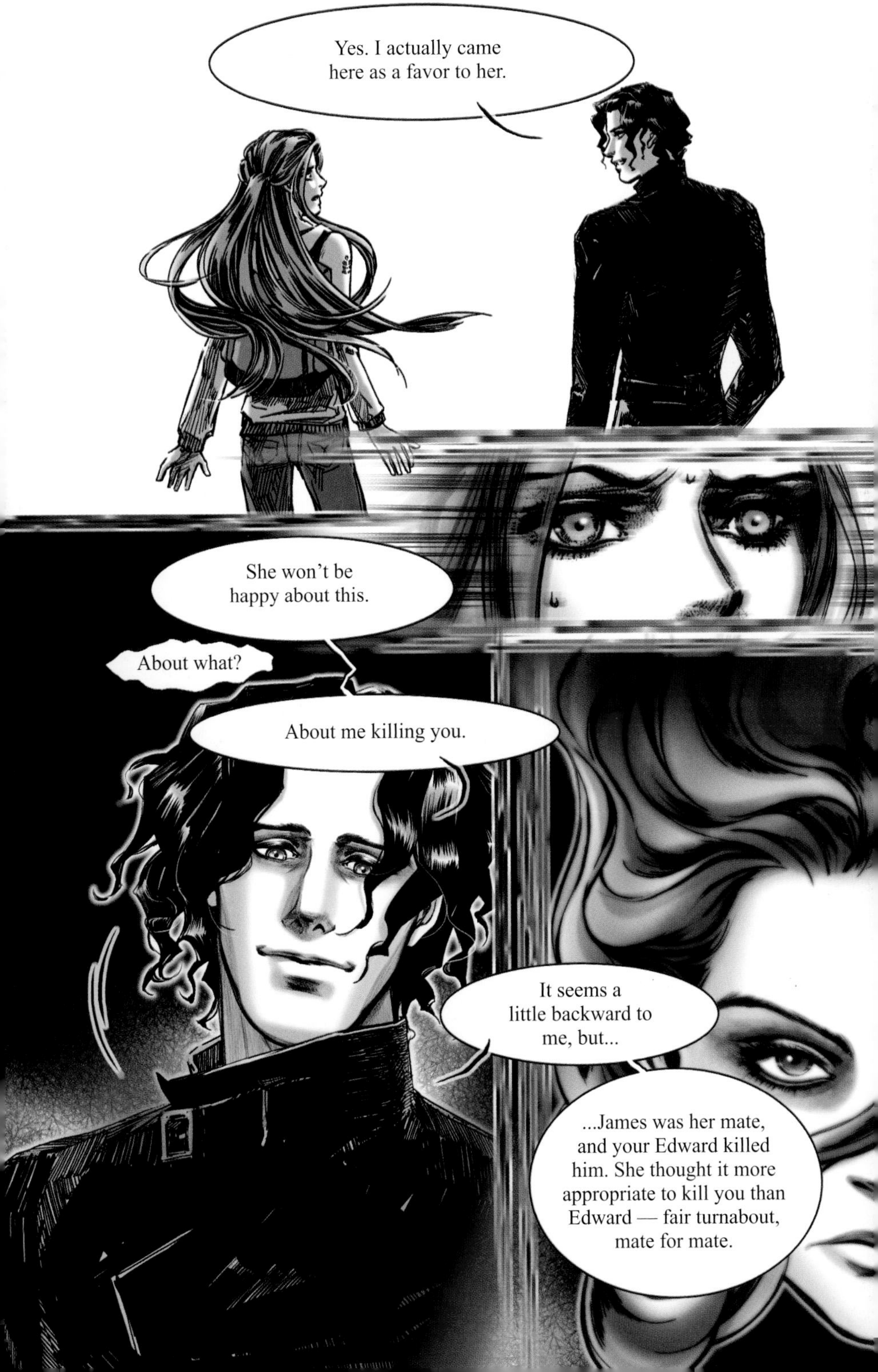
Yes. I actually came here as a favor to her.
She won't be happy about this.
About what?
About me killing you.
It seems a little backward to me, but...
...James was her mate, and your Edward killed him. She thought it more appropriate to kill you than Edward — fair turnabout, mate for mate.

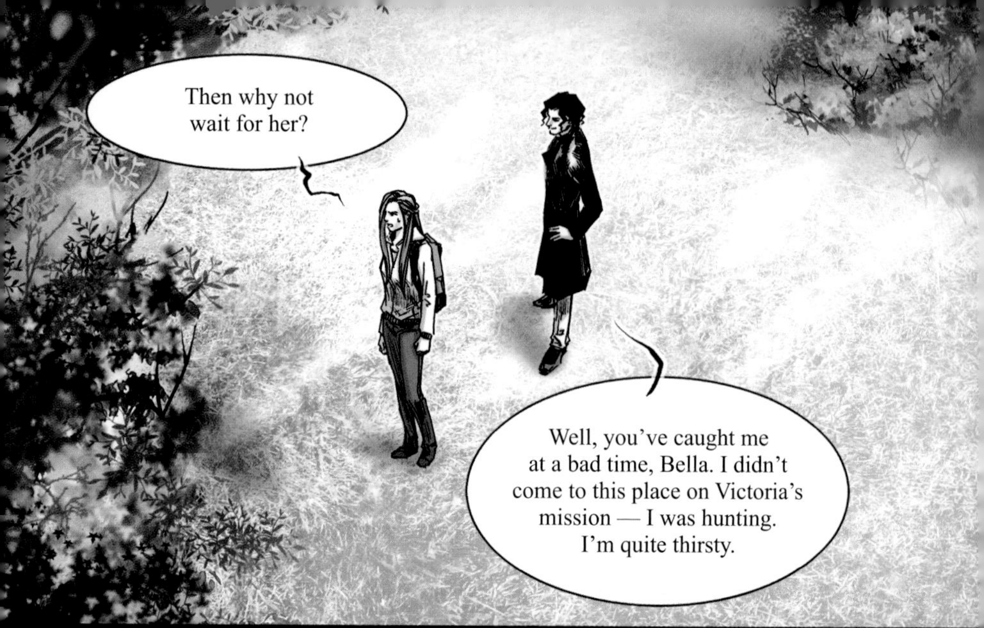
Then why not wait for her?
Well, you've caught me at a bad time, Bella. I didn't come to this place on Victoria's mission — I was hunting. I'm quite thirsty.

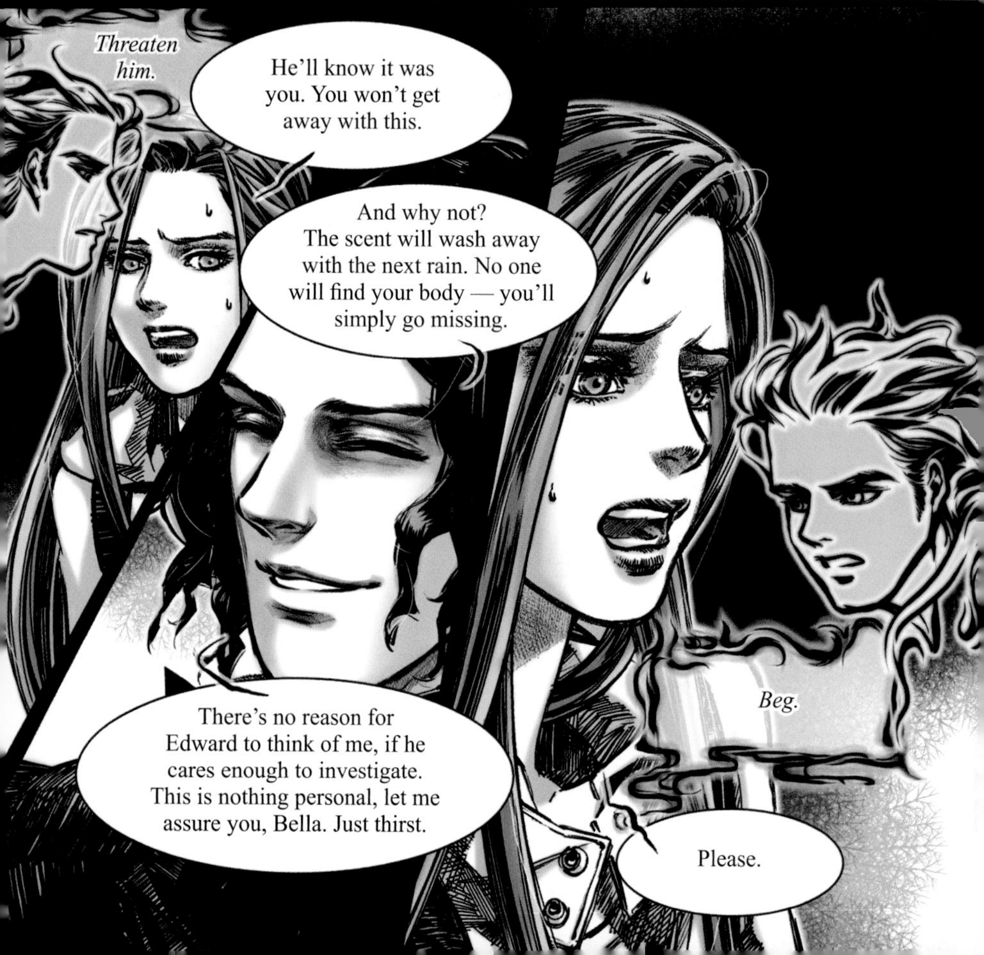
Threaten him.
He'll know it was you. You won't get away with this.
And why not? The scent will wash away with the next rain. No one will find your body — you'll simply go missing.
There's no reason for Edward to think of me, if he cares enough to investigate. This is nothing personal, let me assure you, Bella. Just thirst.
Beg.
Please.

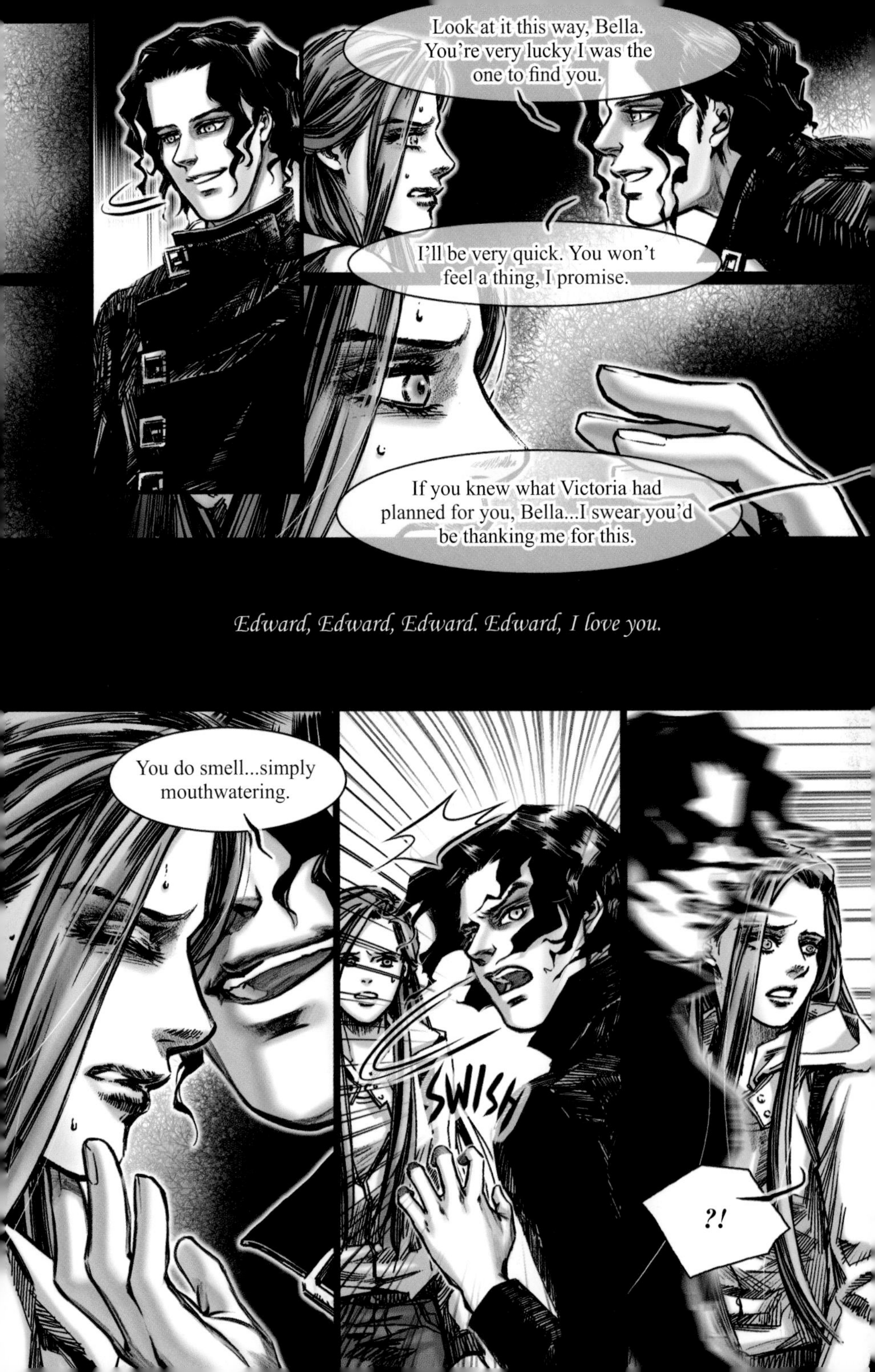
Look at it this way, Bella. You're very lucky I was the one to find you.
I'll be very quick. You won't feel a thing, I promise.
If you knew what Victoria had planned for you, Bella...I swear you'd be thanking me for this.
Edward, Edward, Edward. Edward, I love you.
You do smell...simply mouthwatering.
SWISH
?!

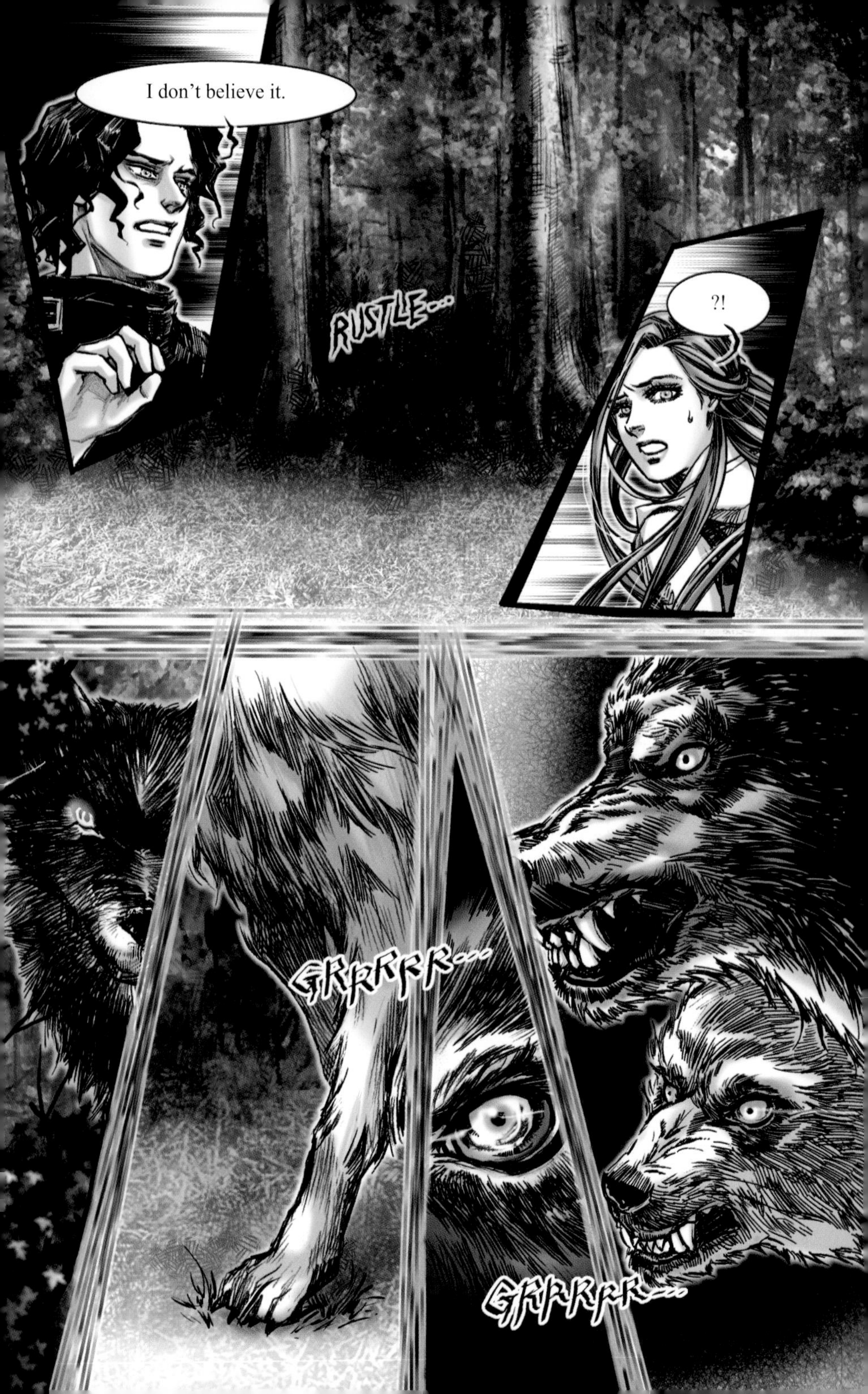
I don't believe it.
RUSTLE...
?!
GRRRRR...
GRRRRR...

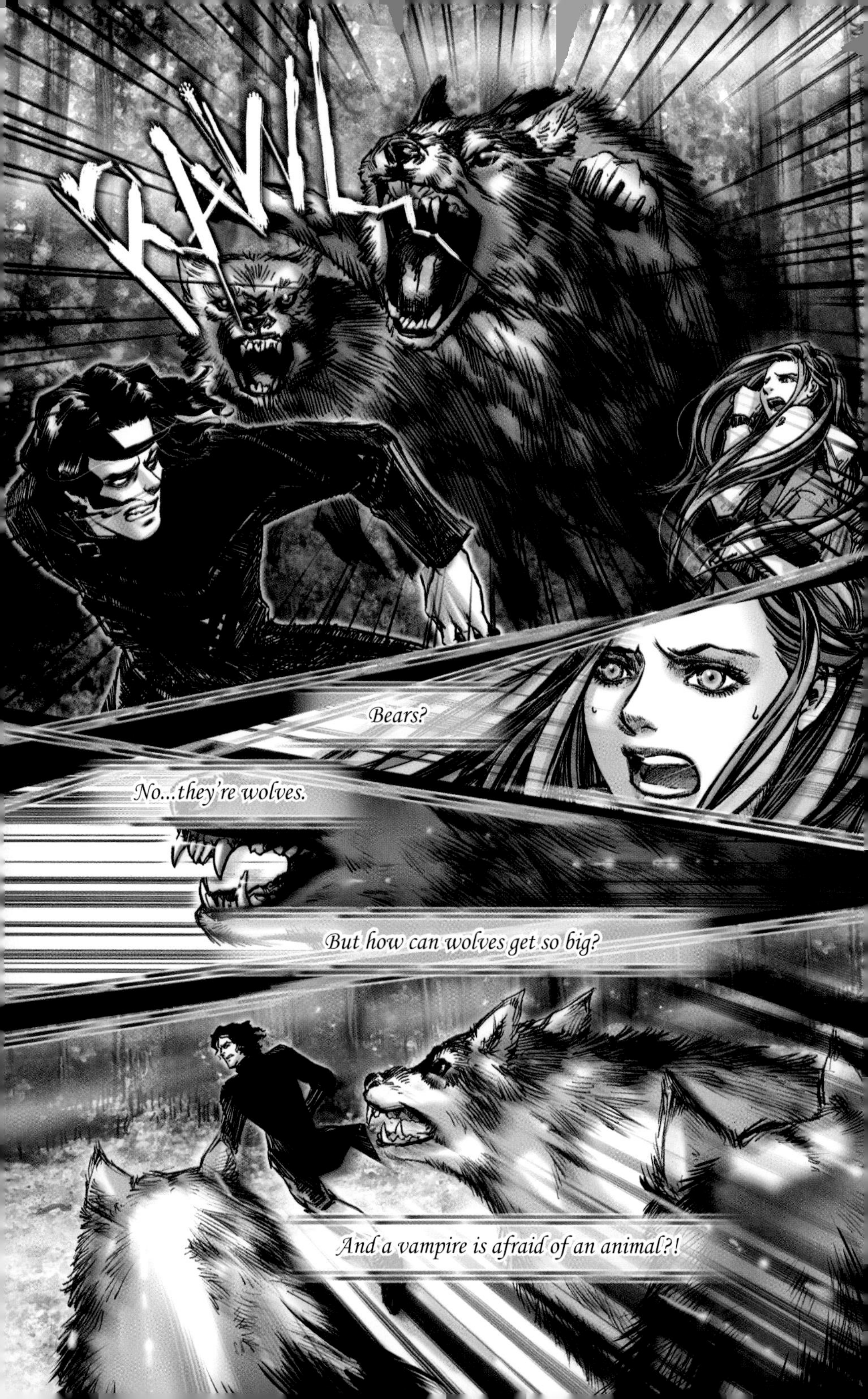
YAWL
Bears?
No...they're wolves.
But how can wolves get so big?
And a vampire is afraid of an animal?!

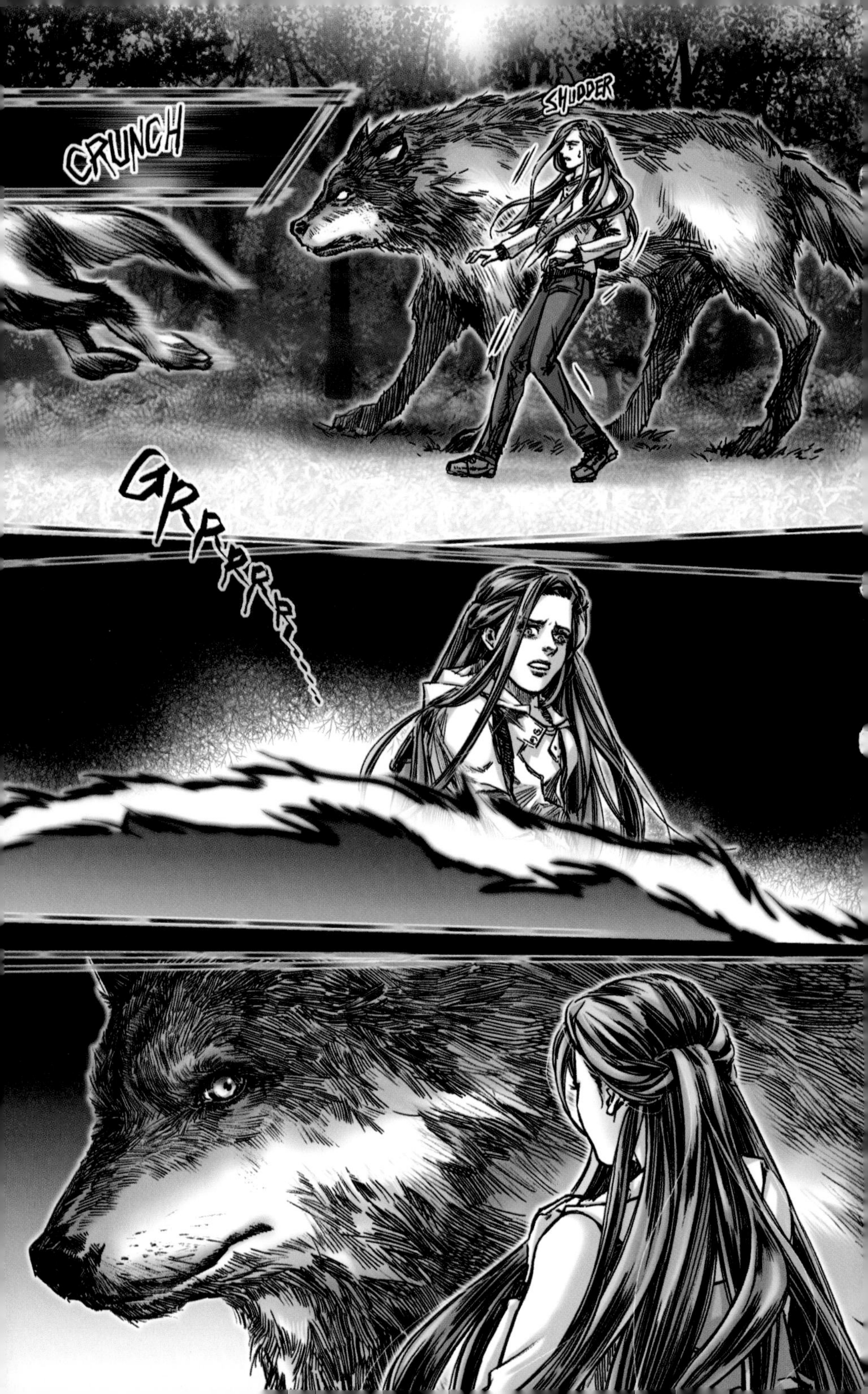

CRUNCH
SHUDDER
GRRRRRR......

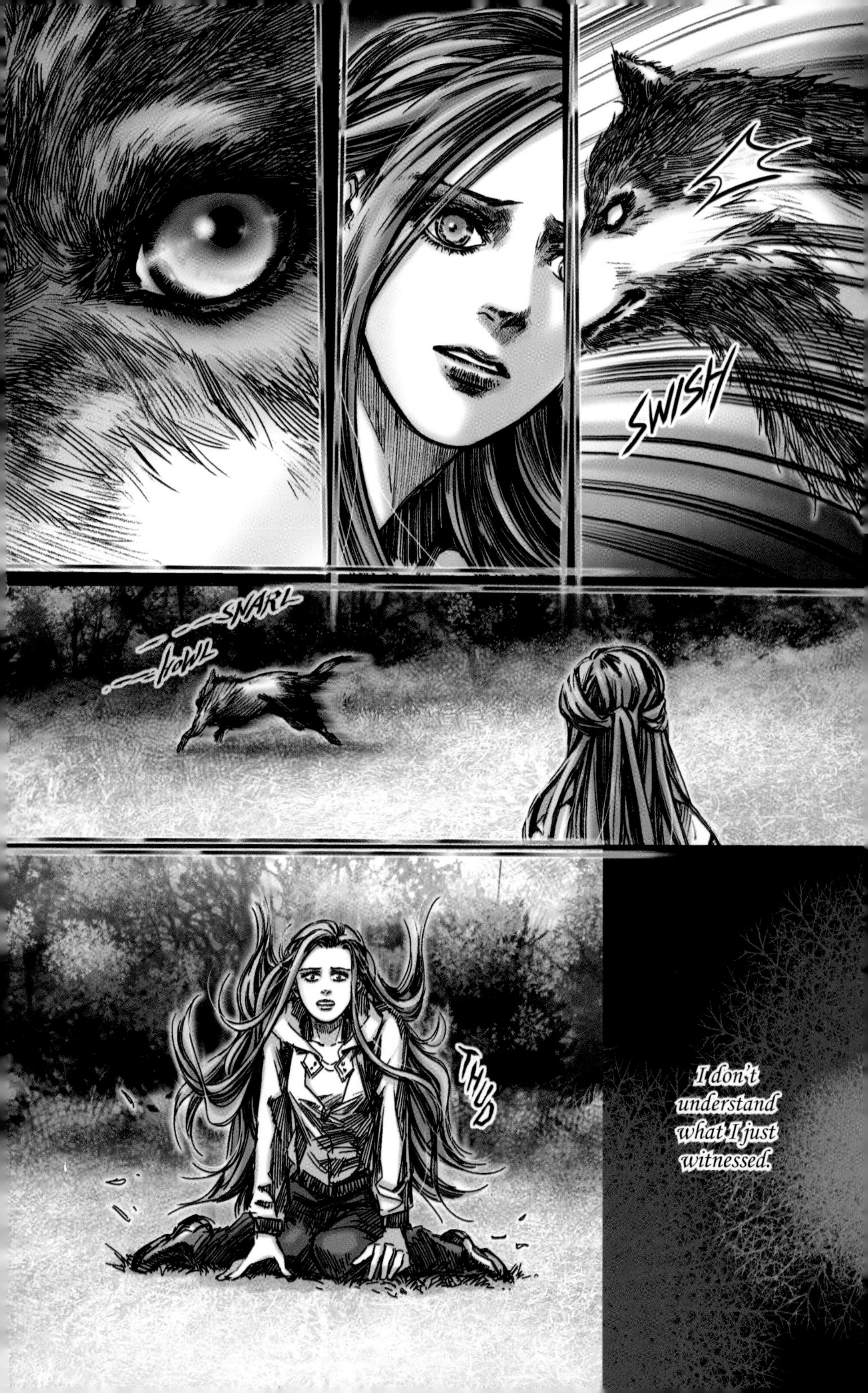
SWISH
SNARL
HOWL
THUD
I don't understand what I just witnessed.

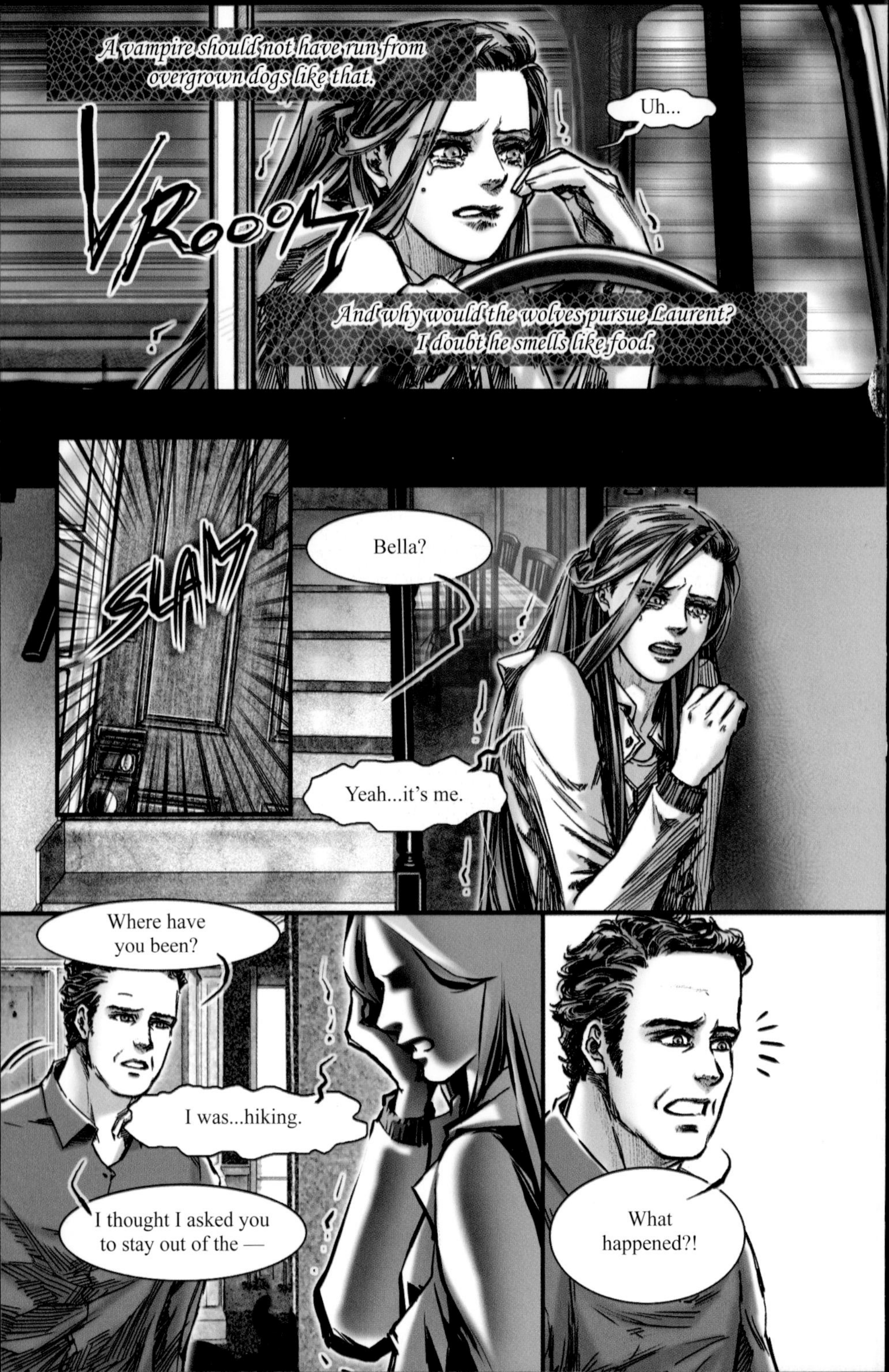
A vampire should not have run from overgrown dogs like that.
Uh...
VROOOM
And why would the wolves pursue Laurent? I doubt he smells like food.
SLAM
Bella?
Yeah...it's me.
Where have you been?
I was...hiking.
I thought I asked you to stay out of the —
What happened?!

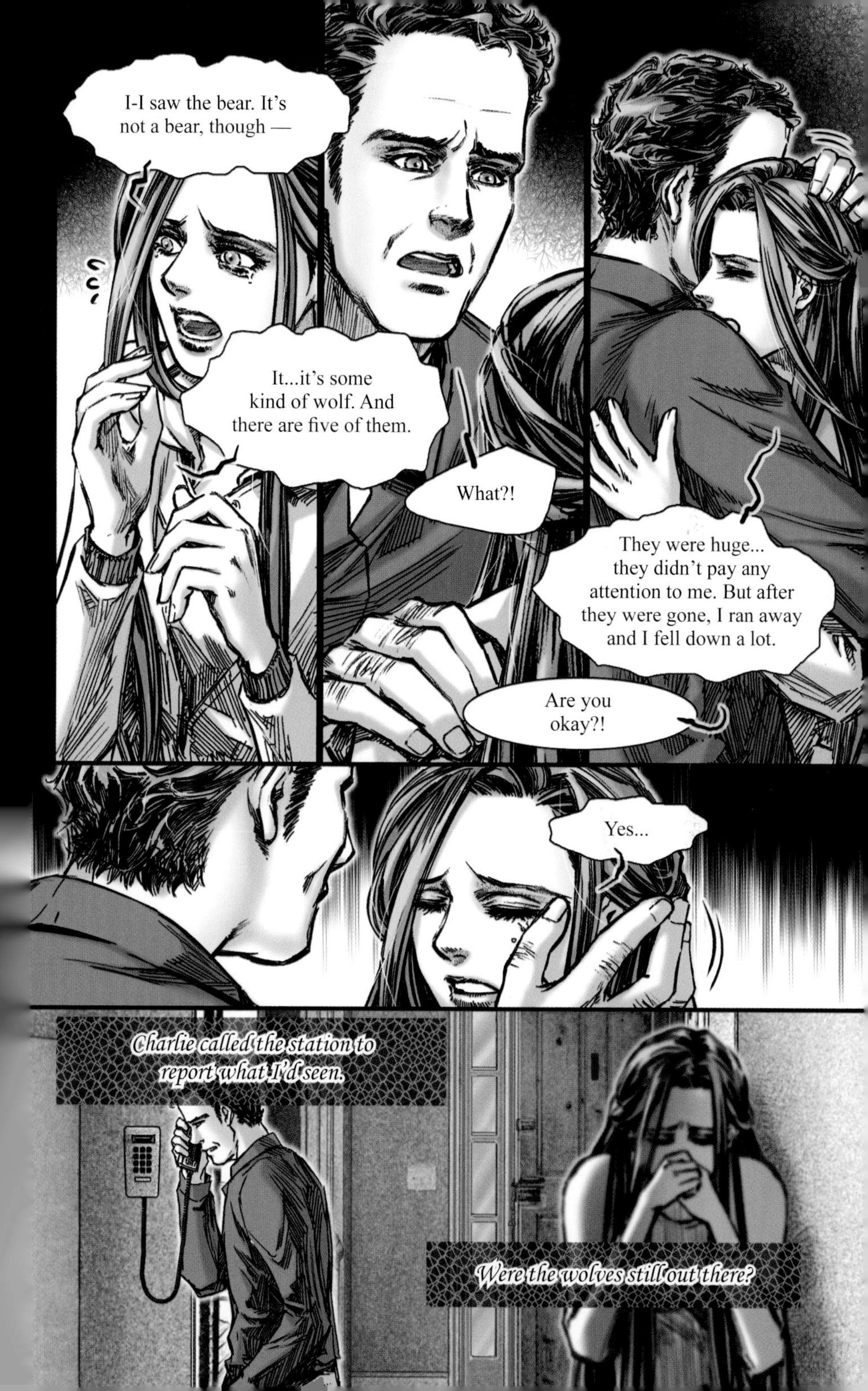
I-I saw the bear. It's not a bear, though —
It...it's some kind of wolf. And there are five of them.
What?!
They were huge... they didn't pay any attention to me. But after they were gone, I ran away and I fell down a lot.
Are you okay?!
Yes...
Charlie called the station to report what I'd seen.
Were the wolves still out there?

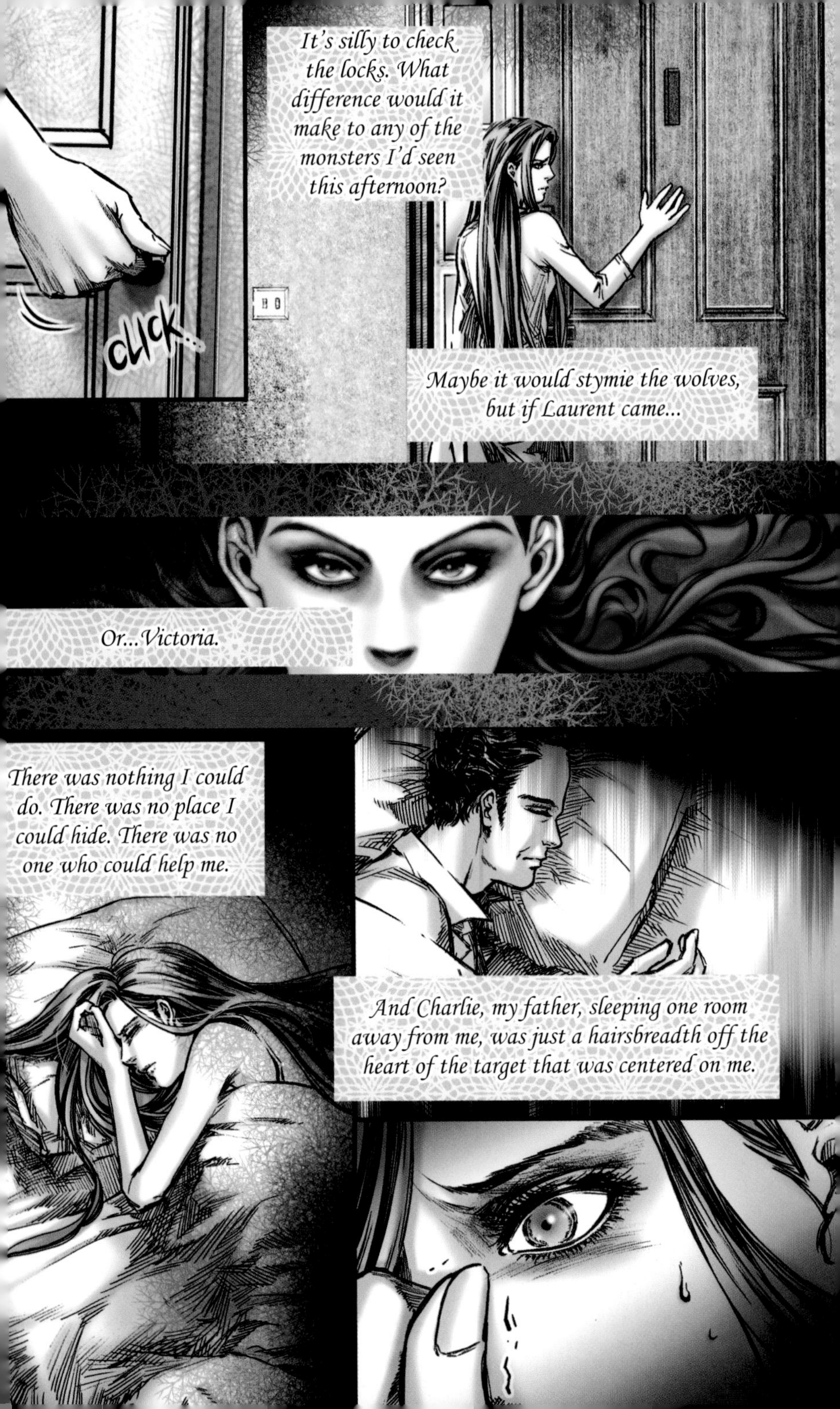
It's silly to check the locks. What difference would it make to any of the monsters I'd seen this afternoon?
CLICK...
Maybe it would stymie the wolves, but if Laurent came...
Or...Victoria.
There was nothing I could do. There was no place I could hide. There was no one who could help me.
And Charlie, my father, sleeping one room away from me, was just a hairsbreadth off the heart of the target that was centered on me.

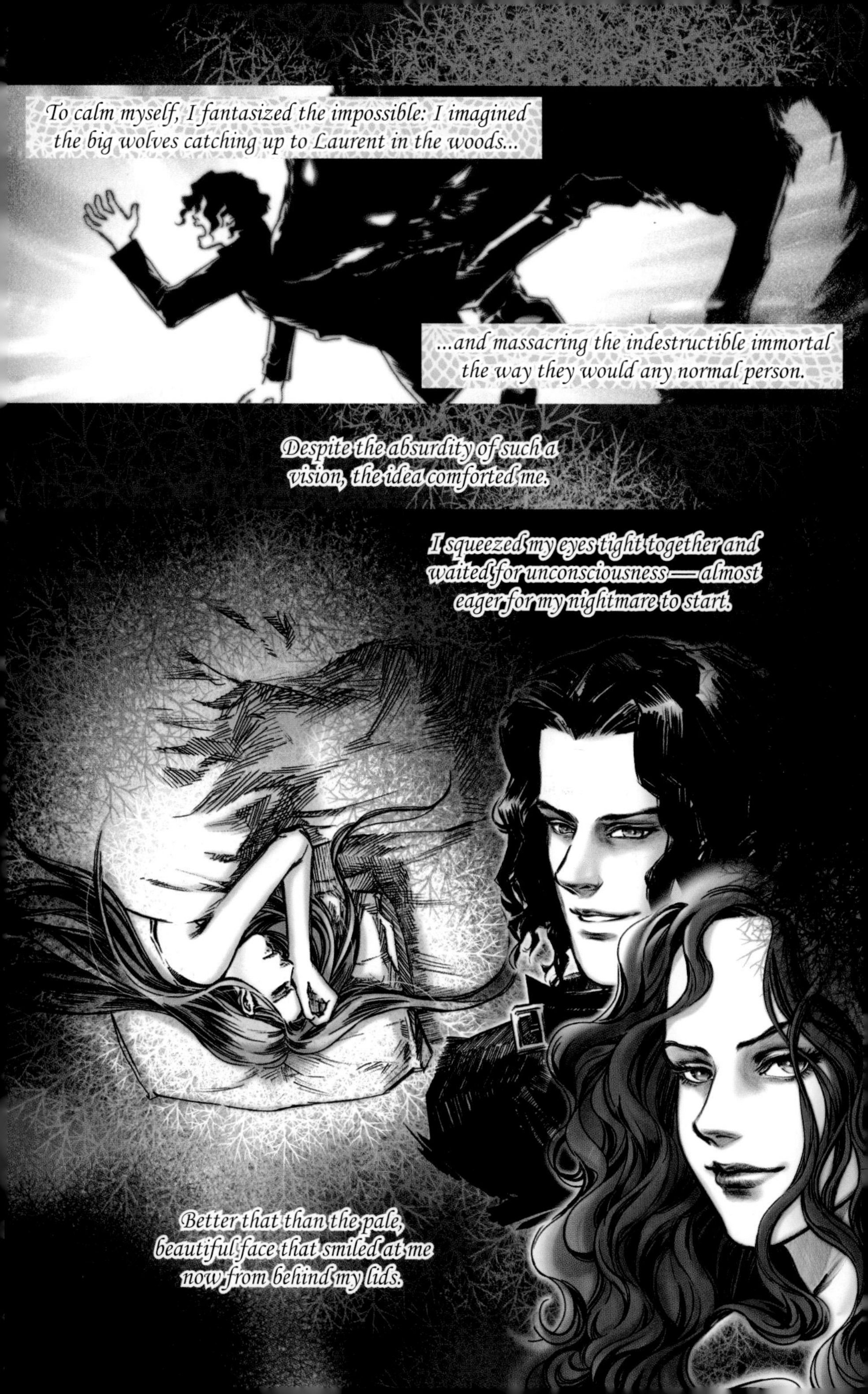
To calm myself, I fantasized the impossible: I imagined the big wolves catching up to Laurent in the woods...
...and massacring the indestructible immortal the way they would any normal person.
Despite the absurdity of such a vision, the idea comforted me.
I squeezed my eyes tight together and waited for unconsciousness — almost eager for my nightmare to start.
Better that than the pale, beautiful face that smiled at me now from behind my lids.

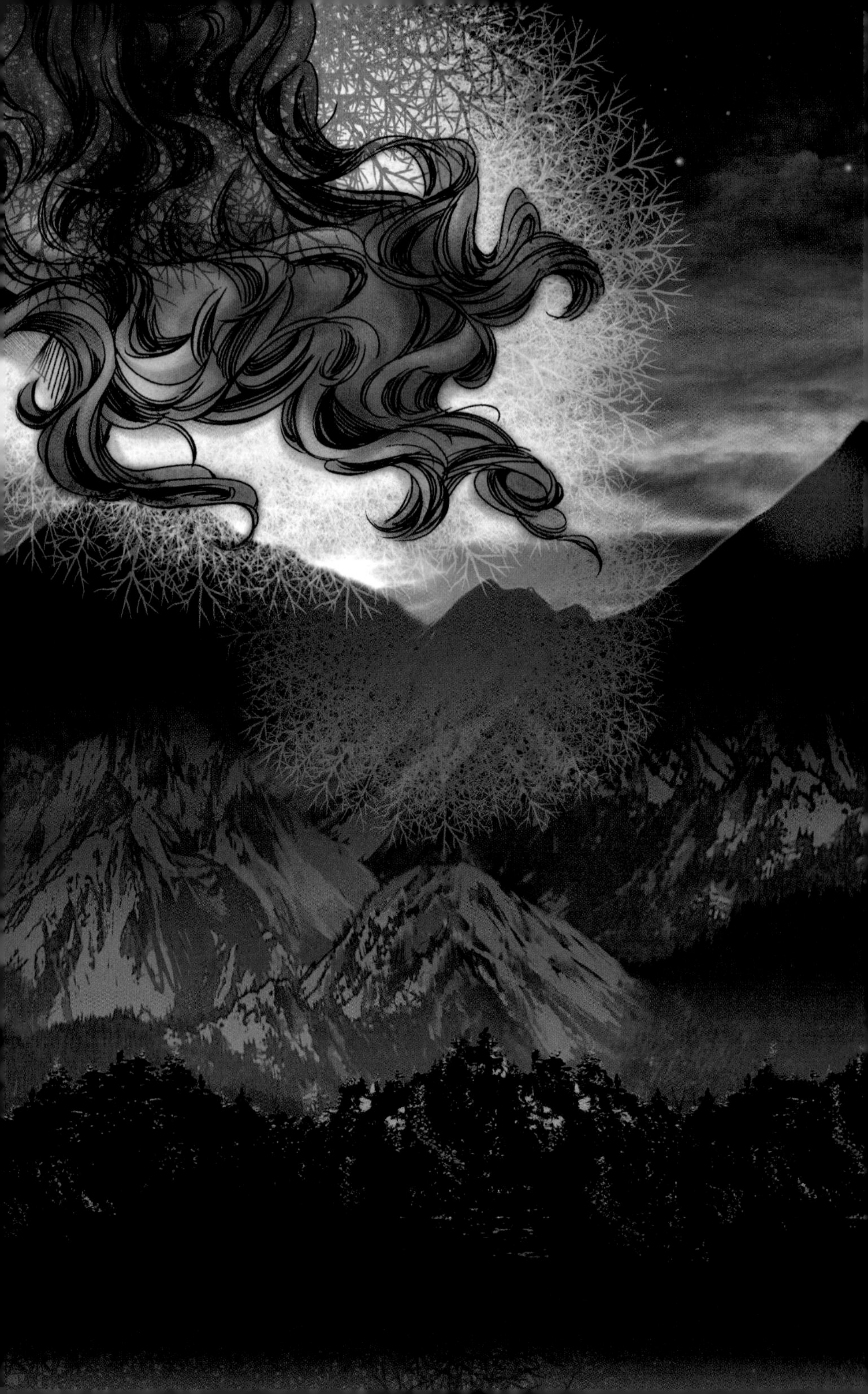

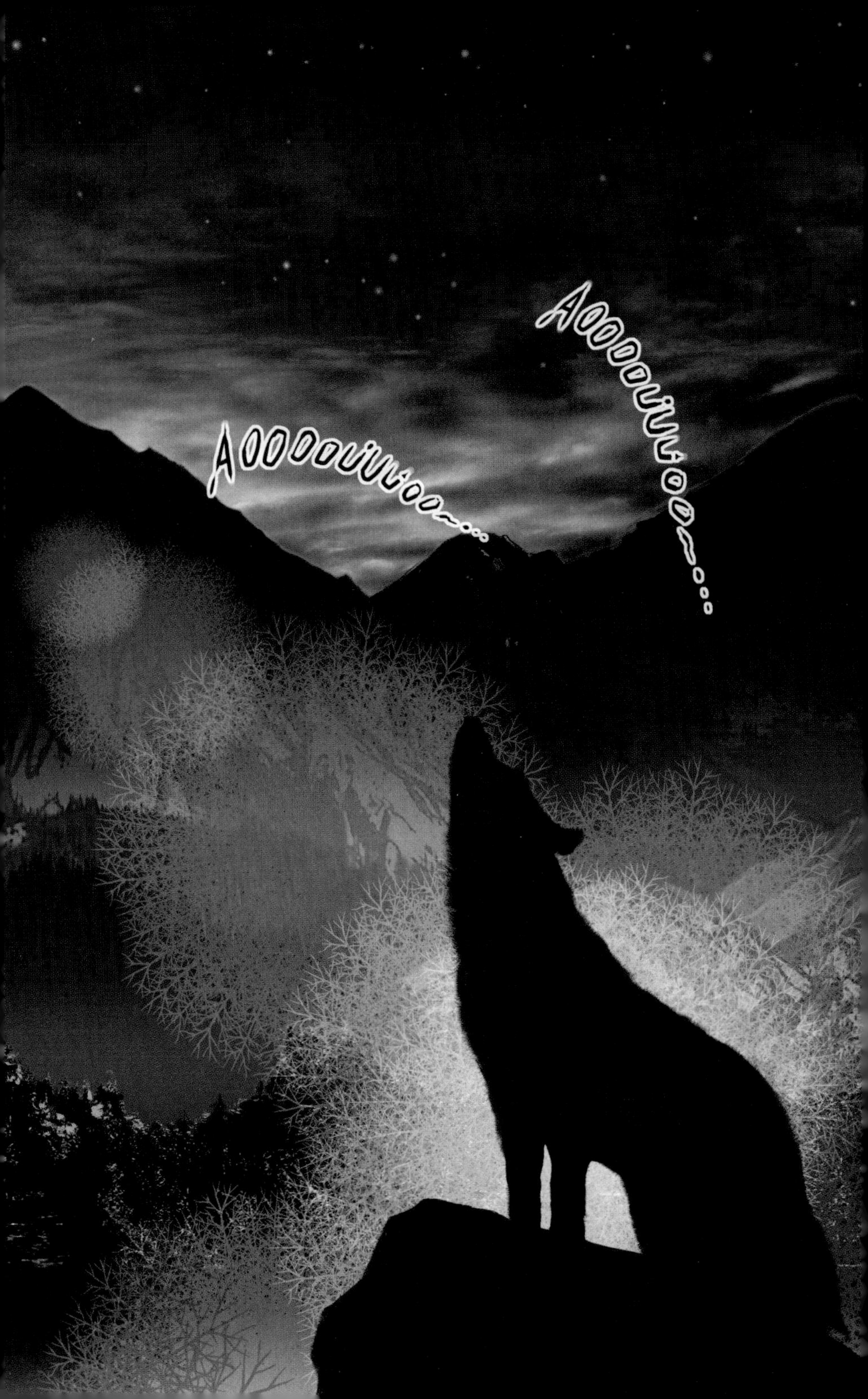
AOOOOOUUUOO~...
AOOOOOUUUOO~...

To be continued in Volume Two...

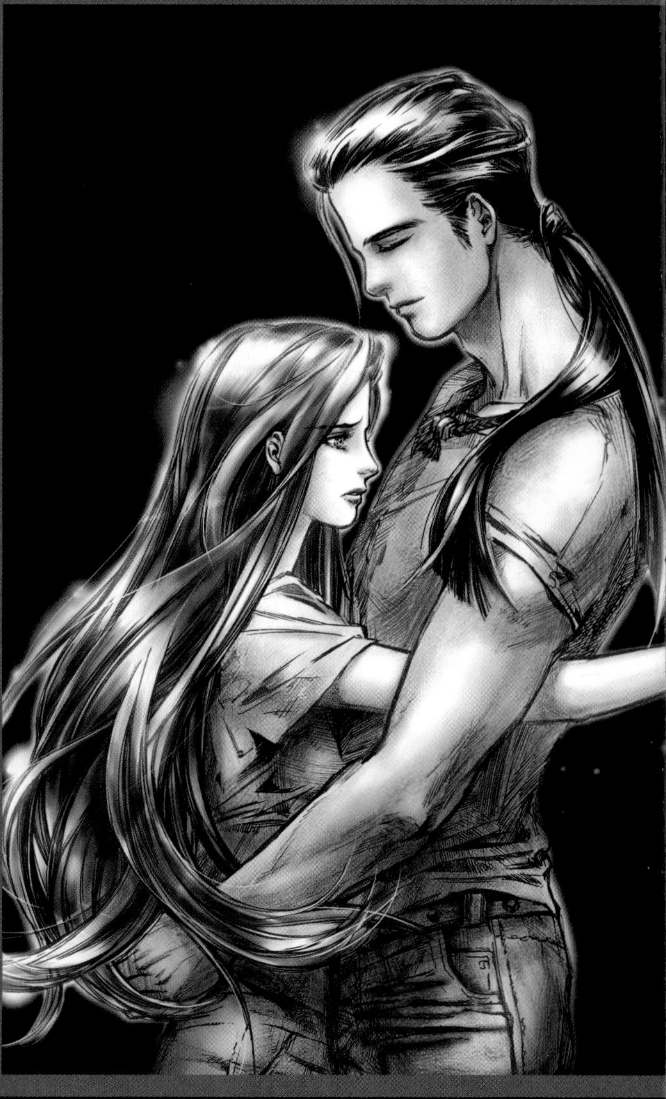

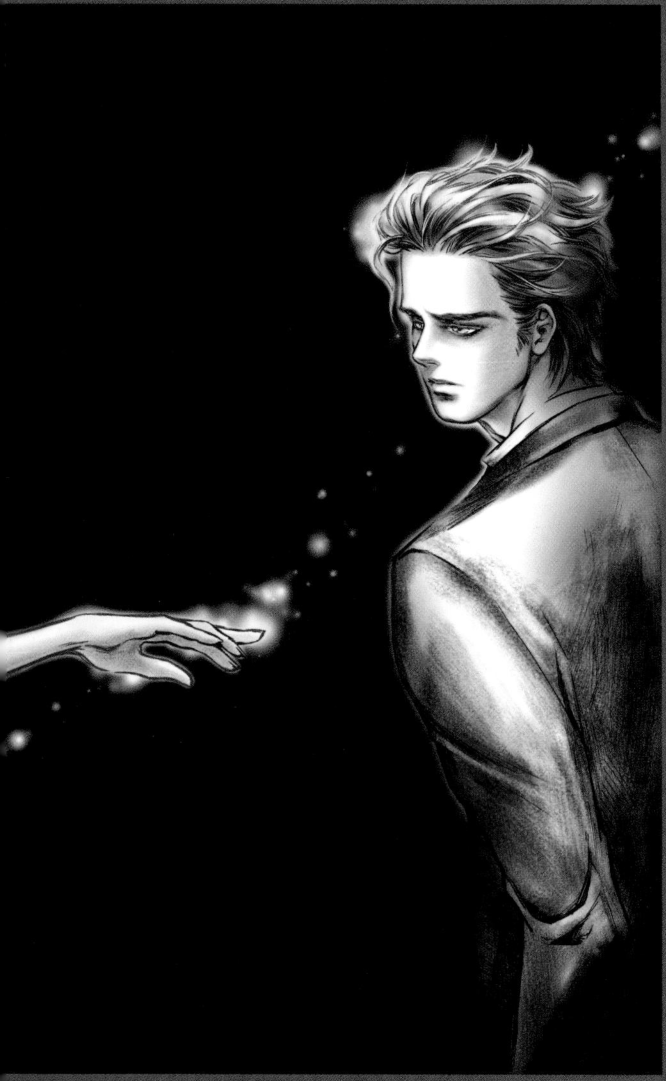

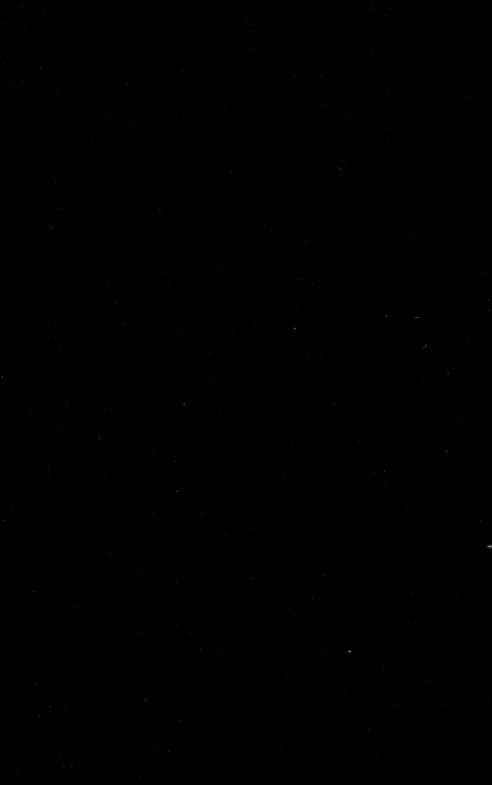